WHEN DARKNESS BUILDS
M. C. SUTTON

To all those who suffer in silence, and to those who touch their hearts without ever knowing it, I humbly and gratefully dedicate this book.

CHAPTER 1

Emma woke up screaming.

"Emma, calm down! You're going to wake up the entire camp."

She opened her eyes and gasped, breathing fast and drenched in sweat, the humidity much thicker than when they'd finally crawled into their sleeping bags only a few hours before. It made it even harder to breathe.

It took a moment to focus through the darkness, shattered every few seconds by an intense flash of lightning. Her husband, Jon, knelt on the floor of their tent beside her, watching her as she struggled to steady the pounding in her chest.

"Are you okay?" he asked. "It sounded like maybe you—"

"I'm fine." Emma crawled out of her sleeping bag and sat up, her chin on her knees.

"Yeah, sure," Jon mumbled, and grabbed one of their bags. "Your pager has been going off for the last half hour. I'm guessing it's Frank. It's been thundering and lightning all night."

Frank? Why in the world would her boss be paging her? "But that doesn't make any sense," said Emma. "I checked the weather before we left and didn't see a storm system for miles."

"I'd tell you just to call him," said Jon, pulling out his phone and glancing at it. He threw it across the tent. "If the *damn* cell phone service ever actually *worked* anymore."

Emma stared at him. It didn't take suddenly finding themselves in the middle of an unexplained storm to tell he was frustrated, though she wasn't sure why. It had been his suggestion they spend Mother's Day weekend volunteering at the camp.

She put a hand on his arm, took her bag from him, and found the pair of jeans she'd worn the day before. Her pager hummed as she pulled it from the front pocket. She had eighteen messages, all from Frank.

"Tornado warning? But how is that even possible?" she said.

Jon scratched his stubbled chin and looked away.

She read through the rest of the messages. "Great. Our alert systems are down again."

Jon stopped trying to shove his sleeping bag into its sack. "So what does that mean?"

"It means," answered Emma, pulling on her jeans and unzipping the tent door, "that we need to warn Riley and start getting all these people to shelter."

She climbed out the door without waiting for a response.

It was chilly in southwest Missouri, even for May. The flashes of lightning in the distance outlined the immense pine trees that circled the camping area and hinted at the denseness of Wakarusa National Forest just beyond. Even in the darkness, the beauty of the surrounding nature was a stark contrast to the camping area. On every available square foot sat a makeshift dwelling in what the locals called "Tent City," an area established for families left homeless after the economy all but collapsed years ago. The land had once belonged to the government, before widespread budget cuts caused the state parks to close.

Her and Jon's tent, an expensive two-person backpacker that sat low enough to the ground to withstand the winds picking up around them, appeared almost shameful compared to the haphazard shanties and army-style tents that shook and swayed in the night. Surprisingly, as far as she could tell, no one else had yet awoken to the approaching storm.

Well, almost no one.

Emma stepped toward their seventeen-year-old son, who sat staring into the dying embers of their campfire. "Mattie?"

He didn't so much as turn around.

"Honey, are you okay? I thought you went to bed hours ago."

"There's a storm coming," he answered.

Emma put a hand on his shoulder. "Yes, I know. I got the warning message."

Matt finally turned to look at her, the green flecks in his eyes glinting in accusation against the brown. Everyone said that his twin brother, Jacob, was the spitting image of their father with his thick, dark hair, square jaw, and rugged features. But when Emma looked at Matt, it was always Jon's strength she saw, even if he hadn't quite grown into it yet.

"So what are we going to do about it, then?" he asked.

"You, young man," said Jon from behind them, "are going to go wake up your brother. Then the both of you are going to the camp host's RV to find Riley. Let him know to start moving people to the bathhouse."

Matt's shoulders fell. "Yes, sir." He stood and headed toward his tent where Jacob lay sound asleep.

"Well, come on then, Dr. Grant," Jon said to Emma, pulling on a sweatshirt. He opened the back of her Jeep parked just in front of their tent site, grabbed two bullhorns, and tossed one to her. "This is what you do, isn't it?"

She narrowed her eyes at him, then shook her head and hurried off to the eastern side of the camp.

"The National Weather Service has issued a tornado warning for this area. Leave your tents and head to the bathhouse immediately!" Emma's voice boomed through the bullhorn. She ran from one section of tents to the next, stopping only long enough to shout a warning and watch for enough movement to be sure her message was received. One at a time, people began to pop out their messy heads.

"Hey, what's all the shouting for?" A white-haired man poked his head out of a family-size tent next to Emma.

"Sir, I'm with McDonald County Emergency Management. This area has been placed under a tornado warning. Please evacuate your family to the bathhouse immediately."

He flinched as a large drop of rain hit him in the face, then nodded and ducked back inside.

It began to pour. Trees cracked in the wind, leaves and small branches blew past Emma's feet. The camp buzzed as people rushed to gather their families and make for the bathhouse.

Jacob appeared on the camp's ATV and skidded to a stop on the wet pavement in front of her. He pushed his dark, wet hair out of his eyes and held a hand to his forehead, the rain now pounding down in stinging sideways sheets. "Dad says that's everyone from the western side, Mom! He says it's time you got up there, too," he yelled over the roar of the wind.

"Go ahead and we'll be right behind you," she shouted back. She had noticed the camp host, Riley, running toward a car trying to make a getaway at the eastern exit of the park.

Jacob hesitated.

"Look, the longer we stand here and talk about it, the longer it's going to take me to grab Riley and get up there," she said, pointing toward Riley, who stood arguing with the driver of the car.

Jacob looked over the hill toward the bathhouse, then up at the sky. "Okay. But I'd suggest you guys don't take your time about it." He turned the ATV and headed up the hill to the bathhouse.

As she stared into the distance after him, at the dark clouds swirling violently against a twilight sky, Emma felt the pressure drop around her. She stood for a brief instant and watched the rotation, the raw power mesmerizing. Her awe turned to panic the second she caught a brief glimpse of updraft.

"Riley!" she shouted. She raced down the hill, skidding across the wet grass toward him.

Riley was still standing beside the car, shouting at the driver through the window. "Look, Tyler, you need to get out of the car and seek shelter *now!*"

"Are you kidding?" the driver yelled back, rain pouring into his car through the open window. "I'm not sticking around here! I'm heading to the emergency shelter in Brighton. We're not risking our lives huddled together with seventy other people in a shower stall!" In the backseat, a frightened little girl no more than four years old sat strapped into a car seat, clinging to a soaked stuffed elephant.

Emma slid to a halt just before slamming into the driver's side door. "Sir, do you see those cloud formations? Do you have any idea what that means?" she said, jabbing a finger at the skyline behind her. "*You* are putting your life, and your daughter's life, in danger if you don't get out of this car right now!"

His eyes widened as he stared past her. Tyler jumped out of the car and sprinted around to the passenger side to pull his daughter out.

Only, for some reason, it took entirely too long to get her out of the car seat.

Riley ran to the other side of the car. "What's wrong?"

"The buckle's stuck!"

"Here, let me try." Riley shoved him out of the way and began pounding on the button and jerking at the straps.

Emma put a hand to her forehead to shield her eyes from the rain as she looked up at the sky. The clouds churned in upon themselves like thick gray sludge in a blender.

Riley struggled fiercely to get the little girl out of the car, which rocked back and forth with the force of the winds. Emma could sense the fear in the girl's teary green eyes as the storm raged around them.

Then in an instant, it all just stopped.

The rain softened, the wind ceased, and everything went silent. Riley paused and emerged from the car to stare up at the sky. Then the almost invisibly-spinning tunnel of clouds which spanned across the western horizon suddenly inverted and touched down, quickly forming a long, snaking tornado. Emma's eyes darted from the frightened little girl to Riley's panicked face. She threw open the back door on the driver's side and dove into the car just as Riley returned to struggling with the seat belt.

"A word of advice, Riley." Emma pulled her knife from her pocket, flipped it open, and sliced through the straps of the car seat. "Get yourself a good pocketknife."

"No kidding," Riley said as he pulled the little girl from the car.

The sound of the approaching tornado was deafening as they rushed toward the bathhouse. The little girl held her hands over her ears, buried her head in Riley's shoulder, and screamed maniacally as Riley, Emma, and Tyler trudged up the muddy embankment.

"Dr. Grant, we're not going to make it," Riley screamed from behind her.

He was right. The debris-darkened funnel was fast approaching. It had already reached the northwest corner of the park. The bathhouse was too far.

They stopped, and Emma turned to the little girl. "What's your name?"

The little girl quit screaming and answered softly, "Maya."

"Well, Maya." Emma rested a reassuring hand on her back. "My name is Emma. It's my job to get you out of here, and that's exactly what I'm going to do, okay?"

Maya nodded slightly.

Emma looked up at Riley, who didn't look so certain. That's when Emma noticed the drainpipe behind him, about fifty feet away, which ran under the road in front of the north side of the park and was big enough to hold them. Rainwater surged out of it, cascading down a rocky embankment into a ditch below. It would be wet and cold, but much safer than being out in the open.

She pointed. "There."

At the same moment, just over the hill behind them, a propane tank from the refill station slammed into the side of the office and exploded.

"Go!" Emma yelled.

They sprinted the short distance to the pipe as the tornado devoured tents and cars on the western side of the park. Somewhere behind them lightning struck a tree with a bright flash and loud crack.

Tyler went first, scrambling haphazardly up the slimy rocks and mud, the water determined to push him back down. Once Tyler was inside, Riley handed Maya up to him. He moved deeper into the darkness, pushing desperately against the rushing water as Riley struggled to climb up the rocks behind him. Emma waited in the ditch below, freezing water up to her knees, and turned to check the path of the tornado. It veered wildly to the south—and headed straight for the bathhouse.

Where her family was.

"Dr. Grant!" Riley yelled.

Emma turned back to the embankment. Riley knelt in the pipe, his hand outstretched toward her. She grabbed it and started to climb.

There was another bright flash, this time much closer. The ground shook beneath her. Her foot slipped on a wet rock, and she lost hold of Riley's hand, splashing into the ditch below. Emma watched, frozen beneath the rush of icy water, as a giant oak tree fell toward her.

An arm wrapped tightly around her waist from behind. It pulled her out of the way of the falling tree, up the embankment, and into the pipe. The long branches of the tree slammed into the ditch with a shuddering crack.

Emma's heart raced. "Thank you," she whispered.

"No problem," Jon answered, breathless.

The five of them braced themselves inside the pipe, fighting to hold their position against the water that surged past them as the storm continued to rage outside. Emma closed her eyes and rested her head against the cold metal pipe, freezing and exhausted.

They crouched there in the darkness and cold for what seemed like forever. Eventually the pipe stopped vibrating underneath them, and the sounds of the storm subsided.

Riley emerged from the pipe first. He snaked through the branches of the downed oak, then turned back to grab Maya, whose father lowered her down. Once they were all out, they surveyed the damage.

Tents and belongings were strewn all over the park. Trees were uprooted. RVs and cars were rolled. A large hole gaped in the side of the brick office building where the propane tank had exploded.

Emma's main concern, though, lay with the bathhouse. She and Jon climbed the hill to find out if it still stood.

The roof had been blown off, but otherwise the bathhouse had held. People were filing out past Matt and Jacob, looking shaken but unharmed. Jacob waved and gave them a reassuring thumbs-up.

Emma breathed a sigh of relief. She knew it could have been much, much worse.

"Well, Dr. Grant," said Jon, shaking his head. "So much for your weekend off."

CHAPTER 2

The creek that ran through the back of Hackett Ranch was still swollen from the storms that had blown through a few days earlier. Sam sat on its bank, watching the muddy water flow through the branches that littered the bottom. For as far back as he could remember, he and his little brother, Toby, had come down to this creek to splash in the cool water while they ate their lunch under the hot east Texas sun, their bare backs baked to a deep orange, beads of dirty sweat running down their cheeks. A faint smile crossed Sam's face as he thought about those times, accentuating the wrinkles that had begun to develop much too early on his sun-weathered skin.

He bowed his head almost shamefully. *My god, things have changed.*

First, and most painfully, Toby was gone. The endless acres of pasture weren't so endless anymore, either. Sam had been forced to sell them off slowly just to make ends meet. It had killed him to do it, but the little bit of extra money had been necessary. Then eventually even the deep-pocketed investors couldn't afford to buy any more. The cattle went up for sale next, till there was only enough left to keep his own family going. He was grateful his father wasn't alive to see it.

Sam looked down at the small leather notebook on the ground beside him, its cover as tan and worn as the hand that picked it up. Inside were pages upon pages of notes, taken not in the cursory scribble of a cattle rancher, but in the carefully attentive hand of a writer. He turned impulsively to the front half of the book, to the page marked with the frayed ribbon, and read.

> *And though I fight*
> *I know, I'll never win*
> *For the battlefront*
> *Comes from within*

He sighed and closed the notebook, shaking his head as if to shake off some distant notion. Shoving the notebook into the back pocket of his faded jeans, he stood, turned away from the creek, and squinted at the small house across the pasture. Claire would be up and making breakfast, and if he wasn't back by the time it was done, she'd start to wonder where he'd gone off to.

He headed toward the house.

Sam was met at the door by the smell of bacon and the haze of dust floating along the beams of early morning sunshine. The light poured through the windows onto the worn wooden floors. As he stepped into the living room, Sam looked up at the canvas painting that hung above the mantel of the large brick fireplace—him and Claire on their wedding day. They looked so young and carefree then. It seemed like eons ago.

He found her at the stove, tucking a strand of golden-blond hair behind her ear as she pushed eggs around the skillet. Clarissa Finch, his high-school sweetheart. It seemed almost a crime that she'd had to change her name to Hackett. That in choosing to spend her life with him, she had gone from something as soft and light as *Finch* to something as hard and abrupt as *Hackett*.

"Hey, sugar," she said with a smile.

He stole a piece of bacon from the plate on the counter, broke off a piece, and popped it into his mouth. "Mornin', babe."

"Breakfast is just about ready." She looked at him sideways as he chewed. "Everything okay?"

"Just fine," he answered with a forced smile.

She turned back to the skillet. "It's the last of the bacon," she said quietly.

Sam turned his eyes to the black-and-white checkered floor. They'd butchered the sow late last year to get them through the winter. The few piglets born that spring had all been carried off during the night by coyotes, probably just as hungry and desperate as anyone else was, Sam figured. Claire had done the best she could with what was left in the freezer—including skipping a few meals herself, he'd noticed. But her culinary ingenuity could only get them so far. With a crop ruined by too much rainfall and the lack of work in town, they couldn't keep the pantry stocked, and they both knew it.

Sam stepped behind her and wrapped his arms around her waist. "It'll be all right, babe. You'll see."

She took a deep breath and let it out slowly before moving the eggs from the stovetop and turning to look at him. "Of course it will," she answered. "Now go up and wake Cole before his breakfast gets cold."

Sam nodded and headed for the stairs.

He found their three-year-old lying asleep in his room, surrounded by stuffed monsters and worn fuzzy dogs. Sam hated to wake him, he looked so peaceful. It had been another rough night, with a low-grade fever and more complaints of chest pain.

Sam knelt beside Cole's bed and ran a hand through his son's sun-bleached hair. Cole stirred slightly and took a few dotted breaths, but didn't wake. Sam smiled. The boy's fever had finally broken. He'd let him sleep a little longer.

Sam glanced at the door before taking a letter out of his pocket. He turned the envelope over in his hand, almost afraid to open it. He'd picked it up at the post office during a trip to town several days ago, and had been hiding it from Claire ever since. Rural mail delivery had been canceled years ago, thanks to gas prices, and this was a rare occasion where Sam was grateful for it. He had wanted to get to the letter before she could.

This letter was their last chance. *Cole's* last chance. They'd appealed to every hospital in Texas with heart surgeons trained to treat Cole's condition. Cole was almost at the age when he'd need to receive his final surgery. If it didn't happen soon...

Sam ripped into the envelope and pulled out the letter.

Dear Mr. Hackett,

> *We regret to inform you that due to current federal regulations, we are unable to accept...*

Sam let the letter drop into his lap. He didn't need to read any more. All the others had started out the same. *We regret to inform you...* It was ironic, really. The federal programs were supposed to help people who couldn't afford healthcare. Like most government endeavors designed with good intentions, though, it proved to work much better in concept than in practice.

Instead of helping, the programs, along with the faltering economy, had put healthcare providers out of business. Cole's cardiologist had closed his doors almost a year ago. Even those doctors and hospitals that were still going would no longer accept federal insurance, thanks to the well-below-market cost-of-service caps put on their contracts by the government due to budget cuts. Eventually they stopped accepting insurance all together and instead switched to monthly membership fees or cash-only payments to lower their costs enough to stay open.

Unfortunately, it was cash that Sam didn't have.

He took a long, deep breath and rubbed a hand across his face. "I'm so sorry, buddy."

"Sam!" came a man's voice from downstairs. "Sam, where are you? Get your backside down here, now!"

Sam shoved the letter into his pants pocket as he hopped to his feet and shot for the stairs.

"Zach?" said Sam.

His childhood best friend stood pacing at the bottom of the stairs, his face pale.

"Zach, why on God's green earth are you carrying on like that? From upstairs it sounded like you were dying."

Zach looked him square in the eyes, leaned in toward him, and lowered his voice. "The feds are raiding Harley's gun shop."

Sam gasped.

He shouted toward the kitchen, "Babe, I'll be back," then grabbed Zach by the arm and hurried out the front door.

The drive into town was quick and wordless, Sam bouncing around in the passenger seat of Zach's truck as they flew over gravel back roads, both too terrified to speak. If the feds had been tipped off—if they were there for the reasons he and Zach both prayed they weren't—then everything was about to come to an abrupt end before it had even begun. They passed the "Destiny City Limits" sign, population 2,346 and falling, and headed straight for Harley's store.

Nestled between Nell's barber shop and the abandoned five-and-dime, it was one of the few places downtown still left open. Sam fully expected to see the tiny gun shop engulfed in smoke and under siege by FBI agents. Instead, most of the agents gathered outside the store wore little badges with an acronym that the folks around here dreaded seeing just as much.

IRS.

"You can't do this!" Harley's wife Selena screamed from the sidewalk as Sam and Zach pulled into a parking spot across the street. One of the FBI guys had an arm around her, holding her back as balding little weasels with badges carried boxes of merchandise out of the store.

"Zach, go find out whatever you can about what they know," said Sam.

Zach nodded. "Will do."

"Hey, let her go!" Sam shouted as he climbed out of the truck.

Selena pulled herself away from the FBI agent and ran to Sam. He caught her just before she stumbled off the edge of the sidewalk.

"Sal, honey, calm down," he said. "Just tell me what's going on."

Selena tried to explain in a rush of Spanish and English, tears streaming down her face. "They took him, Sam! They say we owe back taxes, but I know we don't. There's no way we can. How can any of us owe them anything when no one's making money?"

"Wait—what do you mean, they took him?"

"Harley! They took him, and they won't tell me where he is! They say they're going to take all of it if we don't start cooperating!"

Start cooperating? How on earth could a hundred-and-ten-pound, five-foot Puerto Rican and a fifty-year-old war vet with three kids do anything but cooperate when faced with a small army of federal agents?

"Young man, is there something we can help you with?" said a middle-aged bureau boy whose belly filled out his FBI jacket just a little too well. Sam guessed *he* didn't have a hard time making ends meet.

Selena darted behind Sam, whispering a colorful expletive in Spanish.

Bureau Boy curled a lip. "Now, now, little missy. There's no reason we can't all be civilized."

Sam pushed Selena farther behind him. "My friend here says you've taken her husband. Refused to tell her where he is. You can't just take off with a man and not tell his family what you've done with him. From what I understand, this is still America—though it looks less and less like it every day, from where I'm standing."

"Son, I'm Deputy Director Sanchez with the Federal Bureau of Investigation," said the overweight agent. "In case you didn't catch the FBI part." He smirked and pointed to his jacket.

Sam clenched his jaw.

"Now, your feisty little friend here refuses to answer any of our questions. If you want this to go smoothly, I suggest you talk her into being a little more cooperative. And as for not knowing where her husband is... Well, if the little fence jumper has some difficulty *communicating*... then that's not my problem."

"*Ai!*" Selena shouted, darting toward Sanchez. "I was born in San Antonio, you ignorant *pendejo!*"

Sam grabbed her by the waist.

Sanchez just smiled as he stepped away and motioned to another agent standing next to a van parked just in front of the store.

"Selena, that doesn't help," Sam whispered. "Do you want to find Harley and save your shop or not?"

Selena bowed her head. "Yes."

Sam let her go.

"Mrs. Rankin," said the next little FBI weasel. "Mister…" he added, turning to Sam and offering a hand.

Sam crossed his arms. "Hackett. Sam Hackett."

The guy pulled his hand back. "Mr. Hackett," he said to the sidewalk as he ran a hand through the brightest copper-red curls Sam had ever seen. "I'm Agent Larson. I'm a negotiator with the FBI."

"A negotiator? Why would the FBI feel the need to have a negotiator present for an IRS seizure?"

"Sometimes these things get a little… ugly," Larson answered quietly. He glanced at Sanchez, who was talking to some of the guys with IRS badges by the van. "Look, if you could just answer a few quick questions for me, it would make both our lives a lot easier."

Sam sighed. If it would help them find out where they had taken Harley, then fine. "All right, Larson, what do you want to know?"

"Are you aware of any support, financial or otherwise, given by Harley Rankin to any of the following organizations: Public Citizen, the Movements, Americans for Prosperity, any organization that promotes education about the Constitution or Bill of Rights, or any organization openly against federal healthcare?"

Sam's jaw dropped. "What?"

"Is Rankin an avid supporter of President Saundra? Is he actively involved in any sort of local militia?"

"This is Texas; of course he is," said Sam. "We all are. What does any of this have to do with owing back taxes?"

"Mr. Hackett, has Harley Rankin ever spoken against, or supported organizations that have spoken against, the GOG?"

Sam froze. This wasn't about back taxes at all.

Selena released a blood-curdling cry he wouldn't have thought possible from such a small-framed girl. "*Phoenix, noooo!*"

Sam followed Selena's gaze—and understood her panic. Phoenix, her twelve-year-old son, was squatted just inside the second-story window of Harley's shop, the glint of his bright blond head the only thing visible aside from the AR-15 he had rested in the windowsill.

"I don't know about you, Mama, but I think I've had just about enough of this!" he shouted before firing a single shot into the side of the IRS van.

Agent Larson shoved Sam and Selena behind an unmarked car.

"Son, that was about the dumbest thing you could have done!" shouted Sanchez, squatting with several other agents behind the van and pulling out his sidearm. He nodded to one of the other agents, who disappeared around the back of the van. "Is this how you raise your kids, fence jumper?" he barked at Selena.

Selena glared at him and spat some colorful Spanish Sam had never even heard before.

Sam grabbed her before she could rush at Sanchez again. "Selena, don't let him bait you. You can't help Phoenix, or Harley, from the back seat of an FBI car."

"Then what am I supposed to do, Sam? Just sit here?"

Sam sized up the scene. The agents had all taken cover, but Sam knew it wouldn't last for long. He glanced up at Phoenix's window, then dropped his gaze to the doorway beneath it. "That's exactly what I expect you to do," he answered, then jumped up and ran for the door.

"Sam!" Selena shouted after him as Phoenix began unloading several rounds into one of the other IRS vans parked across the street.

Sam dodged Phoenix's hail of bullets, one whizzing dangerously close to his head. He popped through the door of Harley's shop and didn't look back.

Inside the store it was eerily silent, the familiar scent of old cigars and gunpowder that floated in the air was now coupled with dust, kicked up by all the IRS agents scuffling through. Sam knew exactly where to go. He'd climbed the stairs to the box-filled storeroom dozens of times over the last few months. He locked the door behind him and pushed an old metal shelf over in front of it before heading up.

He found Phoenix squatted just beneath the window, peeking out like a sniper scoping his mark.

"Phoenix Rankin," said Sam. "Do you have any idea how dangerous this is?"

Phoenix didn't take his eyes from the street. "'I prefer dangerous freedom over peaceful slavery.' Thomas Jefferson. 1787."

Sam took a deep breath and one slow step forward.

Phoenix popped off another round out the window.

"You can stop right there, Mr. Hackett."

"Okay, okay," said Sam. "I won't come any closer."

"No, you'll get on out of here. I don't wanna have to shoot ya."

Sam prayed he hadn't already hit someone. "Listen, Phoenix. You can still get out of this. Right now, all they want are the guns."

"'To disarm the people is the best and most effective way to enslave them.' George Mason. 1788."

Sam rubbed the back of his neck. He could tell he'd need to take a different approach. "You could have killed me out there, you know."

Phoenix lowered his head, and his gun, only slightly.

"Your mother is out there. Your father, too, probably. And other people's mothers. Other people's fathers, and brothers, and sons, and daughters. A lot of people out there, just trying to do their jobs so they can go home to their families. All this could have been over in a few hours. But not with you up here like some kind of glorified Lee Harvey Oswald. You really going to get someone killed over a bunch of old boxes of ammo?"

Phoenix finally turned from the window. "What do you expect me to do? Just sit back and watch? I'm sorry, Mr. Hackett. You're a good man. Like my daddy. I know you believe in this country as much as he does. I've heard you talk about it myself. But you also know that in war, sometimes you lose good men."

"War? Boy, just what do you think is going on out there?"

"What do *you* think is going on out there? Maggie Wilkins died last night, did you know that? Of an asthma attack. A friggin' *asthma attack*. Her family hasn't been able to afford the medicine for months. They found her in her bed this morning, stone cold and gone. She didn't want to tell her parents that her asthma had been actin' up, because she knew they didn't have the money. So she did nothing. She was eleven years old, for Chrissake, and she was my friend. And now she's gone. Because no one *did* anything!"

Sam stared at him. "I'm so sorry, Phoenix."

"Yeah, well, don't be," he answered, sniffling and rubbing a hand across his nose. He turned back to the window. "Not for me."

"Look," said Sam, lowering his voice and taking a small step across the old wooden floor. Somewhere downstairs he heard glass break. "You're only twelve, son.

You have your whole life ahead of you. Why don't you just come away from that window and let us handle this, okay?"

"My whole *life*?" Phoenix stood and took a step toward him, pointing the gun at Sam.

Sam stopped and held up his hands.

"'When dictators come to power, the first thing they do is take away the people's weapons.' Ronald Reagan. Today it's our medicine and our guns. Tomorrow it'll be our shops and our farms. What else are they going to take from us before someone finally does something about it? What kind of life do any of us have to look forward to?"

"You sound just like your father," said Sam.

"Good! It's about time somebody did!"

"Yeah? And look where it's gotten him! What kind of life do you think he'll have now?"

Phoenix turned his eyes to the floor.

The sound of boots echoed in the stairwell.

"Kid," said Sam, "if you don't hand me that gun right now you won't have *any* kind of life."

Phoenix stood and aimed the gun at the door. "'It is better to die on your feet than to live on your knees.' Emiliano Zapata."

That's when Sam noticed the laser sights dancing across the dust in the air. "*Get down!*" he shouted.

But it was too late.

The shots were clean and quiet, but unmistakable. For a moment, Phoenix looked confused. He stared down at his chest, at the bright red seeping through the dirty white of his T-shirt. Then he looked up at Sam.

Sam stood frozen. "Phoenix," he whispered.

"Mr. Hackett?" Phoenix answered, in the broken voice of a child. Then his eyes rolled upward.

Sam rushed across the room, but not fast enough. He watched helplessly as Phoenix slumped backward out the open window and slammed onto the concrete below.

His mother screamed and rushed to his side.

"Oh, God," Sam whispered, fighting to breathe. His hands gripped the windowsill, his arms shaking. "Oh, dear God."

Sanchez appeared silently beside him.

"What is wrong with you people?" Sam said quietly, his eyes beginning to blur. "He was just a little boy."

"Not anymore, he wasn't," said Sanchez. "The moment he decided to point a gun at the federal government, he was no longer a kid." He picked up the

AR-15 from the floor and narrowed his eyes at Sam. "He was a threat."

Sam was too numb to respond.

"This is a crime scene now, Mr. Hackett," said Sanchez, turning for the stairs. "I suggest you go home."

Sam's eyes stung as he stumbled across the room and down the narrow stairwell. He could still hear Selena's desperate and broken wails as he stepped through the shop's back door and into the alley, the dust lingering in his nose in a way that made it hard to breathe. His head spun as violently as the bullets that had just torn through Phoenix's chest.

Dear God, he thought, *how did it ever come to this?*

He dropped to his knees and vomited onto the cold, hard concrete.

Zach was waiting for him by the time Sam made it back to the truck.

"Sam! Are you okay?"

Sam looked down at his hands. He didn't want to have to answer that question. "What'd you find out?" he asked instead.

Zach lowered his voice. "There wasn't anything in the shop left for them to find. Harley moved it all out a couple of days ago. But now we have a different problem," said Zach.

Sam looked up to meet Zach's gaze.

"Burt Wilkins is out. You know his little girl died last night?"

Sam glanced over his shoulder at Harley's shop, where the line of little IRS ants had returned to carrying out boxes as if nothing had even happened. It made him want to be sick again. "Yeah. I heard."

"He's not the only one, either. A lot of the others are spooked now. Mackenzie says he can replace them with some of the guys he knows, but I'm not exactly sure I trust him, let alone a bunch of people we've never even met. Especially for something like this."

Sam didn't trust Damian Mackenzie as far as he could throw him, either. But they were quickly running out of options.

"Both Burt and Harley gone? I don't know, Sam," said Zach. "This sure does change things."

An ambulance pulled up into the street between the truck and Harley's shop. Sam and Zach watched as they loaded Phoenix's body into the back.

Sanchez noticed them watching. He tipped his head

17

and smirked.

Sam slipped his hands into his pockets, his fingers closing tight around Cole's rejection letter.

He narrowed his eyes. "This changes nothing."

CHAPTER 3

Jon stood on the back deck overlooking the lake, a can in one hand and a spatula in the other. To him, nothing was better than an ice-cold drink and a hot grill on a warm spring afternoon. He took a deep breath and smiled as he flipped the last batch of burgers.

The rev of a diesel engine purred on the other side of the garage behind him. "Sounds like your granddad's here," he said to their not-quite-nineteen-year-old, Leah, who was sprawled out on the patio sofa next to him reading a book.

She hopped up and disappeared around the side of the garage.

This year's end-of-spring-term cookout came with a bigger sigh of relief than usual. Somehow they had all survived another vicious round of budget cuts at the college where Emma taught part-time, Leah's freshman year at Emma's school, and the boys' graduation.

Jon hadn't seen his father-in-law since spring break, and with all the chaos lately, he looked forward to the visit. He never understood why people didn't get along with their in-laws. Jon had a lot of respect for Richard, an honest man who had worked hard to raise three kids after his wife passed away.

Jon couldn't say the same for his own father.

Richard stepped up onto the deck at the side of the garage.

Jon noticed that Richard's limp—the remnants of a gunshot wound to the hip years ago—seemed even more distinctive than the last time he'd seen his father-in-law.

"Hey there, Jon boy."

"Hey, Dad," Jon greeted him with a hug. He was relieved to have Richard there. Maybe Richard could make some sense out of whatever Emma's deal was lately. Or at least he'd be a sympathetic ear. Richard was all too familiar with Emma's—well, craziness. "It's good to see you."

"You too, son. I would have gotten here sooner if I hadn't had to go twenty miles out of my way just to find a gas station still open. When did Peep's finally close its doors?"

"About three months ago, unfortunately," said Jon, who'd had to cross the state line that morning just to find a few bags of chips and a case of pop for the occasion. "I offered to buy it from him, just to keep it open, but he wouldn't hear of it. Said there's no money in convenience stores when a gallon of gas costs more than a carton of cigarettes."

"Yeah, and it's not too easy on the everyday Joe's wallet, either."

"Honestly, Dad, I don't know why you won't just come stay with us." Jon extended the same offer he did every time Richard came to visit. "We have plenty of room."

"My place on the golf course is just fine, thank you very much. So long as I don't actually have to go anywhere."

Jon knew perfectly well Richard didn't golf. He didn't bother to argue, though. He would just ask him again the next time Richard came to visit.

Emma stepped through the French doors from the kitchen and onto the deck.

Jon checked his watch. Finals should have been over hours ago. What took her so long to get home?

"Hey, you two," she said, crossing her arms. "Are you going to stand around and chit-chat, or are we going to eat?"

"Hey, now. Is that any way to greet your old man?" Richard glanced at Jon and winked.

Jon grinned as he plated the burgers. *You get her, Richard.*

Emma took a deep breath and rubbed her forehead. "You're right, Dad. I'm sorry. How are you?"

Jon saw his opportunity to give Emma and her father a chance to talk, hoping that Richard would pick up on Emma's irritability without Jon having to say anything.

He slipped quietly into the kitchen of the home the Grant family had once fondly nicknamed the Lake House. Built right into the side of the embankment which led to the lake below, its open floorplan, floor-to-ceiling fireplace, picture windows, and use of natural materials in everything from the stone tiles to the mahogany cabinets gave it the feel of a cozy getaway to the woods—as if the house were merely an extension of the scenery surrounding it.

It had taken Jon months to get every detail of the design just the way Emma would have wanted, having secretly commissioned the build as a surprise for her. But over the years he'd grown to love it as much as she did. It had become far more than just a house to them. It was their safe place, a way for them to escape the world, and there was nowhere that he'd rather be.

He sat the plate of burgers on the kitchen island, then, unable to resist, grabbed one of the patties with his bare fingers.

Sarah March, their dearest and oldest friend, walked through the front door and caught him. "Hey, what'd I tell you about watching your cholesterol? You're not getting any younger, you know."

"Speak for yourself, Doc. I'm only forty-five," said Jon. "I don't know why you have to be on my case all the time." Though Jon knew with as much effort as Sarah had to put into keeping the entire Grant family alive and well, in spite of themselves, it was a wonder she didn't have them all shackled.

She glared at him as she dropped her bag onto the loveseat. "And I don't know why you even bother coming in for a checkup if you're not going to listen to anything I say."

He winked at her and took a bite of his burger.

Sarah's twenty-one-year old stepson, Daniel, walked in behind her, staring at his feet as he headed for the French doors, his face barely visible beneath the dirty-blonde hair that fell in front of his forehead.

"Hey, Daniel, how's it going?" said Jon, popping the last of his burger into his mouth and licking his fingers clean.

Daniel stopped in mid-stride right in front of the kitchen island. "Um," he stammered, shoving his hands into his pockets. "Fine?" he answered in that thick British accent Jon always found slightly annoying.

"That's..." Jon said, his mouth still full, not having actually expected a response. He looked at Sarah and raised an eyebrow. "Good?"

Sarah just shrugged.

Daniel offered a weak smile, then cleared his throat and turned his eyes to his tennis shoes, his glasses slipping even further down his nose.

The click-click of the ceiling fan slowly spinning over the living room behind him echoed from the wooden floors up to the exposed beams as Jon and Sarah stared at him.

"Well, okay, then," said Jon. He pulled a cutting board and knife out of a drawer and sat them down on the counter. "I think Leah and the boys are down by the lake. Why don't you go find them and tell them the food's ready?"

Daniel nodded. "Right," he said, as if to himself, then turned, stared at his feet as he passed Sarah, and headed down the stairs leading to the walk-out basement instead.

"What's up with him?" Jon asked Sarah as she came to sit on one of the barstools across from him.

"I have no idea," she answered. "He's been acting weird lately."

"You mean, weirder than usual?" said Jon. "Speaking of weird, wasn't your husband supposed to be here?"

"Um," said Sarah, "Mike couldn't make it."

"Oh, that's too bad. Emma will be disappointed."

Sarah laughed. "Are you kidding? Mike is convinced Emma's avoiding him."

"Why would she be avoiding him?" Jon asked, grabbing a tomato from a bowl on the counter.

Sarah's eyes widened. "Hey, did you even wash your hands first?"

"No, *Mom*, I didn't."

"Don't call me that."

He sliced into the tomato and winked. "Then don't act like it."

Emma threw open the French doors. "Well, look who's decided to join us," she barked at Sarah before grabbing a water bottle from the counter, turning on her heel, and heading straight back out onto the deck.

"Hello to you too!" Sarah called after her.

Jon grinned and leaned toward her. "Yeah. She's in one of her moods," he whispered.

Sarah groaned and rested her head on the counter.

By the time they all fixed their plates and settled down to dinner, it was almost sunset. The teenagers opted to sit on the patio sofas at the far end of the deck by the garage, where it wrapped around the left corner of the house. The adults sat at the deck table to the right of the French doors. Jon left an empty chair between him and Sarah for Emma. But when Emma stepped out of the kitchen with her plate, she glanced at the chair beside Jon, narrowed her eyes at Sarah, then sat across from them instead.

"So, President Saundra was here touring the storm damage from last week, I hear. Mike even said he saw Saundra's entourage up at the college today," said Sarah, whose husband taught on the same campus as Emma.

Emma glared at Sarah, but Sarah just bit into her hamburger like she didn't notice. Or didn't care.

"Greg was on campus today, Emmy?" Richard asked,

rubbing his hip before sitting down next to Jon. "Did he come to see you while he was there?"

Emma glanced at Jon and bit her lip. "I saw him, yes." She turned her eyes back to her plate.

Jon raised an eyebrow. He knew that President Saundra and Richard had worked together as US marshals for decades when Emma was younger. The man had practically helped raise her. But having the president of the United States pay you an unexpected visit wasn't something that happened every day. To anyone.

Richard tilted his head. "And?"

"And what?" she answered.

"What did he want, Emma?"

"What makes you think he wanted something?"

Richard crossed his arms. "He's a busy man, Emmy. I doubt very seriously he just popped in to say hello."

Emma continued to stare down at the table. Jon heard the teenagers laughing all the way around the corner while he waited for her to answer. Finally, Emma stopped pushing her potato salad around with her fork and looked up at Jon.

"The man asked you a question, Em," he said. "I think you should answer him."

She dropped her fork onto her plate with a clatter and leaned back in her chair. "Congress has called a convention for next month, okay? Greg asked me to go as a representative."

Jon clenched his jaw. "Why you?"

"Because I tried to warn them years ago that transporting everything from food to energy across the country wasn't sustainable—that the *entire market* existed on a delicate socioeconomic system that could crumble at any moment, at even the slightest upset."

Jon glanced toward the lake, regretting having triggered a rant. "Are you done, yet, Rand?"

"Not with a bang, but a whimper," she mumbled, crossing her arms. "Everyone kept waiting for some solar flare or EMP—some grand calamity—but all it took was an interruption in the fuel supply to bring it all down."

"And Greg thinks you can help?" said Richard.

Emma rubbed her forehead. "The point of the national convention is to present the states with plans for new policies to deal with the energy crisis and recession, like the plans on transitioning back to more localized markets that *I* outlined over twenty years ago. Greg thinks if I presented them now that they'd listen."

"Whoa, did you just say national convention?" said Jacob from behind them. All five of them turned. Jacob stood just outside the kitchen doors, about to walk in with his empty plate.

"What?" said Emma.

"Well, I could have sworn I just heard you say you were asked to speak at the national convention," he answered, brushing his dark hair from his forehead in a gesture that Jon always thought made him look like a Kennedy. "Is that true?"

Emma turned to Jon as if she were asking him whether to answer.

"Because if so, that would be incredible," Jacob continued.

"Why?" asked Sarah. "What's so special about the convention?"

Jacob's eyebrows shot up. "You're kidding me, right? You mean you guys really don't know?"

"No, Jacob, we really don't know. So why don't you enlighten us already?" said Jon.

"Okay, okay." Jacob grinned. He pulled out the chair next to Jon and sat down. "The reason this convention is such a big deal," he leaned forward and whispered as if it were all some great secret, "is because it's not just some political love-fest like the conventions held by the parties every election year. This is a *Constitutional* Convention. It's one of only two ways the Constitution can be amended, and it's never been done before. The state legislatures have applied to amend the Supremacy Clause, which makes the federal government the supreme law. They want to give more power back to the states because they think they can do a better job themselves."

"Greg wouldn't allow that," said Richard.

"He doesn't have a choice," said Jacob. "Neither the president nor Congress has any power over the amendment process in this case. A Constitutional Convention takes control away from the federal government and puts it into the hands of a state-selected group of elitists. Whatever happens at that convention— no matter what it is—will pass if at least three fourths of the states ratify it. The convention doesn't even have to be limited to a single subject once it's been called, either. The delegates could get down there and propose any changes they want, and the Constitution dictates the boundaries for every law and policy that is or ever could be passed in this country. It outlines the extent of power the US government can have. You control the Constitution, and you control the United States."

Emma's eyes got wide. "Which is why Bennett will be there," she said, almost to herself.

Jon sat up straight. "Wait—what?"

"*Stephen* Bennett?" said Sarah. "As in, poster-boy-for-the-GOG Stephen Bennett?"

Emma looked at Jon but didn't answer.

"How in the world did a Canadian national get invited to an American convention?" Richard asked.

Jacob shrugged. "The states can call any delegates they want to represent them. There were bankers, lawyers, and ministers at the Constitutional Convention held when the United States was founded. If President Saundra asked you, Mom, it means he made sure your name got included through one of the state legislatures."

That didn't surprise Jon at all. Greg Saundra probably had quite a few friends from Virginia and North Carolina he could talk into it. That would also explain why he'd been so secretive about his visit. It hadn't even been mentioned in the local news. Saundra knew he was the only one who could convince Emma to do it—yet if anyone at that convention found out she'd been asked by the federal government to be there, her credibility would be shot.

"But Stephen Bennett?" said Sarah.

"Yes. And that's exactly why everyone's so worried," Jacob explained. "Because the only other time there's been a Constitutional Convention was in 1776, to fix the problems of operating under the Articles of Confederation. Except that, for most of the attendees, their goal wasn't actually to find a way to *fix* the existing government." He picked up his plate and stood.

Jon, Emma, Mike, Sarah, and Richard stared at him.

"Then what was their goal?" asked Jon.

Jacob turned and headed toward the doors. "To form an entirely new one."

They finished the rest of their meal in an eerie silence, punctuated by occasional laughter from the kids around the corner. The sun faded into a deep orange as it disappeared through the tops of the trees on the other side of the lake. The frogs were as loud as Jon had heard them all spring, and there was already a thick stickiness in the air. It would be a rough summer.

Eventually, Jon could no longer swallow the perfectly marbled porterhouse he'd been saving since they slaughtered the steer six months ago, thanks to the large knot that had formed in the back of his throat as soon as he heard Stephen Bennett's name. Every few minutes he'd glance over at Emma, who hadn't so much as lifted her eyes in his direction. He was angry at her for not telling him sooner, though he had to admit she hadn't had the chance.

Finally, he resolved to find something more productive to do than sit there and stew. He got up and headed into the kitchen to clean up.

Sarah followed him.

"Did you bring them?" Jon asked her as he rinsed a plate and loaded it into the dishwasher.

She leaned against the counter next to him. "Yes, I brought them."

Jon went silent as the others began to stream in from the deck. Leah and the boys spread out across the sofa and loveseat in the living room. Richard plopped himself down in the armchair across from them. Jon took a quick glance out the window over the sink to check on Emma. She still sat on the deck alone in the dark, poking at her half-eaten dinner with a fork.

"Then you're okay with it?" he said, turning back to Sarah.

"Of course I'm not *okay* with it," she answered, lowering her voice. "It goes against every ethical code I'm sworn to uphold."

Jon wrinkled his forehead. Sarah was like a sister to him. The last thing he wanted was for her to have to do something that made her uncomfortable. But what other option did he have?

He took a deep breath. "Then I appreciate it even more."

Sarah sighed. "All right. But let's not make a habit of it, okay?"

"Thank you. You know you're my favorite MD, right, Doc?" he said with a smile.

"I darn well better be."

Jon quickly cleared his throat to let Sarah know that Emma was stepping through the French doors behind her. Sarah winked at him and walked off.

"Honey, you didn't have to do this," said Emma, setting her plate on the counter. "You did the cooking and prep work, the least I can do is clean up."

"It's okay. I don't mind." He looked down at her plate. "Em, you barely even touched your food."

"I know. I just don't feel much like eating right now."

Jon looked her over. She had dark circles beneath her eyes, like she hadn't slept in days. Her face was even starting to thin, accentuating the lightly-bronzed complexion and high cheekbones of her mother's tribe. At barely five-foot-four and a-hundred-and-fifteen pounds on a good day, Emma had always been small, but Jon could tell she'd lost some weight. And he knew she would just get worse, which was exactly why he had gone to Sarah when he did.

He turned off the faucet and dried his hands. "Baby, why don't you go downstairs and get comfortable? I'll make sure everything gets taken care of," he said, wrapping his arms around her waist. He noticed Sarah heading toward him from the loveseat, a hand in her pocket. "How about I bring you down a cup of tea?"

"Why are you being so nice to me all of a sudden?"

"What are you talking about? I'm always nice to you."

Emma grinned and shrugged. "Yeah, I guess you're right."

Jon leaned down to kiss her and, as he did, felt Sarah slip something into his pocket.

"All right you two, that's enough of that," said Leah. She glared at her mother, her eyes burning with the same reddish-brown that Emma's would whenever she was mad, and grabbed a bag of chips from the counter. "If I have to behave while everyone's here, then so do you."

"Excuse me, young lady?" said Emma. "I don't see a ring on *your* finger!"

"Come on, Emma," said Sarah, grabbing Emma by the arm and pulling her toward the stairs. "Why don't you show me some of Jacob's latest work?"

Seriously? Jon glared at Leah as Sarah dragged Emma away, luckily before things became any more heated.

Leah shoved the bag of chips into the pantry cabinet, flipped her hair over her shoulder, and walked off.

Jon finished up the dishes, then looked around to make sure he was the only one in the kitchen before making Emma's tea. As he headed toward the stairs with a steaming mug in each hand, he could feel Matt following him across the room with his eyes.

He walked softly down the wrap-around staircase, stopping on the landing at the middle. Sarah stood on the other side of the family room, admiring some of Jacob's latest photography which covered most of the wall behind the piano. Jon glanced down at the sectional sofa just

27

below him. Emma was in her favorite spot, curled up in the corner with a blanket wrapped around her.

Jon shook his head. Almost summer, and Emma was cold. It wasn't a good sign.

He continued down the stairs and handed Sarah one of the mugs of tea. Sarah stared into the cup and raised an eyebrow at him. Jon grinned and winked.

As he turned toward the couch to give Emma the other cup, he noticed her nodding off. She sat with her knees drawn up to her chest and her head resting on the cushion beside her. Unfortunately, falling asleep was never her problem. It was staying asleep that she had such a hard time with.

"Thank you, sweetheart," said Emma, sitting up straight as he handed her the tea.

He smiled. "You're very welcome."

Jon settled down at the other end of the couch, the clock on the wall counting off nine bongs as he sank into the softened leather chaise, not realizing until then how tired he was himself. Sarah sat down on the side of the couch close to Emma. Emma took a long drink of her tea, then yawned and rubbed her eyes. Jon furrowed his at Sarah.

She frowned and took a deep breath. "You look awfully tired, kiddo," she told Emma.

"I'm not as young as I used to be, I'm afraid."

"Oh, you're only as old as you feel."

Emma leaned her head back and closed her eyes. "Then I'm old."

"Hey, I've got six years on you. What does that make me?" said Sarah.

Emma smiled. "Older."

Jon couldn't help but laugh.

Until Sarah glared at him. "Emma," she said, as she pushed a lock of hair over her ear that Jon noticed had become more white than blond over the years, "Jon says you've been having trouble sleeping."

"Well, Jon has a big mouth."

Sarah grinned. "Be that as it may, I still think you should let me give you—"

"No."

"Emma—"

"I don't want to take anything, Sarah!" Emma lifted her head off the cushion and narrowed her eyes.

"Fine," said Sarah. "If you won't let me help you, then I'll just give it to Jon so he can slip it to you when you're

28

not looking."

Jon's jaw dropped. *Sarah, what are you doing?* She had told him she would give Emma the opportunity to accept her help willingly, but this wasn't what he had in mind.

Emma curled a lip. "He wouldn't do that." She brought her cup to her mouth.

Jon felt a pang of guilt as she took a long drink.

"Oh yeah?" said Sarah. "How's your tea?"

Emma choked mid-gulp. She looked first into her cup, then up at Jon, her eyes wide. Jon dropped his head and looked away. Apparently secretly drugging her patients wasn't something Sarah was particularly good at.

I guess this makes us even.

"You traitor!" Emma barked.

Jon shrugged. "What can I say? The woman signs my flight physical."

"Yeah? Well, she's also going to be signing your *death* certificate."

"Okay." Sarah clapped her hands together and stood. "I can see my work here is done. That should kick in pretty quickly," she added, pointing at Emma's cup.

Emma glared.

"You can thank me in the morning," said Sarah.

Jon highly doubted that would happen. "Let me walk you out," he told Sarah.

Upstairs in the living room, the boys had decided to start a movie. Richard had fallen asleep in the armchair, as usual. Sometime in the middle of the night he'd get up and pad down the hall to the guest room. Then in the morning he and Jon would sneak off together to enjoy short stacks and sausage without a lecture about cholesterol.

"Well, boys, we're heading out. Where's Daniel?" asked Sarah.

"Out on the front porch," said Jacob, "with Leah."

Jon clenched his jaw.

Sarah flipped on the light as she and Jon stepped out onto the front porch. Leah and Daniel were standing next to the banister, their arms wrapped around each other's waists, and Daniel's forehead rested on hers.

Daniel quickly dropped his hold on Leah and stepped back.

Jon glared at Leah. "I specifically asked you to cool it tonight, didn't I? Are you determined to see your mother's head explode?"

Leah narrowed her eyes at him, then looked away.

"Oh, don't mind him, honey," said Sarah, stepping

over to give Leah a hug goodbye. "He's just cranky because he's pretty sure he's sleeping on the couch."

Jon might have laughed if it weren't partially true.

"Come on, Daniel. I'll walk you to the car." Leah grabbed Daniel's hand and dragged him toward the steps.

Daniel nodded nervously at Jon as they passed. "Captain Grant," he said, his accent even more annoying when shaky.

Jon crossed his arms. "Daniel."

"You should really cut them some slack, Jon," said Sarah, once the lovebirds were out of earshot. "Don't you remember what it was like to be that age?"

"As a matter of fact, I remember *exactly* what it was like to be that age."

Honestly, Jon didn't mind that the two of them were together. Leah was seventeen when they started dating. Daniel was twenty. Jon and Emma would never have allowed the age difference if it were someone other than Daniel. But still, no sense in letting the kid get comfortable. The longer Jon made Daniel nervous, the less likely the two of them were to make the same mistakes he had.

Sarah smiled. "Yeah, well, he's nowhere near as wild as you were."

"I would certainly hope not." Jon smiled back. He watched Daniel and Leah disappear up the path toward the darkened driveway, then lowered his voice. "Listen, Sarah, about Emma…"

"I know, Jon, I'm worried about her too. If you can manage to slip her a few more of those sleeping pills, hopefully it will help."

"Yeah, *if* I can manage it, now that you've blown my cover."

Sarah frowned. "Yeah, I guess I did, huh? Sorry about that. Sometimes I just let Emma get to me."

"But it isn't just that she's not sleeping. I don't know if you've noticed, but she's not eating much either. I think there's something else bothering her. She's restless and edgy." Jon looked down at the porch, then up at Sarah. "I think she's having the dreams again, Sarah. You know how reckless she gets when she has them. I'm not sure if I could go through that again. I'm not sure if *we* could go through that again."

Sarah sighed. "Jon, things are a lot different than they were twenty years ago. You're both stronger people than you used to be."

"Yeah, I know, but…"

"Look, I know Emma, and I know how… *difficult*… she can be sometimes. But I also know you. I know how much you love her, and your kids, and just how far you'll go for them. I'm sure you'll get through it."

Jon took a deep breath. If only he could be that certain.

"And if she needs anything—if *you* need anything—don't hesitate to ask, okay?"

He nodded.

Sarah leaned up to kiss him on the cheek.

"Thank you, Sarah," he said. "I really do appreciate it."

"What can I say?" She rolled her eyes before turning to leave. "I live to serve."

Leah passed her on the walkway. "Goodnight, Sarah."

"Goodnight, sweetie," she answered.

Leah stepped up onto the porch and slipped an arm around Jon's waist. They both watched in silence as Sarah's headlights disappear up the drive.

"Dad," Leah said form underneath his arm, "did Daniel talk to you?"

"About what, pal?"

"Oh, nothing. Anything, really."

"You know," said Jon, turning them both toward the door. "I actually think that's the most that kid has said to me in months."

Back inside the darkened living room, the boys watched their movie and Richard snored. Jon grabbed a blanket from the loveseat and threw it over Richard before heading to bed. "Good night, boys," he said. "Don't stay up too late."

"Sure thing, Dad," said Jacob.

Jon found Emma curled up on the sectional downstairs, breathing softly, the empty tea cup still in her hand. Jon took the cup from her and set it on the coffee table, then pushed a lock of auburn hair from her face before picking her up gently to carry her to bed.

"You are in so much trouble," she whispered as she wrapped her arms around his neck.

"As long as we both get a good night's sleep," he said, "that's fine with me."

CHAPTER 4

"I don't know why you bother to knock," said Matt, just as Jon raised a hand to knock on his open bedroom door. He sat cross-legged on his bed, a textbook in his lap. "It's not like I have a girl in here or anything."

Jon leaned against the doorframe. "Well, you did just have a birthday, didn't you? You're legally an adult now. I think the least I can do is respect your privacy."

Matt turned a page. "What do you need, Dad?"

Jon hesitated, slightly hurt that his son would think the only reason he'd come to his door was if he wanted something.

Matt sighed and closed his book. "I'm sorry. That was rude. I didn't mean to—"

"No, Matt, it's okay. I know you're busy. I just…" Jon rubbed a hand across his mouth, unable to remember the last time he *had* come to Matt's room for a reason other than needing something. "Have you seen Mom?"

"Yeah. She's been home for a few hours, but she hasn't said a word to me. In fact, as soon as she got here…" Matt took a deep breath and tugged at one of the loose threads of his bedspread, then said, "Dad, she grabbed the peanut butter and went straight up to your studio."

Oh no. Jon closed his eyes and bowed his head.

His studio was the most secluded room in the house. Hardly anyone ever went up there, even him. Emma had always been adamant about staying out of there herself, because she insisted she had put it in the house design specifically so that he would have somewhere to go to be alone. Which was exactly why he never went up there. Jon had never liked being alone. Between being raised in boarding schools and locked up as a POW during the war, he had already spent enough time alone to last him the rest of his life.

And the fact that she was now sitting up there with a jar of peanut butter made it a thousand times worse.

Jon opened one eye, peering at Matt through the locks of dark hair that fell in front of his forehead. "Did she take a spoon?"

"Yeah, Dad. She did."

Great. He thought he'd fixed this. After spending over twenty years together, he could usually work out what was bothering Emma. He seldom understood it, but he could at least get close enough to help. If using the sleeping pills to make sure she was getting plenty of rest and busting his tail around the house so she could work on her presentation over the last month wasn't enough, then Jon was out of ideas. Which meant there was only one thing left to do if he wanted to know what was wrong with Emma.

Ask Matt.

"Matt?" said Jon, sitting down at the end of his bed. "Is your mother... okay? I mean, over the last few months has she... I don't know... talked to you about anything?"

Matt sighed and looked out the window, watching silently as two of the foals chased each other from one side of the pasture to the other. "Dad, I really don't think it's me she needs to be talking to."

Jon *had* tried to talk to her. Plenty of times. But there were some things Emma just wasn't comfortable discussing with him. The same things he wasn't comfortable discussing with her—or anyone else.

"And, no," Matt continued. "She's not okay." He opened his book and turned his eyes back to the page. Jon guessed that was his way of saying he wasn't the person *Jon* should be talking to either.

And he was probably right.

Jon rubbed his hands across his jeans and got up. He stopped just inside the doorway. "Hey, Matt."

Matt looked up.

"If you did have a girl in here, who would she be?"

Matt grinned and shook his head. "I have a lot of reading to do, Dad."

Jon smiled as he left the room.

He took a deep breath and crossed the living room. *Okay, Jon, you can do this*, he told himself as he reached for the doorknob to the stairwell that ran behind the fireplace and up to his studio above the garage. After all, it was just peanut butter, which meant the good old-fashioned kind of stress he could deal with. The going head-to-head with administrators, working out budget cuts, and arguing with Leah over dating habits kind of stress. It wasn't like Emma had come home and tried to figure out where he'd hidden the chocolate again.

The darkness of the narrow stairwell gave way to sunlight when Jon reached the top. Emma sat slouched on the massive sectional sofa which took up the entire left side and back of the room, her arms crossed and feet resting on the coffee table, staring silently out the floor-to-ceiling windows that ran across the dormer overlooking the lake below. It really was a great room, despite its seclusion. He wasn't sure why she didn't just claim it for herself. Jon had never understood Emma's occasional need for solitude. Mostly because she loved being alone for the same reason he hated it.

Because being alone meant no one needed you.

"Hey there, stranger," said Jon.

"Hi," answered Emma quietly, without looking at him.

Jon picked up the half-eaten jar of peanut butter from the coffee table. "Extra crunchy, huh? Must be serious."

Emma didn't answer. She just stared into the distance, mindlessly sliding the dove pendant on her necklace back and forth like she always did when she was nervous.

Jon put down the jar and sat next to her.

"Jon," she said without turning, as if she were talking to the trees across the lake rather than to him, "do you ever wonder who you really are?"

Jon wrinkled his forehead. *Who I really am?*

He looked down at the silver ring on his right hand. The inscription *Tolle Super Nobis Nomen Et Memento* was engraved around the gemstone in the center. The stone wasn't a birthstone like it would be for anyone else who wore one, but a yellow star sapphire with a dark circle beneath, like a great eagle's eye. It was the only one of its kind like it.

And so was Jon.

The ring was a symbol of his commitment to the Order of the Golden Eagle, an organization that was more like a country club than a secret society. It was also an organization that Jon had sworn he'd never have anything to do with. Until the day he needed their help.

After Emma got sick.

Since then, he'd attended the classes, participated in the fundraisers, sworn to the code. He'd even held offices and looked out for other member families. So far, nothing the OGE had asked him to do had ever interfered with his own responsibilities. In fact, they had taught him how to be a better father and husband. Something he'd never learned from his own dad.

So no, Jon didn't have to wonder, any more than Emma did. They'd both been told, years ago, exactly who and what they were. From what Jon understood, the OGE had nearly condemned their marriage because of it, for fear Emma would be a bad influence on him. Ironic, considering that unlike Jon, Emma had been born and raised a believer. It wasn't until they let her down that she lost faith, and it was a long time before she got it back again. But by then it had become more like a bone that had been broken in too many places, never healing to as strong as it was before.

"My grandfather would say," Jon answered, "that we are the choices we make."

Emma squeezed her eyes shut for a moment. "What if I made some bad choices? What if I could have said something, or done something, differently? Something that would have made things better? Made everyone's lives… *easier*?"

Her words echoed inside Jon's head. Not so much what she said, but how she said it. With an incredible tone of finality. He reached for her hand, and only then did she look at him. For the first time, Jon noticed the shimmer of tear stains on her cheeks.

Emma had been crying.

"Something," she whispered, her eyes meeting his, "that would have changed… everything."

Jon pushed a lock of hair behind her ear. She was hurting, and he could feel it. He had no idea why, and it drove him nuts. *Please, Emmy, just talk to me. Tell me what's wrong. Just tell me so I can* do *something about it!*

Emma was scared, though, and he didn't blame her. This stuff made him nervous, too.

"Is this about the convention?" he asked.

She sighed. "The convention," she said, as if it were the furthest thing from her mind. She rubbed a hand across her face and sank back against the cushion. For a while she just stared blankly at the ceiling. Then she got up and walked over to the window.

He followed her.

"I just…" She crossed her arms. "I just don't know if I can do this."

Jon smiled. "You said the same thing when the boys were born."

"Yeah, and I'm still not so sure I can do that either."

"Emmy." He put his hands on her arms. "You are an incredible mother, and a *freakishly* persuasive speaker. You'll do fine."

"It's not the speaker I'm worried about, Jon," she said quietly. "It's the listener."

Jon shook his head and let go of her. "Oh, come on, Em."

"Maybe if I just showed them? Made them

35

understand."

"But that's not what we're here for, Emma."

"Then what *are* we here for, Jon!" she exploded.

Jon stared at her, at the slight tremble of her lip, and the glimmer of freshly-forming tears against the caramel color in her eyes. He knew she was on edge, but he'd had no idea it was this bad. What in the world was happening inside her head?

Emma took in a long, deep breath and turned back to the window. "To watch it all fall apart?" she said quietly to the lake. "To pick up the pieces?"

Jon watched silently as she closed her eyes and rested her head against the glass. Emma was the strongest person he had ever known. He had seen her broken countless times, after losing everything from children to almost each other, and every time she bounced back. Every time, she fought it and moved on. But this time, whatever Emma was up against had her so worried she couldn't even bring herself to talk to him about it.

This time Emma wasn't recovering. She was getting worse.

"Honey," he said quietly, wrapping his arms around her waist.

She let her head sink back against his shoulder. "I can feel it, Jon," she said, "*screaming* inside of me. I just don't know what I'm supposed to do."

He wanted to say "nothing." That there wasn't anything either one of them was *supposed* to do besides live their lives, raise their kids, and grow old together. The entire world could fall apart around them and it wouldn't faze him one bit, as long as they still had each other. But the point of him coming up here was to make her feel better, not push her further away.

"Em…" he said, pulling her around to face him. "You just have to be patient, okay? When the time comes, we'll know. You probably even before the rest of us. Until then, don't get so focused on the distance that you can't see what's right in front of you."

"You mean like you? My incredibly wonderful husband?"

Jon smiled. "For starters."

He could feel the warmth of her breath against his lips as he pulled her in to kiss her. She melted into his arms, as if just being that close to him could make her forget about everything else. Jon completely understood that feeling. It never ceased to amaze him how, even after all these years, kissing Emma could still do strange things to his head.

"You know," he said, slipping his hands into the back pockets of her jeans and pulling her tighter against him, "I could be wrong, but I don't think we've marked this room off our list."

Emma's eyes widened. "Jonathan Grant."

"What?" he answered with a grin. "Come on, Em, it's been over a month."

As he leaned in to kiss her again, his heartbeat quickened. Caused, in part, by the spark he always felt whenever they kissed. He'd noticed it the very first time he'd pressed his lips to hers, and the intensity had never faded.

"That's not my fault," she pulled away long enough to say. "I'm not the one that drugs you every night before bed."

"Well, you're not drugged now." He started to move down her neck, the floral scent of her skin filling his senses.

"And Matt's home."

"So? The room is soundproof."

"I don't think that's going to stop Matt from knowing what *you two* are doing up here," said Jacob.

Emma jumped so fast Jon thought she might scream. Standing at the top of the stairwell was Jacob, a big grin on his face as if he'd just caught them doing a lot more than kissing.

Emma buried her face in Jon's shoulder.

"Is there something I can do for you?" Jon snapped.

"I am *really* sorry to interrupt," said Jacob, brushing his hair out of his eyes, "but Mom, I wanted to let you know I stopped by the library before I left campus and found those statistics you were looking for."

Emma raised her head from Jon's shoulder and drew her eyebrows together. "Really?"

"Yeah, I've got them downstairs. So, whenever you're ready to get started again..."

Jon smiled. Jacob adored his mother and tried hard to find ways to spend time with her. Too bad it always had to involve her work. Emma never seemed to make as much effort with him.

"But there's no hurry or anything," Jacob added as he backed toward the stairs. "Feel free to carry on with... whatever you were doing," he said with a wink before leaving.

Emma narrowed her eyes at Jon. "You know he gets

that cheekiness from you, don't you?"

"He does not," Jon answered, though he knew perfectly well she was right.

He smiled down at her, suddenly realizing how little time they had gotten to themselves over the last month. Jon had no idea how long she'd be in Dallas, but from what he understood about what Jacob had told him of the original Constitutional Convention, it could be months before he saw his wife again.

"Hey, why don't we get out of here, just you and me?" he said. "It's still early. We could drive down to Eureka Springs, spend the night at that little place on White River, and be back in the morning just in time to get you to the airport for your flight. What do you think?"

"I thought that's what the cabin was for," said Emma, referring to the weekend cabin Jon had built on the other side of the lake years ago. They used it during holidays and special occasions when they couldn't travel, or every now and then when they wanted to be alone. Like now.

"Yeah..." He nodded slowly, remembering that no one had cleaned it after the birthday party he let Leah and the boys have up there without telling her. "But then we couldn't go to Ermilio's for dinner." *Or Anglers for breakfast, for that matter.* "So... is it a date?"

Emma sighed. "I'd love to, but..."

"But?"

"I'm not done with my presentation."

"Oh," said Jon, his heart sinking. The thought of spending a night with Emma—a night without kids or school or presentations to interrupt them—had sounded fantastic. *So much for that.* "Rain check, then?"

"Absolutely," she answered, putting her hands on his chest and giving him one of those incredible, bright-eyed smiles that lit up her entire face. It had been months since he had seen her smile like that, and it wasn't until that moment that Jon realized how much he'd missed it. He never would have thought it possible to love someone so much that just watching them smile could fill him up inside. It was too bad she didn't have enough faith in them to tell him what was wrong.

"I love you," he said. "You do know that, don't you?"

"You mean despite my many flaws?"

Jon grinned. "*Because* of your many flaws."

Emma's smile slowly faded, and she rested her head on his shoulder, turning to look out over the lake again as if she had suddenly come to some bleak realization. He wrapped his arms tighter around her and pressed his lips to her hair, breathing deep the familiar scent of awapuhi and almond.

A few dark clouds began to roll in above the tree line.

"Em," said Jon. "This isn't just another convention for you, is it? This is really something you feel like you have to do."

Emma looked up at him. There was a sense of security in her eyes, as if she knew, regardless of anything else, she could always trust him to watch over her. "Yes, Jon, it is."

Jon sighed. "Then I guess you should probably finish your presentation."

Emma nodded slowly, then gave him a long, lingering kiss and headed down the stairs.

He took a deep breath and turned back to the window, watching the trees as the gathering winds blew the leaves light-side up—a sign of the approaching storm.

Over the years, he had learned to live with the eccentricities. The premonitions. The sudden attacks of anxiety and nausea, or the occasional request to turn left when he normally would have turned right. It was the dreams he couldn't deal with. The sleeping pills helped, but they couldn't take away what she had already seen, and whatever it was had had such a profound effect on her that Emma was beginning to snap.

Unfortunately, it wasn't so much *what* she knew, but what she chose to *do* with what she knew that was the problem.

The first time he saw it happen, it had scared the hell out of him. They were both lying sound asleep in their little one-bedroom apartment in Leesburg, Virginia, over twenty years ago. Emma was still working in the field for FEMA, and he had flown for the Guard for close to a year.

It was just after dawn when she woke up screaming.

In a frantic frenzy of blankets, Jon somehow managed to find the lamp on the nightstand and flip it on. Emma was sitting up in bed, coughing and gasping for air.

"Emmy?" He knelt on the bed in front of her, his hands on her shoulders. "Are you okay?"

Just when he was about to call 911, her breathing steadied. But instead of calming down, she did something that caught him off guard completely.

Emma burst into tears.

He had never seen her cry before. Or at least, not like this. Emma was one of the strongest people he had ever met. He'd watched her command entire teams of emergency personnel, snake her way through collapsed buildings, and go head-to-head with high-ranking military officials without so much as batting an eye. Seeing her so vulnerable was unnerving. He held her, her face buried in his shoulder, patting her gently until she finished.

When she looked up at him, her eyes were puffy and red.

Jon wiped the tears from her cheeks. "What is it, Princess?"

In a rush of words, she told him what she had seen in her dream. Emma was able to describe in great detail, from the color of the surrounding cars to the smell of gasoline, a woman driving through a tunnel with her toddler son strapped into his car seat in the back. Until there was suddenly a deafening explosion, and everything went dark. Then the water came. Her eyes began to tear again as she told Jon what it felt like to watch the mother reaching helplessly for her son as the icy water flooded in around them.

No wonder she was so upset.

Jon knew Emma was terrified of water, so he assumed it was just a nightmare. He cradled her in his arms. "It's all right, sweetheart. Everything is fine. You're safe. I'm not going to let anything happen to you." He coddled her unsuspectingly, wanting to do whatever he could to make her feel better. She told him that a bar of chocolate usually helped, which seemed odd, knowing Emma wasn't big on sugar, but he offered to go down to the corner store and bring her back one anyway.

At the convenience store, Jon grabbed the candy bar and headed up to pay. The cashier was staring at a tiny TV on the counter in front of him as if he didn't even notice Jon was there.

Jon cleared his throat.

"Man, I just can't believe this," the cashier said, almost to himself.

"Believe what?" Jon asked.

The cashier looked up at Jon. "Dude, where have you been?" He turned the TV around to face Jon and raised the volume.

Jon watched the newscast live from New York. The cashier had said it right. Jon couldn't believe it either.

When he returned to the apartment, Emma was dressed and standing behind the couch in the living room, watching the same newscast. She hung up her cell phone as he walked through the door. Her pack lay on the floor at her feet.

Jon grabbed the remote and turned up the volume.

"Again, for those just tuning in, there has been an explosion in the Holland Tunnel. There is no word yet on whether this explosion was accidental or a terrorist attack. Emergency personnel report that some people are trapped inside the tunnel, and those people are at significant risk both from structural collapse and from the potential for flooding..."

Jon turned off the TV and threw the remote onto the couch. "Why didn't you just tell me?"

"Why should I, Jon? You've already made it clear you don't believe in any of this. You won't even accept what *you* are. What would make me think you'd accept *this*?"

She was right about one thing. He'd told her from the very beginning that the Mark—the emblem that signified from birth that their kind were *different*—meant absolutely nothing to him. But still, he had a right to know about her gift. Especially considering what she chose to do with it.

"I don't know what I am, Emma," he said, "but I do know what *you* are. You're a Seer. I don't know why I didn't figure it out in Seattle. That's how your team made it there so fast, after the quake. That's how you knew exactly where to go, isn't it?"

Emma picked up the bag at her feet. "Look, Jon, I have to go to New York."

"For *what*, Emma? You just got here!"

"I have an obligation to those people!"

"Fine," said Jon, slapping the candy bar in her hand. "Here's your chocolate. I hope it makes you feel better."

He turned, strode into the bathroom, and slammed the door behind him. He only faintly heard the front door open and close as he started the shower.

Since then, Emma had never again shared with him anything she saw in one of her dreams.

Sarah had been right about what she said on the night of the cookout, though. Things were a thousand times better now than they were back then. But it had taken a war, cancer, and years without the dreams to get to that point.

All Jon ever wanted was a normal life, and he'd grown far too used to it over the last nine years to give it up now. He wasn't about to let her get swept away by some obligation she felt toward everyone else but him. To let everything they'd worked so hard for get taken away just because of some obscure images she'd seen in her sleep.

He'd be damned if he ever came that close to losing her again.

Jon waited for the distinctive click of the studio door closing downstairs, then picked up the phone on his desk.

And called his father-in-law.

"Hey, Dad," he said once Richard answered. "I have a favor to ask. Could you come up and keep an eye on things for a little while? I'm not sure for how long, I just…" He closed his eyes and rubbed a hand across his face.

In the distance, a crack of thunder broke the silence.

"Dad," he said, taking a deep breath, "I'm going to Dallas with Emma."

CHAPTER 5

Emma jumped halfway across the back seat of the car as another bottle shattered against the window beside her.

Jon wrapped an arm around her and pulled her closer. Emma welcomed his protectiveness, so shaken she wasn't even sure she could make it inside the building on her own once they arrived. Even though Jon, the smoothest pilot she knew, had insisted on flying them down to Dallas himself that morning, she had been unnaturally queasy from the moment they took off. And the crowd of protestors surrounding the massive four-star hotel just beyond the window wasn't making her feel any better.

"I thought you guys said this location was supposed to be confidential," Jon said to their driver.

The driver had slowed to a crawl just to get through the crowd, which spanned several blocks of downtown Dallas. "Yes, sir, it was. In fact, we even changed the location last minute because we received a tip the previous one was leaked to the media."

"I guess this location got out, too," said Emma.

"Don't worry, ma'am," said the driver. "I can assure you, we at the FBI have made the security of this conference our top priority."

"And a lot of good that's done, apparently," Jon whispered to Emma.

The inside of the hotel was much quieter, but almost as hectic. Hundreds of people scurried across an extravagant lobby, the marbled floors and lush furnishings contrasting starkly to the chaos outside. Most of the people in the lobby were dressed in what Emma guessed was the hotel's uniform, crisp white button-up shirts and jacquard vests. The others, all of whom were surrounded by their own circles of security guards, were barking orders and being handed glasses of chardonnay.

One particularly stout, grandfatherly gentleman in a dark suit had a much larger and more serious-looking security detail, but insisted on walking out in front of them and shaking people's hands instead.

Jon's "uncle" Jack.

He caught Emma's eye and headed straight for her and Jon.

Emma relaxed slightly at seeing Jack there. Jack, along with Jon's parents, Robert and Alyssa, had been best friends from the time they were young. The three of them were once so inseparable, from what Emma understood, that Jack and Robert had competed for Alyssa's affections. In the end, of course, Jon's father won. Robert and Alyssa were married, and nine months later Jon was born—and Alyssa was gone. Jack had made a special point to look out for Jon from the time he was little, going out on a limb to bail him out of every bad situation he ever got himself into. Emma suspected that Jack's watchful eye over Jon had more to do with the fact that he was Alyssa's son than that he was Robert's.

"Mr. Vice President," said Jon, grinning and shaking Jack's hand.

It still seemed strange to Emma to think that Jack and Greg Saundra had ended up running for office together, considering that she and Jon were the ones who'd introduced them.

Jon glanced at the Secret Service men hovering around Jack and lowered his voice. "I'd hug you if I wasn't afraid I'd get tackled."

"I know what you mean. I'm sorry about all this security."

"We can see why it's needed," said Jon. "What's going on out there?"

"You mean the protesters? Most of them are out of work and have been for a long time. Some of them are here to protest Bennett's presence at the convention. A lot of them don't really even know why they're here, just that they're desperate and angry and looking for someone to blame."

"It's hard to believe it's gotten that bad," said Emma. "I mean, we'd heard about the Movements, but we've never seen one where we are."

"They're much worse in the bigger cities, I'm afraid. More people out of work and fewer resources to go around." Jack put a hand on each of their arms, smiling with a warmth that made his eyes wrinkle around the edges. "Regardless, I'm glad you're here. It's really good to see you."

Jon smiled back. "It's really good to see you too, Jack."

For a moment, Jack stared at Jon with the affection of a father seeing a son for the first time in far too many years. Then he turned his gaze to the front doors. His smile faded. "Well," he said, shifting nervously, "I should probably make sure things are in order. Why don't you go ahead and get yourselves settled in? I'm sure you'd like some rest after your flight. Emma, how about you go on into the atrium and sit down while Jon checks in and picks up your room key?"

Jon looked over his shoulder at the front desk. A significant crowd was gathering just inside the doorway to greet one of the newest arrivals. "Yeah, sure. I can do that."

"Good, good," said Jack, his eyes darting toward the door again. "And Jon—" He pulled him in and hugged him close for several moments before finally letting him go. "I really am glad you're here, son."

Jon raised an eyebrow at Emma.

"Both of you," Jack added quietly, then stepped away, his entourage following behind him.

Jon shrugged and turned toward the front desk.

Emma headed into the atrium. The rush of water cascading down the three-story fountain in the center of the room and the occasional whoosh from the gold-trimmed glass elevators nearly drowned out the clamor of attendees and employees heading this way and that, pushing carts of luggage or staring at their phones. She hugged herself as she caught a chill from the draft off the fountain, feeling suddenly dizzy upon standing amid two dozen floors of ornately detailed mezzanines all ascending into obscurity.

It surprised her how many people were there, considering the level of commitment—and, apparently, danger—involved in attending the conference. Emma barely noticed their inane chatter, though, thanks to the ringing that grew steadily in her head. She scanned the atrium for a secluded place to sit down, but it contained oddly inadequate seating for as spacious as it was. All the chairs and tables were already taken by tailor-suited fat cats shaking hands and clinking glasses.

Through all the commotion, Emma somehow noticed two men in white shirts and hotel vests talking to each beneath the second-floor mezzanine all the way across the room. She wasn't quite sure what about them caught her eye, but she did notice that they were the only hotel employees just standing around.

She walked straight through the atrium to ask them for a bottle of water. One of them was slightly smaller than Jon, probably late twenties, with sun-bleached hair and an east Texas complexion. He smiled at her as she approached. The other one wasn't as friendly. He was big and burly, and looked rather uncomfortable in his small uniform. Emma froze the moment their eyes met. She wasn't sure if it was the stark contrast of the whites of his eyes against his black skin or the snarl that formed on his lip, but she suddenly got the sense that, if he could, he would pounce on her from across the room like a panther.

And that's when it hit her.

In an instant, all the foreboding and anxiety of the last few months swelled into one vicious wave. Her heart skipped a beat, then pounded so hard inside her chest she was sure everyone in the hotel could hear it. A coldness washed over her from head to toe and she fought to breathe, as if her chest were being crushed. Emma closed her eyes and concentrated on taking slow breaths, determined not to have an incident in the middle of all these people.

Come on, Emma. What is wrong with you?

Emma opened her eyes again, just long enough to see the swirling of the marble tile rising up beneath her. The dizziness and nausea were too much. She reached out a hand to catch herself before she hit the floor.

Someone else caught her first.

Emma breathed in deeply, clinging to whomever stood next to her as the final wave washed over. Then she let out a long breath and looked at the person who'd caught her.

It was the young man with the sun-streaked hair and weathered face. "Ma'am, are you all right?" he said with a level of concern in his eyes she wouldn't think possible for a stranger.

She glanced at his forehead instinctively before answering. There was nothing there. "Yes," she said, her voice shaky. "I think so."

"Are you sure?" he said, scanning her face. "You look awfully pale."

"No, it's okay. It's probably the heat. I just need a moment."

He didn't look convinced. "Maybe I should call for the doctor."

Emma's eyes widened. "No, don't," she pleaded. "I'm fine, really." She looked past him to where he had been standing just moments before. The big, burly guy was already gone. "Please," she said. "I don't want to make a scene."

He wrinkled his forehead, then smiled. "All right. What *can* I do, then?"

Emma relaxed her shoulders. She glanced around, relieved to see that apparently no one else had noticed her close call with the floor. "Just help me find a cold drink, and maybe somewhere quiet to sit down, okay?"

"Okay," he said, glancing at the name badge on her collar. "Right this way, Dr. Grant."

Emma smiled and took his offered arm.

The young man led her carefully across the atrium to the door of one of the restaurants, which hadn't yet been opened to guests. He guided her inside, flipped on the lights, and directed her to the closest table, already prepared with half a dozen pristine place settings. Emma sank gratefully into the leather chair and closed her eyes.

"How about a glass of ice water?" the young man said, pulling a small notebook from his back pocket and taking out a piece of paper.

"That'd be fantastic," said Emma. "Thank you."

"No problem." He set his notebook on the tablecloth and unfolded the paper in his hand. "Assuming, of course, one of these codes actually gets us into the kitchen," he added with a smile, then stepped away.

Emma eyed the notebook he'd left on the edge of the table. The worn leather and frayed ribbon told her how much it meant to him. It surprised her that he would leave something so obviously important with a total stranger.

"Well, that wasn't hard at all," he said, returning with a wine glass of water. "Is there anything else I can do for you?"

Emma gratefully accepted the water and took a long drink before answering. There was a hint of green against the brown of his eyes as he stood watching her that reminded her of Matt and somehow made her feel better. "It probably isn't fair at all for me to drag you away from your duties, but would you mind just sitting with me for a little while? It helps if I have someone to talk to."

"Are you kidding? And miss my chance to continue catering to all those pompous windbags? A bunch of guys who are supposed to be 'representing the people' but probably have no idea what it's like to actually be one of those people?" The young man pulled out the chair beside her and sat down. He put his hand on his notebook and pulled it closer. "I could think of a thousand other things I'd rather be doing, trust me."

"Such as?"

He smiled. "Well, writing for one, I suppose."

"Ah," said Emma, nodding to the book tucked under his hand. "So that explains the notebook."

"Well, yes, actually. One of my professors in college

suggested that we get into the habit of keeping a notebook with us. A place to jot down our ideas and whatnot. I took his advice."

"So what happened then? With your writing, I mean."

"Pretty much the same thing that happened to everyone else, I guess. My little brother went off to fight in the war and my father passed away, so I came home from school to take care of the family ranch. I only meant to stay till my brother got back, but…" His eyes dropped to the table.

Emma didn't have to ask what happened to his brother. "You know, I once read that people who keep private notebooks are lonely and restless rearrangers, cursed at birth with an affinity for loss."

He laughed. "It wouldn't surprise me. Does that mean you're a 'lonely and restless rearranger' too?"

"Me? No. I've always been too afraid to keep a notebook. I have this underlying paranoia that someone would find it and know all my innermost personal thoughts."

"Well, you're just going about it the wrong way, then. Most of what's in this notebook isn't mine. It's filled with poems, song lyrics, and what other people have said and written. Kind of like a code. Everything in here has some sort of meaning, some background, but only to me."

"What do you mean?"

"The words are little bits and pieces that remind me of a part of myself, like a freeze frame in time. What I choose to jot down isn't what's important. What's important is how I felt when I wrote it. How it *made* me feel. Like a reminder of the person I was at that time, a way to keep in touch with a previous version of myself. It helps me remember who I was and wasn't, who I am and who I'm not. I guess you could say it's kind of like my totem."

Emma shook her head. "Totem?"

"Yeah, you know, an object that's a representation of ourselves. Something that's familiar only to us, that helps us remember who we are." He added with a grin, "Kind of like that necklace you've been fiddling with for the last five minutes."

Emma hadn't even noticed she was playing with it. She dropped her hand and smiled. "Wow, I didn't realize it was that obvious."

"Only for someone observant. And I'm afraid that's what writers do—observe. So, does that mean I'm right? Or am I really the only one cursed at birth with an affinity for loss?"

Emma's smile faded. She stared into the glass rested on her lap. "I grew up not too far from here, in a little east Texas town. When I was twelve years old, my mother and four-year-old brother were killed in a car accident just a few days after Thanksgiving. We didn't exactly get along, my mother and I, but that Christmas I found a small box under the tree with my name on it. Inside was this necklace, with a note that said, 'Learn to let go.' My father told me she had bought it for me several months before she died."

The young man's face fell. "I'm so sorry, Dr. Grant. I didn't mean to…"

"It's okay," she said. "You're right. I guess it is kind of like my totem. A reflection of someone I once was. This necklace is a reminder to me that the choices we make don't just affect us, but those around us as well. It's a part of me, and it helps remind me of who I am."

He raised an eyebrow. "Are you sure that's all it reminds you of?"

Emma opened her mouth, then swallowed hard and dropped her eyes.

He cleared his throat and stood. "Well," he said, pushing in his chair. "I should get back, before someone starts to wonder about me."

Emma nodded. "You're right. I shouldn't have kept you so long. I'm sorry."

"No, don't be." He tucked the notebook into his back pocket. "I'd much rather be in here than out there, anyway. And you're welcome to hang out as long as you need to. The restaurant won't be opening for a few more hours. I don't think anyone will bother you."

"Thank you," said Emma. "For everything. I'd probably be out there on the floor surrounded by a bunch of gawking, gossiping politicians right now if it weren't for you."

He grinned. "You're welcome."

"Oh, wait," said Emma, just as he was about to turn and leave. "I never got your name."

He paused before answering. "It's Sam."

"Sam, huh? Well, it was very nice to meet you, Sam." She offered him a hand.

He shook it. "It was nice to meet you, too, Dr. Grant."

CHAPTER 6

Jon loathed the fluff of political façade. After hours of polite drivel in the lobby, he managed to make it up to their suite at the very end of the second floor, just in time for a quick shower before having to change. He stood in front of the mirror above the dresser, fumbling with the bowtie of what he so lovingly referred to as his "penguin suit." No matter how many times he had to wear one of these stupid things, he still hated it.

"I really don't see why we have to go to a state dinner, anyway," he said, unknotting his tie and starting over for the third time. "It's not like we're in DC."

"Because this is still a political event, and there is a foreign national here," Emma answered as she stepped out of the bathroom and came over to help him. "Trust me, I'm not exactly looking forward to it, either."

Jon knew full well how apprehensive she was about meeting Stephen Bennett, though he hoped that apprehension was related more to her distaste for Bennett's political views than anything else. "Well, at least I get to see you in that little black cocktail dress."

"I'm glad you're getting a kick out of it." She finished knotting his tie. "Now, if you're done drooling over me, can we please go?"

Jon sighed. "Let's get this over with."

In the elevator, Emma reminded him that this was a diplomatic dinner, and that he needed to be on his best behavior. He knew better than to mention that he had way more experience with this kind of stuff than she did, or that she was the one more likely to fly off the handle anyway.

The banquet hall downstairs where their invitation indicated that the private guest dinner would be held was filled with round tables, each with a bronze-toned tablecloth, an arrangement of freshly-lit tiered candles and hot-pink peonies, and eight formal place settings. Only one of the tables was occupied when they were met at the door by the maître d', a young man with sun-streaked hair and a weathered face.

"Mr. and Mrs. Grant?"

Jon nodded, and the young man led them to the occupied table at the very back of the room.

Jack stood as they approached. "Jon, Emma," he said, shaking their hands. "Emma, I believe you know most of our presenters. Jon, this is Dr. Anna Korvaire, Dr. Najeet Anand, Senator Moses Hendrix, and Professor David Goldberg."

Jon nodded politely to each of them.

Jack then motioned to a young, dark-haired gentleman who appeared entirely too debonair to be dining at a table full of scientists and politicians. "Then, of course, there is our special guest, whom I believe neither of you have met before. Minister, this is Captain Grant, formerly of the Virginia Air National Guard, and his wife, the lovely Dr. Emma Grant. Jon, Emma, I'd like to introduce to you the Canadian Minister of International Development, Stephen Bennett."

Emma reached for Jon's hand.

"It's a pleasure to meet you, Minister," said Jon.

Bennett stood and greeted him with a gleam in his eerie-blue eyes and a smile bright enough to see one's own imperfections in, despite the dimly-lit room. "Oh, I can assure you, Captain," he said, shaking Jon's hand, "the pleasure is all mine."

Jack motioned for Jon and Emma to take their seats, between himself and Bennett. Jon made sure to pull out the chair next to Jack for Emma, so that Jon would be the one sitting next to Bennett instead of her. The maître d' returned and offered them all a glass of wine. Bennett held up his glass, but Jon politely declined.

"Come now, Captain, have a drink with me," said Bennett.

"No. Thank you," Jon insisted.

"Oh, yes. That's right." Bennett smirked and took a sip of his wine. "A man who knows his limits. I admire that."

Jon looked sideways at Emma. What was that supposed to mean?

"Captain Grant, you are a combat pilot, yes?" Bennett asked.

"Not anymore. It's just private charter now, thankfully."

"But you flew during the war, did you not?"

"That's correct." Jon looked down at his plate as the first course was placed on the bronze charger in front of him, a ricotta gnocchi with caviar. Where in the world did they even find caviar?

"Somewhat of a hero, from what I understand," said Bennett.

"There are no heroes in war," Jon answered.

Bennett smiled. "Indeed. Especially one so bloody and

corrupt. A lot of good men and women were lost in that war. Some might say... needlessly?"

Jon simply stared at Bennett, silent, the clinking of silverware against china ringing in his head as the other guest enjoyed their appetizers. This guy sounded more like an aristocrat Sophist than a Quebecker.

"And then, of course, there were those whose lives were so horribly... disrupted." The minister looked this time at Emma, who sat staring at her plate. "Rather unfortunate. So many lost. So many left behind to pick up the pieces. Why, one might almost feel a sense of *betrayal* from the entire ordeal, considering the outcome."

"Yes, well, it was a long time ago," said Jon.

"And hardly a topic for dinner, wouldn't you agree?" Jack interrupted.

Bennett nodded. "Yes, of course, of course." He turned and winked at Dr. Korvaire, whose low-cut evening dress and matching red lipstick seemed a bit provocative for a political dinner, then struck up a conversation with Senator Hendrix about the decline of the transportation sector and the effects of the rising cost of oil.

Jon quickly tuned them out. Bennett's comments about the war had left him uncomfortable, to say the least. He wasn't sure at all where Bennett had been going with it, but he was certain it wasn't something he cared to discuss. He was grateful to Jack for changing the subject.

When the maître d' returned with another waiter to take their plates in preparation for the main course, Emma looked up at the young man's name tag.

"Sam," she said. "And how are you this evening, Sam?"

He smiled. "I'm doing very well, thank you, ma'am."

Emma smiled at him in return.

"Well, then, Dr. Grant," said Bennett, a gleam in his eye as he sat his napkin down and turned to Emma. "Crisis psychology spans multiple disciplines, from what I understand, from the traumas of domestic violence to war. Your specialization is in...?"

"Disaster psychology. It focuses on how people react specifically during and after a disaster."

"Yes, I am familiar with it. Indeed, I have endeavored to familiarize myself with most of your work, Dr. Grant. Quite an impressive career." Bennett picked up his glass and gave her a smirk that, to Jon, felt like nails on a chalkboard. "Considering its... *rocky* beginnings."

Jon clenched his jaw and turned his eyes up to the chandelier, the light ricocheting off of it like a million tiny shards of shattered glass. *Great*, he thought. *Here we go.*

Emma took a deep breath. "I'm not sure I follow you, sir."

"Oh, I mean that only respectfully of course. I am referring to the ordeal with your government's Federal Emergency Management Agency so many years ago, right before the disaster outbreaks. When your recommendations were so *unreasonably* dismissed. It must have been difficult for you, to have to watch the entire scenario unfold, knowing something could have been done."

"I believe that, at the time, decisions were made based on cost-benefit and what evidence was available," said Emma.

Jon knew better, but he admired her effort.

"Evidence, indeed. Though I must say your projections were staggering, to say the least. Considering you had the same amount of *evidence* available to you. I'm no scientist and don't pretend to fully comprehend the research, but I have never been able to ascertain just how you so accurately predicted each occurrence. Perhaps one day you can explain it to me."

Emma's face paled. Jon could almost feel the wave of panic that washed over her. He reached for her hand under the table. It was cold.

"And that is exactly what we're here for, isn't it?" Jack interjected as the maître d' returned with the main course. "To share ideas and experiences? To bring down our boundaries and work together in mutual problem-solving?"

"Yes, absolutely. And aptly put, I must say," said Bennett. "As you know, the GOG's position has ever been to bring down the boundaries that surround our nations in order to work in mutual cooperation for the good of all."

"At the expense of our freedoms and identities?" said Emma.

The maître d' paused as he sat Jon's plate down. The young man glanced at Emma, then at Bennett, before continuing.

"Certainly everything worth working toward requires some sacrifice, wouldn't you agree, Doctor?" Bennett replied. "If we are to achieve a common goal, we cannot hope to continue as isolationists, can we?"

"On the contrary, Minister." Emma looked up at the

maître d' as he set her plate down in front of her. "I believe good walls make good neighbors."

The maître d' grinned.

"Oh, come now, Dr. Grant. Surely you of all people, having suffered personally as well as professionally at the hands of a corrupt system, would be able to appreciate the need for a government restructuring? A government more adequately held accountable to the people it is intended to serve? A government more centralized, with much further-reaching resources?" Then Bennett turned on Jon. "Captain Grant, can you honestly sit there and insist that these are issues you have not, yourself, considered?"

Jon was shocked by Bennett's brazenness. Had he completely forgotten that he sat right next to the vice president of that so-called "corrupt system"?

Emma answered for him. "Minister, it is quite clear that you have done your homework. But one thing you fail to recognize is that my husband and I are patriots. We have both served this country. We have suffered and sacrificed, and we shall continue to do so, under an American flag. Now, if you will excuse me," she said, pushing her chair back and standing. "I seem to have lost my appetite."

Bennett stood too. He spoke with an air of calm arrogance. "Make no mistake, Dr. Grant, the world is changing. And it is seldom... *wise*... to stand in the way of progress."

Emma narrowed her eyes. She dropped her napkin on the table, then turned on her heel and headed for the door.

Jon stood and watched her leave.

"I do hope I didn't offend her, Captain Grant," said Bennett. "It was certainly not my intention."

Jon doubted that. It wasn't a coincidence that Bennett had managed to bring up the very subjects which were the most sensitive to both himself and Emma. "No, Minister," Jon answered anyway, remembering that he was still at a diplomatic dinner, even if Emma seemed to have forgotten. "I must apologize for her abruptness. I'm afraid Dr. Grant isn't exactly... feeling well."

"Think nothing of it, Captain. Do let her know that I hope she recovers quickly." Bennett held out his hand.

As Jon shook it, his gaze landed momentarily on the minister's forehead before quickly looking away. "Thank you. I will be sure to tell her," he said with a forced smile. With a nod to the others at the table, he excused himself to follow his wife. As he stepped out into the hallway, he wondered if he'd really seen what he thought he just saw.

Up in their suite, he found Emma standing at the floor-to-ceiling window, silhouetted against the lights of downtown Dallas. "Well, that was diplomatic," he said as he pulled off his tie and jacket and threw them on the bed.

"Just be glad I didn't punch him."

"Now *that* would have been something worth getting dressed up for."

He joined her at the window. She stood with her arms crossed, staring at the lightning flashes in the distance. Though her face was back to its normal color, he knew she was still upset.

"What do you say we order some room service?" said Jon.

"Actually, I think I'm just going to bed. It's been a long day."

"Suit yourself." He picked up the phone on the nightstand.

She stopped just inside the bathroom door and grinned. "Want to come help me out of this dress instead?"

"Absolutely." He smiled and set the phone down, immediately forgetting about food.

It had been a really long month.

Afterward, Jon stared up at the blank white ceiling above their bed, his arm draped across his forehead, listening to the rain against the windowpane. Eventually he rolled onto his side and leaned up on one elbow to see if Emma had fallen asleep yet. She lay on her back, her eyes closed, her breathing soft and steady. He brushed her hair from her face and kissed her gently before crawling out of bed.

He dressed as quietly as he could in the dark. His plan had been to wait until she fell asleep and then order room service, but the longer he lay there, the more he thought about what Bennett said at dinner, and the less he felt like eating. Jon wasn't even sure why he kept thinking about it. Normally he had no trouble brushing off what other people said. But for some reason it had gotten under his skin, and he couldn't seem to shake it. He had to get up and *do* something.

A few laps in the pool sounded like a good idea.

As he searched through their bag for a pair of shorts, Jon came across the bottle of Ambien he'd secretly stashed in one of the inside pockets. He glanced back at Emma, realizing he'd missed his chance to talk her into taking one. Jon relocated the bottle to his toiletry bag, hoping she wouldn't need it for once, then found his shorts and slipped quietly out the door.

The halls were empty, except for the guys in FBI jackets posted on each level. Jon opted to take the stairs instead of the elevator, hoping they would make it easier for him to avoid security.

He was wrong.

"Sir!" A bald guy with glasses stopped him just outside the stairwell on the first floor. "Is there something I can do for you?"

"No, I'm just heading for the pool," Jon answered.

The guy raised an eyebrow. "Sir, can I see your name badge please? The one you were given when you checked in with security."

Jon sighed. "I don't have it with me, it's up in my room. Besides, this place is like Fort Knox. Do you really think I'd have gotten in here if I wasn't supposed to be?"

"Can you at least tell me your name then?" the man said, crossing his arms.

"Grant. Jonathan Grant. I'm Dr. Grant's husband."

"Oh, Captain Grant." The man slipped his hands into his pockets. "Why didn't you just say so in the first place? I'm Assistant Director William Tanner of the FBI. I'm in charge of security during the convention. Vice President Allred warned me that I should keep an eye on you two. Well, on Dr. Grant mostly."

"For her sake, or yours?" Jon asked.

"A little of both."

"Does that mean I can go now?"

"Honestly, sir, we've received some reports of suspicious activity. I'm not exactly sure it's safe to be wandering around the hotel after dark."

"I'll take my chances," said Jon, brushing past him.

"Sir," Tanner called down the hall. "We're just here to protect you."

Jon stopped and turned around. "Look, Assistant Director Tanner, I'm just a pilot. I don't think I'm the person you should be worried about. You want to protect someone? My wife is upstairs asleep."

He left AD Tanner standing in the hall staring after him.

As Jon stepped into one of the changing rooms by the pool to put on his swim trunks, he felt guilty for being so short with the FBI guy. He was right, after all. They were just here to protect everyone. The truth was, his snippiness had nothing to do with the inconvenience of extra security. It was what Bennett had said that bothered him, a lot more than Jon liked to admit. No—not *what* he said, but what he *hadn't* said. The guy had a knack for dancing around what he really meant.

A lot of good men and women were lost in that war? *Yes, Bennett, I know. I was there. When you were still chasing freshmen around your dorm room, I was there.*

He rested his forehead against the partition, angry at himself for thinking about it. It had been so long since he'd even had to.

Once he finished changing, he stepped out onto the deck and dove straight into the deep end of the pool, ignoring the cold. At the other end, he flipped beneath the water and kicked his legs hard off the wall. Jon soon lost track of how many laps he'd done. Instead of relieving his frustration, though, it only made it worse.

Some might say needlessly? "Needlessly" wasn't the word for it. Those people had been sent to die in a political war. A war over control and lies. They were told they were there to end a dangerous conflict and lift the oil embargo. But the war was never really about any of that. That embargo had been put into place because production had declined, and no one wanted to admit it. The war wasn't about saving lives. It was about saving face.

Breathing hard and shaking from anger as much as exertion, he held himself up on the edge of the pool, resting his head on his arms. *Maybe that wasn't what Bennett meant at all. Maybe he was referring to something more... specific.* Emma was right. Bennett had done his homework. But exactly how much did he know? How much could he know?

When you finally return after having been left for dead by your own government in a jail cell in east Africa for over a year, people don't exactly ask you a bunch of questions about your experience. Jon had never explained to anyone, not even Emma, the responsibility he felt for what had happened to his squadron. The guilt of knowing he was the only one who came back.

Stop it, Jon. Just stop it. He lifted his head and wiped the water from his face. Maybe he was reading too much into it. After all, Bennett didn't say anything about the war that hadn't already been said over and over again. Nothing that he couldn't have read about in the news. The guy was clearly trying to rile them up. *Are you really going to let a sleazeball like Bennett provoke you over something that happened ten years ago?*

Jon pulled himself out of the pool and sat on the edge,

his feet in the water, the moon reflecting dimly from the skylight above. He thought about Emma, his beautiful wife, asleep in their room, and what Tanner had said to him in the hallway. There was a reason why he didn't want her coming to Dallas alone, and why he asked Richard to check on the kids while they were gone. Jon was just as apprehensive about this convention as Emma. Something didn't feel right.

"What am I even doing down here?" he muttered aloud. He should never have left Emma upstairs alone for this long, especially after what Tanner told him. But anger and bitterness had clouded his mind. Bennett had gotten to him, and Jon wondered how someone as levelheaded as himself could have let it happen.

Then he remembered what he saw on Bennett's forehead.

And with a crack of lightning, the lights went out.

Jon grabbed a towel from one of the racks along the wall and headed back to the changing room. He dried off and dressed as fast as he could by the faint rays of moonlight that poured through the skylight above. Just as he was about to open the door, a beam of light passed over the changing rooms. He heard voices.

One of them sounded an awful lot like Bennett.

A woman giggled. "I don't exactly think you brought me down here to talk about the pipelines, did you?"

Steadying his breathing, Jon peered out through the slats of the wooden door. Dr. Korvaire stood by the pool with a dark-haired man in a suit, his back turned to the changing rooms. She held a wine glass. He held a bottle.

"My dear Dr. Korvaire, I can assure you my intentions are purely," the man said, pouring her a glass of wine, "professional."

She took a drink.

"Of course, you do know the importance your research has on our plans. Surely you can understand my *insistence* on your continued cooperation?" he said.

She wrapped his tie around her fingers. "Well, as much as I've enjoyed *cooperating* with you, surely *you* can understand that I am bound by the interpretations of the research. I can only support what I can prove."

"Of course. Well, Doctor, as you say, it is indeed a matter of interpretation. Perhaps you will allow me the opportunity to *alter* your perception," he said, pulling her closer to kiss her. He slid the strap of her bright-red dress off her shoulder.

Jon rolled his eyes and stepped away from the door. *Great.* Any chance he'd had of nonchalantly slipping away had just gone out the window. This could take a while.

He wasn't sure how long he sat there, grateful that the rain pounding against the glass drowned out everything but Korvaire's incessant giggling and an occasional splash of water. Eventually he tuned them out altogether.

Until he heard Korvaire scream. And glass shatter, followed quickly by a scuffling of metal chairs against the concrete pool deck, some of which sounded close to the changing room door. Jon stood, his heartbeat quickening. There was a loud splash.

Then all was quiet.

Jon sucked in rapid breaths. He felt for the door in the darkness and tried turning the knob. It didn't move. He jiggled the handle and pushed hard against the door. Something was blocking it. He stepped back from the door, swung his leg hard, and shattered the wooden frame in one kick.

A chair flew across the deck as the door burst open. Korvaire's companion must have known Jon was there. Or at least, he'd known someone was there.

The hall was dark, but the skylights above provided just enough light for Jon to catch sight of the tail of a suit jacket disappearing into the hotel. Jon started to run after him, then stopped.

Where was Korvaire?

His gaze came to rest on the outline of a figure floating motionless in the deep end.

Jon turned back toward the hallway, then hesitated.

What is wrong with you, Jon? Go after him! If that really is Bennett, you can end this. All of this. You can have him arrested and thrown out of the convention, Emma can do her presentation, and you can both just go home. All of this will be over. No more Bennett, no more threat.

Jon looked back at the pool. *But what if Korvaire's not dead?*

He ran to the pool and dove into the water. In one brisk stroke, he popped to the surface, a half-naked Korvaire in his arms, and rolled her onto the deck. He pulled himself up next to her and put an ear to her mouth.

She wasn't breathing.

"Anna, can you hear me?" he yelled. Not expecting a response, he balled his fists over her chest to start compressions. Jon counted out thirty quick thrusts then tilted her chin back, pressing his lips to hers and forcing two rescue breaths into her lungs.

Nothing happened.

"Come on!" He started over. "One... two... three... four..." He pressed his fists into her chest. "Five... six... Come on, Anna. Come on!"

Her body jerked lifelessly with each compression, blood trickling slowly down the side of her ghost-white face from a gash on her forehead. Jon finished the last few compressions, then leaned over her for more rescue breaths.

Halfway through the second breath she sputtered, and water erupted from her mouth.

Jon rolled her onto her side as she coughed the water out of her lungs. He took a deep breath and narrowed his eyes toward the darkness of the hallway. At least he'd managed to save someone tonight.

Even if it wasn't his wife

.

CHAPTER 7

Emma lay dozing beneath the comforting weight of the bedspread, only faintly aware of the tap of rain against the window and the gentle warmth of Jon kissing her on the forehead before getting out of bed. She opened her eyes for a moment when a flash of lightning filled the dark room. As she started to drift off again, she heard the rustling of Jon getting dressed, then the latch of the door as he closed it behind him.

She continued to lie there under the softness of the sheets, somewhere between wakefulness and sleep. At some point, she became conscious of an increase in the intensity of the storm outside. She rolled over, away from the window, but with each flash of lightning against the white walls, the room became brighter. Eventually, the sound of the storm subsided, but strangely, the lightning didn't fade with it. It continued to light up the room. Feeling there was no way she would be able to sleep, she opened her eyes.

Emma no longer lay in the comfortable bed of their suite. She had no idea where she was, and yet this field was calmly familiar to her—in the same way that a fleeting memory, played repeatedly in the mind, becomes familiar. She stood upon the edge of consciousness, neither seeing nor knowing anything past the rolling hills before her.

As the fog of dissonance began to fall away, she felt a part of herself slipping with it, replaced by something much like it and yet altogether different. Something more ancient, more weighted, more worn.

And then, like so many times before, came the pain. It burned from deep inside her like an old wound that festered but never quite healed. A heartache, deeper and more permeating than anything she had ever known, as if something had been ripped from her very being, never again to be recovered nor comforted.

She sensed him before she saw him coming. He strolled across the open field toward her, as she somehow knew he had done before. The wind blew stronger.

"*Lienna…*"

She didn't turn to face him, but felt his eyes upon her. Those crystal-blue eyes she had seen so many times. She continued to look out over the meadow, her lips pursed tightly as he stopped beside her.

After a silence that seemed almost an eternity, he

spoke.

"You have been told, then?"

Even without looking at him, she could feel the tenderness he held for her, could feel his intensity. She knew that whatever she said to him now would determine the course of what was to come.

She nodded.

"Li?" he whispered. He stepped closer and took hold of her arm.

She instinctively turned to face him. In the shimmering light of the setting sun, his features were even more beautiful. Jet-black hair, olive skin, and those eyes as deeply blue and ominous as an icy sea that overtakes you, washing away all perception until you finally allow yourself to sink, cold and apathetic.

She looked away.

He drew closer to her and brushed a lock of hair from her face. He held his hand there, beneath her chin. She shivered at the icy chill of his touch.

"Come with me." His words were a breath upon the wind. As if fate itself rested upon one sentence, upon one answer, spoken softly under a waning sun, on an obscure hillside, in a distant and forgotten place.

She somehow conjured the strength to calm her quivering lip and meet his eyes.

Those deep, eerily beautiful eyes. Behind them was greatness, strength—but also, she knew, the cold flame of darkness.

And it was into the darkness that she would not cross.

"Torren, I cannot go with you."

She could feel his spirit shatter as he released her. A foreboding crept into her chest and rested itself alongside the burn of sorrow. He stepped away and looked toward the setting sun.

Again, the silence.

A chill accompanied the darkness that crept across the countryside. Did the rising moon bring the icy cold of indifference? Or was it him, her dearest childhood companion, whose heart now ached with hers? Whose heart now ached for her?

"Ren, you don't have to do this. It isn't too late."

As he looked out across the darkening hillside, his words came now without the sweetness with which he'd always regarded her. They came, instead, as a dark serpent in the night, who cares not for his prey but only for himself, and the desperate hunger that nature requires he feed. "You were to be mine, you know. It had been decided."

"Torren." She closed her eyes and breathed in the mist that rolled across the hillside. "I will not betray my father."

He turned to face her. The darkness shrouded him, seeming to pulse from within him. "He is a fool. And you are a fool for following him."

It was then that he walked away from her, away from all that they had ever known, disappearing past the edge of the vastness, and beyond.

The lingering bite of his piercing blue eyes, now cold and hardened, overwhelmed her. She dropped to her knees upon the unforgiving hillside and wept.

Then Emma screamed.

And woke up.

The storm raged beyond the window, her heart pounding as hard as the rain against the glass. The room was completely dark, save for the flashes of lightning and the bit of moonlight that managed to break through the clouds. She tried switching on the lamp on the nightstand, but nothing happened. Was the power out?

Emma sat up, her head still swimming with the images from her dream. It was all so clear. More than any of the things she had seen before. Her body shook uncontrollably, protesting the shock of snapping from one vivid reality to the next. Still enveloped by the bitter pain and cold, she rested her head on her knees and cried. In great, racking sobs.

No. She wrapped her arms around her head as her tears soaked the sheets. *It isn't true. It can't be true.*

She glanced down at the empty bed next to her, then faintly recalled Jon leaving earlier, probably to find something to eat. At that moment, she wanted him more than anything in the world, and she wasn't about to just sit there and wait for him to come back.

A wave of nausea washed over her as she stood. She stumbled to the bathroom to be sick.

If the power was out, she would need a flashlight. Most hotels had a few scattered around, in drawers and underneath cabinets, thanks to the frequent blackouts. She found one in the drawer of the nightstand, dressed, and went to find Jon.

Downstairs, the atrium was empty. *Where in the world is all the security?* she thought as the beam of her flashlight darted across the stilled fountain and empty chairs. She checked the restaurant. It was already closed, but a light shone faintly from the kitchen inside. She knew Jon had the ability to charm his way around the rules when he wanted something. Maybe he'd convinced someone to make him dinner.

The kitchen door was unlocked, and Emma slipped inside. She did find someone, sitting on a stool, leaning on one of the stainless-steel prep tables. But it wasn't Jon.

"Oh, hello, Sam."

"Dr. Grant." He jumped up and closed his notebook, still sitting on the table in front of him. "Um, is there something I can do for you?"

Emma was surprised at his startled reaction. "No. I'm just looking for my husband. I'm afraid he had to cut his dinner short, thanks to me, and I thought maybe he'd come looking for something to eat."

"Yes, I noticed. About dinner, I mean."

"Oh." She glanced at her feet. The tile still shimmered faintly as if freshly cleaned. "I'm sorry you had to see that. My behavior was a little less than professional, from what I understand."

"Oh, no, ma'am, please don't apologize. I was quite impressed with your restraint. I don't know if I could have remained that calm while getting a lecture about corruption from a guy whose watch is probably worth more than my house."

Emma laughed. "I'm not so sure if *calm* is the word I'd use, but thank you."

He smiled at her. "Listen, the kitchen usually closes at nine. I kind of got stuck here when the power went out," he said, jabbing a thumb over his shoulder at the faint glow of the emergency light in the corner. "But I'd be happy to fix you guys a couple of plates to go."

"Oh, no, it's very kind of you to offer, but I don't want to be any trouble."

Sam grinned. "Really?"

"I mean, no more than I've already been."

"Please, it's no trouble. I'd be happy to do it. I've been told I grill up a pretty mean cheeseburger. And I think there may even be some cheesecake in the cooler."

Emma smiled. His eyes were kind and warm and immediately made her feel better. She wasn't sure whether Jon had eaten yet or not but knew he would appreciate the gesture. She owed him big time for all the support he'd shown her—and all the mood swings he'd put up with— over the last month.

"Okay," said Emma. "That'd be great. Thank you."

Sam picked up his notebook and turned toward the freezer at the back of the kitchen. Something fell out of the book as he left, so Emma picked it up. It was a wallet-sized photo of Sam with a young blond woman and a little boy.

He returned with a box of frozen hamburgers and lit the grill.

She held up the photo. "Your family?"

"Oh," he said, placing a hand on his back pocket. "Thank you. I didn't even notice. Yeah. That's my wife, Claire, and my son, Cole."

"How old is he?"

"He's three now, but he was barely two then."

Emma glanced at the photo again. "But he's so tiny."

The grill sizzled as Sam threw a couple of patties on. "Cole's always been small. He was born with a heart defect. He's probably spent as much of his life in a hospital as he's spent at home."

"I'm sorry to hear that." She set the photo on the prep table. "My eighteen-year-old son, Matthew, has a heart condition too. When he was born, the left side of his heart wasn't fully developed. He had to have three surgeries before he was four years old."

"Really?" Sam raised an eyebrow. "It's the same with Cole. We've never met anyone else with his condition. But you said your son is eighteen? Did he have problems after the final surgery?"

"I'd like to be able to tell you no, but I'm afraid it's something he's had to deal with his entire life. He has to be monitored by a cardiologist regularly. There's always the risk that his heart could become too weak and fail, at which point he'd have to have a transplant. But for the most part, we've been lucky. Other than taking a few precautions, like diet and medications, he's had a pretty normal life."

"Cole hasn't had the last surgery yet." Sam took the notebook from his back pocket and slipped the photo back inside. "We're still trying to find a pediatric surgeon in Texas willing to do it. There were already so few of them trained in that kind of surgery, and with the hit on the medical industry, it's made it even harder. To say nothing about finding a facility still willing to accept federal healthcare coverage." He went back to the grill to flip the hamburgers.

As the haze of grease began to dance across the dimly-lit room, Emma realized by the look on Sam's face that he was worried about his son. She didn't blame him. She remembered what it was like for her and Jon when Matt was that age. And that was back when medical treatment for a case such as Matt's was more readily available. They'd also had good insurance and Jon's inheritance to cover it.

"Listen, Sam," said Emma. "I have a friend in Virginia who's a pediatric cardiologist. He did all three of Matt's surgeries. I could talk to him if you'd like. Maybe we could work something out for Cole? Including something to help alleviate some of the costs."

Sam stared at her, wide-eyed. "You'd be willing to do that for us?"

"Yes," she said. "I would."

"Dr. Grant, I don't know what to say."

"Well, you can start by saying yes, so I can go ahead and make the phone call."

"Yes." He nodded. "Of course, yes."

"Well, okay, then. So how about those cheeseburgers?"

Emma was glad that she'd be able to help Sam, but she still couldn't shake the apprehensiveness from her dream. She had thought coming to this conference would mean finally taking control of what she'd been seeing over the last few months, but at the moment she felt worse than she had in all of those months combined. She shifted in her seat, suddenly wishing she knew where Jon was.

"Two burgers and two slices of cheesecake to go," said Sam, returning to the table with two Styrofoam containers. He glanced down at his watch. "Maybe I should walk you up to your room."

"It's just a blackout. I've certainly made my way through worse."

"I don't doubt that at all," said Sam. "But there's no harm in having an escort."

Emma shrugged. "Well, if you insist."

Sam was unusually quiet as they walked through the hotel. In fact, everything was unusually quiet. It was hard to be sure from the faint light of the flashlight, but there didn't seem to be a single other soul awake. She expected there to be several FBI agents scurrying about in the dark, but she didn't even see so much as a security guard out as they climbed the stairs to the second floor.

Sam stopped just short of the door to her room and looked at his watch again. "Well, I believe this is good night, Dr. Grant," he said, his eyes darting nervously to the darkened hall behind them.

"Is everything okay, Sam?"

"Of course." He gave her what she suspected was a forced smile. "Just another blackout, right?"

"Right," said Emma. "Well, goodnight, Sam," she added, offering him her flashlight. "And thank you."

"You're welcome, Dr. Grant." He took the flashlight and darted down the hallway without another word.

Emma set the Styrofoam containers on the dresser in the nearly pitch-black room, then kicked off her shoes. She suddenly felt more nauseated than she had the entire trip. She desperately wished Jon had come back, or that she at least knew where he was.

"Jeez, Emma, get a grip already," she said to herself.

The bedside lamp flickered to life.

Emma's jaw dropped.

The room had been turned upside down. Their suitcases were emptied, the mattress stripped bare, and papers were strewn all over the floor.

"What in the...?" said Emma, her nausea quickly joined by a rapid heartbeat.

Then she noticed the breakfast table in the corner. Spread across it was every bit of research, every notecard, every source, every map, every graph, and every statistic she'd brought with her. And fanned neatly across the top of it all was the typed script for her presentation.

Emma suddenly felt very alone. Where was Jon?

She turned toward the door.

A dark figure in a mask three times her size stood just in front of it.

Emma gasped. He shot her a chilling sneer before lunging toward her. She jumped across the bed and tried to dart past him, but he grabbed her by the wrist and yanked her off the bed. She turned instinctively, kneed him hard in the groin, then threw an elbow into his face as he doubled over in pain.

"Come back here you little—" he gasped as she shot out the door.

She rushed up the hallway toward the mezzanine, rounded the corner, and slammed right into someone.

"Emma!" said Jon, breathing hard and soaking wet. "I need your help."

"Jon! Boy am I glad to see you!" Emma stared at him, wide-eyed, as his clothes dripped onto the carpet. "Wait— what is it? What's wrong?"

"Anna Korvaire's been attacked."

CHAPTER 8

Despite his complete and total exhaustion, Jon still didn't get much sleep. He tossed and turned throughout the night, resting only briefly between broken images of everything from Bennett standing over his bed to discovering Emma unconscious on the floor. Each time he opened his eyes, though, all he found was a dark room, and Emma wrapped around him. Judging by how desperately she clung to him, he guessed she had just as much trouble sleeping as he did.

So when the knock on the door to their room came just after seven a.m., Jon was already wide awake, staring blankly up at the ceiling.

"I'm sorry to wake you, Jon," said his Uncle Jack when Jon opened the door. "I heard you two had a pretty rough night."

Jon yawned and rested his head on the door frame. "I think that's an understatement."

"I know. I was just hoping to ask you a few questions." Jack glanced at the Secret Service guys hovering behind him and lowered his voice. "I thought perhaps you might have remembered some *additional* information since last night."

Assistant Director Tanner had come up to get a statement about Korvaire sometime after midnight before moving them to another room. But Jon had a feeling that's not what Jack meant. "Give me just a second," he said.

Jon pulled on a T-shirt and ran a hand through his messy hair before stepping into the hallway and following Jack toward the window at the end of the hall.

"So how's Korvaire?" Jon asked.

Jack shook his head. "She's stabilized, from what I'm told, but she has yet to regain consciousness. They're afraid she may have gone too long without oxygen."

A twinge of guilt for not having gotten to her sooner warmed Jon's chest.

"Jon, the report said you saw Korvaire down by the pool with someone. A man. But that you didn't see his face. Is that correct?"

Jon stared down at the red and orange ovals that wove in and out on the brown carpet. He had never understood why they always put such ostentatious carpeting in hotels. "Yeah, that's right."

Jack stepped in closer and lowered his voice. "Do you

know who he was?"

Jon wasn't sure whether he should answer.

"Please," said Jack, putting a hand on his arm. "If you have any additional information that might help us…"

Jon took a deep breath. "Bennett. I think she was with Bennett."

"Minister Bennett? But that doesn't make sense. She and Bennett may have left dinner together, but I can assure you their relationship has always been purely professional."

"I don't know, they seemed pretty friendly to me," said Jon, crossing his arms.

"Jon, the minister is a foreign national. Accusing him of having been involved in something like this is a pretty serious allegation. Especially considering the compromising position Korvaire was found in."

Compromising position? Was a potential sex scandal really more serious than attempted murder? "Look, Jack, you asked me who I thought it was, and I'm telling you it was Bennett. You can take that for whatever you want."

Jack paused, then rubbed a hand across his mouth. "All right," he said. "If you're certain. I'll make sure I mention it to Tanner. Thank you."

Jon headed back for his suite.

"Oh, and Jon, there's just one more thing."

Jon stopped with his hand on the doorknob.

"You said Korvaire had been drinking, right?"

"That's right."

Jack shook his head. "That is odd."

"What do you mean?"

"Well, Korvaire has a history of epilepsy. It's entirely too dangerous, mixing her medication with alcohol. She knows that." He shook his head again as he walked up the hall past Jon. "There's something off about this entire thing, Jon," he said quietly.

Emma stepped out of the bathroom wearing one of his Duke University T-shirts as Jon re-entered their room. She glared at him with her arms crossed. "I'm going to stop going to sleep if every time I wake up you'll be gone."

He sat down on the sofa next to their bed. "I'm sorry, babe. That was Jack. He just wanted to ask me some questions."

Emma curled up on the couch beside him.

"Em, did you know Anna Korvaire?"

"A little, yes."

"And have you ever seen her drink?"

Emma laughed. "Absolutely not. Anna is way too conservative for that. In fact, she's a bit priggish. There's a running joke about how none of us have ever seen her have so much as a boyfriend, let alone a drink."

Jack was right. None of this made sense.

Jon stood and walked to the dresser. He leaned against it and crossed his arms. "Emmy, I think it's time we left."

"What?" She shot up.

"We haven't even been here twenty-four hours, and we've already had our room ransacked, and another presenter is in a coma. Look, I just don't think it's worth the risk. I think Bennett was the one who tried to drown Korvaire, and I told you what I saw at dinner. He's dangerous, and I don't think either one of us has any business being here. I think we should just go home."

Emma looked at the floor and shook her head. "Jon, I don't—"

"Emma, I think Bennett is a Pusher. And from what I can tell, he's good, too. Only I think Bennett uses it to promote his own personal agenda."

Emma sat back down on the couch and pulled her knees to her chest.

Jon sat down beside her. "Look, Em. It was Bennett I saw Korvaire with last night. I know it was. And now she's in the hospital. I say we get out of here, while we still can, before something even more horrible happens. To one of the *other* presenters," he said, nodding meaningfully at her.

Emma stared across the room. "Maybe you're right," she said quietly. "Maybe we are in over our heads."

He pushed a lock of hair, turned even more red than brown now from the summer sun, behind her ear and over her shoulder.

"But maybe that's exactly what Bennett wants us to do. Maybe he's just trying to scare us off. I mean, think about it. That crack he made at dinner about those who stand in the way of progress. Jon, this may be our only chance. If I don't stand up and speak out against the GOG, especially now that Anna's gone, then who will?"

Jon looked her in the eyes. They were amber, with dark circles that radiated out like the rings of an ancient tree. Behind them, always, was an incredible sense of responsibility. It was something that had both drawn him to her and driven him nuts at the same time. She usually acted on it without any regard for her own personal safety, and she never stopped to think what it would do to him if anything should happen to her.

Everything inside him was screaming to just walk away. But how could he know for sure if that was really how he felt, or if it wasn't just some notion that Bennett had pushed off on him?

He took a deep breath. "Fine. We'll stay, but we've got to be careful. We don't go near Bennett any more than we have to. Neither of us. And we don't leave each other alone, even for a few minutes. Okay?"

Emma nodded.

He held her chin in his hand so she would have to look him in the eyes. "I mean it, Em."

"Believe me," she said. "The last thing I want is Stephen Bennett in my head."

"All right. Well, I imagine they'll be bringing breakfast up soon."

"Good. It will give me some time to get my research sorted out. I need to go across the hall to gather up my papers. And some clothes."

Jon frowned.

"Don't worry," said Emma. "I had no intention of going by myself."

Emma poked her head out the door to make sure no one was around, then they both padded across the hallway barefoot. The door to their old room was already wide open. A bright light flashed as they stepped inside.

"Um... Is there something we can do for you?" Emma asked the brunette behind the camera.

"I'm sorry. I didn't mean to intrude." The woman shook both their hands. "I'm Rachael Dallin. I'm a photojournalist. You must be the Grants. Allred told me quite a bit about you two. It's nice to finally meet you." She stepped over some papers and took another photo.

"Hey, I've heard of you," said Jon. "Our son Jacob is into photography. He's a big fan of yours."

Emma shot him a surprised glance like this was news to her. Jon ignored her. It didn't surprise him at all that she knew nothing about one of Jacob's hobbies.

"But you're press?" he continued. "I thought Jack wasn't allowing any press in here during the convention."

"He's not—besides me. He invited me personally, to do some PR work to *appease* some of the attendees." She rolled her eyes. "I think what he was really wanted was for me to do a little snooping around. Though I now seem to be serving double duty as a police photographer."

"So I guess that means you were called down to the

pool last night as well?" said Emma.

"Yeah. Pretty crazy stuff, huh? Though I've certainly been in the middle of worse."

"Snooping?" Jon asked. "What kind of snooping?"

Rachael smiled. "Let's just say I have a knack for getting into places and finding out things most people can't."

Jon glanced quickly at Rachael's forehead. He had a pretty good idea exactly where she got her "knack."

"Well," said Rachael, snapping off one last shot. "I think that just about does it. I'm sure you'd both like to gather up your things so you can get dressed." She scanned the mess. "Would you like some help cleaning all this up?"

"Oh, no, thank you," said Emma. "I think we can handle it."

"Well, all right then." She shook their hands again before leaving. "Good luck with your presentation tomorrow, Dr. Grant. I'm sure we'll see each other around."

Jon and Emma gathered up their things and headed back to their room. Jon enjoyed the chance to have breakfast brought up to them and lounge around for a couple hours before going downstairs, though he ended up wishing later he had taken a nap instead. He sat at the table in the back row of the large conference room, surrounded by a hundred people more important than him, trying desperately not to fall asleep in his oddly comfortable chair during the presentations.

"As you can tell from this chart…"

Dr. Anand had already been rattling off statistics for forty-five minutes. Jon rolled his eyes and looked at his watch. Two more hours till lunch. There was no way he would make it. He squinted at Emma, sitting at the table up on the stage just to the right of the podium at the very front of the room. Jon caught her attempting to discreetly stifle a yawn and smiled. *Poor Em.*

He was tempted to sneak upstairs and go back to sleep, but he knew it wouldn't be fair to her. If she could sit through this technical garbage, so could he. But he was going to need some caffeine to do it.

He looked up at the stage once more before getting up. On one side of the podium was Emma. On the other was Bennett. They had agreed they shouldn't leave each other alone, but she wouldn't exactly be alone. And Bennett wasn't going anywhere.

Jon slipped out the back and made his way across the prefunction area. It took a moment for his eyes to adjust to the sunlight which flooded from the floor-to-ceiling windows spanning the front of the hotel. A few people were milling around, whispering amongst themselves by the coffee station, their eyes ever so often darting around the room as they spoke.

The entire scene felt a bit too cushy for his taste. The whole convention had, in fact. From the moment they'd arrived. Cushy chairs and cushy carpets, in a building full of a tad too cushy conversations. Jon wondered if even one of the representatives in that conference room behind him had ever done a hard day's work in their life, aside from Emma. Not being a coffee drinker, nor wanting to get drawn into a political debate, he kept walking. He remembered seeing some vending machines next to the elevators anyway.

As he turned the corner into the room with the vending machines, he almost collided with a hotel employee who seemed to be in an awfully big hurry.

"Excuse me," said Jon, grateful he didn't actually run into him. The guy kind of reminded him of an angry locomotive. Jon faintly remembered seeing him in the atrium on the afternoon they arrived, and remembered thinking even then that something about the guy bugged him.

The guy just huffed and walked away with a toolbox in one hand.

Jon pumped a few quarters into the pop machine and made a selection. Nothing happened. He pounded the button several times, then jiggled the return.

Still nothing.

Maybe it was just sold out. He tried again, putting in more quarters and choosing another kind of pop. But the result was the same.

This time, though, he noticed something odd. The display didn't show the amount that he had put in, like most machines did. It didn't say "Vend" or "Sold Out." It just continued to show the price, no matter which button he pressed.

Something wasn't right, and Jon suspected the burly guy with the toolbox might know why.

It wasn't hard to spot the guy across the prefunction area. He headed down the stairs that ran between the escalators leading down to the second floor, dodging congressmen and other hotel employees. Jon tried to act nonchalant as he trailed after him.

Jon reached the top of the second-floor stairs just as the guy made it to the first floor. The guy glanced over his shoulder and then hastened his stride. Jon sped up, too.

The man slipped through a door that was marked for employees only. Jon followed him anyway. This guy was definitely up to something, and Jon wanted to know what it was.

The door opened into a service hall. The guy was nowhere in sight.

Great. He had lost him.

Jon sighed and shook his head. The best he could do now was report the entire thing to AD Tanner and hope he took it seriously, especially since Jon had little more to go on than an out-of-order pop machine and a gut feeling. At least his adrenaline was pumped up enough that he was sure he wouldn't have a hard time staying awake until lunch.

As he re-entered the lobby, he bumped into someone else. "Oh my gosh. I am so sorry," said Jon.

"No, don't worry about it," the guy said, brushing his drink off his shirt. "It's just water. Maybe it'll help wake me up."

"Yeah, I know what you mean," said Jon.

"You must be Jon Grant." The guy held out his hand.

Jon immediately noticed the OGE ring on his finger.

"I'm Aaron Dallin. Rachael's husband."

"Let me guess," said Jon, shaking his hand. "Vice President Allred just so happened to mention my name?"

"How did you know?"

"It seems to be a habit of his lately. But how did you recognize me?" He glanced at Aaron's forehead.

Aaron winked and lowered his voice. "Don't worry, it wasn't anything I couldn't figure out through conventional means. You and I are probably the only two people in this entire hotel who aren't in a tailored suit, a uniform, or a jacket that says FBI on the back. That... and it's on your name tag."

Jon laughed. "Yeah, I guess that helps."

They headed back up to the conference room together. Aaron seemed like a good guy, a translator attending on personal invitation from Jack. Aaron explained that all the foreign nationals and guest speakers in attendance spoke perfect English though, which meant he was mostly twiddling his thumbs and trying not to fall asleep. Jon understood completely.

They stopped outside the conference room. "Well." Aaron looked at his watch. "I guess we better get back in there before someone notices we're gone."

Jon grinned. He could imagine what Emma would say to him if she happened to look up and realize he had bailed. "Hey, how about you and Rachael join us for dinner tonight?" he said. After last night's fiasco, some good food and good company sounded like a great idea.

"You know, I think we'd both really like that. Yes."

"All right, then. We'll meet you down in the atrium at seven o'clock."

CHAPTER 9

Jon apologized to Emma for the third time as they strolled down the hallway to meet the Dallins for dinner. In his defense, it wasn't his fault his mind kept wandering while she told him about everything she had heard that morning. He didn't understand most of the scientific jargon anyway.

They ended up not even making it downstairs before they met up with Aaron and Rachael. As it turned out, the Dallins' room was up the hall from theirs, close to the second-floor mezzanine. Jon suspected this wasn't a coincidence—that Jack had arranged it to make sure the four of them bumped into each other. In fact, there seemed to be quite a few things about this convention Jack Allred had managed to personally arrange.

The Dallins were only a little younger than him and Emma, mid to late thirties, and he very much appreciated their company. Aaron was a lot like Jon—a down-to-earth, practical kind of guy—and Rachael kind of reminded him of Emma. She was shorter than Em, with long, dark curls as bouncy as her personality. And judging by her wild stories about doing news coverage for the war while in Egypt, where she grew up, she had a knack for getting herself into trouble too.

Once they finished dinner at the restaurant, a Texas-themed steakhouse with the juiciest cut of ribeye Jon had ever eaten, the four of them were enjoying each other's company so much they decided to order dessert. Emma excused herself to the restroom. Rachael, thankfully, offered to go with her. Jon had noticed Bennett and some other guests at a table across the restaurant.

"So, Jon," said Aaron. "Where are you from originally?"

"Originally?" Jon smiled. He hated it when someone asked him that, because of the reaction he usually got to his answer. "Bethesda."

"Whoa. Private schools and country clubs, huh?"

"Yeah, yeah," said Jon. Bethesda, Maryland, just northwest of Washington, DC, was once one of the most affluent areas of the country and home to overpaid government officials—including, at one point, Jon's father and stepmother. "And summers on the Vineyard and weekends in Virginia Beach. But, in my defense, it was only till I was sixteen. Then I went to live with my grandparents in Raleigh."

"Got burned out on the high life, huh?"

"Something like that."

"And what about now? Where was it you guys came down here from again?" Aaron asked.

"Pineville, Missouri."

Aaron raised an eyebrow. "Missouri?"

"I know, don't ask me. It was Emma's doing. She was always a small-town girl at heart, I guess. For years, she tried to talk me into buying a big plot of land in the middle of nowhere. Eventually she won."

"Bet that was quite a culture shock for you. But I take it you adapted."

Jon chuckled. "Uh-huh." *Adapted* wasn't the word for it. He had been *assimilated*. He had gone from high-rise apartment buildings and sandy beaches to sprawling ranches and the rocky banks of what Emma so lovingly referred to as "the crick," from playing rock in the back of bars to directing school plays, and from passing out after an all-night gig to crawling into bed exhausted after helping the local sheriff save his peach trees from an early frost.

He had to admit, though, Emma couldn't have picked a better place to raise a family. There was an incredible sense of community in their little town. People looked out for each other, something Jon wasn't used to. They didn't have to worry about much more than the occasional tornado or ice storm, either. The Bentonville area, less than an hour south, was just the right size for plenty of fantastic restaurants and family entertainment without all the crime. And the extended effects of the war somehow didn't hit the area nearly as hard as the rest of the country, like they were in their own little socio-economic bubble or something. It was a little strange, actually. Almost as if Emma knew.

"But," he added, "I do miss the ocean. There's something about the smell of the sea and a long walk on the beach." He flashed back to his times sailing on the Chesapeake Bay. The feeling of the wind through his hair, the spray of salt water against his face. He had learned to sail when he was very young. Those were the good memories of his childhood. The only good ones he had.

Jon snapped himself out of his daydream. That's when he noticed Bennett glance at him, then look away.

"So, Aaron," said Jon. "Where are you from?" He took a sip of his water. "Originally?"

"Iowa."

"Cornfields and windmills, huh?" said Jon with a grin, noticing for the first time that Aaron's hair was as red as ripe corn silk.

"Yeah, yeah." Aaron chuckled. "And more cornfields and more windmills."

"Then how in the world did you end up in Cairo?"

"The same way every other small-town guy that made it over there did. I got sucked into the war. Don't get me wrong, I love linguistics, but I never meant it to be any more than a hobby, you know? Once all the fighting broke out, though, I got this bright idea I wanted to go off and serve my country. Honor and glory and patriotism and all that."

Jon stared into his glass. He wished his own reasons for ending up over there had been as noble.

"I have to be honest, though," said Aaron. "I saw a lot of crazy stuff over there. Had a lot of close calls. But being a translator, I had it kind of easy. I have a lot of respect for those of you who were out there risking your lives."

"The war was hard on everyone." Jon noticed the girls making their way back to the table and thought about everything Emma had gone through while he was away. "We just did what we had to do to get home."

"Yeah, well, I'll have to admit, if it hadn't been for the war..." Aaron smiled at Rachael as she pulled out her chair. He leaned over and kissed her. "We would never have met."

Once their waiter arrived with their desserts, Jon settled in to another slice of the fantastic cheesecake Emma had brought him the night before. She picked through a bowl of fresh cantaloupe, though Jon couldn't possibly imagine it was anywhere near as good as what they could pull out of their own garden back home.

"Mr. and Mrs. Grant." AD Tanner stepped up to their table just as they were finishing.

"Assistant Director." Jon reached across the table and shook his hand, then introduced him to the Dallins.

"Mr. Grant, I wonder if I might have a word with you?"

"Of course," said Jon. "Have a seat."

Tanner glanced over his shoulder in the direction of Bennett's table, then sat down. He leaned toward Jon and lowered his voice. "Mr. Grant, I wanted to talk to you about what you discussed with Vice President Allred this morning. Are you absolutely certain about who you believe Dr. Korvaire was with last night?"

"Of course I'm certain. I wouldn't have said anything if I wasn't."

Tanner let out a long sigh.

"Why do you ask?"

"Because eventually I'm going to have to go question the guy, and I'm not exactly looking forward to it," he answered, glancing over his shoulder.

Bennett was staring at them now, frowning.

Tanner shook his head. "Well, I guess I should go make a phone call, then. Deputy Director Sanchez is going to have my head. Thank you for your help... I think."

"No problem," said Jon. "If you need anything else, just let us know."

"Yeah." Tanner got up and walked away.

"What in the world was that all about?" Aaron asked.

Jon explained what he'd seen the night before, including who he believed had been with Korvaire when she was attacked. He left out the part about what he noticed at dinner and his suspicions concerning what Bennett really was.

"But why would he try to kill her?" Aaron asked.

"Isn't it obvious?" said Rachael. "Because of her research. Jon, you said she had told Bennett she could no longer support the GOG's work on the pipelines, right?"

"That's right!" Emma's face lit up. "It's like what I told you earlier, honey. According to Senator Hendrix, based on what Anna found she didn't believe the GOG could follow the timelines they promised. She planned on announcing that during her presentation. That is, until..."

"Until he tried to kill her," Jon said quietly.

The others stared at each other in silence.

"Em, when our room was ransacked, you realize what they were looking for, don't you?"

Emma wrinkled her forehead. "My presentation notes. But, Jon, surely you don't think... I mean, he wouldn't be that stupid, would he?"

"Well, I guess that depends," said Aaron.

"On what?" Emma asked.

Jon sighed. "On what he thinks you're planning on saying tomorrow morning."

Jon and Emma looked at each other, then across the restaurant at Bennett. He lifted his wine glass and smiled at them with the kind of crooked expression Jon imagined a spider might make when it's discovered it has a fly trapped in its web. Jon reached for Emma's hand under the table. This was getting a lot more serious than he would have liked.

The four of them returned to the second floor in silence. They stopped just outside the Dallins' room to say their goodnights. Jon shook Aaron's hand and thanked them both for joining him and Emma for dinner.

"It was our pleasure," said Aaron. "Though I wish it could have ended on a better note." He looked past Jon toward Emma, who stood waiting just up the hall with her arms crossed, staring silently at the floor. "Listen, Jon." He lowered his voice and glanced at Rachael beside him. "If you need anything, we would both be more than happy to help you keep an eye on her."

Jon smiled. "Thanks, Aaron. I'll keep that in mind."

Aaron nodded. "Goodnight, Emma," he said over Jon's shoulder.

"Goodnight, you two," she answered.

Jon and Emma returned to their room. The orange tones and rich fabrics suddenly seemed more suffocating than inviting. Under any other circumstance, Jon would have looked forward to the idea of curling up between the soft linen sheets next to his wife and slipping into a deep state of sweet unconsciousness. But he was too restless, and she too apprehensive, for either of them to be able to relax. So they just lay there wide awake, with Emma curled up under Jon's arm.

"Baby?" she said. "I think I owe you an apology."

"For what?"

She propped herself up on her arm and looked at him. "I do have a little bit of a tendency to get myself into these situations, don't I?"

He laughed. "You're just now figuring that out?"

"Well," she said, grinning, "I just wanted you to know that I'm sorry. I can't even imagine the amount of worry I've caused you over the years. I mean, I know before, when the kids were little..."

"Hey." He put his hand on her arm. "Don't do that. Remember what we said?"

"I know what we said. I just want you to know that I never meant to cause you so much grief. And that I really appreciate how supportive you've been this time." She shook her head and turned her eyes to the sheets. "You know, you weren't always..." She stopped, then looked back up at him. "I guess what I'm trying to say is, I'm really glad you're here."

"Me too."

"Well, that having been said, there is something else I need to tell you."

"And what's that?"

"There is no way I'm going to be able to go to sleep."

He grinned. "Then are you thinking what I'm thinking?"

"I'm no mind reader," she said as she leaned in to kiss him, "but I think I have a pretty good idea."

Jon pulled her closer. Maybe being stuck in a hotel four hundred miles from home wasn't such a bad thing after all.

Afterward, he wasn't sure when he finally dozed off or how long he slept. At some point Emma crawled out of bed, turned on the lamp by the couch, and began looking through her presentation. Jon just rolled over and went back to sleep. It must have been hours later when the light finally went out again.

But instead of her crawling back into bed next to him like he expected, she tried to wake him up. "Jon?"

He fought to peel back his heavy eyelids.

"Sweetheart, the power is out."

"It's probably just a blackout. Come to bed already."

"No, Jon, I don't think so." She stepped over to the window and opened the curtain. "Look."

Fighting his tired body, Jon threw back the blankets and stumbled out of bed. He stubbed his toe on the coffee table and limped over to stand beside her.

She was right—it wasn't a blackout. The rest of the city was still lit up.

He looked at Emma. It was hard to read the expression on her face in the dim light through the window, but he had a pretty good idea she was thinking the same thing he was.

They both dressed quickly. Jon found a flashlight in the bedside drawer.

Emma put her hand on his shoulder as he reached for the door. "Honey, I don't know if this is such a good idea," she whispered. "Maybe we should just stay here."

Says the woman who will rush into the middle of a tornado. "Would you rather wait here like a sitting duck, or find out what's going on?" What he wanted to do was leave her behind and go out there by himself, but knew that was an even worse idea.

Emma sighed. "Fine."

As they walked past the Dallins' door on their way down to the atrium, Aaron popped out and scared Emma half to death.

"Sorry, Emma," he said, trying to hold in his laughter. "I take it you guys couldn't sleep either?"

"No," said Jon.

Aaron winked. "Well, what do you say we find out what's happened to the juice, then?"

Rachael pushed through the door behind him.

"Whoa!" said Aaron, stopping her. "Just where do you think you're going?"

"Very funny," said Rachael.

"Actually, you know what?" said Jon. He pointed at Aaron. "You come with me." Then he grabbed Emma by the arm and pulled her toward the Dallins' door. "And you two stay here."

"*What?*" the girls said together.

"Jon!" said Emma.

"No," he answered. "This is not up for discussion."

Rachael opened her mouth to speak.

Jon cut her off. "From either of you. It's too dangerous, especially for you, Em."

"Aaron?" said Rachael.

"The man is right, Rae. Besides, it's best for Emma. No one will look for her in our room, and she shouldn't be left alone."

Rachael looked Emma over and sighed. "Yeah, I guess you're probably right."

Emma crossed her arms and frowned.

"All right, we'll be back as soon as we figure out what's going on," said Jon. "It shouldn't take too long. Emmy, promise me you will not leave this room."

"But Jon—"

"Promise me."

Emma sighed. "All right, I promise. Just *please* be careful."

Jon and Aaron started their search in the atrium. It didn't surprise Jon at all to find not a single FBI agent anywhere. If there had been someone around, they could have asked what was going on and been done with it. But instead they had to sweep through the first floor with nothing more than the dimness of their cheap hotel flashlights.

The more they walked, the more tired Jon became. He kept thinking he would just as soon be in his own bed. This, of course, made him think about home, and his kids. It was kind of funny how, no matter how old they got, he still worried about them.

"You and Rachael ever thought about having kids, Aaron?" said Jon.

Aaron answered quietly, "We did have one, actually. A little boy. He was killed in the riots when we were trying to flee Cairo."

"Oh my gosh. I'm so sorry."

"No, it's okay. We all knew the risks, right? So many of us are afraid to even have kids now, with the world the way it is. But Rachael, she was pretty insistent. I certainly don't regret it. I'm sure you know what I mean, though, having three of them. I imagine Emma got to you too."

"Actually, it wasn't Emma who was the insistent one."

They turned a corner into a hallway, and Jon stopped suddenly. Down the hall, in the darkness, danced a faint red light.

Both men quickly turned off their flashlights.

CHAPTER 10

I can't believe I'm doing this.

Sam sat on the edge of his bed on the top floor of the hotel. Those who had been chosen to work the convention, including himself and the others from his team who had strategically placed themselves in position as hotel employees, had each been assigned a room. The people in charge of security apparently felt it would be easier to keep up with everyone's comings and goings if the people who were supposed to be there stayed there. It had made things much easier on their plans, but much harder on him. He missed his family something terrible.

He stared down at the photo of the three of them in his hand, unwilling to admit to himself that he would probably never see them again. If his team was caught, he would be going to jail for a long, long time. Then, of course, if things went really wrong, there was always the possibility that he wouldn't be coming back at all.

And even if everything went exactly according to plan, then what? He wondered if he *should* go back. If she knew what he was doing, would Claire even let him come home?

He looked over at the phone. He knew he couldn't call her. If he was to keep her out of this, he couldn't contact her now. They would be able to trace the phone records from his room, and they'd accuse her of having been an accomplice. So he had kept her in the dark about everything. It made him feel guilty. He had never once lied to his wife before this. But in order to protect her and Cole, this was the way it had to be.

What he *could* do, though, was write to her. A letter he could get to her later, when everything was said and done. Or someone else could get to her—if the worst ended up happening to him.

He found a notepad and pen in the nightstand.

My dearest Hummingbird,

I cannot even begin to imagine how hard all of this is for you. Please know that I never wanted to deceive you, but you must know why I did. I could not bear for you to have to

*suffer for my decision any more than
I know you already will. I just hope
that one day you will be able to
understand why I chose to do this…*

The knock on the door came just as he finished the letter. He slipped it inside his notebook and returned it to the back pocket of his slacks. He took a long, deep breath before opening the door.

The towering image of Mac stood just outside. "You ready, Hackett?"

Sam nodded.

They stopped a few doors down to pick up Rat. That's what everyone called him, though his real name was Eric Reynolds. Sam wasn't sure where Reynolds got his nickname, though it was easy to guess. Rat was small and shifty, with mousy brown hair and jerky mannerisms, like a rodent incessantly popping its head in and out of a hole in the wall. Where in the world Mac had found this kid, Sam didn't know, but Rat was supposed to be good at what it was they needed him to do.

As they stood just inside the door to the stairwell, they stared down at their watches.

"And three, two, one…" said Hackett. The light beside the door went out.

They took the stairs two at a time, by the soft glow of the red lights they held in their hands. Sam was impressed at how quietly and quickly the other men moved. Given Mac's military background, this didn't surprise him, but he wondered what kind of work Rat had done before this. Rat didn't strike Sam as the military type.

Not a single FBI agent was in sight on the first floor, just as planned. Now they just had to make it across the atrium and to the security office in the back hallway.

They made their way along the outer edge of the atrium, beneath the second-floor mezzanine. Just as they got to the halfway point, however, they heard the startled scream of a woman on the floor just above them. They all stopped and looked at each other, then turned off their lights.

Sam could hear voices above them, though he couldn't make out what they were saying. He glanced at his watch. If they were going to do this, they had to go now. Mac must have felt the same way, because he turned on his light, and the three of them booked it the rest of the way across the atrium and down the back hall.

The door to the security office was already unlocked. Sam guessed that security had been there monitoring cameras just up until the point when the power went out. Where they went after that, he wasn't sure. He knew Mac had a contact on the inside, but still, this seemed a little too easy.

"How much time do we have?" Sam whispered.

"Enough," said Mac.

The security office featured a wall of screens, showing feeds from around the hotel. A backup power source kept the monitors and cameras running, but nearly all the images were black, with the lights in the hotel out.

But they weren't interested in the screens. They needed to get into the small room just off the side of the office. And that door was locked.

Rat knelt in front of the doorknob and pulled a small tool kit from his backpack. Holding his flashlight in his mouth, he set to work picking the lock.

"And voila." The door popped open. "See?" said Rat. "Piece of cake."

"Yeah, that's great, kid," said Mac, pushing him into the room. "Now finish the job."

The room was filled floor to ceiling with cables, electrical boxes, and tubing. What they were looking for specifically was an access point that would allow them to hack into the security cameras and monitor everything that went on inside the hotel.

"How exactly is this supposed to work, Rat?" Sam asked.

Rat dropped his backpack on the floor and pulled out a lantern and a small plastic box. "See this?" he said, holding up the box. "This is a wireless transmitter. Once we get this thing connected to the main line, in there," he said, pointing to one of the metal boxes on the wall, "we'll be able to see everything they see. That way, we can keep an eye on everything that's going on from right inside the conference room."

"Yeah, fantastic," said Mac. He stood just inside the outer door, keeping watch. "Can we get a move on, please?"

Rat worked as quickly as possible. Using the schematic they had been given in advance, he found the main access point and spliced it to his wireless transmitter, which he hid behind some cabling.

"How do we know for sure that it works?" Sam asked.

"We'll have to test it," Rat answered, pulling a tablet

from his pack.

"You just better pray that it does, kid," said Mac. He grabbed the tablet and shoved it back into Rat's backpack, then threw the bag at him. "'Cause we got company."

Sam peered out the outer office door, his flashlight pointed at the floor. Down the hall were two faint yellow lights. Suddenly, they went out.

Sam looked back at Mac and Rat. "Time to go."

Their own faint red lights provided enough light for them to see by, but hopefully not enough to give away their identities. They walked quietly down the hall, away from the owners of the yellow lights, but Sam heard their footsteps following.

The hallway ran behind one of the atrium restaurants, then turned and opened onto the kitchen. Since all three of them were in hotel uniform, Sam figured if they just walked inconspicuously toward the kitchen, they could simply talk their way out of this, even if they got caught.

That option disappeared when Mac suddenly took off.

Mac, you reckless idiot!

Sam broke into a run behind him. He glanced over his shoulder. The two flashlights had turned back on. They had definitely aroused their pursuers' suspicions.

Great.

Just as they raced through the back door into the kitchen, the hotel lights came on. They'd never make it across the atrium now without being seen. Their only hope was to hide in the storage closet off to the side of the kitchen. Sam unlocked it, and the three of them pressed inside and pulled the door shut behind them. They quickly discovered there was no way to lock it from the inside.

Their pursuers burst into the kitchen. "Where did they go?" said a man's voice. "I think we lost them."

"They couldn't have gotten far," said another.

Sam and Mac both stood with their ears to the door, barely breathing. Rat squatted on the floor behind them.

"We should probably just get back upstairs," the first man said. "We've left Emma and Rachael alone too long."

Emma? Sam suddenly recognized that voice. He'd heard it at the private guest dinner in the banquet hall. The man on the other side of the door was Dr. Grant's husband.

"Wait, Jon," said the other voice. "There's a door over here."

Mac clenched his fist around the doorknob and pulled something dark and metallic from behind his back. Even in the dimness of Rat's red light, Sam recognized the object immediately. He grabbed Mac's wrist.

"No!" he whispered.

Mac sneered down at him.

"No casualties! We agreed."

The doorknob began to jiggle. Mac tightened his grip. Sam held his breath and readied himself to take the gun from Mac if he had to. He wasn't prepared to kill anyone. Especially Jonathan Grant.

"Well," said Grant, "so much for that. The door's locked."

"Come on then," said the other guy. "Let's get back up to the room. Maybe they escaped through the atrium."

"Yeah, maybe." Grant sounded disappointed.

"At least the power came back on."

Only when the voices and footsteps faded did Sam release his death grip on Mac. Mac pushed his gun into the front of his waistband, pulled his vest down over it, and rubbed his wrist.

"Holy crap, that was close," said Rat.

"Yeah, too close." Mac glared at Sam. "If they'd found us, it would have blown the entire operation."

"But they didn't find us, did they? And what's with the handgun? Are you trying to get caught?" He started to open the door.

Mac slammed it shut. "I know who that was, Hackett. It was that doctor's nosy husband. He followed me through the hotel earlier today. They're getting too suspicious. I should have gotten rid of him when I had the chance."

"*No*, dammit." Sam shoved Mac against the door and held him there. "No one dies. Not on my watch." He was too mad now to care that Mac was three times his size.

"You're getting soft, Hackett," said Mac. "If you don't have what it takes to get the job done, I suggest you turn it over to someone who does."

Sam pulled Mac's gun from his belt and pointed it right at his face. "This is *my* job, Mackenzie, and *I* will decide how it goes. If *you* can't handle that, then maybe you should walk away. Because the rest of us are not risking our lives because of your stupidity. Are we clear?"

Mac glared at him. "Crystal."

Sam held him there, staring him straight in the eyes.

Mac stared right back.

"Good." Sam let him go and pushed the gun into the front of his own pants. "Now let's get the hell out of here."

CHAPTER 11

"Well, what did you find out?" Rachael asked from the sofa as Jon and Aaron walked into the Dallins' room.

"Absolutely nothing," answered Aaron, plopping down beside her.

"I knew I should have gone too!" she said.

Jon sat down on the edge of the bed where Emma lay curled up on her side, asleep. He pushed her hair from her face. *At least she was finally able to get some rest.*

"I don't know, honey," said Aaron. "I don't think even the famous Rachael Dallin could have sniffed out much in the pitch black down there."

"Well, it wasn't *completely* dark," said Jon.

Rachael raised an eyebrow at Aaron.

"We saw a few people with flashlights, down in the back hallway. We followed them, but then lost them in the kitchen," Aaron explained.

Rachael pouted, as if she were hurt that she couldn't have been involved in the excitement.

"Well," said Jon, "I guess we should get back to our room. Let you guys try to salvage the rest of your night." He shook Emma gently. "Come on, Em."

"What 'rest of the night'?" asked Rachael. "It's six o'clock in the morning."

Jon looked over at the alarm clock on the dresser. Sure enough, it was fifteen minutes after six. The hotel staff would be coming around with breakfast soon. The exhaustion from getting very little sleep for two straight nights suddenly hit him.

He pulled Emma to her feet and guided her down the hall toward their room. He hadn't missed his bed this much since leaving the Guard. All he wanted was to crawl between the sheets of that big, king-sized bed and sleep until this stupid convention was over. If he'd had the energy to do it, he would have picked Emma up and carried her just so he could get there faster.

"Well, well, well," said a voice from behind him. "If it isn't the Grants."

Jon cringed. Just when he thought the night couldn't get any worse. The slimeball attached to that voice was the absolute last person he wanted to run into just then. Jon wondered if he had the energy left to restrain himself from punching the guy right in the nose.

"Captain Grant," said Bennett.

Jon turned around, pulling Emma behind him to put himself between her and Bennett.

"And what exactly are two upstanding individuals such as yourselves doing leaving someone else's room so early in the morning?" Bennett asked.

This meant, of course, that Bennett had made a point of knowing which room was theirs. "We were just visiting a friend," Jon answered. "I'm sure you of all people can understand that."

Bennett narrowed his eyes. "Indeed."

"And what about you, Minister?" said Jon. "What is someone no doubt accustomed to wandering hallways late at night doing up so early in the morning?"

"Oh, I prefer to keep a close watch on my surroundings, as well as those who inhabit them. One might be surprised by just how much is revealed about an individual when they think no one else is watching." He raised an eyebrow at Emma. "I think perhaps you should get your wife back to bed, Captain. It would appear she is completely exhausted. Something that can all too often affect one's judgment, I'm afraid. Yes, I believe she could perhaps do with a nice… long… nap. I'd hate for anything *unfortunate* to happen to her," he said, then smiled that arrogant half-smile that made Jon want to break the guy's face.

Jon glared.

"Enjoy the rest of your morning, Captain," Bennett added, then turned and headed back down the hall.

Jon watched him till he reached the mezzanine and turned the corner. Only then did he unclench his fist and start to breathe again. *I am too old for this.*

"Come on, sweetheart," he said, putting his arm around Emma. "Let's get you back to bed."

His mind was almost beyond numb, he was so tired. If it wasn't for the fact that their little encounter in the hall had pushed his blood pressure through the roof, he might very well have fallen asleep standing up. Instead, he sat on the edge of their bed next to Emma, both of them physically and mentally spent, too tired to move and yet too shaken to sleep. And in less than two hours, Emma had to give her presentation.

What a disaster this has all turned out to be.

"I think I'll go take a hot shower," he said, knowing that if he fell asleep now there was no way he'd be able to get himself back up for her speech. He stood and kissed her forehead. "Why don't you try to lie down for a little while and get some rest?"

As Jon started the shower, he heard someone knock and yell "room service." He was so tired, though, the thought of food just made him feel nauseated.

Jon stood in the steaming shower, his hands against the cool granite walls, enjoying the relaxing sensation of hot water beating against his back. The one thing he could be grateful for through this whole ordeal was that his back wasn't bothering him. It had been more than twenty years since his accident, but it still acted up every now and then. He remembered absolutely nothing about the wreck, just the conversation he and Emma had had several hours before.

"Hey, baby, what are you doing here?" He'd just stepped down off the stage at the back of Charlie's bar after she'd walked through the door. "Charlie, how about a beer for my girl?"

Charlie nodded from behind the bar.

"Actually, I can't stay," said Emma.

Jon narrowed his eyes. She wore her lucky pack over her shoulder. "You're leaving again, aren't you? After everything we talked about this morning?"

"It's only for a few days. Then I promise I'll be back. Hurricane Irving is about to make landfall—"

"No, Emmy," he interrupted. "I can't do this anymore."

"But Jon, I have a responsibility."

"Yeah? And what about your responsibility to me? I told you how I felt about this, Em. I'm not going to wait around for another phone call. What if the next one I get is that you're dead? I'm not going to live like that."

"Jon, you don't understand—"

"No, *you* don't understand! You're being completely selfish." He wouldn't normally lash out at her, but he'd had a few drinks. The scare she'd given him a few weeks earlier, with her accident out in the field, didn't help either.

"No, Jon." She stepped in closer and put a hand on his cheek. "*This* is what I want. To stay here with you. But if I do that, I turn my back on everything I know, everything I believe in. This job is who I am. If I walk away from that for what I *really* want, *then* I'm being selfish."

Jon turned his eyes to the floor, not believing what he was about to say. "You leave this time, Emma..." He hesitated, then looked up at her. "And you don't need to bother coming back."

He could see from the shock in her eyes that he'd

broken her heart. But that was exactly how *he* felt every time she blew into town and then suddenly took off again: as if a piece of him had shattered and fallen away.

She bit her lip. He knew he was asking her to choose between him and something that was so much a part of her, but he simply couldn't do this anymore. If something didn't change soon, they would be split up anyway. Whether she walked out the door now or got herself killed chasing some disaster later. Surely she could see that.

That was the last thing he remembered about that night. He woke up in the ICU several days later.

It's funny how you can spend twenty-two years doing just fine on your own, then someone suddenly wanders into your life and you just can't seem to get along without them, he thought as the hot water washed over him. He couldn't handle the thought of losing her now any more than he could handle it then. It had almost killed him last time. He couldn't imagine what it would do to him now.

Jon stepped out of the shower, stood in front of the bathroom sink, and wiped the fog off the mirror. He stared at his own reflection, at the dark stubble peppered across his face and the small lines beginning to form at the corners of his eyes. Jon wondered if the man in the mirror was any different than that lost kid standing alone at the bar. He was almost grateful he couldn't remember the pain of watching as she'd walked out the door. Emma meant everything to him. She was his companion. The mother of his children. They had been through so much together. If she were gone, then a piece of him would go with her.

And that was why Bennett infuriated him. Jon knew his type and the type he worked with, having been burned before by people just like Bennett. People who were determined to get what they wanted, no matter who they hurt along the way. Jon thought back to what Bennett had said in the hallway: *I'd hate for anything unfortunate to happen to her.* He had no doubt in his mind that Bennett would target his wife—that he probably already *had* targeted her. The question was... how?

If he could only figure out what Bennett had in mind, maybe he could stop it. He was almost certain Bennett was a Pusher. That was most likely how he'd managed to get Korvaire drunk enough to take advantage of her. What in the world would he have said to her to get her to act so unlike herself? Luckily the only thing Bennett had said to Emma recently was that she looked like she could use some sleep.

And then it hit him.

Jon grabbed his toiletry bag and dumped its entire contents into the sink in front of him.

The bottle of Ambien was gone.

How could he have been so stupid?

He hadn't even thought about the sleeping pills. The pills that he himself had asked Sarah to prescribe for her. The ones *he* had brought, that *he* had snuck into their bag.

He'd never be able to forgive himself if…

Jon found Emma asleep on the couch, a teacup still in her hand. He sat down on the coffee table and pushed her hair from her face. She breathed softly, her head resting on the arm of the couch.

Jon took the cup from her hand and examined its contents. There was nothing left but a bit of sediment. He set it down next to their uneaten breakfast.

At first he wasn't sure what to think. It was possible, of course, that she had simply fallen asleep. After all, they *were* both exhausted. There was one thing he should check before deciding whether he was being paranoid, though. If Bennett had just successfully pushed Emma into accidentally overdosing, that prescription bottle was somewhere in this room.

He started with all the areas closest to Emma: the coffee table, side tables, the dresser. He rifled through her bag, finding only a bunch of folders and pens, a first aid kit, a flashlight, her cell phone, and her pocketknife. He wondered how she'd gotten the knife past security. Next he moved to the nightstand.

The bottle was sitting by the lamp, completely empty.

"Emmy!" He sat down on the couch next to her and pulled her into a sitting position. She barely even opened her eyes. "Emma, honey, wake up!"

"What?" she muttered. He had to wrap an arm around her back just to keep her propped up.

"Emma!" He shook her. She opened her eyes a little bit wider this time. "Did you take the rest of these?" He held the pill bottle up in front of her.

"The rest of what?" She squinted at the bottle.

"The sleeping pills, Emma!"

"Jon, I don't know… I don't know what you're…" Her words slurred and trailed off as her body went limp in his arms.

"Emma?" He shook her again. "*Emma!*"

He laid her back down and ran to the phone, dialing the only number he could remember. "Aaron!" Jon didn't even wait for him to say hello.

"Jon?"

"Aaron, find the doctor and get to my room as fast as possible."

"Why, what's wrong?"

"Just hurry, please!" He slammed down the phone.

Jon didn't think, he just did. He grabbed the salt shaker from their breakfast tray and took it into the bathroom. As he filled one of the plastic hotel cups with water, he held the little glass shaker up to eye level to see how much was in there. Thank goodness it was full.

He unscrewed the cap and dumped the entire thing into the cup of water. Stirring it with his finger, he rushed back to Emma and set it on the table. Jon pulled her up again, wrapping his arm around her back to support her. Putting his ear up to her lips, he stopped to listen.

She's still breathing.

He grabbed a trashcan from underneath the side table and set it on the floor in front of her. *Please let this work.*

"Emmy?" He shook her again. He knew it wasn't likely that he could wake her up, but he wanted some indication that she was at least slightly responsive. If she was unconscious, what he was about to try would do more harm than good. "*Ennaso?*" He rubbed her cheek, and waited anxiously for some sigh she had heard him. "Please."

"Jon?" Her voice was barely audible, and she didn't open her eyes.

But it was enough response for him.

He grabbed the cup of salt water and used the hand that was already behind her back to restrain her in case she tried to fight him. Then he tilted her back slightly, put the cup up to her lips, and tipped the salty liquid into her mouth. The first few drops just ran down the side of her cheek.

Somewhere in her subconscious she must have realized what he was doing, because she began to drink the water. Jon waited till the cup was emptied to the very last drop before setting it down on the coffee table. He pulled Emma upright again. "Come on, baby."

Just when he was starting to wonder if he hadn't just given her salt poisoning on top of everything else, she started to cough. He leaned her forward and supported her with one arm under her chest while she emptied the contents of her stomach into the trashcan.

The salt water had done the trick.

CHAPTER 12

"I will have a skinny hazelnut latte with extra foam, please."

Matt stood behind the register at the small coffee house on campus, where he worked. He stared blankly at the short-haired woman across the counter, squeezed his eyes closed, and tried to blink off the haze. "I'm sorry, Professor Churchill, what was it that you ordered?" He tried hard to focus on what she was saying.

"The same thing I order every morning, dear." She cocked her head and raised an eyebrow. "Matthew, are you all right? You don't look exactly... well... coherent this morning."

The truth was that Matthew Grant *wasn't* all right. He hadn't been "all right" for several months now. The anxiety—the foreboding, as his mother called it—had become so overwhelming lately it affected his everyday life. It wasn't so bad that it made him sick, like it did his mom. No, never as bad as his mom. It was more like an echo of a feeling. Kind of like the nausea his dad swore he got each time their mom was pregnant with one of them. It was like a sympathy response. Or, in Matt's case, an *Empath* response.

Matt continued to stare blankly at Professor Churchill. She scanned the room, as if searching for someone to notify in case he should suddenly pass out or go postal. He wasn't sure himself which one he was more likely to do. He was just grateful it was still early and there weren't any other customers in the café yet.

He cleared his throat and tried to focus on the feeling of his hand against the cool granite countertop. He moved his thumb beneath the counter, grasping the edge of it, suddenly feeling like he might faint. It had never been this bad before—usually the feeling faded, or he was able to drown it out through the distractions of school or work. But not this time. This time the sensation washed over him like a wave of dense, suffocating darkness.

Something is wrong.

Then Matt felt a gentle touch on the back of his hand, and the darkness withdrew.

He knew who stood beside him before he even opened his eyes. The instant she had placed her hand on his, he had felt a spark of excitement, a wave of comforting warmth. Alex Romano was the only person in the world who could make him feel like that with a single touch. And because of what Matt was, Alex was also one of the few people outside his own family that he would let touch him at all.

"Hey, are you okay?" she whispered with sweet sincerity.

Matt knew she didn't even have to ask. Words had become nothing more than a formality between them. A courtesy to the outside world. Alex was a Reader, which meant she knew his thoughts before he could even work out the words to express them. She'd told him once that she wasn't usually that good at it, but with him, for some reason, it came naturally to her.

"Here you go, Professor Churchill," said Alex. She handed their English Lit teacher the latte she'd ordered.

Matt knew full well that Alex hadn't been close enough to them to hear the professor place her order, but he was also certain that Alex had prepared exactly what Churchill asked for. It was both against the Code and dangerous for any of them to use their gifts in public, but the fact that Professor Churchill ordered the same thing every morning was probably cover enough.

Professor Churchill thanked Alex and paid for the coffee. She suggested that Matt get up to the Health Center, since he clearly wasn't well. Alex promised she would make sure he saw someone.

"Thanks, Lex," Matt said after Professor Churchill walked out the door. "I owe you one."

"You're absolutely right you do. And you're going to pay me back right now by going straight to Professor March's office."

"Alex." Matt rolled his eyes.

"I mean it, *Matia*."

Matt couldn't help but smile at the familiar Greek term of endearment she had given him years ago. Though he'd heard it around the Romano house plenty of times, Matt still had no idea what it meant. He didn't need to. Just knowing how she felt when she said it was more than enough.

"Look, Matt, I know you've been having a hard time lately—"

Matt opened his mouth to argue.

"And don't you *even* try to convince me that you've been in to see him lately, because I know you haven't."

Matt shut his mouth. He shouldn't have bothered.

"Hey, and besides," she added, wrapping a hand

around his wrist, "I promised Professor Churchill I'd make sure you talked to someone. Don't make me break my promise."

There was a softness in her tone, and the spark in her touch made Matt's heart skip a beat. He relaxed his shoulders. There wasn't any point in arguing with her. Though honestly, if he told her that he already felt better, he *would* be telling the truth. Alex just had that effect on him.

She smiled, wide enough that her blue-gray eyes wrinkled around the corners. He looked down at the floor, realizing that she'd probably "heard" that. Once upon a time that would have made him uncomfortable. But he had come to accept the fact that she knew how he felt about her. She certainly made no attempt to hide her feelings from him.

"You'd better get going if you're going to go," she said. Alex grabbed an apron from the wall and pulled it over her black polo shirt and slacks. Matt loved how the dark uniform contrasted with her olive skin. She tied the apron behind her, flipping the bouncy waves of her long black hair over the straps around her neck. For a brief second Matt caught the sweet scent of chamomile and lavender.

Matt glanced toward the kitchen, where their manager was pulling pastries from the oven.

"Don't worry," said Alex. "You let me deal with Luke."

Matt's smile fell. He noticed the slight elation he got from her whenever she said Luke's name. "Yeah, okay." He pulled off his own apron. "As long as you don't have to agree to go out with him again," he said, narrowing his eyes, "just for my sake."

Alex glared. "Well, it's not like anyone *else* is asking me."

Matt stood there with his hand still on the apron he had just hung on the wall. From somewhere in the café he caught the distinctly bitter smell of burnt coffee, like a forgotten pot of decaf someone had left on a little too long.

Alex sighed. "Sorry, Matt, I didn't mean…"

It was too late. She had gotten defensive, which unfortunately meant *he* would now be defensive, too. It was better that they just get away from each other before one of them said something they'd regret.

"Don't worry about it," he said, slipping through the swinging door at the end of the counter. "I'll see you in

English Lit."

He didn't bother to wait for a response.

Matt didn't blame her for reacting the way she did. She was right. He had made it clear to her that, despite his feelings, he wasn't interested in pursuing their relationship. It hadn't exactly gone over well. He was lucky she still talked to him at all, let alone maintained a friendship. It wasn't fair of him to expect her not to see someone else.

Maybe it was a good idea to pay Professor March a visit after all. Between worrying about his parents and Alex's suppressed resentment, Matt felt worse that he had in years. Almost as bad as the day his father's plane had gone down during the war.

And knowing that was what scared Matt the most.

Though Professor March's office wasn't that far from the café, Matt was soon tired and out of breath from the walk. Of course, it had never taken all that much to wear Matt out. Unfortunately, what was kicking his butt that morning wasn't so much the walk as the heat. Even though it was still early, the sun beat down at a scorching ninety degrees. They had predicted above-average temps for this summer, but this was ridiculous. Matt didn't need to have a heart condition to be worn out. This kind of weather would make an Olympian pant like a dog.

Professor March's office was in the same paint-chipped building as his mom's: the Hopkins School of Arts and Sciences. As Matt walked into the office, he was suddenly surrounded by the musty scent of walnut wainscoting and old books. The professor stood behind his desk, looking out the window.

"Hello, Matthew," he said without turning, in that voice that somehow always seemed simultaneously familial and condescendingly distinguished. Though the professor had been unofficially adopted into the Grant family upon marrying Sarah years ago, and had worked closely with both Matt and his mother as a sort of counselor, the professor still felt oddly distant to Matt. As if he knew more about them than they knew about him.

"Hello, Professor March," Matt replied. He felt a slight twinge of guilt, suddenly realizing he'd been avoiding the professor, mostly because his mother had been too—though he had no idea why.

"Matthew, I'm glad you're here. There's something I've been meaning to ask you." Professor March turned around and walked to the front of his desk, his chocolate loafers clacking against the worn wooden floors. He motioned for Matt to have a seat. Matt sat down, and the professor took the chair next to him.

Professor March leaned forward, folded his hands in front of him, and pressed them to his lips. "Matthew…"

Matt squeezed the arms of the leather club chair as the professor stared at him with his eyebrows drawn. "Yes, Professor?"

The clock at the top of the student union building bonged out a warning to those poor souls who were crazy enough to take a seven-thirty class.

The professor took a deep breath. "Do you like English toffee?"

Matt smiled. "If you're talking about the stuff my mom made you for your birthday, then yes sir, I'd have to say I do."

"Fantastic!" Professor March stood and walked around his desk again. He pulled a large tin from his top drawer. "Don't get me wrong," he said as he sat back down and opened the lid, offering some to Matt. "I enjoy a good toffee as much as the next fellow, but I can't possibly eat all of this by myself. And if I take it home, then Sarah will know that your mum made it for me, and we'd both be in trouble."

"Don't worry, Professor. Your secret is safe with me."

Matt knew from personal experience how Nazi Sarah tended to be with all of them about their diets. He was also well aware that Professor March could easily eat the entire tin by himself. In fact, that's exactly how his mother had known to make him the toffee in the first place. He had devoured an entire plate of it at the OGE's last Christmas party.

But Professor March had offered him the toffee because he knew it would help. Not so much the candy itself, as the feeling associated with it. Professor March, like Matt, was an Empath, so he knew that the quickest way to cheer Matt up was to conjure a positive emotion. Family was the most important thing in the world to Matt, and the toffee was a reminder of the time his family spent together during the holidays.

It also didn't hurt that Professor March himself got so much enjoyment out of the toffee.

Matt relaxed and rested his head against the cool leather as they both sat mindfully chewing the buttery candy. "Thank you, Professor," he said quietly.

"You're very welcome, Matthew. Now." The professor

brushed the crumbs off his lap. "I don't think your mother's toffee is the reason you came to see me today. Something has been bothering you lately. Something that I gather has been eating at you for quite some time now."

Matt sighed. "Yes, sir."

"I do believe I know where part of the problem lies," said the professor. "Miss Romano came in to see me yesterday. She's been coming to my office quite a bit lately."

"Oh." Matt looked at the floor. "I see." He sometimes forgot he wasn't the only ESPer Professor March worked with. Matt wondered exactly what the two of them talked about and how much of it involved him.

"Now, Matthew, I don't have to remind you that anything I discuss with any of my students is completely confidential."

Matt shifted in his chair. "Of course not."

"But I will say this. Whatever your reasons for distancing your relationship with Miss Romano, you're keeping it well hidden, even from me. Of course, it is not at all necessary for me to understand why you're doing it. My only concern is that *you* understand why."

Matt took a deep breath.

"Look, Matthew, I know how hard it can be as an Empath to trust your own emotions. Often we wonder if the feelings we experience come from ourselves or from someone else. I would caution you not to let that distrust interfere with what has the potential to be a sincere and fulfilling relationship, whether it be with Miss Romano or anyone else."

Matt managed a half smile. He didn't doubt that Professor March understood what it was like. Not only did the professor speak from personal experience, he had spent a lifetime training other ESPers to learn how to adapt so their gifts didn't control their lives. But there was one thing the professor didn't know. The one thing that no one in Matt's life could possibly understand.

"Well then, let's move on, shall we?" Professor March returned to his desk to put away the candy. "Something else is bothering you, Matthew. Something not wholly yours, and yet very close to you. My first guess, of course, would be that you are worried about your parents. But I also sense it is something much more than that. Something deeper that's been going on for a few months now. And you're having trouble pinpointing it."

"Yes, that sounds about right."

"Have you tried some of the focusing techniques we've practiced?"

Though Professor March taught philosophy and theology now, that hadn't always been his primary occupation. He didn't talk about it much, but Professor March had spent most of his life working with British intelligence. Matt had no idea precisely how long "most of his life" was, but imagined it was a while. Whenever any of them would ask the professor his age, all he would say was, "I've been on this earth long enough to learn a thing or two."

During that time, the professor had been trained in certain techniques that could help an ESPer turn their gifts from passive to active. Techniques that had made it possible for him to use his gifts to find and gather whatever information he needed. Techniques so advanced that he could *take* what he wanted—feelings, memories, sometimes even more—instead of passively having them pushed onto him. He had spent the last few years trying to teach these techniques to Matt—with frustratingly little success.

"I have," Matt answered, "but I'm afraid whatever it is is just too close. Anytime I've tried, it's like whatever I'm sensing gets all mixed up with my own feelings about it."

The professor smiled knowingly. This very problem was an Empath's biggest downfall. Matt not only had to sense the emotion without letting it affect him, he also had to distinguish it from his own feelings. Some Empaths take a lifetime to overcome it, and many never learn to do it at all.

"Perhaps a little help, then?" said the professor.

Matt breathed a sigh of relief. It wasn't often that the professor offered to help his students directly. Mostly because Professor March strongly believed in learning through experience. But also, Matt suspected, because any direct involvement the professor had with another person's emotions meant that he had to experience them too, which was not only uncomfortable but risked exposing the professor to potentially private information.

Matt would normally have politely declined in order to spare him. But if things were bad enough that he was having fainting spells in public, it was probably time he tried something new. "Yes, sir, I would appreciate that very much," he said.

"Well, then, let's get started."

Professor March picked up the phone and asked the

department secretary to make sure they weren't disturbed, then returned to his chair beside Matt. "All right, Matthew, I'd like to try something a little different. Something we haven't tried before. I'm going to picture very clearly in my mind a specific time in my life in which it was necessary for me to be completely and totally focused. I am then going to place my hands on your shoulders—"

Matt took in a sharp breath before he could stop himself.

Professor March's expression softened. "This will make it much easier for you to fully grasp the sensation," he explained quietly.

Matt wasn't so sure, but he trusted the professor. He nodded for him to continue.

"Now, Matthew, once you grasp it, I want you to use it to your advantage. I want you to use this focus to pinpoint the exact origin of the feelings you've been experiencing and explore them. Use all your resources to analyze what you're sensing."

Matt noticed a twinge of apprehension from the professor, but couldn't pick up on why.

"Matthew, do you understand?"

"Yes, Professor, I understand."

"The sensation might be alarming at first, but I believe you are one of the few people able to handle such a direct exercise."

"It's all right, Professor," said Matt. "If you believe it will help, I'm certainly willing to give it a try."

"All right, then." Professor March stood.

Matt tried to calm his breathing as the professor came to stand behind him. He sank back into the chair and rested his arms on the soft leather. For the first time since he'd walked into the office, he noticed that the window behind the professor's desk was cracked open. A few dark clouds had rolled in, and the clean smell of rain blew through. Matt breathed deep the refreshing scent as he closed his eyes.

"Are you ready, Matthew?" Professor March asked quietly from behind his chair.

"I am."

CHAPTER 13

"Well, if it isn't the cavalry," Jon barked as he answered the door. Between his lack of sleep and Emma's brush with death, it was all he could do to suppress his irritation.

Aaron, Rachael, Jack Allred, and a fourth man—the doctor, judging by his little black bag—stepped into his suite. Two Secret Service agents remained in the hall.

Jon explained to the doctor that he believed Emma had accidentally ingested too many sleeping pills, and that he had successfully induced vomiting to get them back out again.

"I don't understand, Jon," said Jack. "That doesn't sound like Emma at all. How in the world could this have happened?"

Jon scowled. "Why don't you ask Stephen Bennett?"

Jack raised an eyebrow and glanced around the room. "Jon, why don't we step out into the hall for a moment?"

Jon didn't move.

Jack gently put his hand on Jon's arm. "Come on, son."

Aaron looked back and forth between Jon and Jack. "It's all right, Jon," he said. "Rachael and I will stay here with Emma."

Jon sighed and headed into the hall with Jack.

Followed by two Secret Service agents, they once again headed to the window at the end of the hall. Jon could feel the heat already radiating from the glass, even though it was still early. Down below, the crowd of protesters seemed to have doubled in size since their arrival. They held up their signs, shouting their contempt at whoever and whatever would listen to them. There was a distinctive rhythm to their angry cries, as if a collective spirit of contention had descended, pushing out whatever sense of reason these desperate and broken people still had left. How much had been taken from them, he wondered, before they gave up all hope and resorted to shouting their woes beneath the beating rays of an east Texas sun?

The world was going mad around him. He wondered how long it would be before he went with it.

"Jon Jacob." Jack squeezed his shoulder.

Jon turned away from the window. "He had something to do with this, Jack. I know it. That pill bottle wasn't even there last night." He recalled pulling a flashlight out of that same nightstand less than eight hours earlier.

Jack turned to the two Secret Service men. "Gentlemen, can you give us just a moment, please?"

"You know we can't do that, Mr. Vice President," one answered.

"Look, I know you're both a bit new at this. I get that you have to be here to watch over me, but can you please do it from a little bit farther up the hallway? Even my usual boys knew to give me a bit of privacy every now and then."

The two men looked at each other, then back at Jack.

"Please," he said.

They moved only a few feet up the hall.

Jack sighed and shook his head.

"Uncle Jack," said Jon, lowering his voice. "I saw Bennett's mark."

Jack gasped. "You what?"

"I know exactly what he's capable of, and *you* know that Emma would never have taken those pills herself. Hell, she didn't even want me to bring them in the first place."

"Of course I do, but how in the world am I supposed to prove that Bennett had something to do with it?"

"By exposing him for what he really is, for starters."

"And expose *ourselves* in the process?" Jack whispered.

Jon sighed. He was so sick of the cloak and dagger routine.

"Jon, look. I owe you and Emma both an apology. I feel responsible for all of this. I can promise you that for the remainder of the convention you will both have escorts and security posted at your door at all times."

Jon shook his head. A lot of good that would do. "It doesn't matter, Jack. Because we're not staying. As soon as Emma is well enough, we're both getting back on the plane and going straight home." He turned and headed back toward his room.

Jack followed after him. "What about Emma's presentation?"

"Emma's *presentation*?" Jon spun around. For a moment, he actually thought about hitting Jack. *I really must be losing it.* "You've got to be kidding me! Jack, my wife could have *died* this morning. We didn't sign on for this."

"Emma agreed to do this because she knew what needed to be done. She knew the risks involved, and she was still willing to make the sacrifice."

"*Sacrifice?* Don't you dare talk to me about sacrifice, Jack Allred. Do you have any idea what we've lost? What we've *already* sacrificed?"

"What *you've* lost? Jon, we have *all* lost something. We have all sacrificed something—for the greater cause. And we will continue to sacrifice because we understood the risks. We all knew what had to be done and what was at stake if we failed." Jack lowered his voice. "I lost someone, too, Jon. Or have you forgotten that?"

"Of course I haven't forgotten," he answered quietly. Jack's son, Danny, had been the closest thing Jon ever had to a brother. Danny had been part of the first wave in their unit to be called up for the war.

"Son, listen to me." Jack put his hands on Jon's shoulders. "Greg and I have watched out for you and Emma since you both were young. Probably a lot more than we should have. I understand your position. Really, I do. I loved both your parents very much, and I know what it did to your father when he lost your mother. But this is bigger than all of us, and we are running out of time. We can't do this without her, and you know it. We need Emma."

"I need her, too, Jack," Jon told the floor.

"You know what? Fine. You go right ahead and walk away. But just how long do you think you can hide out in your little town in the middle of nowhere? How long do you think it's going to take before someone like Stephen Bennett catches up to you? Because eventually it's going to happen, Jon. They know who you are, and they will see you as a threat. You think they're just going to let that go?"

Jon crossed his arms and looked away.

"So I tell you what, Jon. If you're going to turn your back and leave, you better make sure you talk to Bennett first. You go ahead and tell him that he's already won. Because *you* are giving up," he said, then pushed past Jon and disappeared into the hotel room. The Secret Service men resumed their posts by the door.

Jon clenched his fists, wanting to break something. He didn't know what made him angrier: what Jack had said, or the fact that he was right. He was so completely *done* with this entire thing. But the knot developing in the pit of his stomach told him it was just beginning.

For the first time in years, Jon wished he hadn't

stopped drinking.

"Jon?" said Aaron.

He'd been so caught up in his own thoughts he hadn't even noticed Aaron, Jack, and the doctor leaving his room.

"Hey, are you okay, man?" Aaron asked.

Jon turned to the doctor, ignoring the question. "How's she doing?"

"I think she's going to be all right, Mr. Grant. Her heart rate and breathing are both normal. Other than drowsiness, I don't see any side effects. Definitely nothing to be concerned about. She needs rest, but after that she should be fine. Thanks to you, most of the medication doesn't seem to have been absorbed into the bloodstream. You did the right thing, Mr. Grant."

"Don't you think she should be taken to the hospital?" Jon asked.

The doctor shook his head. "No, not necessarily. They wouldn't do much more for her there than what we've already done here." He took off his stethoscope and dropped it into his bag. "Besides, from what the vice president tells me, we wouldn't want to draw too much attention to the situation. For the sake of Dr. Grant, or the convention."

Of course not. Jon rolled his eyes.

"I'll be back in a bit to check her vitals." He shook Jack's hand and accepted everyone's thanks before turning to leave.

"Well, I guess that means Emma won't be doing her presentation this morning," said Aaron. "I guess Bennett got what he wanted."

"On the contrary," said Bennett. "I was rather looking forward to it."

Jon's blood pressure shot through the roof. Bennett strolled down the hallway toward them in his crisp black tailored suit, his hands in his pockets, sporting that ridiculously smug expression of his.

Aaron stepped between Jon and Bennett. He had apparently picked up on the fact that Jon was struggling not to beat the living daylights out of the guy.

"So the rumors are true, then?" said Bennett. "Dr. Grant won't be gracing us with her skills of persuasion after all?"

Jon tried to hold his breath and count to ten. He wondered why no one was asking Bennett how he'd found out about Emma so fast.

"Yes, Minister, I'm afraid Dr. Grant is not feeling well

this morning. It looks like she won't be able to go forward with her presentation," said Jack. He paused, then added, "At this time."

Bennett shook his head. "Quite unfortunate."

"I wonder if you might be prepared to go ahead with *your* presentation then, Minister? The convention must continue, after all," said Jack.

Had Jon been the only one to notice the glow of satisfaction that flooded Bennett's face?

"Of course, Mr. Vice President, I am prepared. Certainly Dr. Grant is known for her expertise, but she is also, from what I understand, somewhat impulsive. You can never be too certain when one so *emotionally unstable* will suddenly back out on their commitments." He looked Jon straight in the eye and curled a lip. "Or attempt suicide."

That's it! Jon pushed past Aaron and lunged for Bennett. On top of everything else this man was responsible for, Jon wasn't about to let him insult his wife's character.

"Jon, don't!" Jack jumped in front of him, a hand across his chest. "Try to be rational."

Aaron grabbed Jon's arms from behind.

Bennett smiled and stepped closer. Jon noticed the two Secret Service men push back their jackets and place a hand on their guns. Somewhere in the back of his mind— the part that was still slightly rational—Jon wondered why the men in black hadn't already grabbed both him *and* Bennett.

"Well, it looks like emotional instability is a shared trait among the Grants. But what can you expect—" Bennett leaned in, inches from Jon's face. He lowered his voice to barely above a whisper. "—from an alcoholic squadron leader who couldn't even manage to bring his own boys back alive?"

And then something in the air just snapped. In the sudden rush that followed, all Jon was aware of was Aaron letting him go, a flash of black suit jackets, and the crack of knuckles against bone. But when it was all said and done, it wasn't Jon lying face down on the floor with the knee of one of the Secret Service men in his back.

It was Aaron.

What just happened? Jon stared down at Aaron's frame pinned to the carpet. Bennett stood a few feet up the hall, nursing a bloody lip.

The Secret Service guys pulled Aaron to his feet and

held him by the arms. Bennett regained his composure and approached, wiping his mouth with the back of his hand.

"Well, well, Mr. Dallin," he said. "I certainly wasn't expecting that."

Yeah, no kidding, thought Jon.

"What would you like us to do with him, Mr. Vice President?" the guys in black asked Jack.

"It's all right," Bennett answered them instead. "I'll overlook it." He narrowed his eyes at Aaron. "This time."

Jack nodded silently to the two men, who let Aaron go.

Bennett looked down at the bright red blotch on the back of his hand. "Well. Good day to you gentlemen." He turned and walked away.

Jon, Aaron, and Jack waited till Bennett was out of sight before saying another word.

"I'm sorry, Jon." Aaron flexed his swelling hand. "Something about that guy just gets to me."

"Are you kidding, man?" Jon beamed. He couldn't have been happier if he'd punched the guy himself. "That was incredible! In fact, when I get home I'm adding you to my will."

"I believe you owe him more than that, Jon." Jack reached for Aaron's hand to examine the damage. "I guarantee that if you were the one who'd hit Bennett, he wouldn't have been so forgiving."

If I were the one who'd hit him, thought Jon, *he wouldn't have been conscious.*

Still, Jon had no doubt in his mind that Jack was right. Bennett would have loved nothing more than to see Jon arrested and out of the way.

As the three of them stepped into the sunshine-flooded suite, Jon couldn't help but feel an incredible sense of relief. All the pent-up anger he'd been holding in for the last two days was gone, as if whatever fuel had fired his rage had been cut off by a simple act of primal instinct. He had Aaron to thank for that.

Rachael stood and stepped out of the way so Jon could take her place next to Emma on the bed. The doctor had said it was important that they watched Emma for the next few hours, Rachael explained, for any signs of change.

Jack spoke up. "Well, ladies and gentlemen, if you'll excuse me. Despite how it may seem, there are over three hundred other people here whose lives don't revolve around us. I have a convention currently in shambles to attend to. Especially since we have just lost what I consider to be our most important speaker."

He looked at Jon and raised an eyebrow. "Of course, I could always rearrange the schedule so that Emma presented after lunch instead. Assuming you both were still up to it?"

Jon turned to Emma, curled up beneath the blankets behind him, hugging his pillow. Despite everything that had happened, the delicate features of her face shimmering faintly in the sunlight made her look so peaceful. Anyone watching her would have thought she was just sleeping soundly. More soundly than she had in months.

Emma didn't have to be awake for Jon to know what *her* answer would be.

Jon nodded his acquiescence to Jack.

"Thank you, Jon. It means a lot to me." Jack patted Jon's shoulder and headed to the door. "Oh, and by the way," he added, turning. "All four of you are confined to this floor until after lunch. I'll have security posted outside your rooms and at the end of the hall."

Rachael's jaw dropped.

"And you, young man." He pointed at Aaron. "Try to keep your hands to yourself from now on."

"Yes, sir." Aaron looked appropriately chastened, but as soon as the door had closed behind Jack, he and Jon exchanged a grin.

"All right, boys." Rachael crossed her arms and tapped a finger against her elbow. "Why are we now confined to this floor, and what exactly did the vice president of the United States mean by 'keep your hands to yourself'?"

CHAPTER 14

The sensation almost overwhelmed him.

Matt had made every attempt to relax his mind and body before Professor March began the exercise, but he barely had time to notice the warmth of the professor's hands on his shoulders before he found himself floundering in a torrent of vivid emotions.

They slammed into him like a violent ocean surge, washing over his body and mind in brisk, cutting waves. Matt struggled amid the rush of the incoming tide, desperately holding on to what little was left of himself. But the harder he fought against it, the faster the swell of sensory overload came. Until, at last, he could no longer maintain his mental footing, and he slipped beneath the crashing waves of disarray.

Deeper he sank into the emotions that were Professor Michael March. The pain of losing his wife and daughters in the raids on London during the war. The guilt he carried from the choices he'd made as a British operative. The incredible weight of what he knew—about the world, what was to come, and the role Matt's parents played in it.

What about my parents?

"Focus, Matthew," he heard the professor say from somewhere on the distant shore of consciousness.

But Matt was too far gone now, washed away in a great sea of desperation. It tossed him relentlessly until he could no longer tell which way was up or out. He knew only the blackness and the tide, and the bitter froth of what he could only describe as hopeless solitude. He could feel the pressure of it like an incredible weight against his chest. Against his weak, scarred heart.

Was it Professor March's solitude he felt?

Or was it his own?

"It's all right, Matthew. I'm here." The voice pierced like a light through the darkness.

And then, everything was calm. The beating of the waves ceased, and Matt suddenly found himself not amid the torrent, but lying comfortably on the shore, basking in the warmth of the sun-baked sand beneath him.

I'm here.

It had been a subtle reminder that he wasn't alone. That he had never been alone.

He lay beneath the warmth of a cloudless sky, the rays of sunshine enveloping him. The salty ocean breeze blew across his tired body, across his tired mind. The warmth resonated within him and strengthened him somehow. The way his family did.

And he understood. When Professor March had realized that Matt was struggling, Matt had become overwhelmed with the concern the professor felt for him. The affection. It was the same way he felt about his own family.

"I'm all right now, Professor," Matt whispered. He had found his footing, and they could now move on.

Somewhere far away, Matt felt the professor's grip on his shoulders tighten.

His senses sharpened. He could distinctly make out each individual grain of sand, could hear the distinctive click of the beetle that scuttled beside him. The bitter taste of salt in his mouth was fresh and new. Matt felt the flap of every fish in the ocean before him, felt the air buoying the lone seagull floating lazily above. Even the beating of his own heart and the hollow whistle of the air entering and exiting his lungs echoed in his ears. It was fascinating.

So. This is what focused feels like.

"Don't forget what it is you're meant to be doing, Matthew," the professor said.

Matt wasn't sure he wanted to remember. Everything he'd felt over the last few months was like being beneath those violent ocean waves. It had disoriented and overwhelmed him, and Matt didn't want to explore it. He wanted to stay here, where it was calm and warm and inviting. It comforted him, as if it were one of his favorite places in the whole world.

But wait, Matt thought. The beach *wasn't* one of his favorite places.

It never had been. Matt's favorite place in the world had always been home. Whether it was the apartment in Leesburg where he grew up or the house in Pineville, his favorite place had always been wherever his family was. Matt didn't care for the beach at all. It was vast and lonely. So why had his subconscious mind chosen to conjure this place?

Though Matt wasn't fond of the beach, there was someone in his family who was. His dad. And then Matt knew why. What he had been feeling over the last few months reminded him of his father—more specifically, of the dark time in his childhood when his father was gone. Matt didn't like to think about it, to remember the feeling of almost losing his dad. It hurt entirely too much to even try.

Matt was only about seven years old at the time, and he remembered quite distinctly feeling what his mother felt. Though one's gift doesn't usually manifest until early adolescence, the professor had once explained to him that a gift is typically based on personality. Ever since Matt was little, he had been sensitive and compassionate, and therefore he had become an Empath. Just like his brother had always been charming and convincing and later became a Pusher.

But Matt didn't believe that. He hadn't just picked up on the incredible pain she went through. He had felt it. Her heartbreak, her helplessness, her discord—it was the most horrible thing he had ever experienced in his life.

Looking back on it now, though, he realized that maybe her feelings weren't about losing his dad. She had never actually believed he was dead, anyway. She even refused to go to his funeral. No matter how much everyone tried to convince her to accept it and move on with her life, she still held on to the hope that he was alive.

So if it wasn't the horrible sense of separation that his mother had felt, then what was it?

This was the point on which Matt would focus. It was the closest he had come to understanding his feelings over the last few months. It wasn't exact, but it was a start.

He thought back to that time, years ago, that he'd tried so hard to forget. He chose a moment where the feeling had been the strongest, and remembered.

When Matt was growing up, his dad was always there. He was the building superintendent of their apartment in Leesburg, and with Matt's mom so busy with her work, it was his dad who was always there when they got home from school. Up until he was deployed, the only time he ever wasn't home was the few weeks a year when he was out for training.

After his dad was shipped out for the war, Matt and his brother and sister would go to their Aunt Renee's apartment every day after school, a few doors down from their own, and stay until their mom got home from work. Sometimes that was only for a couple of hours. Sometimes she wouldn't come home for days. But every time Matt walked by their apartment, he would turn the doorknob to see if it was unlocked. Because if it was, then maybe his dad was home waiting for them.

On one particularly bad day, Matt hung back behind his brother and sister as they headed down the hallway to

Aunt Renee's. Things had gotten rough at the Grant house lately. His mom was hardly ever home at all, and when she was, she seemed on the verge of a nervous breakdown. He'd overheard quite a few heated phone calls between her and whoever was in charge of looking for his father. They wanted to give up because they thought his dad was dead. She wasn't convinced.

So as Matt watched his brother and sister disappear through the door up the hall, he took a deep breath and put a hand on the doorknob. He closed his eyes and willed the knob to turn. He knew if his dad just came back then everything would be okay again. His mom wouldn't be so sad and upset all the time. The teachers at school would quit whispering and shaking their heads whenever he was around. The doorknob just had to turn, because if it did, then everything would be all right.

It turned.

Matt tiptoed into the apartment, as if he were intruding on someone else's home instead of his own. He held his breath, hoping beyond hope that his father would be there waiting for him.

"Dad?" He was barely able to whisper over the pounding of his heart.

But it wasn't his dad who he found sitting in front of the couch on the living room floor, crying.

It was his mom.

"Matt?" she said, wiping the tears from her face. His mother always tried so hard not to let him or his siblings see her cry. But Matt always knew. "Honey, what are you doing home already?"

Matt sat down on the floor beside her and took her hand. "I was going to ask you the same thing, Mom."

"Sweetheart..." She hesitated as if she wasn't sure whether to continue. "Mommy is... sick."

Matt already had a little bit of an idea about that, but he hadn't wanted to believe it.

"And Uncle Quinn thought it would be a good idea if I took some time off work. Just for a little while. Till Dad gets back."

Uncle Quinn wasn't really Matt's uncle any more than Aunt Renee was his aunt. Matt's mom and Uncle Quinn had grown up together, just like Matt's dad had grown up with Aunt Renee's husband, Danny, who was killed in the war several months before. It was hard on all of them when Danny died. He had always treated Matt and his brother and sister like they really *were* his niece and nephews.

Uncle Quinn was different. He was never at birthday parties. He didn't offer to babysit on Matt's parents' anniversary, or bring over soup and movies when they were sick, the way that Aunt Renee and Uncle Danny did. The only member of the family that had ever been all that close to Uncle Quinn was Matt's mom, and there was something about him that made Matt uncomfortable. Matt didn't like the way Uncle Quinn looked at his mom, and he was sure his dad felt the same way.

"Does that mean you're not going to be gone so much anymore?" Matt asked.

"That's right." His mom tried to smile. "So it's a good thing, really. Isn't it? It means I'll get to spend a lot more time with you guys."

Matt frowned. As much as he loved the idea of his mom being home, he knew that wasn't really how she felt. "If it's such a good thing, then why are you so sad?"

She put an arm around his shoulder and pulled him close. "Mattie, sometimes bad things happen. And as much as grownups don't want it to, as much as they work and they plan, it happens anyway. Sometimes they can prevent it, and sometimes, no matter how hard they try, there isn't anything they can do about it. It's simply out of our control. But even knowing that—knowing you did everything you could to try to stop it or reduce its effect on the people you care about—doesn't necessarily make it any easier to deal with. It's still very, very hard."

Matt wasn't sure what she meant.

"Oh, honey, I know you probably don't really understand. But maybe someday you will." She held him tight. Matt didn't have to hear the occasional sniffle to know she was crying again.

It was at that moment that he felt it the strongest. The horrible sense of hopelessness and turmoil, as if something inside her had split in two. Matt always thought it was because of his dad being gone and her being sick. She hated everyone focusing on her when they should have been trying to find his father. It was true Matt didn't understand what she had been talking about, but he always thought she was referring to the cancer.

Yet looking back on it now, Matt knew that wasn't it. That moment may have been the strongest he ever felt the sensation, but it wasn't the first time. It had been going on long before that. He had been so young at the time, and Matt had never wanted to think about it before. All the arguments, his parents sleeping in separate rooms, and his mom disappearing for days without any of them even knowing where she was.

It hadn't always been like that. Matt remembered how in love his parents had been when he was little. Kind of like they were now. Before all the fighting. Before his mom would wake up crying. Before…

"The dreams." Matt opened his eyes.

It took him a moment to focus on the professor's office. The storm clouds were gone, and sunshine flooded in through the window. Though the clock above the desk said it had been less than an hour since they started, Matt felt like entire years of his life had passed in that room.

Professor March took his hands off Matt's shoulders and returned to his chair. Matt tried to steady his breathing. Physically, the exercise had taken a lot out of him.

The professor waited for him to catch his breath, then said, "Well? What did you see?"

Matt wiped sweat from his forehead. Had it been this hot in here the entire time? "It's my mother," he said. "I think she's having the dreams again. I mean, I already knew she was, I've known for a while, but… She's seen something, Professor. Something she's having a really hard time with."

"You mean, like the dreams she had when she was your age? Before the storm outbreaks?"

"No, not quite like that. These are different, I think."

Matt's mother had never actually talked to him about her dreams. He'd only picked up on bits and pieces of overheard conversations, and things that his great-grandparents had told him. He knew that when she was younger, she used her dreams to help people through her work. Like the tornado at Wakarusa. She had turned her gift from passive to active, in a way. Much like Professor March was trying to teach him to do.

But these new dreams were the complete opposite. She didn't control them; they controlled her. That's what she'd meant when he found her sitting alone on the living room floor that day. She was trying to use what she knew to stop whatever horrible thing was about to happen—or at least try to keep them all safe through it. Just like she had tried so hard to do back then.

"Like before the war…" he mumbled.

"Before the war?"

Matt hadn't realized he'd spoken aloud.

"Did your mother dream about the war?" Professor March asked.

Matt had never thought about it that way before, but it made sense. "Yeah." His eyes widened. "Yeah, Professor, I think she did."

Professor March clasped his hands together and brought a finger to his lips. "And you think that's what she is experiencing now? That she's having these same dreams again?"

My gosh, thought Matt. That was exactly what it seemed like. But if so, that would mean...

Professor March rose and walked to the window again. He was usually good at hiding his emotions, but at that moment he made no attempt to do so. Matt knew exactly what he was feeling.

"Professor?" Matt stood and joined him at the window. "Are you saying..." He took a deep breath. "Are you saying there's going to be another war?"

The professor didn't respond. But he didn't have to. Matt already knew the answer. He could feel it. He had been feeling it for months. And he had a sneaking suspicion he wasn't the only one.

"And it's not just that. It's something much more. Something much... *worse*," said Matt.

Professor March turned to look at him. And for the first time since Matt had walked into the office, he noticed the dark circles under the professor's eyes. He hadn't been getting much sleep lately either.

"But you already knew that, didn't you, Professor?"

Professor March took a deep breath. "We had a pretty good idea, yes."

"We?"

CHAPTER 15

After spending most of the morning in the professor's office, Matt couldn't help but be disappointed. The longer they talked, the more confused and worried about his parents he became. The professor wouldn't tell him much. He just kept making vague references to childhood stories. None of it helped, or even made much sense. Eventually the professor had to excuse himself to get to his next class.

So the only things Matt knew for sure were that something was coming—something that had been brewing for a long, long time—and that there wasn't anything anyone could do to stop it.

Matt and Alex hadn't worked out whether she expected him to come back to the café, but there was no way he was going to. He was too physically and mentally exhausted to go back. Which meant he needed a place to crash until Calculus at eleven-thirty. Unfortunately it wasn't worth going all the way home, and he doubted he had the energy to make it there anyway. But there was one other place he could go. Matt checked his keychain to make sure he still had a key to the apartment Daniel kept on campus before heading toward the complex. The guy was rarely ever there, anyway.

The oversized leather couch called to Matt as he unlocked the front door of Daniel's fourth-floor studio apartment. *Must be nice to be the only son of a tenured professor and a physician*, he thought as he scanned the brushed-nickel and exposed-brick room. Not that Matt's family wasn't well off, but his parents had never offered to pay for an expensive apartment for any of their kids.

It looked like Daniel had actually been there for a change. Books were strewn across the coffee table, and dishes sat in the rack by the sink. It was odd for the place to look lived-in, but even odder for the place to look clean. As a med student, Daniel was usually way too busy studying to be concerned with something as trivial as cleaning up after himself.

Matt dropped his keys and phone with a clink onto the glass coffee table and collapsed on the couch. He passed out almost immediately.

He wasn't sure how long he slept before he heard the front door open. He assumed it was just Daniel, who wouldn't care that Matt had crashed on his couch. After all, you don't give a guy a key to your apartment if you don't expect him to use it, right?

But it wasn't *just* Daniel.

"Don't give me that, Daniel! You've had plenty of opportunities to talk to him. You're just making excuses now," snapped Leah as she and Daniel burst into the apartment, apparently in the middle of a very heated discussion.

Matt sat up and rubbed his eyes. *Great*, he thought. *The last thing I need.*

"But, poppet, I don't think you fully understand what you're asking. It's just *different* for us," said Daniel. "Do you have any idea how hard it would be on you if anything should happen?"

"You know, I'm beginning to think you don't care about me at all," Leah yelled, her face turning as red as it had after she fell asleep on the shore at Virginia Beach last summer. "And stop calling me that!"

"But I thought you liked it?"

"Well, not anymore!"

Daniel sighed. "Darling..."

He tried to put his hand on her arm. She pulled away from him.

I should have just gone home.

At first, the two of them stood just inside the doorway, too engaged in an intense staring contest to notice Matt—Daniel with his look of obviously sincere concern for Leah, and Leah with her glare of consternation.

Then Leah glanced toward the couch. "Matt!"

"Hey." He ran a hand through his hair, trying not to get sucked into her crankiness. "What are you doing here?"

"What am *I* doing here?" she barked. "This is *my* boyfriend's apartment! What are *you* doing here?"

"Daniel gave me a key," Matt snapped back at her. "He was my best friend way before he was your boyfriend, remember?" Though to be honest, the two of them hadn't spent a whole lot of time together since Daniel and Leah started dating.

"Ah, thanks, Matt, I'm touched." Daniel winked at Matt as he dropped his bag on the couch.

"Shut up, Daniel," said Matt. *So much for self-control.*

"What the heck is your problem, anyway?" said Leah. "Why do you care whether I'm here?"

"For the same reason you're so mad that *I'm* here! Because we both know darn well how Mom feels about you two being here alone together."

"Well, Mom isn't here, is she? And besides, I'm nineteen years old, for goodness' sake. She can't tell me what to do anymore."

Matt jumped to his feet. "Leah! She's just trying to watch out for you. And she has enough on her mind without worrying about you two being as reckless and stupid as she and Dad were."

"I am *not* Mom! And she's not trying to watch out for me, she's trying to *control* me." She turned on Daniel. "I wish *everyone* would stop treating me like a child just because I wasn't born with some stupid mark on my forehead!"

Then she spun on her heel and left, slamming the door behind her.

Matt plopped back down on the couch. He now understood why Daniel's apartment was so clean. Leah had apparently been keeping house.

Daniel sat down beside him. "You want to tell me what *that* was all about?"

Matt took a deep breath. "I'm sorry, Daniel. You know it doesn't actually bother me that she's here. I trust you. I know my parents are a little overprotective because she's not like us. But you've definitely got a better head on your shoulders than my dad did when he was your age." Matt cradled his head in his hands. The nap hadn't helped much. He was still exhausted. "I don't know, man. I guess I just haven't been feeling too hot lately."

"You don't exactly look too hot, either."

Matt lifted his head. His friend appeared genuinely concerned.

Matt stood and walked into the bathroom to look at himself in the mirror. His complexion was pale, even more so than usual, and nearly all the color had drained from his lips. The lightness of his hazel eyes contrasted with the dark, puffy circles beneath them. His arms began to tremble as he leaned against the cold, porcelain sink and bowed his head. He looked horrible.

"Matt?"

Matt looked up into the mirror again, at the reflection of Daniel leaning against the door frame.

"Maybe you should let me drive you down to the clinic to see Sarah," said Daniel.

Matt was touched by the offer. It was a two-hour drive to Bentonville and back, and Matt knew Daniel still had classes that afternoon. Ditching a class just wasn't something you did as a graduate student in the med program.

"No, it's all right, I'll be okay," he said, turning from the mirror.

Daniel shook his head. "Well, if you won't go see Sarah, at least let me have a look at you."

Matt smiled. "You're not a doctor yet."

"I might as well be," Daniel answered. "I've spent so much time helping Sarah at the clinic, I could have already finished an internship by now."

Matt nodded. It was better than nothing.

He sank back onto the couch while Daniel went to grab his stethoscope. Matt noticed for the first time the theme of the books spread out across the coffee table. Anatomy and physiology textbooks, medical journals, symptom cross-references. Daniel's obsession with medicine went way beyond what Matt assumed was normal for a med student. It was true what Daniel had said about the time he'd spent at the clinic. It seemed like he was there helping Sarah every waking minute he wasn't studying or with Leah.

"Can I ask you a question?" Matt asked as Daniel returned to the couch.

Daniel smiled. "As long as it doesn't involve your sister."

Matt guessed Daniel had had enough Leah drama for one day. "What made you decide you wanted to be a doctor?"

Matt knew full well why *he* had chosen to study medicine. As a lifetime heart patient, becoming a cardiologist to help others like himself just made sense. Matt also knew he'd have an advantage in school with all the experience he already had with the subject.

But Daniel was the type of ESPer known as a Savant. He had the ability to retain and apply information at an incredible rate. Savants often chose careers in mathematics, engineering, social sciences, linguistics... Daniel could have done anything he wanted. And with the way healthcare was these days, a career in medicine was much less lucrative than it had once been.

Daniel looked down at the stethoscope in his hand. "Actually, it was something your mother said to me."

Matt's eyes widened. "Really?"

"Yeah. She said that if I was serious about your sister, it's something I should learn. That I would..." He looked up at Matt, drawing his brows together. "That I would need it later."

Wow. If the amount of time Daniel devoted to studying was any indication of how much he cared about Leah, then he must be crazy about her.

The Grants had learned to live with the fact that Matt's mom caught occasional glimpses of the future. But the idea that something she knew could have such a direct effect on a person outside of their immediate family was still a little eerie, especially considering Daniel's strong reaction. By the look on his face, it was something he was genuinely concerned about.

It was also something, Matt guessed, that Daniel hadn't told Leah. Matt didn't blame him. Given Leah's shaky relationship with their mother, she probably wouldn't take it well. It was ironic, really, considering the flack Daniel took from Leah for studying instead of spending time with her.

"Well, then, Doc," said Matt. "What say we get on with it?"

"Right." Daniel smiled and pushed the stethoscope into his ears.

As he listened to Matt's heart, Daniel's smile faded. Matt could feel the palpitations pounding hollow in his chest even more prominently while concentrating on them. When Daniel finally removed the stethoscope, he got up and walked across the room and stared out the floor-to-ceiling window, a hand over his mouth. He clearly didn't like what he had heard.

Daniel turned back to the couch. "It's getting worse, Matt."

"I know," Matt answered quietly.

"Have you told your parents yet?"

Matt stared at his hands, silent. A couple of years ago he had asked that his parents no longer accompany him to his cardiologist's appointments. He told them it was because he was older and wanted to go alone. The truth was, he had known something was wrong.

Daniel sat back down beside him. "You haven't, have you? Why in the world not?"

"Because my parents already have enough to worry about without me adding to it."

"Matt, that's ridiculous. You're their son. They have a right to know. Especially if it's as bad as I think it is."

Matt rubbed his hands across his face. He sank back against the cushion and stared up at the repurposed wood paneling, wondering just what its previous "purpose" had been. He took a deep breath, then proceeded to unload the entire story of what he had been feeling over the last few months, and what he'd discovered in Daniel's father's office that morning. *Something* was going on. And the world as they knew it was about to take a drastic change for the worse, with his parents right at the center of it.

"Blimey," Daniel whispered.

"Exactly," said Matt. "My parents have bigger things to deal with right now than me, and that's why I haven't told them yet."

"But Matthew—"

"And that's also why you can't say anything to anyone. Not to my parents, your dad, or even my brother or sister. Understood?"

"Matt, I really don't think—"

"I need you to promise me, Daniel. That this will stay between you and me."

Daniel eyed him warily.

"Please. This is really important to me."

"All right, mate," he said, pushing his glasses up his nose, "if that's what you want."

"Thank you." Matt checked his watch. It was a few minutes after eleven, so he may as well head for class.

He thanked Daniel—both for letting him crash on his couch and for listening to his problems. Daniel reminded him that if he was that worried about his parents, he could always just use the phone in Daniel's apartment and check on *them* the old-fashioned way—by calling them. After all, if an area the size of Bentonville still had cell service, then why wouldn't Dallas?

Matt wondered why in the world he hadn't thought of that.

CHAPTER 16

The doctor came into the Grant's room four more times to recheck Emma before concluding there were no lasting effects of the overdose. He did, however, comment that Jon looked exhausted and suggest he get some rest as well.

Jon was more than happy to oblige. He crawled beneath the sheets and collapsed into a coma-like sleep that lasted until Emma's cell phone rang.

He wouldn't normally answer her phone, except that he already had a pretty good idea who it was. After everything that had happened that morning, he knew they'd be getting a call sooner or later.

"Dad?"

Jon felt a twinge of guilt at hearing Matt's voice, for not having called to check on *them* first.

"Hi, Matt," he said, determined to act as if everything were completely normal. Jon knew he was already at a disadvantage, though, for having answered the phone instead of Emma.

Matt remained silent on the other end of the line, like he was waiting for Jon to say something. Jon knew what Matt was trying to do, and refused to give in.

"Dad, is everything okay?" Matt finally said. "Where's Mom?"

Jon tried to soften his tone as much as possible. He knew he couldn't lie to Matt, but he didn't particularly want to tell him the truth either. "Matthew, do you trust me?"

"Of course I do, Dad."

"Then everything is fine."

"But, Dad, I just…" Matt sighed. "Can I just talk to Mom, please?"

"No, you may not talk to your mother. The doctor said she needs to rest, and besides—"

"The *doctor*?"

Crap. Jon slapped his hand to his forehead. *So much for honesty.* "Matt, your mother is fine, I swear to you, okay?"

This wasn't going at all the way he wanted. Emma had always been better at relating to Matt than he was. It seemed like no matter what Jon said to him, it always made Matt feel worse.

"Listen, son, I know it's hard for you not to worry. But you know that I love your mother very much and I'd never let anything happen to her, right?"

"Yes, Dad, I know that, but—"

"Then you think I can't take care of my own wife?"

"Dad! That's not what I said at all."

"Well, all right, then. You trust that I'll watch over her, and that I'm capable of doing so, so there really is no reason to worry, is there?"

Matt sighed. "No, sir." He didn't sound convinced.

Matt was most likely wishing Emma had answered the phone instead of Jon.

Jon would probably think of a million things later that he could have said to Matt to console him. But right now all he could manage was to remind Matt how much they loved him and to keep an eye on his brother and sister.

As he returned Emma's phone to her bag, she opened her eyes. He sat down next to her on the bed. "Hey there, sleepyhead."

"Hey," she answered with a scratchy voice and a hand to her forehead.

"How do you feel?"

"Like I got hit by a Mack truck." Emma rubbed her hand across her face, then suddenly jolted upright. "Oh my gosh! What time is it?"

Jon squinted at the alarm clock on the dresser. "Um, it's… eleven-fifteen."

"What? Jon! Why didn't you wake me up?" She threw back the blankets and jumped out of bed, losing her balance the moment she stood.

Jon grabbed her before she could hit the floor. "Whoa. Slow down there, hero. I don't think you're in any condition to go anywhere just yet."

"Why? What happened?" she said as he helped her back into bed.

He piled several pillows behind her so she could sit up, and then sat down in front of her. "You mean you don't remember?"

"The last thing I remember is falling asleep in the Dallins' room."

Sarah had told him amnesia was one of the side effects of the sleeping pills, but Jon wondered if something else had caused Emma to suddenly forget.

"Em," he said, taking her hand, "you downed a half a bottle of Ambien this morning."

Emma's face twisted in horror. "*What?* I did not!"

"Yeah. You did."

"Jon, I would never do something like that, and you

know it!"

Jon delicately explained to Emma what Bennett had said to her in the hall that morning, the state in which he'd found her on the couch, and what he'd done to get her to throw up the medication. He agreed there was a possibility it had been slipped into her tea, though he didn't mention how unlikely that was, given how little had been absorbed into her system. Either way, he assured her it didn't matter. He knew she hadn't purposely taken it herself.

Emma pulled her knees up to her chest. "Well, I guess that would explain why my throat burns," she said quietly, her eyes beginning to tear. "I'm so sorry, Jon. I never should have agreed to come here."

"You did what you felt like you had to do, sweetheart. Just like always."

"Yeah, and a fat lot of good it did! Bennett is probably downstairs right now convincing everyone in that conference room of the superiority of the GOG and how unreliable the federal government can be—all while using me as a perfect example."

"Well, you'll get your chance to prove him wrong. Jack rearranged the convention. You'll be speaking at three o'clock this afternoon."

When lunch was delivered to their door a half hour later, courtesy of Jack, neither of them were even remotely interested. They just lay there in bed, not really awake and not really asleep. Every now and then Jon would feel Emma shudder next to him. She would then scoot closer to him and pull his arms tighter around her. Eventually he must have finally fallen into a deep sleep, because the next thing he knew it was after two o'clock and Emma was standing at the end of the bed getting dressed.

Jon got up and dressed as well. Jack arrived to escort them down to the lobby shortly after. A full entourage of Secret Service and FBI accompanied them.

As they walked, Jack glanced sideways at Jon several times, as if there was something he wanted to say but was waiting for the right time to say it. Jon guessed his hesitation had something to do with the nervous expression on Emma's face. Her heart was beating so fast he could feel it through her fingers.

The prefunction area was emptier than it had been since their arrival. Other than when Jon had been out at night, there were typically quite a few people milling around and talking, even during the presentations.

Instead it looked as if anyone wandering around was being ushered to the conference room by guys in FBI jackets.

They reached the room and stopped just outside the doors. Emma closed her eyes and took a deep breath.

Jon put his hands on her arms. "Hey, I want you to know that no matter what happens in there, you tried your best, okay? After all, you can only ever hope to lead the horse, right?"

She offered a small, uncertain half-smile.

"You're giving them an option, Emma. That's all you're here to do. It's still ultimately their choice what to do with it."

She sighed. "Yeah, I know."

"Here," said Jon, untying his white-shell bracelet. He took Emma's hand and tied it around her wrist.

Emma wrinkled her forehead. The bracelet had been given to him years ago, though she didn't know by whom. All she did know was that the shells were supposed to bring the wearer safely home, and that the only time Jon ever gave it to her was when she was going out into the field and there was a possibility she might not come back.

"What's this for?" she asked.

Jon shrugged. "Luck, I guess. Certainly can't hurt, can it?" He held her tight and kissed her forehead before releasing her.

"And Em," he said just before she walked through the door. "Whatever you do, just *please* don't say 'I told you so.'"

Emma smiled and disappeared into the conference room, an FBI agent close behind her.

Before Jon could follow her, Jack grabbed his arm and whispered, "Jon, Assistant Director Tanner is dead."

Jon snapped his head around. "What?"

"Heart failure. They found him in his room, just this morning," said Jack, then added before stepping into the conference room, "Something is very wrong."

Great, thought Jon. *And you tell me this now?* He shook his head at the ceiling before slipping through the door.

Emma headed up to the stage, then took her seat at the table next to the podium. Jon trailed after her, stopping against the wall across from the bottom of the stairs. He was joined by Aaron, who nodded to him silently.

The conference room was fuller than it had been for the earlier presentations. Or at least, the ones he had been to. Even some of the hotel employees were lined up against the back of the room. As he looked out across the somber faces, his gaze rested momentarily on Bennett sitting up on the stage just to the left of the podium.

Jon couldn't help but wonder if the slimeball had had this kind of a turnout. Then again, even though Emma was a well-known speaker, it did seem odd that so many people had made a point of showing up for her presentation. He wondered exactly what they were all expecting—and what rumors Bennett had floated about Emma since that morning.

As Jack introduced Emma as the final speaker, the color drained from her face. She stood and stumbled to the podium unsteadily, apparently shaken from the effects of the medication and a lack of food. As she stared down at her notes, Jon tried to determine whether she was concentrating on what she was going to say or on not throwing up. Off to the side, Bennett watched her with an oddly intense look of concentration that made Jon uneasy.

Emma took a deep breath.

So did Jon.

"Good afternoon. As Vice President Allred indicated in his very gracious introduction, I am Dr. Emma Grant, Associate Professor of Psychology and Head of the Emergency Management Department at Franklin University. I have served as an instructor and researcher at the Emergency Management Institute in Maryland, as well as an Incident Commander for the organization formerly known as FEMA. My research and contributions to the fields of Emergency Management and Crisis Psychology span two decades, and yet…"

She bit her lip and looked down at the podium.

"I find myself at somewhat of a loss. You see, ladies and gentlemen, the fact of the matter is, we were not prepared. We were not prepared to deal with the extensive loss and damage resulting from the natural disasters that continue to ravage our planet. We were not prepared for the widespread economic downturn in the aftermath of a world war. Nor were we prepared for the extended energy crisis that we now find ourselves faced with. As we all have seen, the effects of these occurrences are global and extensive. Something must be done, and it must be done now."

Jon shook his head. *So much for not saying, "I told you so."*

"First and foremost, we *must* awake to a sense of our awful situation. Those present on this stage with me today,

127

as well as those men and women standing out in the street just beyond the doors of this building, would attest to the severity of it. My colleagues and I have been asked only to present you with options. Invariably, it is up to you to make the final decision. By the end of this convention, you will no doubt have heard many compelling arguments. I ask only that as you consider each one of these solutions, you keep in mind those whom you are obligated to represent. For ultimately it is they—your neighbors and friends, brothers and sisters—who will be most affected. It is they who will either benefit or suffer from your choice.

"Any experienced emergency manager will tell you that the most efficient way of dealing with a crisis is through the process of *mitigation*. Just as prevention is the best medicine, systems and processes put into place beforehand to help reduce the impacts of a disaster are always the most effective. However, we are long past that point. We are now faced, instead, with the impending task of picking up the pieces of a failed system and working together to build a new, more sustainable one. We are now faced with the task of *re-localization*—and re-localization is exactly what I would like to speak to you about today."

While Emma delved into the background of how the Cuban people flourished after the collapse of the Soviet Union by growing gardens on their rooftops and riding bikes—a story Jon had heard more times than he could count—Aaron leaned over and whispered to him.

"Hey, do you smell that?"

"What?" Jon turned to him. For some reason, it was difficult to focus on his face.

"That smell." Aaron sniffed the air. "It smells kind of like my dentist's office."

Before Jon could conclude that Aaron had lost his mind, he picked up on the scent too. They both scanned the room, trying to determine where in the world the faintly sweet odor was coming from.

As Jon looked around, he noticed that Emma had stopped talking. She stood on the stage, staring intently at the podium, her hands clasped tightly around its edges. The entire room had fallen into an eerie silence—aside from a faint hissing sound.

"Jon, look!" Aaron grabbed his arm and pointed at the ceiling. A thin, gray mist floated down from the vents.

One of those vents was right above the podium.

Jon looked down at Emma just in time to see her knees buckle beneath her. She collapsed to the floor. Several of the other presenters up on the stage were already slumped over in their chairs.

A voice deep inside Jon's head told him to get everyone out of the room. But no matter how much he willed himself to act, he simply couldn't. He was faintly aware of Aaron shouting his name, but the urge to act had almost instantly given way to euphoria. Jon suddenly didn't care at all about what was happening to the people around him. For a second he got the distinct feeling he was the only one there, even though across the room he could still make out the blurry images of several of the hotel employees and FBI agents passing out.

Then his body became heavy, and everything went dark.

CHAPTER 17

Matt was just about ready to give up.

If he thought he felt bad before, he felt terrible now. His fears had been confirmed as he spoke to his father in the few minutes before leaving Daniel's apartment. Something *was* wrong. Whether his dad would admit it or not. His mother was sick, or hurt—or worse—and it had to be bad if his dad felt like he needed to hide it.

He didn't even care about going to class anymore. But somehow his feet managed to put themselves one in front of the other until he found himself at the classroom door. Ultimately, it was for the best. What he needed right now was a distraction. Something cold and hard and emotionless to take his mind off everything.

Ninety minutes of calculus proved to be perfect for that.

Afterward, Matt had an hour before English Lit to grab a bite to eat. He wasn't hungry, but skipping a meal would only make him feel worse. Normally he would just go to the café, but he wasn't ready to face Alex, in case she was mad at him for not returning to work after seeing Professor March.

So he stopped into the student union for a sandwich, which he forced himself to finish. As Matt sat quietly in a corner, he noticed there weren't as many students wandering around as usual, even for a summer term. His mom had said enrollment had dropped because of the economy, but he'd had no idea it was this bad. Sheltered in their small town in south Missouri, it had been easy to overlook just how far things had gone downhill. But after what he'd learned that morning, it was all beginning to make sense.

He couldn't help but feel a twinge of anger toward his mother. She had known all along that something was going on, even before these last few months. That was why she had been so careful in all her preparations. Why she had pushed their father so hard to uproot their entire family and move them to the middle of nowhere after the war.

She knew it would be safer.

Matt forced himself back out into the afternoon heat. The storm clouds that had rolled in that morning hadn't lasted, and there was now nothing left to offer any relief from the intense rays of summer. The sun burned through his dark hair and the back of his neck like some great judge that had weighed the world and found it wanting. He wiped the sweat from his brow as he walked.

He made a special point not to step into the classroom until just before class started. That way, if Alex were already there waiting for him, she wouldn't have time to corner him. Matt slipped through the door and scanned the large, auditorium-style room. Alex was sitting toward the back. He glanced away quickly before she could give him a look of… well, whatever way she was planning on looking at him. He grabbed a seat in the front row.

"Good afternoon, class," said Professor Churchill. "Please turn your textbooks to chapter five so that we may begin our in-class discussion."

Matt had read the assignment, and he tried to concentrate on the discussion. But his mind wasn't cooperating. He couldn't, for the life of him, remember anything he had read. As he sat there silent, his classmates around him actively participating in the class, he began to rethink his decision to sit in the front row. It gave the professor a chance to stare directly at him, as if she were waiting for him to jump into the discussion at any moment, like he usually did. It also made it easy for Alex to glare at the back of his head, and Matt didn't have to turn around at all to know she was doing it.

Somehow he managed to make it through the class discussion, and Professor Churchill began her lecture. Matt glanced at his watch. It was almost three o'clock. He only had to get through thirty more minutes. He might actually make it.

Or so he thought.

Out of nowhere, Matt was overcome with another intense wave of anxiety and nausea. It crept across his skin like the unwelcome brush of a stranger in a crowded room, a gesture that would go unnoticed by anyone else but him. It was even worse than what he had felt that morning in the café. This time, he didn't *think* he was going to pass out. He knew he was.

He closed his eyes and grabbed the arms of his chair. He had to get out of there. But he couldn't do it until he got control of himself. If he stood up now, it would be only a matter of seconds before he hit the floor.

He tried to steady his breathing, to calm his heart. It didn't do any good. A cold wave washed across his skin, as if all the warmth had been drained from his body, the way it does when you go too long without eating and your blood sugar drops.

He wasn't going to make it.

"Matthew," a voice said quietly.

Matt opened his eyes. Professor Churchill was standing right in front of him.

"Matthew, are you all right?" She reached out a hand to put on his shoulder.

Matt hopped up before she could touch him. "I, uh…" The room started to spin. He grabbed the back of the chair to steady himself. "I'm fine. I just… I'm not feeling well, is all."

"Well, I'd say so, dear."

Matt could feel the entire class staring at him now.

"You look absolutely dreadful." Professor Churchill pulled her purple, horn-rimmed glasses from her nose and scanned the room. "Miss Romano," she said. "Perhaps you would be so kind as make sure that Mr. Grant actually *gets* to the Health Center this time?"

"No!" Matt shouted.

Professor Churchill snapped her head back around.

"I don't… I don't need any help." He could feel his face burning with embarrassment. "I just…" He turned to look at Alex. "I've got to go."

He grabbed his backpack and kept his eyes on the floor as he stormed out of the classroom.

As the son of a department head, he was certain he'd be the topic of conversation at the next faculty meeting. But at least the adrenaline rush of having so many people focused on him at one time, and the anger of Professor Churchill having pointed him out—especially to Alex— was enough to get him halfway up the hall.

"Matthew Grant!" A door slammed behind him.

Oh, come on, Alex.

If he could have gotten his legs to cooperate, he would have broken into a run to get away from her. But he had never been good at making his body do what he wanted at the time he really wanted it.

Alex apparently didn't have that problem. "Matt!" She jumped into his path. "What the heck is wrong with you? You should have seen the look on Professor Churchill's face when you walked out." She folded her arms and glared at him.

Well, I guess that means she's mad. "Look, Alex." He had to put a hand on the wall to steady himself. The adrenaline rush was wearing off. "I can't…" He grabbed his head. "I can't do this right now, okay?"

"Hey." Alex uncrossed her arms. "Matt, are you all right? You look terrible."

Why does everyone keep reminding me?

"What happened to you this morning, anyway? I kept waiting for you to come back to the café and let me know you were okay, but you didn't."

She put a hand on his face. The warmth of her palm was calming against his cool cheek.

"I was really worried about you, *Matia.*"

Matt took her hand from his face, but didn't let go of it. Instead he intertwined his fingers with hers and held her hand to his chest.

"I'm sorry, Lexi." He had been too concerned about whether she was mad at him to even consider the fact that she might be worried. But he had scared her, and he didn't have to be an Empath to know it. He could see it in her eyes. She was terrified at the thought of something happening to him—and he hated that. He didn't want Alex to have to worry about him. He never wanted Alex to be scared, or sad, or upset. He didn't want her to ever be anything but happy.

He was so tired of being a constant source of pain for the people he loved.

"Oh, Matt," said Alex, biting her lip.

He thought for a minute she might cry. But that wasn't Alex's style. She was strong, and opinionated, and vibrant. Everything he wasn't. She threw her arms around him instead.

It surprised Matt that she would make such an open show of affection toward him. But with the warmth of her body pressed against his, the anger and anxiety he had felt—from his mom, from Professor March, and from everything they knew but refused to tell him—began to melt away.

Matt closed his eyes and wrapped his arms around her, too. He breathed in the sweet, floral scent of her hair as she rested her head against his shoulder. Matt knew he continually sent her on an emotional roller coaster just by allowing her to be a part of his life. But at that moment he was so grateful she cared about him enough to want to be a part of it anyway. He should have known she would be more concerned about his well-being than her own feelings. She had always been there for him, through the good and the bad. She was his beloved Alex—his dearest and closest friend.

And so much more.

"Matt?" she said, her eyes darting across his face. "You are going to be all right, aren't you?"

He could still feel the intense pounding of his heart against his chest, but he knew that, for the moment, it had more to do with her than it did anything else. "I think I will be now," he said.

She smiled at him—that warm, bright, incredible smile of hers. Matt pushed a lock of hair behind her ear and put his hand on her cheek, brushing his thumb lightly across her lips. She gave him that look, the same look she had given him on the back deck of the cabin his parents had rented in Colorado during spring break their junior year. The night when she first became so angry with him. He could feel her pulse growing more rapid now, with his. But unlike the erratic, fleeting rhythm he was used to from his own heart, hers was strong and steady.

Maybe it was the constant spinning in his head. Or maybe it had something to do with the intense heat of the sun shining through the window across the hall. But at that moment, Matt decided to do something completely crazy. The one thing he had held himself back from doing—had held himself back from even *thinking* of doing—a hundred times before.

He kissed Alex for the first time.

It wasn't passionate or seductive. Matt didn't think his heart could have handled that even if that's what he intended, which it wasn't. His and Alex's attraction was something much deeper than physical. No, this was a kiss that was sweet, and soft, and tender. Like the first strawberry of summer. The one that you savor slowly because you know that it will be an entire year before you can experience it again. That's what Matt wanted. To savor it. To be able to freeze time in that one precious instant they had both waited so long for. Because in this moment he could forget about his heart, and his parents, and the war. In this one single moment, life was about nothing more than him and Alex.

Too bad it had to happen in the hallway of the liberal arts building.

"Well," said Alex, smiling up at him once he was finally able to pull himself away from her. "It's about time."

Matt grinned, his mouth still tingling with the sensation of his lips against hers.

"So," she said. "I guess this means…"

But Alex didn't finish her sentence. She drew her

brows together, her delicate smile melting into a look of panic. Her expression reflected the sensation that washed over his body at that very moment.

The moment when his heart stopped.

Matt felt the color drain from his face and continue all the way down to his feet, with nothing but an icy chill to replace it. His entire body tingled, like little electrical explosions dancing across every muscle. When his heart finally started again, it beat harder and faster than he had ever felt it before. As if something had gone wrong inside him and it was trying desperately to escape before all hell broke loose.

"*Matt?*" Alex looked terrified. "Matt! What is it?"

"Lexi," he said, fighting himself to keep from hyperventilating. "I think something's wrong."

"*What?*" She grabbed him as he started to sway.

Matt's vision was beginning to go white. "Alex, find the professor." He put a hand against the wall to steady himself.

"Matt, I can't just leave—"

"Go, Lex." His knees began to buckle. "Please."

Alex put her hands on his chest and looked him in the eyes. "Don't you dare die on me, Matthew Grant," she said. "Or that will be the last time I ever let you kiss me."

He grinned between labored breaths. "I'll keep that in mind."

As much as Matt knew she didn't want to, Alex left him there to go find help. He was all alone now. If he was going to die, right then and there in that empty hallway, he was going to die alone.

So much for the war.

At least he got to kiss her first. Maybe it wasn't such a bad thing that it had happened in the middle of a hallway. Otherwise, it might have never happened at all.

Matt leaned against the wall and slid down it, his legs finally giving out. He'd always thought when he did go, it would hurt more. But he had pretty much lost all sensation at this point, as well as all sight. He couldn't even feel the coolness of the tile beneath him, and the only thing he could see was the sunshine pouring through the window.

Matt did feel one thing, though. Guilt. Kissing Alex was going to make it harder for her when he was gone. Which was exactly why he had never done it before. He had always known this was going to happen one day, and the last thing he'd wanted was to hurt her. Now here he was, about to die, about to leave his family and everything he cared about, and all he could think about was how selfish and inconsiderate he had been to kiss her. He wasn't even going to get the chance to apologize.

He closed his eyes.

I'm so sorry, Alex.

CHAPTER 18

Emma's mother clutched the steering wheel. "Emma Elizabeth Scott, I said drop it!"

Twelve-year-old Emma huffed and threw herself against the back seat of the family station wagon. They cruised down the interstate, headed back home from Christmas shopping. Rain came down in sideways sheets, smacking the side of the car angrily. Emma knew her mother was already frustrated enough from fighting the holiday traffic and the crowds at the mall. Having grown up on a reservation in western North Carolina, her mother always got nervous driving through a big city like Dallas. The storm made it even worse.

But Emma didn't care. She was mad, and she wanted her mom to know it.

She tossed a toy car at her little brother, who sat in his car seat next to her. "No, Adam, I said I don't want to play with you right now!"

His eyes welled up, and he began to cry.

"Emma!" her mother yelled. "He's only four years old! He didn't do anything to you. Don't take it out on him just because I wouldn't let you get that necklace."

"But I don't understand *why* you wouldn't let me get it, Mom! Do you have any idea how long I saved up to buy that necklace? Besides, you're the one who's always telling us we should embrace our heritage. It's a dove. Just like the name that Pow'wah gave me."

Emma's grandfather had once been a tribal elder, so when Emma was born he gave her a tribal name, as was the tradition. The name he had chosen for her was very special to Emma. It meant *Soaring Dove*.

"Yes, Emma, I know the dove is your spirit guide. I never said I didn't want you to have the necklace. All I said was that I thought you should wait to buy it, that's all."

Adam sputtered as he began playing with his toy car.

"But why, Mom? We never come into Dallas, and you know the mall is the only place I've found that has that necklace!"

Her mother shook her head. "Listen to me, Emma. There are some things you don't understand yet—but just because you don't understand them doesn't mean things won't work out. This is not the world according to Emma. You have got to accept the fact that ultimately you are not the one in control here, and trust that the person who *is* in control knows what they're doing. Let it go, Emmy."

Emma folded her arms and stared out into the darkness surrounding them. Her eyes began to tear, but she wasn't about to let her mother see it. In the reflection of the window, Emma noticed her brother holding his little toy car out to her.

"Here, Emmy," he said. "You can hold my car if you're sad."

Emma ignored him.

"Here, Emmy, here." He held it out further to her. The car dropped onto the floorboard. Emma pretended not to notice, which made Adam cry again.

"Oh, Emma, please get his car for him."

It was starting to get late, and Emma knew Adam was already tired. But she defiantly continued to face the window.

"Oh, for goodness' sake!" Emma's mother reached a hand back to feel around on the floor for the toy car. She turned her head back for just a second to try to find it.

In that same moment, the red brake lights lit up on the car in front of them.

"Mom, look out!"

Emma's mother gasped and slammed on the brakes. The station wagon skidded across the wet pavement, veering to the right, and clipped the back corner of the car in front of them, throwing them into a spin. Adam's cries were joined by a screech of metal as the passenger side of the car slammed into the guardrail, throwing Emma hard against the door. Christmas packages flew around them as the car flipped right over the rail.

Over and over they rolled down an embankment, the windows shattering. Emma screamed and grabbed Adam's hand. With each second, each shard of glass that struck her body, Emma pleaded for it to stop. For it to be over. Instead the entire scene continued to play out as if in slow motion.

Until they hit the river.

Emma's head kept spinning even though the car no longer was. Once she realized what was happening, she panicked. They were sinking fast. She screamed for her mother as she struggled to get out of her seat belt, the freezing water already flooding in around her feet. Emma was having trouble focusing, though. Something warm ran down her face from just above her right eye.

Her head pounded painfully. In a hazy fog, she looked over at her baby brother, and then at her mother. Adam's hand had gone limp in hers. Neither he nor her mother moved.

Sobbing uncontrollably and struggling to keep her eyes open, Emma knew she would soon be out, too. As she began to lose consciousness, all that she was aware of was the sensation of icy water washing over her body.

The cold seeped into her. Deeper it ran until she could feel it down to her core. It reminded her of something she knew. Not something she had known then, as a child, but something she knew *now*. Something she had felt. Something she had seen.

It reminded her of *him*.

And then Emma could no longer see her mother, or smell the river. She could no longer feel the pain in her head. She could no longer feel anything. Even the darkness was gone somehow. All that was left was the cold. It called to her to let go.

To give in.

I don't want to let go, she cried out from deep inside the darkness of her own mind. *I don't want to die*.

Then the world faded, and in the darkness, a bright light appeared.

"Dr. Grant?"

Emma gasped and opened her eyes. She was lying on the stage in the conference room. The fluorescent lights shone in her face, blocked partially by the shadowy outline of a figure hovering over her. She coughed and fought for air. There was a pinching in her arm, then something burned through her veins—something that told her to struggle. But whoever it was kneeling beside her had already anticipated the reaction. Her arms and legs were pinned against the carpet.

"Emma, it's all right. Just breathe," a familiar voice said. She focused enough to distinguish the dark-red hair of the person holding her down. It was Aaron, kneeling beside her, his forehead wrinkled.

That's when she noticed the intense pain above her eye and the bag mask over her mouth.

"You're going to be all right, Dr. Grant," said the man above her, squeezing and releasing the respirator over her face. "Just try to calm down."

Emma didn't *feel* all right. She felt cold and shaken from having so vividly relived the nightmare of her mother's and brother's deaths. And she didn't want to calm down. What she wanted to do was cry. To break down and scream the way she had done when she was told that she was the only one who had survived the accident.

Emma fought to hold back the anger and stinging tears. She squinted up at her shadowy helper, but no matter how hard she tried, she just couldn't seem to focus on his face.

She pushed the mask away from her mouth and tried to sit up. Aaron helped her. She cradled her head in one hand, touching the spot on the right side of her forehead from which the pain radiated. There was a bandage there.

"I'm afraid you hit your head pretty hard when you passed out," said her unidentified caretaker.

Emma looked at him again, her vision no longer blurred by the lights. No wonder she couldn't see his face before. Her soft-spoken rescuer was wearing a black ski mask.

Emma shrank away from him, away from the hand he had put on her shoulder. It was hard to tell with the mask, but she thought she saw hurt behind his eyes when she pulled away.

"Don't worry, Dr. Grant, no one is going to get hurt." He scooted closer to her, whispering just loud enough for her to hear. "Well, not any more than they already have," he added. Putting his hand back on her shoulder, he looked her directly in the eyes. There was something warm and friendly about them. "I give you my word."

Emma didn't understand what about the masked figure felt so familiar. Then again, Emma didn't understand most of what she felt these days. But she knew there was *something* about those hazel eyes.

The man picked up his med kit and the gun sitting on the floor beside him and walked away.

"Emma, *are* you okay?" Aaron put his hands on her shoulders and scanned her face. "You were crying, and mumbling about how sorry you were. Then you just stopped breathing."

Emma shook her head. *So much for holding back the tears.* "Yeah, I think I'm okay," she said. *Apart from this horrendous headache.* "Aaron, what in the world is going on?"

He drew his brows together in a look of seriousness that she wouldn't have thought possible for someone so laid back. "Emma, I don't know who these guys are, but they've taken over the convention. They're all wearing masks and toting AR15s like they're some kind of terrorists. But as far as I can tell from their accents and speech patterns, they're American."

Emma didn't want to believe him, but one look around the room told her he was telling the truth. Across the conference room, people were slumped over in their chairs and across the tables. The terrorists, whoever they were, were moving from one person to the next, administering shots. Whatever was in the syringe jolted people into consciousness, some of them kicking and screaming. It was surreal. Like something you only saw on the news where you couldn't help but be sympathetic for the people involved and secretly thankful it was them instead of you.

Just below the stage, the masked men had moved the presenters' tables to the floor and set one of them up with half a dozen monitors and a few laptops, each showing what looked like feeds from inside and outside the hotel. Whatever these guys were doing, they had come prepared.

My god, who are *these people?*

Emma quickly realized there also wasn't a single FBI or security agent in sight. Where had they all gone? Worse yet, what had the terrorists done with them?

There was also someone else she didn't see.

Jon. Where was Jon?

Emma scanned the room frantically, faintly recalling what had happened before she blacked out. The sweet floral smell, the buzzing in her head... and the look of horror on his face.

Emma heard Jon before she saw him, down against the wall, with Jack beside him. Jack was still out, but it looked like Jon had just been given the shot. He came back to consciousness much more violently than she did, complete with a few colorful expletives. It took three guys just to hold him down, and even they appeared to be struggling.

Then with a burst, Jon threw them all off and tackled one of them. They wrestled around on the floor, the two other guys trying to pull Jon off the third. Emma heard bones crack. She tried to scream at Jon to stop before he got himself killed. Before she could manage to steady her spinning head enough to do it, another one of the guys in masks grabbed Emma by the arm, yanked her to her feet, and pushed his gun into her side. Emma winced at the pain of the cold metal barrel between her ribs. She hated guns. She could deal with storms and earthquakes and evacuations, but she *abhorred* guns.

"Grant!" the guy holding her shouted.

Jon stopped fighting as soon as he caught sight of Emma. The terrorists grabbed him by the arms again. This time, Jon didn't struggle.

The masked man who had helped Emma with the respirator walked over and took her by the other arm. "That's enough, Mac," he whispered as he pulled her away. He walked her off the stage and over to Jon.

He gestured for the guys holding Jon to let him go. "If everyone cooperates, no one gets hurt. Are we clear?" he barked at Jon.

Jon glared at him, his jaw clenched.

"Now I suggest the two of you sit down and try not to cause any trouble." He shoved Emma toward Jon and walked off.

Jon caught her before she could stumble and fall. He cupped her face in his hands and scanned her forehead. "Are you okay?"

"Yeah, I'm fine. Just a bit dizzy."

The big guy called Mac, the one who had shoved the gun into Emma's ribs, yelled at them from up on the stage to shut up and sit down. Jon's jaw and the muscles of his arms tensed, the signs of a fierce storm brewing underneath. Though Jon often doubted his own abilities, Emma was well aware of what he was capable of when desperate.

Especially when it involved her safety.

"Jon," she whispered, putting a hand on his cheek.

He turned to look at her.

Don't, she told him with her eyes. *Not here. Not with all these people.*

Jon sucked in a deep breath, scanned the crowd, and then nodded reluctantly.

Many of the other hostages were conscious now, and most of them looked scared and confused. Emma and Jon sat down against the wall next to Jack, who was awake too. Aaron stepped down from the stage and took a seat on the other side of Jon.

"What do you think they injected us with?" Jack whispered.

Emma cradled her head again, her headache pounding so hard she could barely think. "Naloxone, maybe?"

"Naloxone?" Aaron asked.

"Yeah. It's typically used to counteract the effects of a morphine or heroin overdose. Using it on us would reverse the effects of the inhibiting agent in whatever gas they used almost immediately, so they won't have to worry about any of us suffocating or going into cardiac arrest."

"And how in the world do you know that?" Jon asked.

"They used it during the Nord-Ost siege in Moscow in '02. I did a dissertation on it," Emma answered. "Fifty Chechen terrorists took a theatre of eight hundred and fifty people hostage for three days. So the Russian police pumped a knock-out gas into the theater to subdue everyone and get the hostages out. The whole thing was an emergency management mess. Let's just say they weren't particularly well organized."

"Yeah, well, these guys are," said Aaron. He explained to them in a low whisper how the terrorists flooded into the room the instant everyone began to pass out. Those few who hadn't fainted were "recruited" to help prop up all the hostages and make sure everyone was still breathing. Anyone wearing a security uniform or toting a gun was dragged out of the conference room. Aaron had no idea where they'd been taken. As soon as nearly everyone was knocked out, the terrorists put fans up just inside the doors to clear out the gas. And they managed to accomplish all of it systematically, within a matter of minutes.

"So I take it the gas didn't work on you?" said Jon.

Aaron smiled. "It doesn't work when my dentist tries it, either."

The terrorist with the hazel eyes hopped onto the stage again. "Listen up, everybody." He waited till they were all looking up at him. "As long as everyone follows directions and stays on their best behavior, we'll all come out of this okay. We'll get what we want." He motioned to the other terrorists standing on the stage with him, then made a special point to glare at Jon. "And you won't die."

Jon narrowed his eyes.

"From this point forward, we operate on the buddy system. The person sitting to your left is your new best friend. You try to be a hero, and you're not just putting your own life in jeopardy. We'll shoot your buddy, too."

Jon's jaw dropped. He looked at Emma.

"You got it, tough guy," said Mac, addressing Jon directly. "We so much as suspect that you're planning something, she dies. Plain and simple."

Emma could tell by the way Jon dropped his shoulders and leaned his head back against the wall that it was over. Whatever plan he had been hatching, whatever idea he'd had in his head, was gone. Jon wasn't about to do anything that would risk her life. The terrorists, whoever they were, had known exactly what to say to subdue one of the few people in that room who could possibly get them all out of this.

Mac jumped down from the stage and joined the guy who was staring at the surveillance monitors.

"Em?" Jon whispered, his eyes meeting hers.

There had only been a handful of times in their marriage when she had ever seen Jon genuinely worried. This was one of those times.

"Did it end well?" he said. "In Moscow?"

Emma took his hand, suddenly wishing she had been awake to talk to Matt when he had called earlier. "No, honey. I can't say that it did."

CHAPTER 19

"Matthew, can you hear me?"

Matt didn't know how long he'd laid there, passed out on the hall floor. He tried to open his eyes to identify the person talking to him, but he couldn't seem to fight against the weight of his own eyelids.

A different voice spoke. "Matt, honey, it's Sarah."

He still couldn't manage to peel his eyes open, but it didn't stop Sarah from doing it. She lifted each lid and shined a light directly at his pupil. Matt winced at the brightness but didn't try to turn away.

He felt a slight prick on his left arm, then something cold burned through his veins. A moment later he could feel the warmth of a hand wrapped tightly around his. Matt had a pretty good idea who that might be.

"Dr. March, his hands are freezing."

"He's in shock, Alex," said Sarah.

"Is it his heart?"

"No, I don't think so. Not based on what Mike told me. Though I'm sure it probably didn't help."

What? Matt tried to ask but couldn't manage to form the word. If it wasn't his heart that did this to him, then what in the world could it have been?

"Matt?" He felt Alex's hand against his forehead. She must have picked up on his thoughts and realized he could hear them talking.

He finally managed to force his eyes open, though it took him a minute to focus.

Alex was leaning over him, smiling at him through red, puffy eyes. "Welcome back." She ran her fingers through his hair. "I was afraid I was going to lose you there for a minute, *Matia mou*."

Matt conjured a weak smile and squeezed her hand. "You weren't the only one."

Sarah cleared her throat. Matt had almost forgotten she was there. She glanced back and forth between him and Alex, then winked at him.

"Feeling any better?" she asked.

He laughed. "Compared to what?"

With the help of Alex and Sarah, he managed to sit up against the wall. Alex continued to keep a tight grip on his hand, as if she had just gotten him back and wasn't about to let him go again. Matt rested an elbow on one knee and cradled his head in his hand. He had the worst headache of his life.

"Jeez, Lexi, what did you do to me?"

"I don't find that even remotely funny, Matt," she answered, but grinned anyway.

Sarah checked his blood pressure. He sat still while she did it, which wasn't easy, he was shaking so badly. All he could think about was how much he wished he had a blanket to wrap up in. Ironic, considering the heat.

Sarah pulled the stethoscope out of her ears and nodded. Matt guessed that meant his heart rate was back to normal again. Or as normal as it was going to get for him.

Matt had every intention of just sitting there with his head in his hand and Alex rubbing the back of his neck for as long as it took to get his strength back. But the sweet silence of the empty hallway was interrupted by the sound of loafers clacking against the tile. Then Professor March was standing over him, an expression of grim sobriety on his distinguished face.

"Sarah, we've got to go," he said.

Sarah bit her lip. "Matt, do you think you can walk? If Alex and I help you?"

"I guess so. Where are we going?"

"Home, Matthew," the professor answered.

Matt was starting to get worried. What had just happened to him? And what did Professor March say to Sarah that would make her think it didn't have anything to do with his heart? What was she even doing there, anyway? There was no way she could have gotten all the way up to campus from the clinic that quickly. Did Professor March call her? Had he already known something was wrong?

With quite a bit of help, Matt managed to get to his feet. Professor March waited silently while Matt put an arm around Sarah's and Alex's shoulders just so he could make it down the hall. He knew the professor didn't offer to help because Matt couldn't usually handle anyone outside of his own family touching him. Sarah didn't count. She had been the Grants' family doctor since before Matt was even born. She had even come with them to Missouri from Virginia after her divorce, so as far as he was concerned, she *was* a part of the family.

But Matt still got the distinct impression that something else was going on with Professor March as well. He seemed anxious. His eyes kept darting around as if he expected someone to jump out at them. Even though, oddly enough, there wasn't a single other person even in the hallway.

As soon as Sarah nodded to the professor that they were ready to go, he turned on his heel and strode up the hall. He pulled out his phone and dialed a number as they followed.

Matt wondered how he even had cell service here.

"Daniel," the professor snapped without even a hello. "Is Leah there with you? ... Then I want you to find her immediately and take her straight home. ... I don't care if she's in class, Daniel. Pull her out." He shoved the phone back in his pocket.

Matt couldn't take it anymore. "Professor, what in the world is going on?"

"I don't have time to explain, Matthew." He spoke without turning. "All I can tell you is that we need to get you home."

Matt was getting really tired of no one telling him anything. "No," he said, taking his arm off Sarah's shoulder and stopping where he was.

Professor March turned around and stepped closer. "Excuse me?"

"I'm not going anywhere until you tell me what's going on," said Matt.

Sarah bit her lip, and out of the corner of his eye, Matt saw Alex staring at him with her mouth open.

Professor March had an expression Matt had never seen before. It frightened him, like the look on his dad's face last year when he found out Jacob had totaled the car, only much worse. But at that moment Matt didn't care. He was more angry than he was afraid.

The professor's eyebrows were drawn, and the muscles in his neck twitched. Matt waited. He had always been smart enough to never openly defy his parents. He couldn't imagine the consequences of defying a former British operative.

The professor took a deep breath. His eyes softened. "Matthew, something has *happened*... in Dallas. I can't tell you any more than that right now. All I can tell you is that it is absolutely vital that I get you and your brother and sister home immediately."

Matt thought his heart might stop again. He swallowed the lump at the back of his throat. He knew now why he'd fainted. The same thing had happened to his mom a couple of years ago—just before they got the phone call that his great-grandmother had passed away.

"Professor March?" Matt struggled to even get the words out. "Are my parents dead?"

Alex took in a sharp breath. Matt didn't want to turn to meet her stare. He kept his eyes on Professor March. It was hard to read anything from his expression, though. The professor had years of practice in keeping his emotions hidden.

Alex tightened her arm around Matt's waist.

"Matthew." The professor stepped right up to him and lowered his voice. "I can assure you that as bad as you may think you feel right now, if both your parents were dead…" He looked him right in the eye. "You would feel much, *much* worse."

Matt bowed his head. He understood what the professor meant, but it didn't make him feel any better.

Professor March sighed. "Matthew, I need you to trust me right now, all right? Please. Just let me do my job."

Matt wondered what that job was exactly, but he was past the point of asking questions. It wouldn't do any good anyway.

"Now, where is your brother?"

Matt had to think about what day it was. He was still a little dazed. *Friday.* Jacob didn't have any classes on Friday, but there was something else his brother was doing today. "He took my dad's truck, and he and Emily went to Springfield this morning."

"Emily *Burbank*?" Professor March's eyebrows shot up.

So much for controlling his expression, thought Matt, though he doubted the professor's reaction had anything to do with suddenly finding out Jacob's high school crush was back in town.

The professor gave Sarah a knowing look Matt didn't understand, pulled out his phone, and handed it to her. She nodded and walked away.

The professor turned back to Matt. "Come on then, Matthew," he said with a smile. "Let's get you home."

Professor March took Matt's other arm and draped it across his shoulder. Matt was a little alarmed at first, but not nearly as much as he had been that morning. Unlike what he'd experienced the first time the professor put his hands on him, Matt felt only a wave of calm creeping across his mind. He was more relaxed than he had been in a long time—far more than he should be, considering the circumstances.

His body grew heavy. Every so often he would

stumble as they walked, and Alex and the professor would have to support the majority of Matt's weight. It surprised Matt a little each time it happened.

Wow. The professor's pretty strong for an old dude.

"Professor, is he okay?" Alex asked.

"He's fine, Miss Romano. Let's just get him to the car."

The professor and Alex helped Matt into the back of the Marches' Mercedes. Matt rested his head against the cool leather seat and smiled. *Sarah always did have a thing for comfort,* he thought.

Now thoroughly convinced his sudden drowsiness was the professor's doing, he decided he might as well give in. Soon all he was aware of was the gentle hum of the engine and the warmth of Alex's fingers intertwined with his. It was nice to have her there. To have her support.

Too bad Matt knew it couldn't stay that way.

It was a forty-minute drive from the private university campus in Neosho to the Grants' property out on Big Sugar Creek, and by the time they finally pulled into the driveway, the effects of whatever the professor had done to Matt had pretty much worn off. He almost wished they hadn't. For the last few miles of the drive from Pineville out to the Lake House, Matt kept glancing sideways at Alex with an incredible sense of guilt in the pit of his stomach.

This wasn't going to work, and he knew it. He wanted it to. He *really* wanted it to. But he kept replaying in his mind the look of terror on Alex's face just before she left him alone in the hall. She cared about him. A lot. And he cared about her just as much. But that was the problem. Matt cared about her way too much to let her get close, knowing one day he was going to leave her. He couldn't stand the thought of hurting her like that.

The way his father had hurt his mother.

Matt turned to look at her, to revel in the curves of her face, the gentle curl of her mouth as she watched the horses run across the pasture beside the car. She absentmindedly put her fingers to her lips and smiled. He sensed her heart flutter a little and imagined she was thinking about their first kiss only an hour ago.

She must have realized he was looking at her. She turned to him and winked. Matt smiled and squeezed her hand. He knew he was going to have to break her heart eventually. But maybe he didn't have to do it just yet.

When they pulled up to the house, Matt wasn't surprised to see his grandfather's truck already in the driveway. With Grandpa Scott's connections, if there was something going on at the convention, he would have found out before anyone.

Matt was able to make it to the front door without any help, but Alex still kept a death grip on his hand. Was it because of the scare he had given her in the hallway? Or was it more because of a fear that, now that he'd kissed her, he was going to tuck tail and run? Again.

"Mike." Grandpa shook the professor's hand as they entered.

The TV was turned to the news. Either that was a good thing and meant that whatever was happening in Dallas didn't directly involve his parents—or it was very, very bad.

"You've managed to track down Jacob?" the professor asked.

Grandpa nodded. "He was dropping Emily off in Anderson when I talked to him. He should be here soon."

Matt grabbed the remote and turned up the volume on the TV.

"Ladies and gentlemen, we are here with crisis psychologist Dr. Riviera Rodriguez, who has been kind enough to join us today as we try to make sense of the situation that is unfolding as we speak. A short time ago we received word that the Constitutional Convention, which had been moved to an undisclosed location in Dallas, Texas, has now become hostage to terrorist forces..."

Alex gasped and threw a hand over her mouth. Matt tightened his grip on her other hand.

"Dr. Rodriguez," the anchorwoman said. "I'm not even sure I know what to say to this. Exactly what degree of severity are we looking at here?"

"To be blunt, Connie, it's bad. We're talking about the majority of our nation's leaders—representatives, senators, heads of the financial and corporate sectors, scientists, educators, even the vice president—gathered together to address the issues that are crippling our economy, despite the obvious and, as we can see, very *real* risk to their own personal safety. And now they have all been taken hostage by this domestic terrorist group calling themselves 'The Republic.'"

"Dr. Rodriguez, do we know anything, at this point, about who these people are or what they want?"

"We do know one thing. That this group, whoever they are, is very well organized. This convention has changed locations multiple times and had extensive security in place. Yet somehow they managed to pull it off smoothly and strategically. They didn't even wait for us to find out something was wrong. Federal law enforcement and the media were notified immediately after they took control, complete with warnings on exactly what would happen if anyone tried to end the siege by force. Which means they had help."

Professor March and Grandpa glanced at each other.

"Dr. Rodriguez, I'm going to have to interrupt you for just a moment. I've just been told that we've received a copy of the terrorists' demands video. We're going to play that for you now."

The image on the TV changed from the news room to what looked like a small office. Facing the camera were two people Matt recognized immediately. One was a journalist Jacob idolized. The other was Stephen Bennett.

"Hello. My name is Rachael Dallin. I'm a photojournalist currently on special invite by Vice President Allred at the national convention being held here in Dallas, Texas. To my left is Stephen Bennett, the Canadian Minister of International Development. Please know that we are *all* alive and well, and no harm will come to any of us if The Republic receives total cooperation from federal authorities and there are no attempts to remove any of the hostages by force."

Matt sighed. So, his parents were at least alive. Though he wished they were on the screen so he could know for sure.

"I have been asked to read to you their list of demands." Rachael unfolded a piece of paper and began to read.

"We call ourselves separatists. We believe that you can't mix things properly until you've held them separate long enough to test their qualities. Their values. You've got to find your own identity, and I mine. You've got to prove yourself. So, what have we proven? We are Texans. We are the grand testament of the lone striker. We are the children of the Alamo. We are strong, and honest, and proud. We are King and Country. We are friends and family. We are tired, and weathered, and worn, but we continue on, because we know who we are and what must be done. We have proven our value. Can the same be said for you?

"We've all lost something to the federal government. We've lost our livelihoods to agricultural regulations we can't meet. We've lost our lands and homes to taxes we can't afford to pay. We've lost friends and family to a war that should have never been fought. How much more will we lose? How much more are we willing to lose before something is finally done? Is there anything even left?

"We, the people of The Republic, are here to tell you there is still something left. There is freedom. We have the freedom to act. We have the freedom to think, and to plan, and to carry out. We have the freedom to stand up for a belief. A belief against excessive reliance on the market economy. A belief against globalism. A belief in self-reliance. A belief in liberty. But sadly, we also believe that this freedom is slowly fading, and with it goes our time to act. We stand before you God-fearing men. We love our families. We love our lands. We love Texas. We are the last to ever suggest war, but that is exactly what we have on our hands. For what are wars but politics turned bloody? Today, we declare war on oppression. We declare war on rule by the few over the many. We declare war on injustice and on blind tolerance.

"Today we, on behalf of all those who have been wronged, on behalf of all those who are tired and worn, demand..." Rachael stopped and stared at the paper, then looked at someone off-camera. "You can't possibly be serious."

"Just read it!" said a voice.

Rachael swallowed hard. "We demand a total and complete secession of the state of Texas from the federal government, or there will, indeed, be war..." She lowered the paper and looked directly into the camera. "And every single hostage in this building will die."

Grandpa turned off the TV.

"Sarah?" Professor March said quietly. He took her hand.

"It's all right, Mike," she said. "I know."

Matt had never seen the two of them look at each other the way they did just then. They'd been married for about five years, though it was sometimes hard to tell. Matt knew not every couple was as affectionate as his parents, but he'd always gotten the impression the professor and Sarah's marriage was based mostly on mutual respect. As if their entire relationship stemmed from a simple need for companionship rather than romantic interest.

The concern in their eyes at that moment only increased Matt's fears.

The professor let go of Sarah's hand. "Is everything

ready, Richard?" he asked Grandpa Scott.

"Yes. I think they're waiting for you."

"And you appreciate the importance of your objective?"

Grandpa glanced at Matt. "Objective? For goodness' sake, Mike. They're my grandchildren."

The professor looked at the floor. "Of course." And without another word, he turned and headed out the door.

Matt looked to Alex, who appeared just as confused as he was.

What the heck was going on?

"Professor March, wait," said Matt, following him out onto the front porch. "Professor March!"

The professor stopped at the bottom of the steps but didn't turn.

"Where are you going? How can you just leave at a time like this? Do you not care about my family at all?"

The professor turned around. Matt fully expected Professor March to look at him the same way he had in the hall, when Matt had refused to go with him. But he didn't. His eyebrows were drawn and his mouth was turned down in concern. The expression might have made Matt feel guilty for his tone if he hadn't been too angry to care.

"Matthew, I have to go right now," Professor March said quietly. "There are some people I need to talk to. I can't tell you where I'm going or who I'll be meeting with or even how long I'll be gone. I know that you're worried about your mother and father. I am too. But you must trust me. There is much more at stake here than the lives of your parents."

Matt had no idea what the professor was talking about, nor did he care. To suggest that anything could ever be more important than the lives of his own family was both insulting and infuriating. He crossed his arms. "Why should I trust you? I'm not sure I even know who you are anymore."

Professor March dropped his eyes.

"Fine," said Matt. "If you won't tell me what's going on, then I'll just find out for myself. I mean, you taught me that much at least, right?"

"I have no doubt at all in your ability to obtain the information yourself, Mr. Grant," the professor said. "I would, however, appreciate it if you didn't try."

Matt looked away. He didn't want Professor March to see just how angry and frustrated and worried he was. Not that it mattered anyway. The professor probably knew.

The professor always knew.

Professor March stepped back up onto the porch. "If I tell you where I'm going, then will you trust me enough to allow me to leave?"

Allow him to leave? He couldn't stop him even if he tried. But Matt got the sense that the professor didn't want to go until he knew for sure that the two of them were on good terms. Knowing how important that was to Professor March made it hard for Matt to stay mad.

He slipped his hands into his pockets and nodded.

"Matthew." The professor lowered his voice. "I am part of a... council. A council composed of people like us. In light of recent events, including the current situation with your parents in Dallas, it has become relevant for us to discuss certain... *actions* that must be taken. Actions that have been planned for such a time as deemed necessary by members of the council. When events might align in such a way that would signify a *shift* in the status quo. That is where I must go now. To meet with the other members of the council."

Matt's heart beat faster. Not because of what the professor was saying, but because of what Matt was picking up between the lines. Professor March didn't just say "the current situation in Dallas." He very specifically included Matt's parents in that. As if they were involved somehow. As if they were in the middle of it.

And that's when Matt got it.

"It's all connected, isn't it? What's happening in Dallas. The GOG. The problems with the economy. My parents. All of it." All the pieces that had been staring him in the face for the last few months. The things they had been trying to keep from him. Everything he had seen and heard and felt. All of it led back to one thing. "My mother's dreams. That's how it all comes together, isn't it? That's why you're leaving now."

Professor March remained silent.

"But you already knew that. Didn't you, Professor? You and your *council*."

"No," said the professor. "Not with any certainty. Not until..." He stopped, then looked down at the porch. "Not until you came to talk to me this morning."

There weren't many strong emotions that Matt had experienced firsthand. He knew what true anger felt like only through the eyes of others. Like how Jacob had felt when Emily was dragged off to live with her father in

Canada against her will. Or when his dad found out the school board voted to cancel the music program, despite how hard they had all worked to raise the money to save it. But at that moment Matt knew what real anger felt like, because he now knew why his mother had been avoiding Professor March. She hadn't wanted him to know what she was seeing.

So he had tricked Matt into telling him instead.

"How could you do that to me, Professor? How could you do that to *her*?"

"Matthew, we had no choice. There was too much at risk. We couldn't know for sure until we knew what she knew. But your mother has never trusted anyone except your father."

Matt glared. "I can't imagine why."

"We only did it to protect you, Matthew. You and your brother. Leah and Daniel. Your parents. Everyone. That's all we ever wanted to do. Protect you."

Matt fought to hold back the hot sting of tears. "Protect us, huh? So, that's what you meant, isn't it! About this being a job? That's all we ever were to you, Professor MI6? A job!"

The professor's face fell. "Oh, Matthew, no."

Alex stepped out onto the porch. "Matt, is everything okay?" She looked back and forth between him and the professor as if she knew darn well it wasn't.

Matt took a deep breath. "Everything's fine," he said. "The professor was just leaving."

Professor March sighed. "I'm so sorry, Matthew. The choices we make are not always easy when charged with the responsibility of others. I hope one day you'll understand that."

That was the last thing Matt wanted to hear.

Professor March turned and headed to his car.

"*Matia mou*?" Alex said quietly.

He met her gaze. There was an incredible bleakness behind those beautiful blue-gray eyes. As if they had both just discovered that their entire world was nothing more than a desperate lie.

"Everything's not okay," she said, teary-eyed. "Is it?"

Matt held out a hand. She took it, and he pulled her closer. They wrapped their arms around each other then. The feelings they shared in that moment—the betrayal, the helplessness, the fear—were the only things left to them that were real.

"No, Lexi," said Matt. "It's not."

CHAPTER 20

"Put your cell phone in the bag, lady."

The scrawny guy in the mask held out a cloth sack. He and a couple other terrorists were walking around collecting everyone's phones to keep them from communicating with the outside world. This guy had started with Rachael, and then turned to Bennett, who had the unfortunate luck of being plopped down next to their little group after he and Rachael had come back from helping the terrorists videotape their demands.

At first Emma felt bad for Rachael, for being dragged off to help them, then quickly realized Rachael hadn't minded at all. As soon as she returned, she leaned across Aaron and excitedly whispered to them her account of the entire experience, including the terrorists' outrageous demands. She then, with a flip of her dark curls, pulled out her phone and attempted to discreetly bang out a quick email to the media before the scrawny guy demanded she turn over the phone.

Then he took Aaron's phone as well. He moved next to Jon, who coolly told the guy he'd left his phone up in their room. It didn't take a whole lot of convincing. Emma recognized this terrorist as one of those who'd attempted to hold Jon down earlier—and who'd gotten his nose cracked for it. Emma couldn't help but smile at the thought of it.

How's your face feel, kid?

"Come on," he said, holding the sack out to her. "You'll get it back at the end of class."

You've got to be kidding me. "I don't have it." She rolled her eyes. "It was in my bag up on the stage before you guys moved everything."

He glanced over his shoulder. Her bag was gone. "You really expect me to believe that *neither* one of you has a phone on you?"

"That's right, slick," said Jon.

The kid glared at Jon, then turned back to Emma. "Yeah, all right." He smiled and winked at her. "I guess I'll take your word for it."

"Gee, thanks."

"Then again..." He looked her over with a leer. "I could always just frisk you for it."

Jon shot to his feet, inches from the kid's face. "You sure you really want to do that?"

"Careful there, tough guy. You wouldn't want anything to happen to your pretty little wife, now would you?" He grinned and pointed his gun at Emma. The little punk seemed an awful lot cockier now that he'd been given the okay to shoot if there was trouble.

Emma saw the muscles in Jon's arm twitch and felt a tingle of impending explosion, like static in the air. It must have taken everything Jon had to hold himself back. She felt like punching the kid herself.

A couple of the guys who had been hovering behind the computer screens turned to face the commotion. Mac put a hand on his gun.

Jack stood up and stepped in between Jon and the kid. "Look, son," he said to the terrorist. "She already told you she doesn't have her phone. If you really want it, then go find it."

"Stay out of this, grandpa." The kid pointed his gun at Jack.

"I don't think you want to do that, young man," said Jack in an eerie, hollow tone Emma had never heard from him before. He put his hand on the guy's arm.

Emma held her breath. She was sure Jack was about to get himself shot, but instead the kid's eyes went glassy, the twitching in the corner of his mouth stopped, and his stare went blank. Then he simply walked off.

Jack turned back to Jon. "*Sit down*, Jon Jacob," he said before returning to his own spot against the wall.

Jon stared after the kid for a minute without moving, his fist still clenched by his side. Emma reached up and slipped her hand into it. He looked down at her, then finally sat back down beside her.

Emma wasn't sure exactly what had just happened. Or what *hadn't* happened. Apparently Jack was a Pusher. It made sense—most of the Marked who went into politics were. Still, though Emma had never known what Jack Allred's gift was, it seemed odd to think that he had the ability to manipulate people. Jon's Uncle Jack had always been so kind. He had gotten Jon out of trouble more times than Emma probably even knew about. It was hard to imagine him as someone who could make you do just about whatever he wanted.

Too bad it only worked on one person at a time.

Bennett leaned over Rachael and whispered, "Wow, Captain, that was brilliant. What's your next strategy? Threaten to meet him out in the parking lot after school?"

Jon leaned his head back against the wall, ignoring

him.

Aaron answered instead. "Hey, Bennett, how's your lip?"

Jon smiled at that one.

Emma squeezed his hand, and he turned to meet her gaze. Emma loved Jon's eyes. They were a deep, rich brown, but with a fire behind them. Not like the cold, blue flame of the eyes she saw in her dreams. No, Jon's eyes burned with warmth, and light, and everything good and honorable, giving him an air of nobility. Which was fitting. He was her knight in shining armor. Her great protector, from the very first day they met. That was the first time he'd saved her life, and it wouldn't be the last.

Emma was working for FEMA when the big one hit the Pacific Northwest. The devastation was record-breaking. Entire cities were leveled. But Emma and her team were ready for it. In her first real assignment as an incident commander, she gathered hundreds of field agents and volunteers and set up search-and-rescue and emergency shelters. She even had an entire unit from the Virginia Air National Guard at her disposal. Everything went just as she planned—until the storm hit.

Her superiors wanted to pull out until the storm blew through. Emma didn't. She knew there were still people stuck outside in the elements who might not make it through the night. It took a great deal of convincing on her part, but she managed to talk them into letting her make one last run to look for survivors. Under one condition. She had to find a pilot willing to take her. Emma knew the storm would be bad enough for people on the ground. She wasn't sure how to convince a pilot to fly in it. But as it turned out, she didn't have to.

Emma had a volunteer.

And that's how she and Jon ended up spending their first night together, sheltered from the storm in some random basement in Seattle, soaking wet and trying desperately not to freeze to death in the freakish cold of late September. It was strange, the familiarity she felt with him. They had never so much as said a word to each other before that night—although she *had* caught him staring at her on multiple occasions. Which, of course, meant she was looking his way as well. Almost like they were drawn to each other. And the more time they spent together, the stronger that attraction became.

They were picked up the next morning, and no matter how hard she tried to forget about him and go back to the craziness that was her life, Emma just couldn't get Lt. Jonathan Grant out of her head. They were connected somehow.

And had been ever since.

"Thanks, Sparky," she said, winking at him.

Jon chuckled. It had been a long time since she called him that. "You're very welcome, Princess."

Emma resigned herself to staring at the clock above the stage. The seconds passed. Tick, tick, tick. Perfectly synchronized with the pounding in her head. Then the seconds melted into minutes. And the minutes into hours. She pulled off her blazer jacket, covered herself with it, and rested her head on Jon's shoulder. There were only two things in life that Emma had little tolerance for. One was indecisiveness. The other was waiting.

Jon's stomach rumbled. "If I'd known we were going to be held hostage all night, I'd have eaten something this morning," he said.

Emma rolled her eyes. Only Jon could think about food at a time like this. Her stomach was so knotted it was all she could do to keep from throwing up. "Are you serious?" she asked.

Jon shrugged. "I'm hungry. Not everyone can go freakishly long periods of time without eating."

"So how about we actually do something to get out of this instead of just sitting here, then?" she whispered.

"We're not going to *do* a thing." Jon glanced around, then lowered his voice. "You heard what they said, Emma. *You* may not care what happens to you, but I do. Not to mention, we have three kids at home waiting for us. So for once, please, just let someone else be the hero."

Emma sat back and huffed.

Jon shook his head and stared at the ceiling.

"Pardon me for interrupting you in the midst of your marital tension, Captain, but I do believe Dr. Grant has a point," said Bennett. "We should probably do something more than just twiddle our thumbs."

Jon rolled his eyes. "Yeah, Bennett, and the fact that you think it's a good idea makes me just want to jump at the opportunity."

Bennett glared. "Look, Grant, I know you're not particularly fond of me, and to be quite honest I'm not too keen on you either, but the fact remains that we are all in this situation together. I think it would be mutually beneficial if we came up with a way to get out of it."

Jon closed his eyes and rested his head against the

wall.

Emma loathed Stephen Bennett, but at that moment she agreed with him. Someone needed to do something, and she didn't want to rely on the feds to be the ones to do it.

She leaned over to Jack. "Jack, can't you talk some sense into him?"

Jack was scanning the room, a glazed look in his eyes. "I can't believe it's come to this," he whispered, as if to himself.

"Jack?" she repeated, putting a hand on his arm.

He blinked a few times and turned to her. "I'm sorry, what?"

"Are you okay?"

He smiled. "Yes, of course. And I completely agree. Something should be done." Emma was about to turn to Jon and say "I told you so" when Jack stopped her. "But not necessarily the way I think you're suggesting. It's not always wise to go in with guns blazing. Even if we did have guns. Which we don't."

Good point.

"But what we do have…," he raised an eyebrow, "is you."

"Excuse me?" Jon opened his eyes.

"I think I know where you're going with this, sir," said Aaron.

Jon snapped his head around to glare at him.

"Well, just think about it, Jon. I'm no expert, but I do know the first thing we need to do is assess the situation. And Emma's a crisis psychologist, right? I don't know about you, but I'd consider this a crisis."

"Fine," said Jon. "Just so long as you do a *visual* assessment. From here."

Emma cocked her head at him. "How else would I do it?"

"I don't know, but with you, there's no telling."

She shook her head. *Whatever.*

Emma closed her eyes and took a deep breath. If she was going to get an impression of these guys without talking to them, she was going to have to use a lot more than just her skills of observation to do it. She would have to do what she did best: feel her way through it.

She started with the terrorists who were walking around the room, keeping an eye on the hostages. They pointed their guns toward the ceiling, and every now and then would stop and curl a lip in satisfaction at one of the congressmen, whose brows were covered in sweat. Emma could tell that a few of the terrorists were enjoying watching the representatives squirm a little too much. Most of them looked like little more than lackeys, though—there to follow orders, and nothing more. All except for the gangly one with a broken nose. Emma got the impression that he possessed a dangerous combination of overconfidence and sheer stupidity.

Then there was the kid sitting behind the surveillance monitors. Emma couldn't explain how she knew he was young, just that he was. He watched the screens, every now and then pointing out something to the guy standing behind him. The guy would nod, and the kid would go back to staring at the screen.

Which brought Emma to the guy standing behind the table. He was one of the only two who mattered when it came down to it. Clearly the leader, though she sensed there was some friction between him and the one he'd called Mac. He stood with his arms crossed and a hand over his mouth, nodding each time the kid pointed something out to him.

As she watched him, he looked over at her, and their eyes met.

Emma expected him to look away, but he didn't. He just stared at her with this look in his eyes. What was it? Concern? Regret? Second thoughts about what he was doing? It was hard to tell behind the mask.

She frowned at him. He turned his eyes back down to the screen.

Emma sighed. Just based on their interactions, she knew he was the worst type of terrorist they could be dealing with. He was calm and confident, and believed thoroughly in the righteousness of his cause. He wasn't just doing this for himself. He cared about other people, which was why he'd promised her no one would get hurt.

She wondered whether he'd be able to keep that promise.

Despite the terrorist leader's determination to do what he thought needed to be done, he didn't frighten her. Quite the opposite, in fact. There was something friendly and familiar about him. Emma got the sense that deep down inside he was a good man, a man who had simply come to the end of his rope and felt he had no other choice.

Emma knew that feeling. She almost wished, for his sake as well as her own, that everything would turn out the way he hoped. But something told her it wasn't going to.

She turned next to the man who did frighten her. Mac. Based on his build and the remnants of his busted lip, she knew who he was. He was the guy she'd caught ransacking their room. But more importantly than that, she knew his type. Being a Seer, Emma could often get a sense about people.

Sometimes she felt like one of those crackpots who call themselves psychics, who claim to know who you are as well as who you'll become, though they are seldom right. Because the future itself is always changing. It isn't set in stone. It's formed by the choices people make. And when a person's heart and mind are open, their future isn't clear. There is always the option for them to make a good choice or a bad one.

But for people who become dark and hardened—people like Mac—you can almost guarantee that something will go horribly wrong. Because, in the end, there are no bad people. Just bad choices. And when bad choices are made, those who make them aren't the only ones that suffer for it.

They take others down with them.

Emma slipped her hand back into Jon's. "Em, what is it?" he whispered.

She didn't answer. She just squeezed his hand and forced herself to look at Mac.

He was up on the stage, scanning the crowd. Emma half-wished he wouldn't look her way. She didn't want to meet his eyes. She wondered if Jon had brought any chocolate with him, then realized if he did, he'd have eaten it by now.

Finally, Mac turned to face her. She took in a sharp breath, the intensity of what she felt at that moment overwhelming.

Emma felt pain. Suffering. Destruction. Cruelty and malice and hatred. But not anger. Anger stemmed from reason. From a desire to avenge some injustice. Something that can be resolved or worked through or rationalized. Anger would have made sense. But what Emma felt in him made no sense at all. It was the icy sting of cold and darkness. Stronger than she'd ever felt it in a person before. Whatever part of him that had been human had disappeared long ago. Cut off and buried. Or driven out.

"Emma?"

Jon sounded distant. And worried. She didn't have to ask why. She'd broken into a cold sweat and was starting to hyperventilate.

Her lip trembled. "Jon?"

She tried to break eye contact with Mac. But for some reason she couldn't do it, like he was holding on to her somehow. Emma didn't even know that was possible, but Mac seemed to. He sneered.

And then the icy cold slammed into her.

Unlike the gradual descent into the river, this iciness hit her with the force of a tidal wave. Emma was floundering in a torrent of blackness, bitter and cold. She gasped frantically to suck in each precious, icy breath as she tumbled beneath the weight of darkness and despair.

The conference room disappeared in a wave of panicked euphoria. What replaced it was blurred and faint. Total darkness, except for a wash of red and white. Her mind was showing her something, and Emma felt an incredible need to know what it was. It was important, for some reason. She tried to calm herself, to focus on what she was seeing, but the harder she tried, the blurrier the image became. She could make out only a tinge of brown against the blurred outline of her hand. Nothing more.

And then she was overcome with the urge to pull out. The way she pulled out of her dreams just before something terrible happened so as not to become a part of it. Watching people burn to death in an apartment building or drown in a flood was bad enough without having to learn what it felt like yourself.

But it was too late. The red and white shattered and fell away into a million tiny pieces, blasting toward her in a great ball of orange flame. It passed painfully across her body, burning her bare arms and face. A shock wave followed. Emma screamed as it slammed into her.

Then everything went dark.

"Emma!"

Emma gasped and opened her eyes. Jon knelt in front of her, his hands on her shoulders. She was drenched in sweat and struggling to breathe.

He stared at her, his eyes wide with concern. Panic. "Baby, are you okay?"

Emma wondered if he ever got tired of asking her that.

She closed her eyes again and tried to collect herself. She'd never had a vision before, and she had to stop hyperventilating before she could even answer him, though she wasn't sure what she was going to say. She wasn't okay. At all. Every muscle in her body ached and she couldn't stop shaking. Like she'd been thrown up against a wall. She covered her face with her hands, determined not to allow the tears she felt creeping up on her.

"Dr. Grant, are you all right?"

Emma opened her eyes. The terrorist leader was kneeling in front of them.

The muscles in Jon's arms tensed. "Why do you care?"

But the terrorist *did* care, and Emma could see it.

He glared at Jon. "What's wrong?" he asked her quietly. The concern in his voice contrasted almost comically with his semi-automatic and ski mask.

It was apparently more than Jon could take. "What do you *think* is wrong with her?" he exploded.

Emma jumped, afraid he was going to grab the guy and shake him.

"She hasn't been well since we got here, hasn't eaten anything since yesterday, and then you guys come along and pump us all full of whatever the *hell* was in that gas you used and the needles you stuck us with, and you think she's just supposed to be *okay*?"

The terrorist looked taken aback. "Mr. Grant, we took every precaution. I don't know—"

"Every precaution? Are you freakin' kidding me? You don't know? You're right, you don't know. Because you're all a bunch of sorry sons of—"

"Jon!" Jack grabbed him by the arm before he could burst into an array of colorful metaphors. "That doesn't solve anything." He lowered his voice. "Besides, I think we have a more pressing matter to deal with."

"And what exactly is that?" Jon barked, pulling his arm away.

"Emma," Jack said quietly.

Something in Jack's voice made her turn and look at him. He was staring at her lap.

"Emma, honey," he said, barely above a whisper. "Your arms."

She looked down. Her arms were covered in cuts and burns. With all the aches in her body, she hadn't even noticed the stinging pain in her arms—until now.

She took in a sharp breath.

"How did…?" The terrorist stared, wide-eyed.

Jon took her hand and lightly touched the inside of her arm.

Emma winced.

"Did you…" he said, then glanced at the terrorist before whispering, "Did you *see* something?"

Emma bit her lip. She was starting to feel nauseated.

"It's all right, Emma," said Jack, taking her hand from Jon. "I think we should probably get this taken care of, don't you?" He turned to the terrorist. "What do you say, son? You have a med kit, right?"

The terrorist looked stunned. As if he was as amazed by their reaction as he was by Emma's arms.

"Young man?" said Jack

The guy shook his head. "Yeah, of course. A med kit. It's up on the stage." He glanced over his shoulder. Mac was still watching them, his gun in his hands. The terrorist lowered his voice. "I'll go grab it and get these bandaged up."

Jack put a hand on his arm. "Perhaps the washroom would be a better place for this. After all, you don't want to make a scene."

Emma wrinkled her forehead. What exactly was Jack trying to do?

"Yeah," said the terrorist, looking blankly at Jack as if he didn't see him. "Yeah, the washroom. That's a good idea." He got up and headed for the stage.

Jack leaned close and whispered in her ear. "Emma, listen," he said. "I don't want you to worry about me, all right?"

What?

"You just do what you always do," said Jack.

The terrorist returned with the med kit. "All right, Doc, let's get you fixed up." He held a hand out to help her up.

Jon started to get up, too.

"And just where do you think you're going?" The terrorist glared at Jon. "I said I'd take *her* to the bathroom. You will stay here and wait."

Jon tightened his jaw. "Like hell I will."

"Jon," Jack snapped. There was a fierceness in Jack's eyes that even Emma wouldn't dare cross. "She'll be all right. Just stay here."

Emma could tell that Jon was just as freaked out by all this as she was. Between the burns on her arms, what she had seen, and the look on Jack's face, Emma was now completely unnerved. She *needed* Jon. Needed him to be her voice of reason. Because that's what Jon did—kept her grounded when she wasn't thinking clearly. And at that moment, she wasn't thinking clearly at all. In fact, all she could think about was trying not to throw up.

"It'll be all right, son," Jack said quietly. "Let her go."

Jon took a deep breath, then sat back against the wall.

"Don't worry, Cap," the terrorist said as he pulled Emma up. "I give you my word I won't let anything happen to her."

Jon crossed his arms. "Yeah, like that means a lot."

CHAPTER 21

The man in the mask led Emma out of the conference room and down the hall to the restrooms. She stumbled as she walked. He caught her, slipping an arm around her. Casually. Instinctively. Almost as if he knew her.

"You know, you don't act like a terrorist."

"That's because I'm not," he said quietly, with the same hurt in his eyes that she'd seen earlier.

"You're not, huh? Then what do you call someone who knocks out a room full of people, then holds them hostage and makes outrageous demands in exchange for their safety?"

"A revolutionary," he answered, ushering her into the ladies' room.

Emma turned on the faucet and ran her arms through the cold water. The sting was even more painful now. The cuts weren't that bad, but the burns bubbled up and blistered.

"Here," the man said behind her. "Hop up on the counter and let me get them treated and wrapped properly before you give yourself an infection."

Emma raised an eyebrow at him. She wasn't sure she could even get up onto the counter, she was so dizzy and nauseated. But she understood what he meant. She'd grown up in Texas. She knew how inefficient the water treatment systems could be. The water had been so bad in her hometown that if you wanted to make fun of another kid you called them a tap-water drinker. It had never been a problem in the bigger cities, like Dallas, but it would be a known issue for anyone from a small east Texas town.

"Would you let me help you?" he asked.

Emma took a deep breath and nodded.

He put his hands under her arms and lifted her up slowly, careful not to brush against the tender areas of her skin. When she was situated comfortably, their eyes met again. Emma noticed a fleck of green against the brown.

He quickly turned away.

He set his med kit on the counter next to her and pulled out a can of antiseptic spray. "This happen to you a lot?" he asked with a grin.

"Not really," said Emma, her gaze dropping to her lap. "Or at least, not since I was a teenager."

He scanned her face. "I see."

He sprayed one arm at a time, cradling each gently in

his hand. Emma tried to hide how much the cold of it stung.

"It's kind of like an allergic reaction," she said, in a weak attempt to put his suspicions to rest. "Probably the shampoo in the carpet or something." She was a terrible liar.

"Well, whatever it was, it looks pretty painful. I'm really sorry, Dr. Grant."

"It wasn't your fault. I seriously doubt you'd ever hurt anyone. At least, not intentionally."

"Oh yeah?" he said, pulling a roll of gauze from his kit. "You think because you're a psychologist, you know me?"

"As a matter of fact, I do."

"Really? And what exactly do you know about me?"

Emma didn't want to admit it, but it was too obvious to avoid. "I know you're a husband and father. I know that your family has a ranch not far from here…"

He paused as he wrapped her arm.

"I know that you wanted to be a writer, until your brother died in the war. But most importantly, I know that you would never, ever be doing this unless you believed you had no other choice."

He finished bandaging her arms in silence, then rested his hands on the counter on either side of her. "I knew if anyone was going to recognize me, it would be you."

"Sam…"

He stepped away from her, pulled off his mask, and threw it on the counter.

Emma hopped down, ignoring the pain of the pressure it put on her arms. "Why are you doing this?"

"It's exactly like you said, Dr. Grant. Because I have no other choice."

"That isn't what I said at all. I said you *believed* you have no other choice. But it's not true, Sam. There is always a choice."

He stared at the floor. "Not for people like me."

"And what is that supposed to mean?"

Sam took a deep breath. "I looked you up, Dr. Grant. You and your husband. After you offered to help Cole. I wanted to know if you were sincere, and if you even had the means to do it."

"And?"

"And I came to the conclusion that you probably have every intention of following through on your offer. I found out you have an entire foundation set up to make

168

donations for research and treatment for everything from cancer to conditions just like Cole's. You're wealthy and connected. But that's exactly the problem with people like you and the rest of the power elite, Dr. Grant. You're wealthy and connected, and you always have been. Your families grow up together, marry each other, join the same clubs and run the same companies, and you're completely disconnected from the rest of us. Can you honestly tell me there has ever been a time in your life when you've struggled? When you haven't had some senator or president or massive inheritance you could fall back on for help?"

Emma knew he was right—mostly. Jon's inheritance hadn't been dropped at his feet in some massive chunk at age sixteen when his father died. It had come to him in segments, spread out over twenty years, and Robert Grant had made darn sure Jon had to jump through hoops to get it. So, yes, Emma and Jon absolutely knew how hard it was to make ends meet. But they never had to do it alone. There had always been someone there they could fall back on if they became desperate enough.

"Sam, look," she said, stepping right up to him. "I know how you feel, okay? I know what you're trying to do. Believe me, I know. Better than anyone in that room— better than anyone else on the planet—I know. But you have got to trust me when I tell you that this is *not* the way to do it."

Sam glared at her and lowered his voice. "You have *no idea* how I feel."

Emma turned back to the sink and rested her hands on the cool granite countertop, speckled light and dark brown like cigarette burns in the sand. "You see it all falling apart and feel like you have no control," she said. "Like the entire world is going nuts around you, and as much as you'd like to think you can stop it, you know deep down inside there is absolutely nothing you can do. And as it all goes to hell, you're terrified that it's going to take everything you've worked for—everyone you care about—with it."

Sam put a hand on her shoulder. "Dr. Grant."

"I was like you once," she said, turning to him. "So convinced I was right that I was ready to just grab them all by the shoulders and shake them till they saw it my way. And why shouldn't they? I *knew*. So thoroughly and completely I knew. I could show them the error of their ways, and they'd all be better off for it. But that was the problem, Sam. You quickly learn that everyone is just as passionate about what *they* believe as you are about what *you* believe. Everyone thinks they're right. Because no one ever sees the world the way you do. No one ever *knows* what you do.

"So all you can really do is stand back and let it blow up in their stupid faces. And pray that the debris doesn't land in your front yard."

Sam stared at her, wide-eyed. "Dr. Grant, I'm sorry. I'm sorry you feel that way, and I'm sorry you had to get mixed up in all of this. But I can't just walk away. I don't have the money, and I don't have the means, and I'm not even sure I'd want to. I'm not just terrified that they'll take away everything I care about. It's already happening. Those of us at the bottom of the food chain—me, my friends, my family, everyone I love—we're already suffering for it. And we continue to suffer every day. So, no, I can't just do nothing. I'm not going to just go hide. This is very much a part of me. It's who I am. And I can't ignore that."

"Your situation doesn't define you, Sam. It's what you choose to do with it."

He rolled his eyes.

"Look, you're a writer, right? Or at least, you wanted to be once. What method do you use for character development? How do you show your reader what kind of person your character is?"

Sam shrugged. "You use verbs. You want to show what kind of person your character is, you do it through how they act. What they do and say."

"That's right," said Emma. "It's the same way in criminal profiling and risk assessment. If you want to get an accurate picture of a person of interest, you look at how they act. What they do. It's supposed to matter even more than how they dress."

"Yeah, okay, but I'm not sure what this has to do with—"

"Well, I don't believe that. I believe you can tell just as much about a person by what they're wearing or where they live or what kind of car they drive. And do you know why that is?"

He narrowed his eyes. "Honestly, Dr. Grant, I have absolutely no idea, and I'm beginning to think you're just stalling."

"It's because…" she said, putting her hands on his arms, "it's because in the end it's not about what you do or what you wear. It's about the choices you make. Because everything we do—from getting dressed in the morning to holding a room full of people hostage—everything first requires a choice.

"You are the choices you make, Sam. So, what's it going to be? Are you the guy who recognizes when the train is about to speed out of control? Or are you the one who feeds the flame?"

"You know what, Doc?" he said, stepping in close enough to her that she had to press herself against the sink. He put his hands on either side of the counter and leaned in. "You have no idea what I've gone through to get where we are right now. You have no idea what I've watched the people I care about go through. So you can keep your psychobabble, Dr. Grant. Because in the end, you don't have the slightest inkling of who I really am."

"You're right, I don't," she said quietly. "And neither do any of the other people in that conference room. All we see is a guy in a mask with a gun who's about to get a building full of innocent people killed."

Sam's eyes widened. He stepped back. "That's not going to happen."

"Look, Sam, it's not important that anyone else knows who you are. The only thing that matters is that *you* know. That your family knows. Your wife and son."

He turned his eyes to the floor.

"So what you should ask yourself when this all goes bad—because it will, I can promise you that—is what are they going to think of you? When the kids at school tell Cole that hundreds of people died at the hands of his terrorist father, will he understand enough to even *want* to defend you? When Claire cries herself to sleep at night because you're not there, is she going to wonder if you even loved her enough to stop and think about how this would affect them? Or will they both just plain hate you for it?"

Sam's eyes darted up to meet hers. "Dr. Grant, I just… I just want things to change. I don't want to hurt anyone."

Emma closed her eyes and sighed. "Then it's not too late, Sam. It's not too late to stop all this. My father is a US marshal. I have friends in the FBI. I can make sure—"

"Hackett!"

Emma's heart jumped into her throat. Standing just inside the doorway was the scrawny kid with the broken nose.

She wanted to scream at him.

"What are you doing?" the kid said as he stepped into the room. He curled a lip and ran a finger slowly down Emma's arm. "Having a little fun?"

Emma pulled away.

"Though I think I would have left my mask on if I were you, man. She knows your face now."

Sam clenched his fist, a hint of disgust as well as anger in his eyes. "What do you want, Rat?" he said, retrieving his mask.

"Mac sent me to find you. That FBI guy is on the phone again. Deputy something-or-other Sanchez. He wants to discuss our demands."

"Fine, you found me. Now go wait outside."

Rat didn't move. He just stood there, undressing Emma with his eyes.

Sam punched him in the arm. "Hey, kid, enough. I said go wait outside."

"All right, jeez," said Rat, rubbing his arm. "Get some for me too, then. But make it quick. I don't think Sanchez is the type of guy who likes to be left waiting."

As he walked out the door, Emma suddenly had the urge to shower.

"We should get back," said Sam. "It's going to look bad enough as it is."

"Yeah. For your sake, I hope that Rat kid doesn't go running his mouth, or Jon's going to kill both of you."

Sam smiled. "And I wouldn't blame him for it. But it's much better than them knowing what was really going on in here."

"You mean me trying to talk some sense into you?"

Sam glared at her. "Nothing changes, Dr. Grant. Unless you know something I don't, I think you're just scared. It's understandable. But I have absolutely no reason to believe that things won't go exactly as planned."

You have no idea. Emma didn't doubt at all that things would go according to plan. The question was, according to whose plan?

"We are the choices we make," she whispered.

"You're absolutely right, Doc. And this is my choice. No matter what sacrifices I have to make for it. And if you're convinced that the best way to deal with this is to hide and wait it out, then I think you're no better than anyone else in that conference room."

Emma narrowed her eyes at him. "And if *you* continue to go through with this, then you're no better than him," she said, nodding toward the door. She was tired and nauseated and angry at herself now. She'd lost him, and she knew it. If she was going to stop all this, she was going to have to find another way to do it.

Sam shook his head. "Come on, Doc, let's go," he said, reaching for her arm.

"No." Emma pulled away from him.

"Are you really going to make me drag you out of here at gunpoint?" He glared at her for a moment, then dropped his eyes, as if he was embarrassed to even have entertained the idea.

"I just..." Emma sighed. "I just need a few minutes, okay? I'm afraid if I step back into that conference room now I'm going to throw up all over the floor."

Sam rubbed his forehead. "All right, fine. Ten minutes. That's it. Rat will be right outside the door. I've got to go take a phone call."

"Yeah, tell Victor I said hi," she mumbled.

He pulled his mask back on. "Ten minutes. Not a second more. And don't do anything stupid, either. I'd hate to have to..."

"What, shoot me? Guess you'd be breaking your promise then, wouldn't you?"

Sam rolled his eyes. "Hell hath no fury..." he muttered, then walked out the door.

And Emma lost it.

"Damn it!" She slammed her hands down on the countertop. She wanted to curl up into a ball and cry. She could have stopped it. She could have stopped it! *Now* what was she supposed to do?

"Think, Emma, think," she said. She turned on the faucet and cupped her hands beneath the water. She took a long drink and splashed her face.

We are the choices we make. It was the same thing Jon had said to her only days before. It felt more like months. But it wasn't the first time she had heard it. She already knew. Probably better than anyone. And that's what worried her.

That doesn't help, Emma. Yes, it worried her. More than anything else. But at that moment, that wasn't what was important. At that moment, there were more pressing things to worry about.

Like Victor Sanchez.

Yes, she had friends in the FBI. People she liked. People who did their job, and did their job well. People who were patriots, who would lay down their lives for their country and their leaders. But Victor wasn't one of them. He was an arrogant prick who had no idea how to deal with a hostage situation. On the few occasions when she had been forced to work with him, it hadn't ended well. People died. Innocent people who didn't have to. And it hadn't bothered Victor at all. Take out the threat, get the job done—that was his only objective. Anything outside of that was just a bonus. Pair that with a guy like Mac, and you'd have an accident waiting to happen.

A bomb waiting to go off.

Emma needed someone on the outside she could trust. Who cared about what happened to the people inside that building. Someone she could talk to who would believe her when she tried to warn them what was going to happen.

But how in the world was she supposed to pull that off?

"All right, come on, Emma," she said to her reflection. "What do I do?"

What you always do.

Emma wrinkled her forehead. *What you always do?* It was the last thing Jack had said to her before she left the conference room, and even now it made no sense. What in the world was it she always did?

And that's when she saw it. She looked up at the corner of the mirror, at the reflection of the ceiling behind her. She turned and stared at it, wide-eyed.

There was a vent just above one of the bathroom stalls.

"What is it you always do, Emmy?"

Whatever you have to.

CHAPTER 22

"Hey, where's your hot little friend?" Rat leaned against the wall outside the bathroom, a sucker stick hanging out of his mouth.

He looked like an idiot.

Sam smiled and winked. "She needed a few minutes to, uh... compose herself." The words disgusted him, but he had to keep up the façade. Any form of kindness toward one of the hostages would be seen as a sign of weakness. It was sad to think that to these men, there was more dignity in dragging a girl off and having your way with her than there was in showing her some decency.

Where did Mac find these people?

"Wow, that was quick. She shouldn't need too long to recover," Rat said with a laugh. He got a crazed look in his eye. "How about I go help her?"

"Leave her alone, man. She's already had enough."

"Not until I'm done with her, she hasn't. But, hey, I get it. She's gorgeous, and you want to keep her all to yourself. Didn't your mamma ever teach you to share?"

That was as far as Sam was willing to let it go.

He slammed his fist against the wall, right next to Rat's head. "I said leave her alone."

"What the hell, man?" Rat's jaw dropped, the sucker falling from his mouth.

"I mean it, Rat," said Sam. "You're going to stay here, and you're going to keep an eye on this door. But if you touch her, I swear to God, I'll shoot you. Do you understand?"

"You wouldn't do that," said Rat, narrowing his eyes.

Sam backed up and grinned. "You're right. I won't have to. I'll turn her husband loose on you instead."

Rat reached up to lightly touch his nose.

Sam smiled as he headed back to the conference room. It was a good thing Reynolds was a hormone-crazed pervert, or he might have picked up on what Dr. Grant had been trying to do. What she had almost been successful in doing.

Talking him out of it.

In the end, it didn't matter. Things had already gone too far. He didn't care who she thought she was or what kind of connections she had. There was no way she could get him out of this now. And what about Zach and the other boys he'd brought in? They'd already broken too many laws. If they turned themselves in, they'd never see the light of day. All their work, all their sacrifices, would be for nothing. And even if, somehow, they could all just walk away—if they could just lay down their guns, say they were sorry, and head home—what would there be to go home to? A dying country? A dying ranch?

A dying son?

As he stepped through the conference room door, Sam made a special effort not to look toward Jonathan Grant, though he could still feel the man's eyes on him. Grant was no doubt furious to see that his wife hadn't come back from the bathroom with him. But Sam had someone else to deal with.

Someone who was a lot more dangerous when mad.

"Where have you been?" Mac barked at him from the stage.

"Taking care of something," Sam snapped back.

"Where's the girl?"

Sam ignored him and picked up the phone. "Yes?"

Mac sneered at him and walked off.

"Ah, well, look who finally decided to join us," came Sanchez's slimy voice.

Sam tightened his jaw. Out of all the people in the FBI he could be dealing with, why did it have to be the pot-bellied jerk he'd met in Destiny? "Sorry, I was busy accosting one of your hostages."

Sanchez was silent for a moment. *Good.* Sam wanted him to understand he was serious, not someone he could push around.

"Not one of the important ones, I hope," said Sanchez.

What was that supposed to mean? "I guess that depends on who you consider important. Friend of yours, from what I understand. She says to tell you hi."

Sam could hear the muffled sounds of Sanchez holding his hand over the phone. As he waited for the guy to respond, he noticed Zach staring up at him. Zach glanced warily across the room at Mac, then back at Sam. He and Zach had been best friends long enough for Sam to know exactly what that look meant.

Something was wrong.

Sanchez came back. "Look, Boss," he said. "Can I call you Boss?"

Sam didn't answer.

"All right, listen. Before we start to wheel and deal, I need to ask you something."

Wheel and deal? Seriously?

"Exactly how far are you willing to go?"

Sam hesitated. "Excuse me?"

"I mean, I can appreciate your efforts. Really I can. All of us out here are suffering too. We want to see some changes made just as much as the next guy."

Sam highly doubted that. These were government employees, with government health insurance and fat pensions waiting on them. When the cutbacks started, did they touch the paychecks of the bureaucrats? The FBI, the CIA, the NSA? Any of the people in that conference room? No. They took it straight from the average American. From Social Security, assistance programs, even military pay.

This guy didn't care. He didn't care at all.

"But," Sanchez continued, "I just don't think what you're asking is feasible."

"What are you saying, Sanchez?"

"What I'm saying is, do you have any idea how ludicrous your demands are? I mean, think about it, Boss. What in the world makes you believe, even if we could manage to pull everyone we'd need together to discuss it, that they would come to an agreement in a realistic time frame? These are politicians we're talking about here. And who's to say the Texas governor and half his cabinet aren't already in there with you as it is?"

Sam had to smile at that one. No, the Texas governor wasn't there. Or a single member of his cabinet. They'd made sure of that. But it did tell Sam one thing. This guy had no idea how Texas really worked.

"Sanchez, where are you from, anyway?"

"Chicago."

"Well then, you find me a Texan."

"What?"

"I'm done talking to you, Deputy Director. You want to 'wheel and deal,' as you say, then you get me someone who gives a damn."

And with that, Sam hung up.

"What's wrong?" he whispered to Zach.

"I found something," said Zach, nodding toward his laptop.

Sam quickly scanned the room to look for Mac before turning his eyes to the screen. Pulled up was a floor plan of the hotel, with a little blinking light in the middle of it.

"What does that mean?" Sam asked.

"It's an alert I set up. Someone is trying to make an outside call."

Sam's jaw dropped. "From where?"

"The registration room around the corner, it looks like. I take it from your expression it isn't one of our guys."

Sam shook his head. *Really, Doc? I give you ten minutes, and this is what I get?* "Look, Zach, I need you to find me everything you can on Dr. Emma Grant. Anything we can use as leverage."

"Why?"

Sam lowered his voice to barely a whisper. Mac was coming their way. "Because if you don't give me some reason to keep her around, Mac's going to kill her."

"What did Sanchez say?" Mac boomed.

Sam stood up straight. "He said he'd call back."

Mac glanced at Zach's monitor as he stepped up to the table. "What does that blinking light mean?"

Sam and Zach exchanged a look.

"Come on, kid," said Mac. "What does it mean?"

Zach swallowed. "It means someone is making a phone call from inside the hotel."

Fury filled Mac's eyes. He spun to leave.

"No!" Sam put a hand on Mac's chest. "*I* will deal with this."

Mac shot daggers at Sam, then glanced over at Jonathan Grant.

Sam followed his gaze. "Don't even *think* about touching Grant until I get back, Mac. Is that clear?"

Mac curled a lip. "Crystal."

CHAPTER 23

"Jon, can I ask you a question?" said Aaron.

Jon kept his eyes on the doors, willing Emma to reappear. "Sure."

"Was it true what Bennett said earlier?"

Jon braced himself for an uncomfortable conversation.

"Were you really an alcoholic?"

"Oh, that?" Jon turned to him and smiled in relief. "Yeah. But that was a long time ago. I haven't touched the stuff in over twenty years."

"Wow. It's just, well, kind of hard to believe. You seem like such a strong person. It's hard to imagine someone like you could struggle with something like that."

"You'd be surprised," said Jon, turning back to the doors. "Sometimes it's the strongest people who need the most help."

Then the guy in the mask stepped back into the room, without Emma.

And something inside of Jon snapped.

In the few seconds it took the terrorist leader to make his way to the monitors, Jon contemplated no less than thirty-seven different scenarios in which he took down every gun-toting guy in the place, starting with the ones on the stage. For a split second he even thought about grabbing Bennett and using him as a human shield. After all, this was an American convention. It seemed only fitting that if anyone was going to have to die, it should be the Canadian.

And the representative of the GOG no less. He could take out two birds with one stone.

Jon pushed himself up on his toes and squatted against the wall behind him, coiling his body. One of the terrorists walking around the room was about to pass by. As soon as he got close enough, Jon would pop up, grab the guy's gun, slam an elbow into his face, maybe grab Bennett too—not really, but it was fun to think about—snipe the ones on the stage, there'd be some confusion, take out the one behind the monitors, throw his gun to Aaron—maybe he should warn Aaron, but there was no time—grab the pistol Jon knew the terrorist kept at his ankle...

The guy was only a few feet away now.

Jon took a deep breath and held it, every muscle in his body tensed.

Three…

Two…

"Jon Jacob."

Jon turned to Jack. There was a tenderness in his voice, and a warmth in the hand he put on Jon's shoulder that made him relax.

The terrorist passed by. Jon didn't even notice.

"Jon Jacob, there's something I want you to know," said Jack.

Jon smiled at him. His Uncle Jack. The man he'd looked up to his entire life. The man who always welcomed him into his home, always saved a place for him at the dinner table. Who'd tried to teach him that, no matter how badly his father treated him, he was still worth something. When Jon was little, he wanted to be just like Jack.

Did Jack even know that?

"Your father was a good man, Jon. Now, I know typically you'd argue with me about that…"

Jack was right—he *would* argue. He'd say that the only thing his father had ever taught him was how to invest. And the only thing he'd ever given him was a black eye. But in that moment Jon didn't say anything.

He just stared at Jack.

"… but we all have that one weakness. That one thing that, if we lost it, we'd have nothing left to live for. Nothing left to fight for. Ally was your father's one thing, Jon. When your mother died, something just went wrong inside him. And what was left was no more than a shell of a man. Now, I loved your mother very much. You know that. It killed me when we lost her. But I loved your father too, and watching him die slowly inside every day, knowing how angry he would be at himself for the way he treated you… that was even worse."

Jon frowned. He didn't want to listen anymore. It made him mad, but more than that, it hurt. He hadn't thought about it, hadn't dealt with it in a long, long time. He'd heard it all before—that when his mother died, his father lost anything worth living for. But what about him? Was his own son not worth living for?

Jon tried to turn away. There was something he was supposed to be doing, something important. But he couldn't remember what it was.

"Jon, do you remember the summer when you were six years old?" Jack took Jon's arm. There was a deep nostalgia in his eyes. As if when he looked at Jon, he didn't see the man, but a young boy who wanted nothing more in the world than to know that someone loved him.

"That was a long time ago, Jack."

"Well, I remember," said Jack. "You had this cat you toted around. It was white with black spots. I think you named her Bessy, because she reminded you of a cow. You loved that cat. You found her in the tobacco fields out behind the house. Carried her around like a baby. I remember being completely amazed that she let you tote her around like that—most cats aren't that docile. But she didn't seem to mind at all. You begged us to let you leave her at the house, because you knew your father would never let you bring her home."

Jon smiled. "Yeah, I remember."

"Do you remember what happened to her?"

Jon's smile faded.

"We found out she was sick. I explained to you how uncomfortable she was. How much pain she was in. I told you that everything you had done for her, how you had loved her and taken care of her, was good for her. That it had helped her to not feel so bad. For a little while. But her illness was beginning to take over, and we needed to do something about it."

It was almost forty years ago, but the way Jack talked about it made it seem like it was only yesterday. Jon could see himself then, as a six-year-old boy, in the fields out behind Jack's house, carrying around a ball of fur as long as he was tall. The vet had already come and gone, declaring there was nothing more he could do. Jon remembered holding her and feeling so helpless. He did love her. This sweet little animal that had wandered into his life, that had become completely dependent on him. That had let him hold her and pet her and purred with an intensity so great it was as if she thought he was the most important person in the world.

"You know what we have to do now, Jon Jacob?" his Uncle Jack had told him, the syringe in his hand. Uncle Jack towered over him, twice his size. He knelt in front of Jon and wiped a tear from his cheek.

"Will it hurt her?" Jon asked.

"No, it's not going to hurt her. In fact, quite the opposite. She's in a lot of pain right now. This is going to take all that away."

"Do you think she'll be scared?"

"Not if you stay with her."

Jon nodded. He didn't want to be there. He didn't

want to have to watch her go. To lose the one thing he loved more than anything in the world. But he stayed. He could be brave for her, because he didn't want her to be alone.

Jon held her in his lap, cradling her in his arms like a newborn. She looked up at him while Uncle Jack gave her the injection. Jon watched the light slowly fade from her eyes. And in the second just before she was gone, he could have sworn he saw a flash of gratitude.

Jon took in a sharp breath.

Jack was kneeling on the conference room floor beside him, his hands on Jon's arms.

"Jack?" Jon's head spun. He felt as if he'd been shoved back in time, then quickly snapped forward again.

"Jon, do you remember what happened about a week later?" Jack glanced over his shoulder. The terrorist who'd taken Emma out of the room was having a discussion beside the surveillance monitors with the bigger guy—the one Emma said they called Mac.

"Um, I don't know," said Jon, putting a hand to his head. What just happened?

"We found out she belonged to a family on the other side of the fields, remember?"

Jon stared. "Yeah, that's right. She had kittens. She'd gone out into the field to die because she knew she was sick, and she didn't want them to get sick, too."

"That's right. She did it to save them. But you didn't understand that then, did you?"

"Of course not. I was six."

"But you understand that now, don't you, son?"

"Jack, I..." Jon shook his head. He looked over at the terrorists. The smaller one had his hand on Mac's chest. They both were looking at Jon and Jack.

"Listen to me, Jon. Sometimes we lose people. People we care about. Sometimes bad things happen and we don't understand why. We can choose to be bitter and angry, like your father. We can turn our backs on the world. Or we can remember that just because we don't understand why it happened now doesn't mean we won't understand it someday."

"Jack, what are you saying?"

The smaller terrorist turned and ran for the door.

And Mac turned toward them and smiled.

"Jack, no," said Jon, a chill washing over his body as he realized what was going on.

Nothing had happened to Emma. If it had, he would

have felt it.

The reason that Emma hadn't come back from the bathroom—the reason the terrorist leader had been hovering behind the surveillance monitors and then suddenly shot out of the room—was that Emma had found her opportunity to do something. Something reckless and stupid. Something that was about to get her killed.

And now Mac was headed their way. Not for Jon, because Jon wasn't the one who had been sitting to her left.

Jack was.

"Jack, please, don't," said Jon.

He wanted to pull away from Jack's hands still on his arms, but every time he thought about it, the notion would linger for only a split second before being driven out by the comforting knowledge of how much Jack cared for him. By the reassurance that this was a man he trusted implicitly, and that it would probably be best if he just did whatever Jack said.

"Jon Jacob." Jack put a hand on Jon's cheek.

Jon was only faintly aware of the tear that rolled down his face. *No.*

"Jon, I want you to know how very proud I am of you. You are an incredible husband and father. And a better man than I could ever be. I am very glad to have known you. To have been a part of your life. But there is something I need you to do for me, Jon. I need you to have faith. I need you to trust in the things that we have taught you. I need you to trust in Emma, trust that she knows what she's doing. And right now, Jon, I need you to trust *me*. You do trust me, don't you, Jon?"

Mac was only about fifteen feet away.

"Yes, Uncle Jack. I trust you."

And then Jon was eight years old. They were sitting on the shore at Virginia Beach. The sun was warm and the tide was calm. There was a cooling breeze.

"Jon Jacob, I need you to stay here. Can you do that for me?" said Uncle Jack.

Danny had waded out too far from the shore again, and Jack was going to have to go after him.

"Yes, Uncle Jack," Jon answered. "I can do that."

"This is very important, son. You have to stay in this very spot and not move. No matter what. Now, are you sure you can do that?"

Jon smiled. "Yes, sir. I will stay in this very spot and not move."

"Everything's going to be all right, Jon. I promise."
Uncle Jack tussled his hair, then ran toward the water.

As Jon watched Uncle Jack swim away, he pulled his knees up to his chest and shivered. The sun was starting to go down, and it made him lonely. The breeze blew cold across his back. There was something in that breeze, something in the air, that just didn't seem right. He started to get scared. He wished that his Uncle Jack hadn't had to leave him.

Somewhere in the distance, he heard a single gunshot.
And he began to cry.

CHAPTER 24

As soon as Richard Scott found out that Victor Sanchez was heading up the situation in Dallas, he knew he couldn't just sit back and watch.

"And where do you think you're going?" Sarah snapped at him.

Jacob, Alex, Daniel, and Leah were sitting around the television in the living room behind her, their eyes still glued to the news. Matt stood leaning against the back of the loveseat.

Richard shoved his old US marshal jacket into a duffel bag. "I can't just sit here, Sarah. I've gotta do something. You heard what they said on the news. I can't leave Jon's and Emma's lives in the hands of Sanchez."

"Well you can't leave me here alone with *them*, either!" said Sarah.

"Hey, I don't know if anyone's noticed," said Matt, "but we're not exactly toddlers anymore."

"You're right," said Richard. "You're not." He unzipped his bag, pulled out his handgun, and handed it to Matt.

"What in the world is this for?" said Matt.

"Peace of mind."

Matt eyed the gun warily.

"Jacob!" Richard barked.

Jacob jumped up and came over. "Yes, Grandpa?"

"I need you to call one of your dad's pilots and get me a flight to Dallas."

"Sir?"

"Now, Jacob."

Jacob and Matt exchanged glances. Matt handed the gun to Jacob. Jacob slipped it into the back of his pants and pulled his shirt down over it. "Yes, sir," he said, and headed toward the phone in the kitchen, pushing his hair from his eyes as he left. Jacob's shaggy locks compared to Matt's tapered cut was an outward reminder of how contrasting their personalities were, despite being twins. Jacob was fairly laid-back and, when it came right down to it, always did exactly what he was told. Matt usually needed further convincing.

"Let me come with you, Grandpa," said Matt.

"Absolutely not. Your mother would kill me."

"Please. They're my parents."

"Yes. And they're my kids."

Matt shook his head.

"Look, bud, I know you're frustrated. But I need you to trust me right now."

"That's exactly what Professor March said just before he took off and left us, too."

"Yeah, well there's a difference between me and 'Professor' March." Richard pulled Matt close and hugged him. "He's not your grandpa."

Matt sighed and pulled away. "I just don't understand, Grandpa. I don't understand what's going on, and I don't understand why no one can tell me."

"How old are you now, Mattie?"

"Eighteen."

"Good. Then we'll tell you when you're nineteen."

Jacob returned from the kitchen. "All right, Grandpa. Bill says he can be ready to take off in about thirty minutes."

Richard checked his watch. It was just after eight thirty. "Perfect. Listen, Jacob." He put his hands on Jacob's shoulders. "You do whatever you have to to keep 'em safe. You understand?"

Jacob looked him in the eyes and nodded.

"All right, boys, I've gotta go. I love you both. Keep an eye on Sarah and your sister, okay?" He glanced at Leah, who was sitting next to Daniel on the loveseat. She had fallen asleep with her head on his shoulder. "Everything's gonna be all right, I promise. Just you wait and see."

He turned and headed out.

Sarah followed him onto the porch. "Richard, this is crazy!"

"I've never been much for sanity, Sarah," he said as he limped to the truck, his bum leg even more irritating at the moment.

"Richard, please. Your job was to keep the kids safe. You're breaking protocol!"

Richard flung open the driver's side door and chucked his bag across the seat. "Screw protocol, Sarah. I'm not going to just sit back and let them die." He paused and took a deep breath. "Besides, if they're gone, what good is protocol going to do us then, huh? What chance do you think any of us have without Jon and Emma?"

Sarah met his eyes, then looked away.

He climbed into the truck and shut the door.

"Just be careful, okay?" she said.

Richard pulled out the pistol he kept in his glove box.

He handed it to Sarah through the window. "You too."

It was a forty-five-minute drive to the municipal airport in Bentonville where Jon's charter company housed their planes. As Richard passed by the Walmart home office, he pulled out his phone and checked for a signal. His clout would at least get him on the scene, but technically he was retired and no longer had any kind of authority. If he was going to do this, he was going to need some help.

He knew just the man to call.

A couple of hours later Richard landed at a private airport outside Dallas after a bumpy flight. He tipped his head to Bill, who had told him that he'd be praying for Jon and Emma and hoped that everything would turn out okay. Richard thanked him before stepping out onto the tarmac.

He didn't have a black sedan or a guy in a suit and earpiece waiting for him.

But what he did have was Ephraim Grey.

Ephraim leaned against the side of his SUV.

"Heya, slick," said Richard, throwing his bag in the back seat.

Ephraim was thirty years old, six foot two, and black as midnight. He had a tendency to leap before he looked, and a mouth that made you want to smack him, but he was the best deputy marshal Richard had ever had the pleasure of training. He'd also do anything for Jon and Emma.

"Hey, old man."

"Now, what have I told you about calling me old man?"

"Well, what have I told you about calling me slick?"

Richard smiled. "I see you're still cruisin' around in this gas-guzzling monster. Does Uncle Sam pay you enough to keep the tank full, or are we going to have to push it most of the way?"

"Nah, I thought we'd just hitch 'er up to yer tractor and haul 'er," he answered, mockingly slipping into Richard's accent.

"And how's that gonna work if I'm sittin' in the back seat, Jeeves?"

Ephraim laughed. "Whatever, man, just get in the car."

Richard was grateful to have Ephraim with him. There were checkpoints for miles outside of downtown Dallas, stopping people trying to get out as well as trying to get in. More than once Ephraim had to flash his badge to get through.

As traffic slowed to a crawl, Richard looked around at all the abandoned shops and buildings. The city whose skyscrapers used to sparkle in the sunlight had fallen into filth and disarray. Newspapers covered windows. People sat on the sidewalk holding cardboard signs. Even the plants that lined the streets were dying.

If a city like Dallas could be this bad, then what did the rest of the country look like?

Richard's phone rang. It was a Dallas number, but not one he recognized. "Hello?"

"Dad!"

"Emma?"

"Dad, listen, I don't have a lot of time. There's a bomb in the hotel."

Richard froze. "What?"

"You've got to tell them to get everyone out of the building."

"I don't understand. The terrorists have a bomb?" There wasn't anything about that in the information he'd received. "Is it on one of them?"

"I… I'm not sure where it is, Dad. I don't think one of them has it, but…"

"Then how do you know?"

"Because," Emma said quietly, "I saw it go off."

Richard swallowed hard. "So what do we do?"

"Get everyone out," she said. "Get everyone as far away from this building as you can. It's not going to be easy. Sanchez is heading up the negotiations. I've got to be honest, Dad. I kind of wish you were out there right now instead of him."

Richard smiled. "I think I may be able to arrange that."

Emma paused. "You're in Dallas, aren't you? Jon asked you to stay with the kids."

"I know."

"Thanks for not listening to him."

"You're welcome."

"Look, I've got to go. But there's something I need you to do for me, okay? If this thing goes bad—if Jon and I don't make it home—I need you to tell the kids—"

But Emma didn't finish her sentence.

Richard pulled the phone away from his ear. The line had gone dead.

He didn't want to think about why.

"So what's the plan, Chief?" said Ephraim.

"How far are we from the hotel?"

Ephraim scanned the line of cars in front of them. "I don't know. Ten blocks, maybe."

Richard grabbed his bag from the back seat, pulled out his US marshal jacket, and slipped it on. "All right then. I'll meet back up with you after you've made your way through this mess."

"Why? Where are you going?" Ephraim asked as Richard hopped out.

"To find Victor Sanchez."

CHAPTER 25

Emma went into crisis mode.

For the first time since Wakarusa, the anxiety worked for her rather than against her. For a moment, she forgot about her nausea, forgot about Jon in the other room, and focused instead on doing the one thing she'd always been good at, the one thing that always made her feel better—saving lives.

She climbed onto the toilet seat, used what leverage she could find within the stall, and hoisted herself up, teetering with a foot on each of the partition walls while she removed the cover of the vent. She pulled herself up into the darkness of the air duct and crawled army style until she came to a fork.

She glanced first right, then left, and closed her eyes to listen to her instincts.

"Which way, Emmy?"

Left.

"Left it is, then."

She crawled through the pitch black until she noticed light penetrating through a vent just in front of her. She stopped and peered through the slats. Below her was what looked like a registration desk. A phone sat on top of it.

She popped through the vent and dropped to the floor, grabbed the phone, and ducked beneath the desk.

She'd only gotten in a few minutes of speaking with her father before the line went dead.

"Well, look what we have here." Sam's head appeared upside down just above her. "Come on, Doc," he said, frowning. "Let's go."

Emma set the phone back down on the desk before crawling out.

Sam picked it up and flung it at the wall.

Emma slipped her hands into her pockets. "Gee, Sam, you seem a little upset."

"Who did you call?" he asked coldly.

"I ordered a pizza. We're all getting pretty hungry in there. It'll be here in about thirty minutes or it's free. Honestly, I think the pizza place is getting gypped. There is no way the delivery guy is going to make it through those barricades in thirty minutes."

Sam crossed his arms. "Who did you call?" he repeated slowly.

Emma looked away. "I called home, okay?"

"What?"

"You know, to say goodbye. I mean, what would you do if you knew you were about to die?"

Sam turned his eyes to the carpet, his chest rising and falling in angry, frustrated heaves. "Go," he said quietly, pointing toward the conference room.

Emma bit her lip. "Sam, please…"

"Just—" Sam raised a hand to stop her, then shook his head. "Just go."

Emma kept her eyes downcast as he herded her back to the conference room. She had managed to accomplish her goal, but she had lost Sam's trust in the process. He was angry, and that wasn't something she could afford.

"I'm sorry, Sam," she said. "I had to try."

He didn't answer.

She stopped mid-stride and spun on him. "I can't just sit back and let these people die."

Sam held his AR-15 in his hand. Would he have shot her if she'd tried to run?

"I already told you, Dr. Grant. I'm not going to let that happen."

"And what makes you think you can stop it? Do you trust the men in that room? Do you trust Mac? Deep down inside, do you think he cares at all what happens to us? Or even what happens to you?"

Sam narrowed his eyes. "I don't care what Mac thinks. I am overseeing this operation. Me, not him. I am the one who controls what goes on here today."

Before Emma could argue, a gunshot sounded from inside the conference room. She froze, unable to move. Unable to even breathe. Sam stared at her, wide-eyed.

There was only one person in that room Emma could think about at the moment.

"Jon," she whispered.

They both ran for the door.

Emma tried to keep the tears from her eyes. *No, no, no.* If Jon had been shot, then *she* was the one who had gotten him shot. She was the one who had quite possibly just gotten him *killed*. Emma hadn't thought about what they might do to him if she tried to pull something.

They pushed through the door, Emma's eyes darting to where she had left Jon. She fully expected to see him lying on the floor, covered in his own blood. But he wasn't. He was seated against the wall, Aaron on one side of him and Rachael on the other.

Emma headed toward them.

Sam ran past her toward the stage.

"Honey?" Emma said once she reached Jon. He sat with his arms wrapped tightly around his legs and his chin on his knees. Rachael had her arm around his shoulder.

Emma knelt in front of them. "Jon?" she said, her hand trembling as she pushed a lock of dark hair back from his face. His eyes were red and puffy, his cheeks tear-stained. He stared past her as if she weren't there.

Emma looked him over, still half-expecting to find a bullet hole, but saw nothing. She turned to Aaron. "What happened?"

Before Aaron could answer, his eyes widened and darted to a spot above her head.

Mac grabbed her by the arm.

She kept her eyes fixed on Jon as Mac dragged her up the steps and across the stage, then shoved her to the floor against something soft—against something sticky and wet. She held a hand in front of her eyes and stared at the bright red on her skin. Emma had been on the scene of dozens of horrific tragedies in her life, but she had never seen blood quite so red.

She forced herself to turn. To see who it was that was lying behind her. Based on the traumatized look in Jon's eyes, she already knew. It could only be one person. The one person in the world that he had looked up to and loved his entire life.

Emma had thought she'd gotten Jon killed, but she was wrong.

She'd gotten his Uncle Jack killed instead.

"Jack," she said, trying to steady her hand as she put her fingers to his throat to check for a pulse. *Is that…?* Maybe. The slightest hint of a heartbeat. But it was sickeningly faint.

And there was an awful lot of blood.

Emma turned back to Jon. She was only faintly aware of Sam standing in front of her, asking her something. "Barely," she answered him quietly without thinking, but she couldn't bring herself to take her eyes off Jon. He just sat there, staring at nothing, his face pale and distant. Emma had never seen him like that before. Never seen him that completely devastated. Like a child who'd just lost a parent.

She knew Jack must have done something to Jon, must have Pushed him to keep him from interfering and getting himself killed, too. That's why he was acting the way he was now. Jon would never allow himself to be that emotionally exposed, no matter what had just happened. He'd keep a straight face, determined to be strong for everyone else. But that wouldn't change what he was feeling.

And Emma had been the cause of it.

It made her want to throw up.

"I'm going to enjoy this," said Mac, stepping in front of her. He pointed a handgun straight at her head.

"Go ahead," said Emma, closing her eyes and resting her head on her knees. It didn't matter now anyway. Her hope was shattered. As shattered as the inside of Jack's rib cage. She cradled her head, determined not to let Mac see her cry. This was all her fault. When Jon snapped out of it, when he realized what had happened, what was she going to say to him? How was she going to face him? Judging by the heartbroken look on Jon's face, he might as well have been shot in the chest himself.

"No," said Mac, pulling her to her feet. He dragged her to the front of the stage and dropped her back down with a thud. "That's not how this is going to work, Doc. If I'm going to enjoy this, then you have to give a damn."

Emma stared up at him, expressionless.

"Fine, you don't care if you die? Then maybe you'll care if *he* does," said Mac. He hopped off the stage, walked over to Jon, and grabbed him by the arm.

Emma gasped. "No."

Mac dragged him up the stairs and threw him down on the stage right in front of her. Jon shook his head. "Em?" he said, his voice thick with confusion.

Emma scooted closer to him. "Honey, are you okay?"

"Yeah, I guess," he said, resting his head in his hand. "Except for this massive headache. Emma, what the hell is—"

Mac stepped in front of them.

And pointed his gun at Jon.

Jon looked up at him. "Emma," he said, turning back to her. "What did you do?"

Emma's eyes began to tear again. She shook her head. *I'm so sorry, Jon.*

The haze of whatever Jack had done to him lifted from his eyes. It was replaced by a level of outrage Emma hadn't seen in him in a long time. Jon grabbed her by the wrist and yanked her closer. "Damn it, Emma. Do you have some kind of death wish?"

As she stared back at him, unable to answer, Jon glanced briefly toward the back of the stage. For a

193

moment, he seemed not to realize what he'd just seen. Then his shoulders fell. He let go of her wrist and turned his eyes to Jack.

"Jack?" Jon whispered.

Emma started to reach for Jon's arm, but she stopped herself, her hand trembling in mid-air.

Jon looked at Mac. "You bastard."

"I take it he was a friend of yours?" said Mac.

Jon glared. "I swear to you, before this is all over, I am going to kill you myself."

"You know what?" Mac said with a smile. "I think I'll go ahead and shoot her first after all." He turned his gun on Emma.

But Emma looked only at Jon.

Jon, you've got to do something, she pleaded with her eyes.

His jaw was clenched, his cheeks bright red. Emma wasn't sure what was worse. Having a gun pointed at her head, or having Jon look at her the way he was right then.

Then Emma turned to Sam. He was standing next to the surveillance monitors, talking to someone on the phone. She gave him the same pleading expression.

He just stared at her.

Finally, she dropped her shoulders. She had thought she could convince him. She had thought she could stop this. But all she had done was make things worse.

Emma closed her eyes. She listened for the sound of Mac cocking his gun, then realized that she wouldn't hear it. The last sound she was going to hear was the pop of the bullet just before it shattered her skull, if she heard anything at all. Emma wondered if she would be dead before she even noticed.

No, Mac didn't have to cock his gun. He'd already used it to kill one person that day.

And he was about to kill another one.

CHAPTER 26

Sam's eyes darted to the side of the stage as he stepped into the conference room.

Good, Grant was still alive.

But if Grant wasn't the one that Mac shot, then who was?

Sam ran past Dr. Grant, who had stopped just inside the doorway. Out of the corner of his eye he watched her heading slowly for her husband. Sam let her go. Her little scheme was no longer his biggest problem.

Keeping her alive was.

At the back of the stage lay a body, surrounded by a ton of blood. From this angle, all he could see was the soles of an expensive pair of leather shoes, but couldn't tell who they belonged to. He could worry about that later. Right now he had to prevent a second murder.

"Zach, please tell me you found something," said Sam, stopping at the surveillance desk.

"I'm sorry," said Zach. "I'm trying, but there just isn't much."

Sam peered over Zach's shoulder at the screen. "What do you mean there isn't much?" He had found plenty of information about the Grants when he'd looked them up while trying to figure out if they could help Cole.

"Sure, there's tons of stuff about *them*. Him being captured in the war. Coming home to find her in the hospital. Her recovery. The Grant Foundation. Lots of stuff in the newspapers about their story, but nothing specifically about her past. At least, nothing useful. In fact, there are entire periods of her life where she just kind of disappears."

Sam scratched his itchy, sweaty forehead through his mask. He looked over his shoulder to see Mac dragging Dr. Grant up onto the stage. "Zach, please. You've got to get me something. Anything."

"I can get you some of her basic information. Birth certificate. Profile sheets. She did work for the government for a while."

"Whatever you can find. There's got to be something I can use. She's from Texas. Maybe they're from the same friggin' hometown or something."

"All right, man, I'll see what I can do."

Sam jumped up onto the stage. Dr. Grant was leaning over the victim's body, her hand to his neck. The old man's face was sickeningly pale. It was then that Sam recognized who Mac had shot.

My god. We've just killed the vice president of the United States.

"Mac, don't do this," said Sam, taking him by the arm.

Mac pulled away. "We told them if they tried anything, this is what would happen. Do you want them to know we're serious or not?"

Sam looked down at Dr. Grant, who stared blankly across the room with an expression of shock and helplessness. "Is he still alive?"

"Barely," she mumbled without meeting his eyes, as if he wasn't there.

Behind him, the phone rang.

Sam turned to Mac. "Just wait a minute, okay."

Mac glared at him.

Sam hopped down and picked up the phone. "I'm not really in the mood right now, Sanchez."

"We heard a gunshot."

Was that even possible? "Your little friend isn't being particularly compliant, I'm afraid," said Sam. He watched as Mac dragged an oddly apathetic Jonathan Grant up to the stage too.

"Yeah, that sounds about like her," Sanchez said casually.

Sam tightened his jaw. Sanchez cared about what happened to the people in that room about as much as Mac did.

"Look," said Sam, "I thought I said I was through talking to you."

"Now hold your horses there, cowboy. I've found you somebody else to talk to, okay? A Texan. Somebody who 'gives a damn,' as you say."

Up on the stage, Mac had both Dr. Grant and her husband on their knees in front of him, his gun pointed right at her head. Sam swallowed hard. If it came right down to it, would he use force to stop Mac from shooting her? Would he jeopardize everything he'd worked for to save their lives? Or would he let them die?

Sam wasn't sure. He hoped he wouldn't have to find out.

"Hello?" said a voice on the other end of the line.

"Yes?"

"Young man, my name is Richard."

"Nice to meet you, Richard."

"Can I ask your name?"

Sam didn't answer.

"Son, it's hard to trust a man who won't even tell you his name."

"And what difference does it make whether you trust me?"

"Because if you and I are going to work together to get those people out alive, we're going to need to trust each other."

Sam sighed. Finally, someone he could talk to. "Sam. My name is Sam."

"Nice to meet you too, Sam."

"So you're from Texas, Richard?"

"Born and raised."

"You're not one of those bloodsuckers from the FBI, are you?"

"No, Sam, I'm not. I'm a US marshal."

Sam turned back to the Grants. Dr. Grant stared at him pleadingly, her lip trembling, her eyes red. Then her shoulders dropped and she turned her eyes to the floor, almost as if she had accepted the fact she was about to die. It broke Sam's heart to see her just give up like that.

And know he was responsible.

"Sam," Zach whispered.

Sam leaned in and put a hand over the phone. "What've you got, Zach?"

"Not much, just basic information, but maybe there's something here," he answered, pointing at the monitor.

"Let me have it, then," said Sam. He pulled the phone away from his ear.

Zach read the screen. "Emma Grant, born Emma Elizabeth Scott. Originally from Kilgore. Parents: Richard and Narhianna Scott. Graduated from Western Carolina. Height, weight, date of birth, blah, blah, blah."

"Wait, what?" said Sam.

"I know. She's like forty-four. She doesn't look that much older than us, does she?"

"No," said Sam. "I mean her father's name."

"Richard. Richard Scott. He's a retired US marshal or something."

Sam's jaw dropped. He narrowed his eyes at Dr. Grant.

So—her phone call wasn't exactly what she had led him to believe it was. He should have known she was smarter than that. When she told him she had called home, he assumed she'd called her own house, to talk to her kids. But she had called her father. And not just to say goodbye.

To get help.

Sam returned the phone to his ear and curled a lip. "What's your last name, Richard?"

Richard was silent.

"It's hard to trust a man who won't even tell you his last name."

"Scott, Sam. My last name is Scott."

Sam picked up the base of the phone and stepped up onto the stage. He put a hand on Mac's shoulder.

"Richard," he said, loud enough for Dr. Grant to hear him.

Her head snapped up.

"Richard, Sanchez has a friend in here. Hasn't been particularly cooperative. We caught her trying to make a phone call. He doesn't seem to care whether she lives or dies."

Mac eyed Sam, but his gun never wavered from Dr. Grant.

Sam squatted down in front of her. "Do *you* care whether she lives or dies, Richard?"

"Yes, Sam," he answered quietly. "I care very much."

Sam smiled. The cold, hard smile of knowing that he was back in control. "Then perhaps you'd like to say hello."

He held the phone up to her ear. "Why don't you say hi, Doc?"

She glared at him, then turned her eyes to the floor. "Hi, Dad," she said quietly.

Sam jerked the phone away and stood. "You want her alive, Scott? You've got exactly three hours to comply with our demands."

Richard sucked in a sharp breath. "Three hours? Sam, if you're as much of a Texan as I am, you know I can't pull that off in three hours!"

"Three hours, or we start shooting hostages. And I want updates every hour. Is that understood?" Sam had no intention of anyone else getting shot, but knew that he was no longer dealing with a bureaucrat with an agenda. He was dealing with a father trying to save his child's life. Sam knew better than anyone what level of desperation that could drive a man to.

"I understand," said Richard.

"Good. Then I expect to hear from you in an hour."

"Sam, wait. Sanchez said there was a gunshot. Is anyone hurt?"

Sam glanced at Vice President Allred's body. "Yes," he

said quietly, suddenly nauseated. He turned away. "There was an... *incident*."

"Are they still alive?"

"For now."

"Sam, let me send an EMT in to help them."

"Out of the question." It wouldn't matter anyway. Judging by the amount of blood, not even the best physicians in Texas could save Allred now.

"Sam, look. You want me to help you pull this off? You've got to give me something to go on. I can't do this by myself, and I have to convince these guys that the greatest chance of getting those people out alive is to comply. If you start killing hostages, they're just going to cut their losses and try to take you by force. So please, let me send someone in there."

Sam looked over his shoulder. Mac had moved Dr. Grant and her husband against the wall at the back of the stage, by Allred. Dr. Grant knelt next to the vice president, feebly trying to apply pressure to the wound.

Sam sighed. "Fine. You can send in the EMT."

"Thank you, Sam. Maybe you're a better man than I thought."

Sam squared his shoulders. "Three hours, Richard."

"Three hours."

Chapter 27

Richard Scott had exactly two hours and fifty-eight minutes.

The abandoned coffee shop a block up the street from the hotel had been taken over by the FBI for use as a command center. Though what exactly they were "commanding," Richard wasn't sure. The place was chaotic. There were people staring at surveillance monitors, maps and papers spread out across tables, agents on phones, and guys in jackets running this way and that, none of them seeming to get anything accomplished.

Richard grabbed one of them as they rushed by.

"Listen, young man," he said. "One of the hostages has been shot. I need you to find me a negotiator, all right? And get me a couple of EMTs along with him."

The kid stared blankly back at him.

"Go, son," said Richard. "Now!"

The kid ran off, passing Sanchez, who was making his way toward Richard. Richard wondered where in the world Sanchez had disappeared to while he was on the phone with Sam.

"Just like old times, huh, Scott?" said Sanchez, rubbing a belly that seemed even bigger than the last time Richard had worked with the guy.

Richard narrowed his eyes. Sanchez knew darn well this wasn't the type of thing Richard was used to. He'd spent his career chasing down fugitives and protecting court officials, out there on the front lines risking his hide to keep his country and the systems that kept it going safe. Not hiding behind some desk in a cushy DC office getting fat off the taxpayers' dime, like Sanchez. Because unlike Sanchez, Richard actually cared what happened to all those people who had to live outside the protection of those bureaucratic brick walls.

"Oh, that's right," said Sanchez, smiling. "This isn't something you normally do, is it?"

"Look, Sanchez, there is a bomb in that hotel. We're going to have to get everyone out of there as soon as possible."

Sanchez smirked. "A bomb? Where'd you get that intel?"

"Let's just say I have my sources."

"Yeah, and so do I. Tons of them. I have literally

hundreds of pieces of intel pouring into this room every second, and not a single bit of it leads me to believe that there is a bomb anywhere near that hotel. Unless, of course, you've heard something I haven't?"

Richard stared down at the stained concrete, dusty and darkened with grime.

"Oh, wait, I get it," said Sanchez. "Little Miss Crazy Town told you, didn't she?"

Richard sucked in a long, deep breath just to hold himself back from socking the guy right in the nose.

"Oh, stop the presses," said Sanchez, throwing his hands in the air. "Let's notify the American people that we're all going to just lie down and surrender to the will of some crazed terrorist group, all because Emma Grant had one of her freaky little vibes again."

"Look, we don't have time for this! I'm going to need—"

"No, Richard, I don't believe you will. Because, if I'm not mistaken, you're retired. And even if you weren't, I don't recall asking the marshals for help."

"You asked for *my* help, remember? Something about them refusing to do business with you? So it sounds to me like you could use all the help you can get."

"And it sounds to me," said Sanchez, stepping in closer, "like your little girl's in there, and you're willing to make whatever deal it takes to get her out."

So that's what Sanchez had been doing. He'd gone off to listen in on the call—no doubt to catch Richard saying something he could use against him. Typical sleazy Sanchez. The guy probably had surveillance cameras set up in his own house.

Sanchez put a hand on Richard's shoulder. "But hey, it's understandable. I mean, I'm sure I'd do the same thing in your situation. If I, you know, had a daughter. Or any family at all."

"It doesn't really matter anyway, does it?" said Richard. "They're not going to negotiate with you."

"They don't have to. Because from what I understand, Jack Allred's been shot. And in my book, shooting a vice president effectively puts an end to the negotiation process."

Richard's jaw dropped. *Jack?* Sam hadn't mentioned who'd been shot. What made Sanchez think it was Jack Allred?

"As for your help, Scott, I do appreciate it, believe it or not. You've given us exactly what we needed."

"And what is that?"

"Time."

Just then the kid Richard had sent off returned with a couple of guys in EMT uniforms. One was a short Indian kid who couldn't have been more than twenty-five years old or so. His badge read Chris Capitan. The other EMT was nearly twice his age, and had a head full of dark-red curls. His badge said Michael Ashcraft, but Richard knew darn well that wasn't his real name. Because Richard already knew this guy's name.

It was Quinn Larson.

"Sir?" said Quinn, glancing only briefly at Richard before turning to Sanchez.

Richard tried to hold in his satisfaction at seeing Quinn there. And why wouldn't he be there? He was an FBI negotiator, after all, and Quinn and Emma had once been practically inseparable. Just because they'd had a falling out didn't mean he wouldn't still care about her. It was too bad, really. Richard had no idea what had happened, but it had to have been pretty bad for Emma to completely walk away from a guy who'd been her best friend since preschool.

"Yes, Mr. Ashcraft?" said Sanchez. Apparently he didn't know who Quinn really was.

"Sir, we were told that one of the hostages has been shot."

Richard could have kissed him. When Quinn heard that Richard had sent for a negotiator along with the EMTs, he must have caught on to the plan. Posing as an EMT wasn't something a negotiator would normally do, because of the risks involved. If Sam or any of his boys found out Quinn was FBI, they'd probably shoot him on the spot. But it was essential that they get someone on the inside to try to defuse the situation, and Sanchez would probably never go for that. Richard knew that, and apparently Quinn knew that too. Which was why he'd taken it upon himself to sneak in.

Sanchez turned to Richard. "You can't be serious. You're willing to risk sending in *more* potential hostages?"

Richard shrugged. "Hey, it's your operation, remember? I guess if you want to be known as the guy who could have saved the vice president's life, but didn't want to take the chance…"

Sanchez glared. "You boys understand how dangerous this is, right?" he said to Quinn and Chris. "I'm not going to be held responsible if you don't come back out again."

Richard shook his head. How did this guy even get his job?

"We understand, sir," said Quinn. "We just want to help."

Emma sure knew how to pick her friends. Too bad she didn't know how to hold on to them.

"All right, fine. You go do what you have to do. But if anything happens, I just want you to remember whose idea it was to send you in there in the first place." Sanchez looked meaningfully at Richard.

Richard ignored him. "You'll be fine, boys. You just do your jobs the best way you know how, like you always do. And I'm sure your country, and the people you help, will appreciate it."

"Thank you, sir," said Quinn.

Chris simply nodded.

"Well then, gentlemen, what are you doing still standing here?" said Sanchez.

Quinn looked to Richard for confirmation.

Richard nodded. "Good luck, boys."

Quinn and Chris turned and walked out the door, the old coffee shop bell left ringing behind them.

"You too, Scott," said Sanchez.

"Excuse me?"

"Go on. You've served your purpose. Go find a golf course somewhere and let the big boys handle this one."

Richard raised an eyebrow. "You know, one of these days, Sanchez, that arrogance of yours is going to come back to bite you right in the keister."

"Is that a threat, Scott?"

"Of course not." Richard laughed. "Consider it more of a prediction."

"Whatever. Just get out of here." Sanchez turned to go.

"Victor, wait," said Richard, grabbing Sanchez by the arm. "Before you run off, there's something I need to know."

Sanchez stared at Richard's hand on his arm. He didn't say a word until Richard let go. "What?"

"What do you intend to do about that bomb?"

Sanchez scoffed. "There is no bomb in that building. I have absolutely no intention whatsoever of giving these lunatics a single thing they want. And if they don't like that, I'm sorry, but they can shoot every last person in that conference room. The federal government does not yield to terrorists." And with that, Deputy Director Victor

Sanchez turned on his heel and walked away.

"So that's that, I guess," a voice said behind Richard.

Richard turned to find Ephraim standing nearby. He must have stepped in unnoticed.

"That's that," Richard answered.

Ephraim took a deep breath. "You ready?"

"Yep."

And with that, Deputy Marshal Richard Scott and Deputy Marshal Ephraim Grey stopped by the closest table, grabbed a copy of the building plans for the hotel, and slipped out the front door.

CHAPTER 28

It wasn't her fault, Jon.
It wasn't her fault.

It was all Jon could do to keep it together. He sat at the back of the stage, his arms wrapped around his knees, rocking back and forth in an attempt to stop himself from shaking. Lying next to him was the closest thing he'd ever had to a father. The man he'd looked up to more than anyone else in his entire life. Who had accepted him for who he was, even when no one else would.

And that man was about to die.

Jon had seen some pretty disturbing images in his life. Men tortured and beaten. Women and children burned to death. People he'd served with blown to pieces right in front of him. But there was something about Jack lying there on the grey and gold paisley carpet, cold and pale, the life slowly draining from his body, that Jon just couldn't handle.

Damn it, Emma. Why the hell do you feel like you always have to be the hero?

Jon was so mad he wanted to scream. To yell at her about how this never would have happened if she hadn't tried to pull something. But deep down he knew the person he was really angry with was himself. Because the problem wasn't that she had done something—it was that he *hadn't*. He could have stopped all of this from the very moment it began.

But he'd been too worried about her.

Jack's hand lay limp beside his body. Jon wanted so very much to reach out and take it—to hold on to his uncle before he slipped away. But Jon was afraid that Jack would use whatever energy he had left to Push some image of the ocean, or a sunrise, or Christmas, just to comfort him. Because that was the kind of man Jack Allred was. He put others before himself.

Maybe Jon could have done something. Maybe. Maybe not. The truth was, the only time he had ever been able to successfully use his abilities was when it meant keeping Emma out of danger.

And right now, he was too mad at her to care.

"Honey?" Emma whispered.

Jon ignored her.

"Jon," she said, a little louder.

"What?" he snapped under his breath.

She shrank back.

Jon took a deep breath. "What?" he repeated, forcing a softened tone. Judging by the hurt and guilt in her eyes, though, she already knew how angry he was.

"Look," Emma whispered.

She nodded toward the doors of the conference room, where two men in EMT uniforms stood, one of which he recognized immediately. Jon would know that baby-faced, copper-top anywhere.

Was Quinn completely nuts?

"What is this, Hackett?" said Mac to the other leader. The two men waited at the front of the stage, watching the EMTs approach.

So the other one's name is Hackett.

Hackett hopped off the stage without answering.

"We heard someone was shot," said Quinn. He caught Jon's eye, but quickly scanned past him like he didn't exist. Jon didn't care. He knew Emma was the real reason Quinn was there.

"You're the EMTs?" said Hackett.

"Yes," said Quinn. "Who else would we be?"

Hackett glanced over his shoulder at Mac. He looked uncertain.

"Look, pal, I'm just here to make sure that man doesn't die," said Quinn, motioning toward Jack. "And the longer we stand here and wait, the more likely that is to happen."

"Fine," said Hackett. "Go help him."

Jon scooted closer to Jack as Quinn and the EMT neared. It was the first time Jon had gotten a good look at the gaping hole in Jack's chest. A dizzying chill washed over his body in a reminder of how long it had been since he'd last eaten.

Quinn and the other EMT—Chris, his name badge said—knelt on the opposite side of Jack, next to Emma. "Are you all right?" Quinn whispered to her.

"I'm fine," Emma whispered back. "Just help him."

Quinn turned his attention to Jack. "How is he?" he asked Chris.

Chris had his stethoscope out and was listening for a heartbeat. "We need to get him out of here," he said.

"I don't think so," said Mac.

Jon looked up. He hadn't even noticed Mac and Hackett hovering over them.

"Look, it's a miracle he's lasted this long," said Chris. "I can't do anything for him here. We've got to get him to a hospital if there's to be any possibility at all of saving his life."

Mac squatted down next to Jon and stared Chris right in the eyes. "Then here's an idea," he said, curling a lip. "Let him die."

Jon had to restrain himself from beating the hell out of him.

"For heaven's sake, man," Chris pressed. "He's the friggin' vice president. You really want to be known as the guy responsible for his death?"

Hackett knelt next to Emma. "If you get him to a hospital, do you think there's a chance they can save his life?" he asked Chris.

"A better chance than he'd have lying here, I can tell you that."

Jon wanted to scream. Or cry. He wasn't sure which.

"Please," said Emma. She put her hand on Hackett's. "Please don't let him die just because I screwed up."

Hackett studied Emma. He sighed. "All right," he said quietly. "You can take him."

"Thank you."

"*What?*" Mac exploded. "Have you lost your mind? You really think I'm just going to let them walk out of here with one of my hostages?"

"*Your* hostages?" said Hackett.

"Yes, *my* hostages. You lost any say in this operation the minute you got cozy with the doctor over there."

Jon tensed. *What the* hell *does that mean?*

"What if I stayed?" said Quinn. "If it saves Vice President Allred's life, then let him go, and I'll stay here in his place."

"No," Hackett snapped.

"What do you mean, no?" said Mac.

"I mean *no*. The vice president leaves. *Both* the EMTs go with him."

Mac narrowed his eyes. "If you're going to let one of the hostages go, why can't we keep that guy in his place?"

Hackett erupted on Mac. "Because I don't *want* him here! And to be honest with you, Mac, I don't give a damn what you think. This is still my operation, and you are going to do exactly as I say. Is that understood?"

Mac took a long, deep breath. It reminded Jon of the wind blowing through an old organ in an abandoned church. One of those mid-century gothic things that makes the hair on the back of your neck stand up.

"All right," Mac said coldly. "We'll do it your way. If Sanchez doesn't call back in the next thirty minutes—if they don't meet the timelines that *you* set down for them—then I am going to do *exactly* what you told them we'd do. I'm going to start shooting hostages. And I'll begin with your little friend over there." He pointed at Emma. "And if that means I have to shoot both you and the tough guy over here"—Mac nodded toward Jon—"then so be it. I'm getting sick and tired of these games."

He shouldered his rifle, stood, and headed to the surveillance monitors.

Chris stepped away to retrieve the stretcher he and Quinn had wheeled in with them.

"Okay. Does somebody want to explain to me what is going on?" said Jon under his breath. Why was everyone suddenly acting like they knew each other, and what did Mac mean about Hackett getting cozy with his wife?

"Yeah, that's what I'd like to know," Quinn said to Hackett. "Why don't you just let me stay? That guy doesn't exactly seem like the type you'd want to piss off. Besides, I'm an EMT. I could help if there's trouble again."

"Because, *Agent Larson*," Hackett replied, rubbing his masked forehead, "you're about as much of an EMT as I am a terrorist."

Quinn stared at him, wide-eyed. "I'm sorry, have we met?"

"Sam," said Emma, putting her hand on his again. "This has gone far enough. Don't you see there's no way you're going to be able to keep any of us from getting hurt?"

Seeing Emma's hand on Hackett's burned Jon up inside. And how in the world did she know his first name? "Well," he said coldly, "now that we've established that we're all buddy-buddy, can we please get back to what's really important? Like keeping Jack alive."

"It's nice to know I haven't been forgotten," Jack whispered softly.

Jon leaned toward him. "Uncle Jack?"

Jack barely even opened his eyes. His face was so pale it looked like something out of a horror movie. "Son?"

Jon was terrified that whatever words were about to come out of Jack Allred's mouth would be his last. But when Jack did speak, it wasn't to Jon.

It was to Hackett.

"Young man," he said, taking Hackett's other hand.

Jon's eyes burned into Hackett. *This* was the guy about to use up whatever few precious moments Jack had left?

"Yes, sir?" said Hackett.

"He isn't going to let *any* of you out of here alive," said Jack, so quietly Hackett had to lean in closer. "You know that, don't you?"

Hackett shook his head. "Everything is going to be all right, Mr. Vice President. These guys are going to get you out of here and get you all fixed up, okay?"

"No!" said Jack, suddenly jerking himself upright.

Jon slipped an arm behind his back to support him. He couldn't believe that Jack even had the strength to move.

"Everything is *not* going to be all right! Don't you see that now?" said Jack, his pale cheeks flushing with the slightest hint of red.

Hackett glanced uncertainly between Jon and Emma.

"How many have to die before you get that through your head, son? What happens to me doesn't matter anymore. This convention doesn't even matter anymore. *Nothing* matters now except keeping Jon and Emma alive, and *he's* not about to let that happen. He *will not* let that happen. Do you hear me?"

Jack broke into a fit of coughing and sank back down to the floor.

"Uncle Jack, please don't," said Jon.

But Jack ignored him. "You've got to make me a promise, young man. You've got to stop this. You've got to put an end to it right now, before things get any worse. Can you promise me you'll do that, Sam? Can you promise me you will keep Jon and Emma safe? That you'll do whatever it takes to get them out of here?" He added, slow and raspy, "Consider it a dying man's last request."

Hackett still didn't respond. He just stared blankly at Jack.

Jon's eyes burned. He sucked in slow breaths, his anger the only thing keeping him from breaking down completely. Emma's hand still rested on Hackett's, and it ate at him. Badly. Not because Jon was jealous—he'd learned long ago that her strange affinity for people was always more benevolent—but because it represented everything that had ever infuriated him about Emma. Because her own husband's uncle was lying here dying, and she was still attempting to console some guy she hardly knew.

Because she still thought she could save everyone.

Hackett noticed Jon staring. He pulled his hand away from Emma's.

Chris returned to the stage, pulling the stretcher

behind him. He slapped Quinn on the shoulder and nodded to Jon. "You two, help me get him onto the stretcher."

"No," said Jack. "Not yet."

Chris's jaw dropped. He was clearly as amazed by Jack's sudden recuperation as Jon was.

"So what's it going to be, Sam?" said Jack. "Will you give me your word? You'll do whatever it takes to keep them alive?"

Hackett met Jon's eyes. For a moment the two men glared at each other, both just as straight-faced and unforgiving as the other.

"We are the choices we make, Sam," Emma said quietly. She rested a hand on Hackett's shoulder.

He turned to her. A look of sincere vulnerability washed across her face—an expression she'd normally only share with Jon, when she was being completely open with him about how scared or upset or worried she was. Like the night before the convention. And it was a look even he didn't see very often.

"Sam," Emma continued, "I don't want to die. But that's not up to me. It's up to you. Please don't be the reason Jon and I never see our children again."

Hackett turned his eyes down to the bandage covering Jack's chest. He stared at it as blood seeped through it with each of Jack's labored breaths, like fire ants pouring from a dilapidated anthill.

Then something in Hackett's expression changed. His mouth softened. His shoulders sank. He closed his eyes and dropped his head. This wasn't at all the look Jon had been watching for since Jack took Hackett's hand—the look of a man being Pushed into something. It was the look of a man who'd been thoroughly convinced he knew exactly what he was getting himself into.

And who'd realized he was wrong.

"Yes, Mr. Vice President," said Hackett. "You have my word."

Jack closed his eyes. "Thank you," he said. "Thank you."

"Okay," said Chris. "If you're all done now, do you mind if I finish trying to save his life?"

Jon and Quinn helped lift Jack up onto the stretcher. Jon stayed with Jack as long as he could, gripping his hand as Quinn and Chris rolled the stretcher across the stage and carried it down the steps to the floor below.

Jon wanted his uncle to say something, anything,

before they parted for what would likely be the last time. But Jack didn't speak. He didn't even move. He just lay there, his eyes closed, with the most serene, peaceful look on his face that Jon had ever seen. As if Jack had managed to complete his final objective in life and was now ready to move on.

Jon tightened his grip on Jack's hand. "I'm so sorry, Uncle Jack."

Finally, Jack spoke. "It isn't your fault, son," he whispered. "And it isn't hers, either. This was my choice. I want you to know that. I want you to remember that in the end, I chose you." Jack turned his head toward Jon and opened his eyes. A tear rolled down his cheek. "Because I believe in you."

The image of Jack's familiar face was blurred by the tears welling in Jon's eyes.

Mac stepped in front of the stretcher as they neared the conference room doors. "That's far enough, Grant," he said, motioning toward the wall with his gun. "Sit down."

Jon didn't argue. He returned to his seat between Aaron and Rachael, who he was sure had been watching him from the moment he left their side, waiting for some cue to jump up and do something. But that cue hadn't come, and likely never would, because Jon was now even more lost and heartbroken than before.

Emma stood on the stage, staring after Jack. Quinn looked back at her, his forehead wrinkled. Her expression remained unchanged, as if she refused to even acknowledge that he'd ever been there at all. Eventually, Quinn stopped looking.

Rachael took Jon's hand.

Jon was grateful for the gesture.

"We're going to get out of here, Jon," said Aaron. "Even if it means Mac has to take on all four of us. We're not going to let them get away with this."

"All *five* of us," said Bennett, leaning over Aaron. "I may be many things, Mr. Grant, but I'm not heartless. They'll get what's coming to them in the end, I assure you."

Maybe Stephen Bennett wasn't as out for blood as Jon had thought he was. At least Bennett had never killed someone he loved right in front of him. Not yet, anyway.

Emma came down the steps and took a seat on the other side of Rachael. But Jon kept his eyes on Hackett. The guy just stared at the floor, at the bloodstain on the carpet. Then, as if sensing Jon's eyes on him, Hackett looked up.

Again, the two men stared at each other, but this time their expressions weren't hard or unrelenting.

They were grave and broken.

"What do we do now, Jon?" said Emma.

Jon didn't answer. He knew the question now wasn't what *they* were going to do.

The real question was whether or not Sam Hackett was a man of his word.

Chapter 29

Dr. Grant had been right. He was about to get them all killed.

Sam couldn't get the image of Allred out of his head. Every time he closed his eyes it was there, like a scene from the very first horror movie he ever watched. The one he knew he was entirely too young to see but his parents let him anyway. The sight of Allred lying there, blood pouring from his chest, had played through his mind for the last half hour, until it was no longer Jack Allred he saw.

It was Emma Grant.

"They're late, Hackett," said Mac.

Sam willed the phone to ring. As if by simply ringing it would solve all his problems. But he knew that wasn't true. Even if Sanchez or Richard Scott or whoever called, it wouldn't change anything. The fact of the matter was, Mac was determined to see the Grants dead.

And Sam had a feeling he was going to get his way.

Sam squared his shoulders. "You're right, they are."

"So what are you going to do about it?"

Sam pulled his gun from where it hung over his shoulder. "Exactly what I said I'd do."

Mac followed as Sam walked over to the Grants. They stopped just in front of Dr. Grant, their figures overshadowing her like a child beneath an oak tree.

"Dr. Grant," said Sam. "Stand up."

"Sam?"

"Now."

She stood.

"You too, Grant."

Grant just sat there, his arms resting on his knees, staring across the room.

Mac grabbed him by the arm and pulled him up. "The man told you to get up!"

It figured Mac would finally show Sam some support once he thought he was about to kill someone.

"All right, let's go, you two," said Sam.

"No!" barked the man who had been sitting next to Grant—Rachael Dallin's husband. He jumped to his feet.

Stephen Bennett jumped up too. "We're not going to just sit back and watch you kill them the way you did Vice President Allred."

"Oh yeah, tough guy?" said Mac, pointing his gun at Dallin. "And how exactly are you going to stop us if you're already dead?"

"Wait," said Sam, putting his hand on Mac's gun. "Not here. Let me take them to another room."

Mac narrowed his eyes. "Why?"

"For the same reason you never should have shot Allred! Because of this," said Sam, nodding toward Bennett and Dallin. "Because if you shoot them in front of the other hostages, what's to stop them from rising up? Right now, they still think they have a chance of getting out of here alive. But if you start killing off their friends right in front of them, they'll have nothing to lose."

Mac crossed his arms, then nodded.

"I will take them out of here and deal with them myself," Sam continued. "That way the other hostages have no idea whether they're alive or dead, which will make them even more terrified to try something. It will also eliminate the ones who've been such a problem in the first place." He glared at the Grants.

Then he called for Zach, who was still behind the surveillance monitors.

Zach jumped up and ran over.

"Forward any calls to the front desk. I'll take them down there."

"Yeah, sure thing, buddy," said Zach.

"And you three are coming with us too," Sam told Bennett and the Dallins.

Rachael Dallin's husband pulled her to her feet.

"Why?" she asked.

Sam smiled. "Because thanks to your husband's lame attempt to be a hero, you've all just volunteered to be next in line after I'm done dealing with the Grants."

Sam noticed Mac open his mouth as if he were about to protest, suspicion showing clearly in his eyes.

"Rat!" Sam shouted.

Rat stood nearby, pretending to hover over some of the hostages in a sad attempt to listen in. "Yeah, boss?"

"You're coming too." Sam turned toward the door.

Mac grabbed him by the arm and whispered. "No funny business, Hackett. You put an end to them now and stop jerking around."

Sam yanked his arm away. "Consider them already gone."

Chapter 30

Jon followed behind Hackett, glaring so intently at the back of his head that it was a wonder it didn't explode. Perhaps if he concentrated hard enough, Hackett's head would pop like a watermelon wrapped in a thousand rubber bands. Jon doubted it, though. With as high as his blood pressure was, his own head was more likely to blow first.

Emma walked beside him through the prefunction area outside the conference room, every so often glancing over at him. He felt guilty for how he'd treated her. He shouldn't have gotten so upset with her. He knew she felt responsible enough as it was.

It had become clear to him now, though, that Jack had arranged the entire incident. For what purpose, Jon wasn't sure. To give Emma the chance to make that phone call? To get Jon worked up enough to do something? To convince Hackett that things weren't going to turn out as he'd planned? There was no way of knowing what Jack had been thinking, or whether he knew his plan would get him killed.

And Jon was never going to get the chance to ask him.

"I'm sorry, Em," he said. "Things are bad enough without me biting your head off. I'm sorry I snapped at you earlier."

"You had every right to," she told the floor.

"No, I didn't. I was upset about Jack, but that's no excuse to take it out on you. Can you forgive me for being a jerk?" Jon held out a hand.

She took it and smiled. "Considering we're about to be shot, how could I possibly not forgive you?"

"Good," said Jon. He raised his voice at the back of Hackett's head. "Because I would hate to die thinking you were mad at me."

"Oh, you people make me sick," said Rat. "Will you just shut up and walk?"

"Don't pay any attention to him, Jon," Aaron said from behind him. "He's just upset because ol' Sammy up there is about to shoot the woman of his dreams."

Bennett laughed. "Well, isn't that pathetic? Don't you have children older than him, Grant?"

Jon wasn't sure if that was an insult about how young Rat was or how old Jon was.

"I mean it!" said Rat, his voice shaky. "Shut up or I'm

going to pop you right in the back of the head!"

Bennett stopped suddenly and turned around. "I would just like to see you try, young man. Do you have any idea who I am?"

"No, and frankly I don't give a crap."

Hackett stopped too. He stepped between Jon and Emma and walked straight up to Rat. "That's enough, Rat. Knock it off."

"What?" said the kid. "You heard them, boss. I'm the one with the gun. I'm not just going to stand here and let them talk to me like that."

Hackett leaned in, inches from Rat's face. "I said that's enough. I don't care if they call your mother a trailer park tramp, you're not shooting a single one of them. Is that understood?"

"Why not? They're all about to die anyway. What difference does it make if you shoot 'em or I do?"

"I just told you, you're not shooting anyone," Hackett answered coldly.

Rat's fingers trembled against the trigger of his gun.

Jon pulled Emma closer to him.

"You want to know what I think?" said Rat. "I don't think you have any intention of killing anybody. I think you've gone soft."

"You want to see how soft I've gone?" said Hackett, raising his gun at Rat.

Jon watched Aaron pull Rachael behind him. Aaron nodded toward a hallway to their left. Jon nodded back. He wasn't sure exactly where it went, but it would be their best bet if things went south. And judging by the panicky look in Rat's eyes, that's exactly where they were headed.

"You won't do it," said Rat. "You couldn't even handle watching that old guy die. What makes you think you could kill a man in cold blood?"

"What, a creepy little pervert like you?" said Hackett, pressing his gun into Rat's chest. "It would be tough, but I think I could stomach it."

Jon wrapped an arm around Emma and pulled her into his shoulder. She looked up at him and shook her head. He knew she was still convinced she could talk Hackett out of this, but Jon didn't have the kind of faith in people she did. There was entirely too much at stake to rely on the conscience of a guy who wasn't afraid to hold hundreds of people hostage. If Jon had to, he'd throw her over his shoulder and carry her down the hall kicking and screaming.

Jon turned to look for Bennett. He didn't care for the guy, but he wasn't about to run off and leave him.

Apparently, Bennett didn't feel the same way about him.

"Hey," Jon said before he could catch himself. "Where's Bennett?"

It was enough to stop Hackett and Rat from arguing. They turned toward him.

Great, thought Jon. He wanted to kick himself.

Hackett looked around. "Where'd he go?"

"Beats me," said Aaron. "Honestly, we were just about to run off ourselves."

Why in the world would you actually tell him that? Jon thought.

"Oh really?" said Hackett. "And exactly which way were you planning on going?"

Aaron looked at the floor. "Through that hallway," he said, pointing back toward the prefunction area—the complete opposite direction of where they were planning to go.

Jon had to commend Aaron on his integrity. Even though Bennett was a sleazebag who cared more about himself than everyone else, Aaron was still trying to give him half a chance to get away. Jon wasn't so sure he would have done the same.

Hackett turned to Rat. "Go follow him," he said, nodding toward the stairs.

"But that guy just said he went back the other way."

"And you believe him?"

"Well… no, I guess not."

"Then go."

Rat didn't move. "What are you going to do?"

"What do you *think* I'm going to do?" Hackett grabbed Rat by the arm and shoved him forward. "I'm going to take them to the front desk."

"All right, fine," said Rat, heading toward the stairs. "But don't shoot them without me. And I personally think we should pop that guy first," he added, pointing at Jon.

Jon glared at him.

Hackett didn't move, didn't even appear to breathe, until Rat was completely out of sight. Then he took one long, deep breath and let it out slowly.

"All right, let's go," he said, motioning toward the hall.

Jon wrinkled his forehead. Was Hackett for real? There were four of them and only one of him now. What made him think they were just going to follow him to their death, even if he did have a gun?

Emma winked at Jon before turning toward the hallway. Aaron and Rachael followed her.

"Come on, Cap," said Hackett. "Get moving."

Jon started walking.

As they moved, Jon dug his fingernails into his palms, infuriated with himself for having ruined what quite possibly was their only chance to escape. *It wasn't your fault*, Jack had told him. But how could any of it not be? How could he have agreed to let Emma come here in the first place? To have let it all go on for this long? To have just sat there and watched someone he loved be gunned down right in front of him?

Then Jon realized Jack was right. None of this was his fault.

It was Hackett's.

He whipped around, grabbed Hackett by the shirt, and shoved him. Hackett's gun fell to the floor, the clank of metal against tile muffled by the crack of Hackett's body slamming hard into the wall.

Aaron quickly picked up the gun and pointed it at Hackett.

"Jon, please, stop!" said Emma. "Can't you see he's trying to help us?"

Jon tightened his grip on Hackett's shirt and pushed him up the wall. The guy squirmed and gasped under the intense pressure of Jon's forearm against his chest. "Help us?" said Jon. "Emma, he's going to kill us! How exactly is that helping us?"

"He's not going to kill us," she said, putting her hand on his arm. "You're just going to have to trust him, Jon. Please!"

Jon could feel his heart beating inside his temples. He stared right through Hackett, knowing he could break the guy. Crack every bone and burst every blood vessel, until Hackett was no more than a bruised and battered mess. Until *he* was the one lying on the floor bleeding to death.

The way Jack was.

"Jon?" Emma said quietly beside him.

Jon forced himself to look at her.

"You're just going to have to trust *me*."

The white-hot flame of rage burned inside him in a way he hadn't felt in a very long time. He wanted to rip Hackett apart. To make him hurt as much as he was hurting. He wanted the guy to know his pain.

Jon tried to focus on that rage. Tried to remind himself that he was in control of it, and not the other way around.

He wiped the sweat from his brow and answered as calmly as he could. "Emma, do you remember when I told you that sometimes you just need to walk away? Well, now would be one of those times."

"I'm sorry, Jon," she answered. "But I can't do that."

His arm shook against Hackett's chest. "Look, you're asking me to trust him? How exactly do you expect me to trust a guy when I can't even see his face?"

Emma turned to Hackett. "Sorry, Sam, he has a point." She reached for the top of his ski mask and pulled it off in one brisk tug.

Jon's jaw dropped. "The waiter?" he said, stepping back.

Hackett crumpled to the floor, breathing hard and clutching his chest. "Jeez, Grant. You're even stronger than you look."

Jon narrowed his eyes. "You have no idea."

"Sam, are you okay?" said Emma, dropping to the floor beside him. "For God's sake, Jon, you could have broken his ribs."

Jon looked away. *One could only hope.*

"I'm confused," said Aaron. "Whose side are you on again?" he asked Hackett.

"I don't know about sides," Hackett said as Emma helped him up. "All I know is that I told Vice President Allred I'd get the two of them out of here, and that's exactly what I intend to do."

"See, Jon?" said Emma. "I told you he was going to help us."

Jon turned open-mouthed to Aaron. Aaron just shrugged.

"I could be wrong," said Rachael, "but I think he's telling the truth."

Jon looked at the ceiling and shook his head. Every single one of them had lost their friggin' mind.

"We'd better get moving," said Emma. "Eventually someone is going to notice that he didn't take us to the front desk."

Jon crossed his arms. "So some guy makes you dinner and all of a sudden you trust his judgment over mine?"

"No, it's not like that."

"Then tell me, Emma, what is it like?" He grabbed her by the arm, a little bit harder than he should have, and pulled her aside. "Exactly what is it with you and this guy?" he whispered.

"I feel sorry for him," she said. "He has a son. A three-year-old. Who was born with the same heart defect as Matt. Can you even imagine what that would be like nowadays? He's just scared and desperate and doesn't know what to do."

"Oh, Emma," said Jon. "That still doesn't excuse what he's done."

"I know that. It's just…" Emma looked back at the others. Aaron still had the gun pointed at Hackett. "He's a good man, Jon," she said. "Even good men make mistakes sometimes. And sometimes, you have to give them the chance to make up for it."

Jon rubbed a hand across his face, half ready to strangle her. *Oh my god, woman! You're going to be the death of me.*

"Hey, I don't mean to interrupt, guys," Aaron called over, "but whether he's helping us or not, Emma's right. We can't just stand here. They're going to come looking for us."

"If you're serious about getting us out of here," said Jon, stepping up to Hackett, "then how exactly do you intend to do it?"

"The same way *we* were planning on getting out of here," Hackett answered. "Through the subway. There's a sky bridge on both this floor and the one below us. It's connected to the old convention center across the street. Beneath it is an access point for the subway system. The city closed that section down during the war because of a bombing, but it should be cleared out just enough to make it a few blocks."

Jon glanced at Aaron.

"But I know what you're thinking, Grant, and you're going to need my help getting there," he added. "The sky bridge is guarded pretty heavily on both floors. This floor has a bunch of Mac's guys on it, but I know the guys downstairs. If we can get down there and make it across, I can talk them into letting us pass." He raised an eyebrow at Aaron. "Though I seriously doubt I'd get the chance if I walked up on them with a gun pointed at me."

Jon looked to Emma. She nodded.

"Look, Grant, I know you don't trust me. I can't fix what happened to Allred. But what I *can* do is keep the promise I made to him. You can shoot me right here and now, and I wouldn't blame you for it. But I don't think you will. Because I don't think these people would have risked their lives to keep you safe unless you were a better man than that. And I also don't think you'd let Allred die in vain because you were too proud to accept my help. Because that's exactly what you'd be doing if you don't."

Jon clenched his jaw, hating what he was about to do. "Aaron," he said. "Give him his gun back."

"Are you sure?" said Aaron.

"No, but I don't guess we have much choice, do we? How many guys you got spread out through here, Hackett?"

"Fifty, at least."

"Well, then, there you go," said Jon.

"Jeez, fifty?" said Rachael. "Are we even going to make it out of here?"

"Oh, you'll make it out of here," said Hackett, taking the gun from Aaron. "I made Allred a promise, and I never go back on my word."

"And I suppose you expect us to thank you?" said Jon.

"No," said Hackett, pulling a nine-millimeter out of the holster at his ankle and slapping it into Jon's hand. "I don't."

Chapter 31

They were running out of time. Emma could feel it.

Foreboding was no longer a strong enough word for the heaviness that settled into her chest. The word now was dread. Like that long walk down the hall to the principal's office. Or to face your parents. Or your boss. When you're about to come face to face with the vast accumulation of many, many bad choices. Some of them yours. Some of them not.

None of them ending well.

"Hey, are you okay?"

Emma turned, expecting the question to have come from Jon, who had asked her that more in the last few months than he had in the last few years. It was hard to tell who was talking to her just by the voice, though. Emma had disappeared into a fog. Everything was hollow and echoey, like their footsteps in the empty stairwell as they made their way downstairs. But Jon was half a flight in front of her with Sam and Aaron, waiting at the door that led out onto the second floor. He'd gone into combat mode, and how she felt was now most likely the furthest thing from his mind.

"Emma," said Rachael, putting a hand on her arm. "I asked if you were okay."

"I'm fine." Emma struggled to focus. Why was it so dark in this stairwell anyway?

"I think the power's out," said Jon, as if to answer her question. He had cracked the door and was peering out.

"Another blackout?" Rachael asked.

"Most likely Sanchez," said Emma. "Knowing him, he's cut the power." She hugged herself in an attempt to pull it together. For some reason, despite putting her blazer back on, she was suddenly freezing.

"Does that take away their advantage then?" Aaron asked.

"That would be the idea," said Emma. "But something tells me Mac probably prepared for it."

"Yes, unfortunately for us, he did," said Sam. "There are backup generators on all our surveillance systems. The hallways will be darker though. That might help some."

"All right, Hackett," said Jon. He slipped the handgun into the back of his pants and pulled his jacket down over it. Emma knew it probably killed him not to have it out, but if they were going to get through Sam's men, he didn't have much choice. "Our lives are in your hands. I hope you know what you're doing."

Sam looked back at Emma. "Yeah, me too."

As they slipped out into the hallway, Emma realized that it was the first time she had even been on this side of the second floor. The layout was like the floor above them, with a long open hallway that ran across the entire front of the hotel. There was a line of boardrooms to their right and floor-to-ceiling windows to their left, framing what was usually a brightly-lit city of Dallas. Right now, though, most of it was completely dark. She wondered if there were snipers on the roofs of other buildings, but then decided all the other buildings must be too far away.

"Not really," said Jon.

Emma hadn't realized he was right beside her. "What?"

"The snipers. You'd be surprised from how far away, and with how little light, they can hit their target."

"And how did you know that's what I was thinking about?"

"Because I know you," he answered. "Because from the minute we stepped into this situation you started running every worst-case scenario you could possibly think of. We've been together for over twenty years, Em. If I can't read your mind by now, then what good am I?"

Emma smiled. She only wished her head was clear enough to have been running through scenarios this whole time. "I see. So what am I thinking right now?"

"That we're not going to make it out of here."

Emma stopped smiling.

They were coming up on the alcove with the elevators. Past that was a bend in the hallway where the entire building curved to the right. The hall was narrowed by a floor-to-ceiling stone partition that ran perpendicular to the windows, creating a sitting area beneath the large staircase just beyond. It was hard to see any further, but if anyone was going to stop them, it would likely be there.

"And?" she said.

"And I refuse to accept that."

Sam was walking in the lead, about twenty feet in front of them. He suddenly held up a hand, then crept back to the others. They darted inside the doorway of one of the boardrooms.

"What?" Jon asked in a low voice.

"I saw something."

"What do you mean, you saw something?"

"A figure. Just around the corner by the elevators."

"One of yours?"

"Most likely. Though I can't guarantee they're friendly. I know the guys stationed over by the sky bridge at the end of the hall, but this may be a patrol—in which case, it's one of the guys Mac brought in."

"So, what you're saying is you're not so sure you can get us past him?"

"I have no idea whether Rat has made it back to base or what Mac has communicated to the patrols by now."

Jon and Aaron exchanged glances. Jon pulled out his gun. "Let me and Aaron go, then."

"Why?" Sam asked.

"Because if it *is* one of Mac's guys, and you go rushing in there with your gun pulled on him, then the jig is up and they're going to know you've turned on them. But if Aaron and I go, then you can always say we overpowered you. It may give us the opportunity to figure out something else later."

"Or give Mac the opportunity to shoot you himself," said Sam.

"Maybe. And if that happens, I don't care if you have to use yourself as a human shield, you *will* get the girls out of here. Is that understood?"

Sam looked at Emma. "Yes."

"Good." Jon took the rifle from Sam and handed it to Aaron. "Stay with him, Em."

Emma shifted closer to Sam. He offered her his arm, and she was grateful for the gesture. Her head was so fuzzy it was all she could do to walk straight.

"Hey," said Jon, cocking his gun. "That doesn't require physical contact."

Sam pulled his arm away. "Fine. Protect her, but don't touch her. I get it."

Jon turned to Aaron. "You know how to use that thing?"

"Aim and pull the trigger?"

"Pretty much."

"I'm not so sure this is such a good idea, Jon," said Emma.

"Hey, if I can't protect my own wife…"

"… then what good are you?"

Jon grinned. "Exactly."

As he and Aaron disappeared around the corner, Emma wrapped her arms around herself and scooted between the wall and Sam's back, partially for the warmth, partially for balance. Her heart was pounding inside her head, and the dimness of the hallway, lit only faintly by the light of the moon, wasn't helping her dizziness. She wanted to tell herself that she wasn't sure why she felt so bad, but that would be a lie. Her anxiety was getting progressively more severe. Something was wrong—wrong in a way that was even worse than having your life threatened by a group of deranged terrorists.

Emma didn't even want to think about what that meant.

"Sam," she whispered. "Can you see anything?"

Sam peered around the doorframe. "No, not really. Just give them a minute, okay? Given what he just did to me back there, I'm pretty sure your husband can handle himself."

Emma rested her head on the wall as another wave of dizziness washed over her. "You're certainly right about that."

"I'm sorry, by the way."

"For what?"

"For this. All of this. I never meant for any of this to happen. I never meant for anyone to get hurt. Especially Vice President Allred. You know he tipped me a hundred bucks at that dinner you guys had together the other night? Then the next day he came up to my room and personally thanked me for making sure that you and your husband were taken care of after you stormed out. He was a really nice guy. He didn't deserve to meet his end the way he did."

"Jack was alive when they wheeled him out of here. He might still make it," said Emma.

"Dr. Grant, I could tell that you guys were pretty close, but there's no point in holding on to false hope."

Emma tightened her jaw. "There's no such thing as false hope."

Beside her, Rachael whispered, "They're coming back."

Emma stepped quietly around Sam to peek down the hall. Sure enough, past the elevators, three dark figures were headed toward them.

Sam searched for what Emma could only guess was another gun holstered somewhere beneath his vest. She took a deep breath and held it, waiting for the figures to get close enough to know whether the stranger was friendly. Even in the darkness, she could pick out Jon and Aaron. But the third figure...

"Oh my gosh, E, am I glad to see you!" Emma rushed out into the hall and threw her arms around Ephraim's neck.

He squeezed her tight, so tall he lifted her up off the floor. "Come on now, Emmy. You didn't think the old man would leave the two of you to deal with this mess on your own, now, did you?"

"And believe me, no one's more grateful than we are," said Jon. "But I'm not so sure sending someone in was a good idea. If we hadn't already been on our way out, there's no way you would have been able to get to us."

"What do you mean?" said Ephraim. "Richard didn't send me in to get you. I'm here to defuse the bomb."

Emma's heart dropped. She put a hand on the wall to steady herself.

"What bomb?" said Rachael.

"Yeah, Emma," added Jon. "What bomb?"

Emma only faintly heard them. "If Dad sent you in, I take it he isn't in charge anymore."

Ephraim shook his head. "No. And Sanchez has absolutely no intention of complying with their demands."

"Then what *does* he intend to do?" Aaron asked.

"I don't know. All he said was something about Richard buying him some time."

Emma sucked in long, calculated breaths. She was determined not to slip into a panic attack.

"I don't understand," Sam said quietly. "Mac talked about using a bomb as leverage in case they decided to storm the building, but I refused to allow it. What makes you think he planted it anyway?"

"Because," Emma answered, her lip shaking. She raised her eyes to meet Jon's. "Because I saw it."

Jon rubbed a hand across his mouth and turned away.

"Wait," said Rachael. "If Sanchez used Richard to buy him more time, then that suggests Sanchez is going to try to take the terrorists by force. And if there's a bomb…"

"… then Mac will blow this entire place sky high," Sam finished.

"Unless we do something about it," Emma added.

"*No,*" Jon snapped. The intensity in his voice made them all turn. "Now that's enough, Emma."

"Jon, there are over three hundred people in this building!"

Jon stepped in closer to her, pushing Sam away. He rested a hand on the frosted-glass wall beside her head and leaned in. "I don't care," he said quietly. "This is not our fight, and we are not getting involved. Do I make myself *absolutely* clear?"

Emma's anger temporarily pushed aside the knot in the pit of her stomach. "Jon, you know as well as I do the unlikelihood Ephraim can stop that bomb from going off on his own. I've *seen* it. But if we help him—if *you* help him—there's a chance we can still save everyone."

"Wait a minute," said Aaron, staring wide-eyed at Jon's hand. At Jon's ring, judging by the look on his face. "You're the—"

Jon shot a dangerous glare at Aaron.

Aaron shut his mouth.

Jon handed the gun to Sam. "We're leaving, Aaron," he said, his jaw set. "Now."

He headed down the hallway toward the sky bridge. Aaron and Rachael followed. Sam, with an uncertain look at Emma, trailed after them.

"Look, Emmy, maybe Jon's right," said Ephraim. "Maybe you should just—"

Ephraim didn't get to finish his sentence. There was a burst of gunfire, and he crumpled to the floor.

"Ephraim!" Emma screamed, dropping down beside him. Shattered glass rained down from bullets hitting the wall above her head. She felt a sharp pain in her back.

Sam grabbed her by the arm and pulled her away. "Dr. Grant, come on!" he yelled.

"But what about Ephraim?" she said. Or at least, she thought she did. Between the gunshots, the shouting, and the intense ringing in her head, it was hard to tell.

Jon darted into a doorway and fired back up the hall. Mac's men took cover in a sitting area by the stairwell. With Jon laying down cover fire, Aaron grabbed Ephraim and dragged him after Sam and Emma.

The dizziness and nausea took over again. Emma wanted to be sick.

"Jon!" she shouted, kicking and fighting against Sam, who had wrapped an arm around her waist and was dragging her down the hall, away from Mac's men.

"Let's go, Grant!" Sam yelled at Jon.

Jon stepped out from the doorway and fired again at Mac's men, taking one of them down. The others fell back.

"We've got to get out of here before they call for backup," Jon yelled as he ran toward them.

Sam froze in his tracks. "I think it's a little late for that," he said.

A dozen of Mac's men poured from a stairwell thirty feet in front of them.

Jon grabbed Emma by the wrist and dragged her into the sitting area beneath the staircase leading to the third floor, leaving her on a bench before joining Sam and Aaron behind a stone planter. Rachael helped Ephraim into the relative safety of the sitting area and dropped beside him. He pulled the duffel that hung across his chest over his head and unzipped the bag.

Emma grabbed her shoulder as a white-hot pain shot across her collar. That's when she noticed the blood all over her jacket.

She had been shot.

In the course of her career, Emma had been broken and bruised in more ways than she could remember, but she'd never been shot before.

"Jon!" she tried to shout, but could only manage a whimper.

Somehow Jon heard her anyway. He rushed back to her and passed his gun to Rachael, who knelt beside Ephraim, helping him wrap his leg.

"Just try to buy us some time, okay?" Jon said to Rachael.

Rachael nodded. She shoved Jon's gun in her waistband, then grabbed Ephraim's gun, as well as a handful of extra clips from his bag, before joining Sam and Aaron by the side of the escalators.

"Jon," Emma whimpered as he knelt in front of her, the warmth of her tears even more noticeable against her cool cheeks.

Jon put a hand on her face. "Emma, honey, listen to me. You've been hit. I'm going to have to take a look, okay? But I need you to stay calm. I need you to stay with me. Can you do that?"

Emma nodded. She knew how important it was that she didn't pass out, but no matter how hard she tried, she couldn't stop shaking.

Why is it so unbelievably cold in here?

Jon gently slipped her blazer off her shoulders and slid the strap of her camisole down her arm. He sat down beside her and wrinkled his forehead as he examined the damage. "Well, the good news is it looks like there's an exit wound. The bad news is," he added, his voice shaky, "you're losing a lot of blood."

Ephraim lifted himself up onto the bench beside Jon and handed him a pressure dressing. Emma shuddered on the edge of consciousness as Jon wrapped it under her arm and across her shoulder, pulling it tight.

"Grant!" Sam called over the hail of gunfire, his voice echoing inside her head as hollow as if they were still in the stairwell. "We're going to run out of ammo eventually! We can't hold them off forever!"

Emma knew it was nothing short of a miracle they had even made it this far. If they were caught, they were dead. Period.

"Go," Ephraim said to Jon.

Jon turned to him. "What?"

"You heard me. I said go. I'll cover you. Just take them and get out of here!"

"And then what, E? You going to shimmy up the elevator shaft? Or climb out the window and scale down the side of the building?"

"No. I'm going to do what I came here to do. Stop a bomb from going off."

"Oh, right. And how exactly are you going to do that with a busted leg?"

Ephraim looked down at the bandage wrapped around his thigh, now more red than white.

"He can't," Emma said. "And you know he can't. Not without our help."

Jon clenched his jaw. "I said *no*, Emma."

"Damn it, Jon! Since when did you turn your back on the world?"

"*When they turned their backs on us!*" he shouted. "Fifteen months, Emma. Fifteen long months they left me over there while you lay in a hospital bed dying. Haven't we already done enough? Haven't we already *lost* enough? Let someone else be the hero for once, because I'm done."

Emma pulled away from him. The sudden movement made her dizzy, but she wasn't in the mood for his temper.

Jon softened his voice. "I'm sorry, okay? But you're in shock, and you're not thinking clearly. We have got to get you out of here and to a hospital. You and Ephraim. And what about Jack, Emma? He sacrificed himself to save us, you know."

"So that we could *lose* ourselves in the process?" snapped Emma, her head spinning, gun shots ringing in her ears.

It was becoming harder and harder to focus on Jon's face, flushed pale by the moonlight that flooded through the window behind him.

"Hundreds of people will die when that bomb goes off. Probably more. What do you think he would say if he knew we could have stopped it? What do you think he would say if he knew that he saved us just so we could turn around and only save ourselves? Why do you think he even did it in the first place? Because he believes in us. Because he believes in *you*. Do you really want to be the one to prove him wrong?"

Jon's face fell. "Emmy, I didn't ask for any of this. I don't *want* any of this. All I want is to go home, with my wife, to my kids. Why is that so bad?"

"Because that's not who we are, Jon. And you know it."

Jon stared down at his right hand, his forehead wrinkled. He sucked in long, deep breaths. "We are the choices we make," he whispered.

"That's right," said Emma quietly. "And we made a choice, remember? Maybe it's time we stopped hiding from who we really are."

When Jon looked up at her, there was a sad combination of defeat and acceptance in his eyes. He brushed a lock of hair from her face and leaned in to kiss her. Emma relaxed as the energy of it radiated through her body, warming every part of her, alleviating the anxiety and pain.

He pulled away from her and smiled. The way a man smiles at that one person, the only person in his entire life, who has always been there and always knows.

Then he squared his shoulders and stood. "But that doesn't change the fact that we've got to get you out of here before you bleed to death."

"*What?*"

"Hackett!" Jon called.

Sam rushed over. "Please tell me you guys have more ammo."

"Give me a status update."

"Aaron and I are out," Sam answered. "I've counted seven men down the hall, but that's just a start. Any second now Mac's men are going to be crawling all over this floor."

"Emma," said Jon. "I need you to tell me what you know about the bomb. You said you saw it. Where?"

"I don't know, exactly. All I remember is…" She squeezed her eyes closed to think, then found it hard to open them again.

"What? All you remember is what, Emma?" Jon shook

her lightly.

"Red," she said, forcing her eyes open. "Red and white."

"Red and white?" He looked at her blankly, then realization flooded his face. "The pop machine."

"The what?" asked Sam.

"Hackett, your guys guarding the sky bridge—do you think they're still down there?"

"Absolutely. I gave them explicit orders not to move from that spot, no matter what."

"And you trust them?"

"With my life."

"So you're certain that not only are they still there, but you can get past them without a fight?"

"Yes."

Emma interrupted. "Jon?" she said, suddenly noticing an eerie calm. "They've stopped firing."

They all turned to Aaron and Rachael, who were squatted behind the planter at the side of the escalator, breathing hard, their guns still in their hands. Rachael was loading what Emma was sure was their last clip into her gun.

"Grant!" Mac's voice boomed from the somewhere above their heads. *"You've got exactly sixty seconds to come out of there, or we're coming in after you!"*

Jon's face flushed with terror. He glanced at Sam.

"And why should we, Mac?" Jon yelled back. "You're just going to kill us anyway!"

"I don't want to lose any more of my men, Grant. Oh yes, you're going to die, you better believe that. But I tell you what—if you give up without a fight, I'll spare your wife. Do we have a deal?"

Jon's eyes darted to Emma's as if, for a split second, he actually considered the offer. Then he gestured for Aaron and Rachael to join them.

"All right, listen to me very carefully, Hackett," Jon whispered, taking the gun from Rachael. "You, Ephraim, Rachael, and Aaron are going to head for the sky bridge."

"What about you?" Sam asked.

"Don't worry about me," Jon answered with a wink. "I'm more resourceful than I look."

Sam shook his head. "I don't know, Grant…"

"Look," said Jon. "You're the only one who can get them across that sky bridge, and I'm the only one with any kind of training who isn't already bleeding to death. We don't have time to argue."

"Thirty seconds, Grant!" yelled Mac.

Sam looked at Emma, then nodded.

"Rachael. Aaron. Help Ephraim," said Jon.

Aaron and Rachael pulled Ephraim to his feet. Emma noticed that, despite his dark skin, Ephraim was starting to look a little pale.

"And Hackett..." Jon added. "Just one more thing. What I said earlier about keeping your hands off my wife?"

"Yeah?"

"Well, for the moment at least, you have my permission to touch her."

Sam looked as confused as Emma felt. "Why?"

"Twenty seconds!"

"Because," Jon answered, "you're going to have carry her kicking and screaming if you're going to get her out of here."

Emma leapt to her feet, furious. *"What?"*

Sam grabbed her.

"Jon!" Emma whispered. "That's not what I meant, and you know it!"

"Emma, shut up and listen to me," said Jon, cupping her face in his hands.

"Ten seconds, Grant!"

"The more you struggle, the faster you're going to lose blood. And one of us has got to make it home."

"No, Jon. I will *not* leave without you! *Please.* Sam, let me go!" Tears streamed in hot streaks down her face as she fought against the pressure of Sam's arm across her chest.

"Tell the kids I love them, okay?" said Jon, an odd tingling sensation radiating from his fingertips.

Emma's eyes grew suddenly heavy. "Jon! *Don't... you... dare...*"

Then Jon leaned in close and whispered, "Sleep."

And everything went dark.

CHAPTER 32

Jon was amazed it even worked.

"Dr. Grant!" said Hackett, catching Emma before she collapsed to the floor.

"Just take her, okay? She'll be fine. Just get her out of here."

"That's it, Grant!" Mac boomed. *"We're coming down! Don't say I didn't give you a chance!"*

"Ephraim," said Jon, "please tell me you have a flash bang or a smoke grenade or something."

Ephraim nodded. "Here," he answered, tossing his bag to Jon. "Front pocket. The rest of my gear is in the last elevator shaft on the left."

Jon sighed in relief as he pulled out the smoke grenade. "Thank God," he said, slipping a finger into the pin. He looked at Hackett and nodded.

Hackett scooped Emma into his arms, and he, Aaron, Rachael, and Ephraim moved toward the left side of the staircase.

Jon pulled the pin and rolled the canister across the floor, just past the stairs, on the opposite side of where Hackett and the others would make their break for it. As the hall began to fill with smoke, Jon popped out from under the staircase and fired up into Mac's men, lingering only long enough to make sure he was seen before running up the hall away from the sky bridge. As the smoke began to fill in around them, Jon caught a glimpse of Hackett darting away with Emma in his arms. He wondered if he would ever see his wife or kids again.

"Grant!" Mac yelled from somewhere behind him. "That was the stupidest thing you could have done!"

Jon bolted down the hallway and didn't look back.

As he rounded the curve toward the elevators, an idea popped into his head. He darted into the alcove with the elevators and hid in the darkness of a corner.

Perhaps Mac's men would run right past him.

It was an incredible risk, but it had to be better than a mad, uncovered dash down a dark hall.

As footsteps thundered past, he held his breath and pressed his body as far back into the darkness as he could. He prayed silently that none of Mac's men had seen Hackett and the others make a break for it, and followed them.

He stood there for what seemed like hours rather than

minutes, motionless and unbreathing. Just as he was about to decide that all of Mac's men had already passed and if he stayed there much longer he'd be giving them an opportunity to circle back and look for him, soft footsteps came down the hall and stopped just outside the elevator alcove.

Jon rested a finger on the trigger of his gun.

The figure stood there, motionless. Then he turned slightly, revealing in the moonlight a clearer outline of his lanky build. It was the kid whose nose Jon had broken. The one they called Rat. Jon suddenly remembered Bennett's comment about the kid being not much older than Matt and Jacob. He didn't want to have to shoot him.

Just keep moving, kid, he thought, trying to will him on.

"Hey, Rat!" called another of Mac's men. More footsteps approached, and a second guy stepped into the moonlight beside Rat. "It looks like we might have lost them. You got something?"

Keep moving. Just keep moving.

The kid paused as if listening. "Nah," he finally said. "There's nothing here. Let's just keep moving."

Jon breathed a sigh of relief and removed his finger from the trigger as they disappeared up the hall. He slipped his gun into the back of his pants and set to work prying open the door of the elevator with his bare fingers. Jon still found it hard to believe that Ephraim had managed to get onto the roof of a twenty-four-story building and down the shaft without anyone noticing. He'd have to remember to ask him about it later.

Assuming, of course, there was a later.

Jon was more than relieved to find Ephraim's rappelling equipment still hanging undisturbed inside the elevator shaft. The elevator car was on the first floor just below, a glow stick on top of it, radiating a soft green. A crowbar lay next to it. Jon dropped down onto the roof of the car.

He knew he needed to cover his tracks, but it took almost as much effort to get the door closed as it had to get it open, and Jon felt the seconds ticking away. His greatest fear was that Mac would go after Emma. Based on what the guy had said to Rat in the hall, they still hadn't found her and the others, but that didn't mean they were out of the woods yet.

He's not going to let you out of here alive, Jack had said. What did that even mean?

Jon finally got the door closed in one strained push.

He grabbed the crowbar and hooked it through his belt loop, threw Ephraim's bag over his shoulder, and climbed the rope to the third floor. Jon positioned himself just beneath the elevator doors and used the crowbar to pry them open gradually, an inch at a time, just enough to peek out. Soon realizing that there wasn't ever going to be enough light to be completely sure that no one was waiting for him, Jon opened the doors and pulled himself up.

No sooner had he set foot on the third floor than he heard the unmistakable sound of Mac's voice.

"Come on, I said *move*!"

Jon pressed himself against the wall.

He heard nervous chatter and shoes scuffling across the carpet—moving away from him. They definitely didn't sound like Mac's men. Were they hostages? And, more importantly, was Emma among them?

He had to know.

Stepping softly, he eased down the hallway toward the voices. He kept his body pressed up against the wall till he reached the point where the hallway opened into the prefunction area. He peered out from the shadows.

Mac was herding a group of about twenty or thirty men and women in suits toward the stairwell. Where in the world was he taking them?

That's when Jon heard the gun cock right beside his head.

"Hold it right there, Grant," said a voice behind him.

Jon froze.

"Hand me the gun and turn around."

Jon passed the gun, reluctantly, to whoever was standing behind him. He put his hands up and turned around slowly.

"And just what do you think you're doing?" the guy said.

He was wearing a mask, but by his voice and build, Jon recognized him. It was the kid who had watched the monitors. Hackett's friend.

"I thought the boss took you and the others downstairs. What'd you do, hero? Pop him and come back for the rest of us?"

Jon shook his head. "Look, kid, I don't know what you might have read in the news, but I'm just a retired pilot. I'm only here because your buddy let us go."

The guy tightened his grip on his gun. "I don't believe you."

"Well, he's *your* friend, you tell me. You really think your pal Sam would be okay with Mac blowing up a building full of people?"

The kid's eyes widened. "You mean Mac really *did* plant the bomb?"

"That's right, slick."

"My god," he said. "I mean, I knew the guy had lost it. Shooting hostages and all. But blowing up the entire building?"

"Wait, you mean he's shot someone else?"

"Yeah, as soon as Sam left with you guys. He said something about a list. Then he gathered a bunch of people up, shot a few of them, then took the others. He didn't say where."

"And you just *let* him?"

"I didn't know what else to do!"

Jon suddenly realized just how young the kid really was. "Listen," he said, softening his voice, "you need to go figure out what Mac's done with those hostages. Keep him from shooting anyone else. Do you think you can do that?"

"No, but I'll try."

"Good enough. Now go."

"Mr. Grant," the kid said weakly. "We never really meant for anybody to get hurt."

Jon shook his head. "Yeah," he answered. "No one ever does."

CHAPTER 33

Emma wasn't sure what woke her up first, the intense heat radiating through the glass Sam had propped her against, or the sound of Mac's men banging on the metal doors leading to the sky bridge.

"Aaron, I can't hold it much longer!" Sam yelled as Aaron rushed past her with an arm chair. Sam grabbed it and used it to barricade the doorway. Emma doubted it would last long against the force of Mac's men.

"Come on, Doc," said Sam, scooping her up.

Emma wrapped the one arm that wasn't numb around his neck as he ran across the sky bridge toward the convention center. Behind them, the mangled metal doors burst open, and three of Mac's men pushed through. Before Emma could shout a warning to the others, she heard the distinctive pop of bullet through glass and watched as the three men dropped and lay still.

Wow, there really are snipers out there, thought Emma. *I guess someone is on our side after all.*

Her relief was short-lived. Two bodies lay just inside the hotel behind them. *Sam's friends.*

"Sam?" she said quietly.

Sam didn't respond. He just kept running, his eyes straight ahead.

When they had crossed into the second floor of the old convention center, he set her down. "All right, Aaron," he said, "you're good to go from here. Just circle around this floor until you come to the stairwell on the other side. From there, you'll be able to get to the ground floor."

"Wait a minute," said Emma. "Where are *you* going?"

Sam ignored her. "Just stay along the south wall—it's the clearest. Once you get downstairs there shouldn't be much blocking your path. Keep going south and it will lead you to the entrance of the parking deck. From there—"

"Sam!" Emma yelled.

Sam closed his eyes and took a deep breath.

"I asked you where you were going," she said quietly.

He squatted down in front of her and put a hand on her knee. "I've got to go back," he said.

Emma opened her mouth to argue.

"Look, I know what you're going to say, Doc. But I've got to go anyway. My best friend's in there, and I can't just leave him. I've got to try to talk Mac out of this. Everyone in this building, from the hostages in that conference room to the guys I brought in, is in danger because of me. I don't want anyone else to die. This is my mess, and I've got to try to clean it up."

Emma was too tired, too dizzy, and in too much pain to stop him, and she knew it. She rested her trembling hand on top of his. "Jon has a bracelet just like that," she said quietly, noticing for the first time the bracelet on Sam's wrist.

"Cole made it for me," said Sam. "It's supposed to be good luck."

She smiled weakly. "Maybe it will work."

"You were right, you know. About what you said. In writing, we have something called M/R Units. Motivation and Response. But between that motivation and response is a space. And it's the choices we make in that space that define us. Those choices mean nothing, though, until we act on them. The only thing I've managed to do so far is get a building full of innocent people almost killed. And that's not who I want to be."

No, Sam. Please, no. Emma cried out from deep inside her own head, but she couldn't form the words. If she had been more coherent, if she hadn't already lost so much blood, she would have argued with him. No—she would have done a lot more than argue with him. She'd likely have knocked him over the head and dragged him out of there herself, insisting that he, Claire, and Cole would all thank her for it later. Instead, she did something she'd only done on very few occasions where there seemed to be no hope, no control left.

She surrendered to the unfortunate inevitability.

"Did you mean what you said?" Sam asked. "About helping Cole?"

"Every word."

"And you'll make sure he's taken care of?"

"I promise."

"It'll be all right, Dr. Grant," he said. "You'll see." He rose and headed back across the sky bridge.

But that's exactly the problem, Emma thought numbly as Rachael helped her up. *I do see.*

Emma was pretty much gone now. Rachael was patient with her, supporting most of her weight as they stumbled around in the dark, trying to make their way down the hallway that wrapped around the building. Every now and then Emma would lose consciousness, then snap back again. Only Rachael kept her from hitting the rubble-riddled floor.

"Look, Emma, we're almost there," she said, out of breath.

Emma opened her eyes, not even remembering when she'd closed them. Fifty feet ahead, moonlight poured through the exit into the parking garage, somehow making the surrounding area seem significantly darker. She couldn't be sure, but she thought she saw a few people standing just beyond the exit.

"Yeah," said Aaron, who was struggling to keep Ephraim, half a foot taller than himself, upright. "And with any luck, whoever that is out there brought a couple of stretchers with them."

Luck, thought Emma.

Rachael plopped her down and ran for the exit. Emma tried to follow her with her eyes but couldn't keep them open. Her mind wandered, replaying the image of red and white exploding in a fiery ball in front of her. *Luck*, she thought again. She looked at her hand just before the flames burst toward it—and realized what that tinge of brown around her wrist was.

It was Jon's bracelet.

Emma opened her eyes. If it was the bracelet she saw on her hand, then maybe, just maybe, this time she'd managed to change things. Maybe this time, everything would be all right.

In the dim moonlight, she looked down at her hand.

The bracelet was gone.

"Where is it?" she cried.

"Where's what?" Aaron asked. He hovered over Ephraim, unconscious on the concrete.

"Jon's bracelet!" she said. If it wasn't around her wrist, then where in the world was it? If it wasn't *her* hand that she had seen in the vision, then whose?

"Emma, calm down. Are you talking about the bracelet with the white shells?"

"Yes."

"It's okay," he said. "I'm pretty sure Jon has it."

"What do you mean?"

"I saw him pick it up off the stage. It must have fallen off when Mac dragged you up there."

"Wait. Are you sure?"

"Positive," he said.

Rachael reappeared just then with a couple of EMTs. Aaron helped them load Ephraim onto a stretcher. For a moment, everyone was distracted.

Emma hopped up and slipped away into the darkness.

If she were anyone other than who she was, she'd never have found her way back. The convention center was so dark she couldn't even see the floor beneath her. Running on nothing but adrenaline, her mind reeling with one simple goal, Emma used every ounce of her ability to know which way to turn, which step to take, and what part of the path to avoid to get back to the hotel. It was one thing to acquiesce to Sam and his need to put right what he'd done wrong. It was another thing entirely to let the father of her children go out in a violent blast of glory.

Screw the unfortunate inevitability.

She reached the spot just outside of the sky bridge where Sam had left them. She didn't know where the bomb was, just that Jon had said something about a drink machine. The vending machines on the third floor were the only ones she knew of. If Jon wasn't there, then she'd just have to search from floor to floor.

She darted into the stairwell that led up to the second level of the sky bridge. Though her desperate need to get to Jon in time had enabled her to push through the pain and disorientation, she wasn't thinking nearly as clearly as she should be. A second before she popped out of the stairwell she suddenly remembered Sam saying that Mac's men were guarding the sky bridge on the third floor.

"Hi, Doc," said Mac, standing in front of the door as if he'd been expecting her.

Emma turned to run.

"I don't think so," he said, grabbing her around the waist.

She opened her mouth to scream, but a dark, suffocating hand closed over it. Emma struggled to get away, struggled to even breathe, against the intense pressure of Mac's python arm.

"I wouldn't do that either, Princess," Mac whispered in hot breaths against her ear.

Emma froze.

"That's right, I know," said Mac, his hot, sticky breath condensing against her skin. It made her sick. "*He* told me. He told me everything about you, and your husband. He even told me exactly what the good captain is up the hall trying to do right now. And I think you and I both know that there's *nothing* he can do to stop it." He pulled back her bandage and pushed a finger into the bullet hole in her shoulder.

Emma screamed out in dizzying agony against his hand.

"And that's for my lip," he added.

The familiar iciness started at Emma's toes and crept slowly up her body. She struggled desperately against it, against Mac's grip on her, but with each labored breath, each pulse of pain, the sensation grew stronger. With each gasp for air, his hand closed even tighter around her mouth, his arm around her chest, until it was impossible to breathe.

"Don't bother to fight it, Doc," he said. "You and your kind, you think you're so great with all your power and all your abilities. But *he* has power too, you know. And in the end, the cold will win. In the end, it *always* wins."

Then Emma, tears streaming down her face, sucked in one last desperate breath before the barrel of Mac's gun came crashing down against her skull.

CHAPTER 34

Mac grinned in immense satisfaction. He scooped her limp body into his arms and stared down at her disgustingly fragile frame.

"It's too bad, you know. You really are incredibly beautiful," he said, his eyes scanning every delicate curve. Then he frowned. "For one of *them*."

Throwing her over his shoulder, he started across the sky bridge to the hotel with a total and elating awareness of what he was about to do. A tingle of anxious excitement washed over his body, the way it always did when he thought of the sheer destructive power, the magnitude of complete control, that they were about to show the world.

Like a drug, it fed his elation to the point that the sniper's bullets tearing through his leg and arm didn't even faze him. The good doctor lying limp across his shoulder would keep them from hitting any major organs, he knew, but it didn't matter now anyway. This body was weak, temporary, and he would soon be rid of it. What he would gain in return for his sacrifice would be immense and eternal.

He continued to the alcove with the vending machines, where he knew Grant would be trying to unravel everything they'd accomplished. Mac chuckled as he imagined the captain staring at the drink machine, his brow furrowed, sweat running down his face, contemplating the sheer impossibility of his task.

He stopped just outside the doorway to the darkened alcove, pulled the doctor off his shoulder, wrapped one arm around her chest to keep her upright in front of him, then cocked his gun and pointed it at her temple.

"Grant," he said coldly. "Why don't you come out and face me like a man?"

It was Hackett who stepped out instead, his gun pointed straight at Mac's head.

That was, of course, until he saw the girl.

"Dr. Grant," he said, his face falling as he lowered his gun.

Mac smiled. "That's right. I thought her husband might like to see her one more time before we all die. Where is he? I know he's here."

Hackett hesitated, then raised his gun again. "Why, Mac? Why are you so determined to kill them that you're willing to die in the process? What'd they ever do to you?"

Mac threw his head back and laughed. "You don't have the slightest clue, do you, Hackett? You're just as bad as Grant. Him and his *filthy* kind, with all their power and all their knowledge. They believe they're here to make things better. They think they're here to save us, when all they're really doing is screwing it up worse, with their stupid wars and their stupid politics. They think they're so much better than us? They know absolutely nothing! This isn't about what they have or haven't done to me, you moron. It's about what they've done to *him*. It's about what they *would* have done to him"—he pressed the gun harder against her temple—"if I didn't stop them. But more importantly, it's about what he's promised me."

Sam wrinkled his forehead. "He who?"

"I'd suggest asking your girlfriend here," said Mac. "But I don't think she's going to get the chance to answer your question."

And neither would Mac.

The bullet entered the back of his skull in a great, fiery, roaring pop. He fell to the floor like a collapsing building, taking Dr. Grant down with him.

Sam stared into the darkness, unable to breathe. "You actually killed him."

"He's not the first," Grant said quietly, reemerging from the hiding place he'd slipped into across the hall before they'd even heard Mac's footsteps.

"I still don't get how you knew he was coming."

"I just did," said Grant, dropping to his knees beside his wife. "Now help me."

Together, they rolled Mac's body off her.

Grant cradled her in his arms and listened to see if she was still breathing.

"Is she alive?"

"Yes." He ran a hand across his face and stood. "But she won't be for much longer. None of us will. Not unless we get this thing open," he said, stepping toward the drink machine. He pulled a crowbar from a duffel bag at his feet.

Sam looked down at Mac's body. "Do we still need to do this? Mac's dead now. He can't trip the bomb if he's dead."

"Have you, at any point in the last twelve hours, seen a detonator in his hand?"

"Well, no, but that doesn't mean he doesn't have one. Maybe we should check his body—"

Grant grabbed him by the arm. "No! We're running out of time."

Sam hadn't yet seen the man quite this unnerved. Grant was breathing hard, his hand shaking, as if he was under an unseen pressure so great he was about to explode at any moment.

"How do you know that?" Sam asked quietly.

Grant looked back at his wife, who lay silent on the hall floor. "I *just* know, okay? Now stop asking stupid questions and help me get this thing open."

They positioned themselves to pry the thing open, Sam with the crowbar jammed beneath the lock, Grant pulling as Sam pushed. Between the two of them it took less than a minute to get the drink machine open.

Sam stared in shock at the glow of chemical-filled canisters and wash of monochrome wires. He swallowed hard. A timer was nestled at the right side of the machine. They had less than four minutes left.

Running out of time was an understatement.

"Hackett?" Grant said quietly.

"Yeah?"

"Do you know how to disarm this thing?"

Sam swallowed hard and stepped up to the bomb. He studied the layout of the components, his eyes repeatedly darting to the ticking timer. He pushed wires out of the way, attempting to distinguish what each one did, trying desperately to remember all the different schematics Mac had gone over with him.

"Oh, no."

"What?" said Grant.

Sam stepped back and wiped his brow with a trembling hand. "Mac knew he would have problems getting ahold of strong enough explosives to get the bang he wanted. The feds have that stuff all so tightly regulated now."

"Less bang is good, right?"

"It would be..." said Sam.

He looked at the timer. Three minutes nineteen seconds.

"... if this were the only bomb."

Grant's jaw dropped.

"Some of the wires are sequencers," Sam explained. "There are over a dozen of them, which means Mac must have bombs spread throughout the entire hotel—maybe farther. My god, he must have been setting all this up for months. With that amount of explosives, positioned just right, he could level half of downtown Dallas."

Grant ran a shaking hand through his hair.

"I can't stop this bomb from going off," said Sam. "There isn't enough time to disarm it, even if I could remember how. But I can lessen the impact. I can cut the sequencers. I know how to do that much, at least." He looked at Dr. Grant's small frame lying motionless on the floor. "That should give you guys just enough time to get far enough away."

Grant's eyes met his.

Sam pulled his diary from his back pocket. "There's a note in here for my wife," he said, barely able to choke out the words. "Give it to Dr. Grant. She'll know what to do with it. And tell her—" He hesitated, holding out the diary. "Tell her that I know it's all going to be okay."

Grant took the diary from Sam's hand. "I'm so sorry," he said quietly. "I tried. I'm just not..." He trailed off, shaking his head at the floor.

"Jon," said Sam, putting a hand on his shoulder. An odd calm washed over him. "I don't know what Mac was talking about out there, but I'd have to be stupid not to see that something way bigger than me is going on here. I don't have any idea who or what you are, but what I do know is a lot of good people have sacrificed themselves to keep you two safe, and I'll be damned if I'm going to be the reason they fail. Now, I'm sorry for the part I've played in all this. Truly, I am. But it's still my mess. And, ultimately, it's my responsibility." He tipped his head toward Dr. Grant. "And she's yours."

Grant took a deep breath. "Thank you, Sam Hackett," he said, offering his hand.

Sam shook it. "You're very welcome, Captain Grant."

"I may not be able to stop it myself," said Grant, lowering his voice. He squeezed Sam's hand, an odd gleam in his eyes. "But maybe I can help."

Sam suddenly remembered every schematic and bit of information Mac had ever shown him on bomb-making.

Grant smiled. "Good luck."

Sam nodded.

And with that, Jonathan Grant scooped up his wife and disappeared into the darkness of the hallway. The Grants, whoever they were, were gone.

Sam was alone.

He took a deep breath and pulled a pair of wire cutters from Grant's duffel bag. Glancing at the timer every few seconds, he carefully snipped each of the sequencing wires in order, one by one, as if he'd been doing it his whole life. He'd already made it to the seventh one when he heard a voice behind him.

"Well, now, isn't this inspiring."

Sam turned. Standing at the entrance to the alcove, his face illuminated in the glow of the chemical compounds, was Stephen Bennett.

"Minister?" said Sam.

"Hello, Mr. Hackett."

Sam checked the timer. There was less than a minute left. "Sir," he said, "you've got to get out of here. This thing is going to go off any second. You've got to get as far away as possible!"

But Bennett just stood there, grinning, as if Sam had just warned him that he was about to miss a sale at Macy's. He eyed the timer. "Oh, now, that won't do, I think," he said. He pressed a few numbers on the keypad beneath the timer. It paused. "There we go. Give us a chance to chat."

Sam's jaw dropped. "You mean it was *you*? *You're* the one Mac was talking about? You're the one who told him all that stuff about the Grants? You're the 'he'?"

"Not quite," said Bennett. "That *he* that you are so irreverently referring to—I am not worthy enough to even latch his shoe, as the saying goes." He narrowed his eyes. "But I will be soon."

Sam's thoughts turned to the gun holstered at his side.

Bennett grinned. "Don't give yourself, as you call it, 'false hope,' Mr. Hackett."

Sam sucked in a sharp breath.

"Oh, you'd be surprised at the things I've seen. The things I know. Far more than that idiot Mac. And I just so happen to know that you won't be going anywhere. In fact," he said, putting a hand on Sam's shoulder, "I don't believe you'll be doing anything at all for the next forty-five seconds." He glanced at the wires Sam had cut and frowned. "We can't have you causing any more damage than you've already done."

Sam wanted to run. He wanted to scream. He wanted to do anything other than stand there frozen with Bennett's slimy hand on his shoulder. But for some reason, he couldn't move. For some reason, he could no longer even think.

"There now, that's better," said Bennett, cocking his head. "You people really are quite small, aren't you? You think yours is the only world? Yours is the only universe. But you're wrong." He stepped in closer and lowered his voice. "So very, very wrong."

Bennett punched something into the keypad, and the timer resumed its countdown. He closed the door of the drink machine and dusted his hands off as if he'd just taken out the trash. "I don't suppose Grant will ever know just how close you came to stopping me. Pity. I'm sure he'll be beating himself up years." He smirked. "Now you be a good little Native and stay right here," he said, then strolled away.

Sam couldn't move. He could only stare motionless at the drink machine, his vision blurring, until all he could see was a wash of red and white. He tried hard to focus his mind on it, to climb out of the fog and understand what he was seeing, what was going on. His mind was screaming at him to do something. To see something. But what was it that he needed to do? What was it he needed to see?

Summoning all his strength, he managed to reach out a hand.

But it was too late.

The red and white shattered into a million tiny pieces and came blasting toward him in a great ball of orange flame.

The last thing he saw was a tinge of brown against the blurred outline of his hand.

Nothing more.

CHAPTER 35

Are you frightened?
No.
You should be.

Emma opened her eyes slowly. Jon held her in his arms, bounding down a darkened stairwell. She wanted to ask him to stop jiggling her, for fear she would throw up all over the front of his shirt. But she could feel his anxiety, his heart pounding wildly in his chest, and knew they were running out of time.

At the bottom of the stairwell, Jon dropped her to her feet as he cracked the door open and peered out. "Damn it," he said, resting his head against the door. "Mac's guys are everywhere."

Emma felt more disoriented than she had all night.

Jon squared his shoulders and drew his gun. "Well, if we're going to do this, we better go," he said, taking her by the wrist.

Emma pulled away. "Wait, Jon." She looked up the stairs. "Something's wrong."

"You're damn right there's something wrong. We're in a twenty-four-story building with a bomb that's about to go off. That's what's wrong! We've got to go!" He reached for her hand again. "Right now!"

Emma stepped out of his reach. "No. It's something else." Her eyes followed the stairs up into the darkness. She glanced at Jon—

"Emma!" His eyes widened. "Don't you dare!"

—and ran up the stairs.

"Emma, wait!"

She'd made it as far as the next landing when the building blew up around them.

All Emma remained aware of before blacking out was a deafening ringing in her ears and the feeling of being crushed, as if she were trapped inside a car in a compactor.

When she finally opened her eyes, the first thing she saw was the glint of her wedding ring on her own limp and bloody hand. She had no idea whether moments or hours had passed while she lay there unconscious, buried beneath a cold claustrophobia of mangled steel and concrete.

"Emma!"

She thought she heard Jon—thought she heard someone—call for her in the distance.

"Em-maaaaa!"

"Jon," she managed in no more than a whimper. She tried to take a deep breath, but was met by a painful inability to inflate her lungs.

He's not going to find you, you know, said a voice in her head. *No matter how much he searches, no matter how much he tries, you're already lost to him. You always have been. And the sooner you realize that, the sooner you give in, the better off they'll all be.*

No! I don't believe you! Emma screamed to herself. *He will find me! Jon always finds me!*

"Emma?"

This time the voice came from just above her head.

It was Jon.

An incredible warmth washed over her as he slipped an arm through a crack above her and took her hand.

"Emmy, honey, it's going to be okay," he said, then shouted, "Richard! Quinn!"

Emma tried to move, but she couldn't manage so much as an inch beneath the rubble. She thought she heard scuffling and shifting of the debris above her, but couldn't tell for sure. It was getting harder and harder to focus on anything but the gurgling in her own chest.

It was also getting harder to breathe.

"Baby girl?" Her father's voice came this time. "It's okay, sweetheart. We're here. You're going to be all right."

"Dad," she gasped, sucking in a lung-full of dust. She broke into an excruciating fit of coughing, filling her mouth with thick, rusty-tasting phlegm.

"Come on, boys," said her dad, his voice growing more distant. "Let's get her out of there."

Jon let go of her hand, and Emma suddenly felt more lost and alone than she ever remembered feeling in her life. As if she were descending into the darkness of a great and endless well, never to be seen or heard from again. *No!* she wanted to scream. *Please don't leave me. Please don't leave.*

And then Emma saw images she had never seen before. She saw Torren, and the Great War, and cities burning, and people dying, and the fall of mankind. She saw the beginning and she saw the end and she saw more disturbing scenes than she would ever remember—or ever want to.

And she heard Jon's voice, from what seemed to be an eternity away.

"Do you hear that?" he said.

The pile of debris where Emma imagined her father

stood stopped moving. "It sounds like water."

"Emma!" Jon called down.

She choked and gasped desperately for air, but she couldn't answer. Her chest rose a little less each time she tried to breathe as her body began to give in to exhaustion.

"I think she's drowning," said Jon, his voice thick with panic. "Quinn, go find someone! Go tell them to shut off the water!"

Before Emma lost consciousness, before she surrendered to the suffocating darkness, all she remained aware of was the realization that it wasn't water slowly filling her lungs. It wasn't water that Jon and her father could hear trickling through the cracks and crevices around her body.

It was blood.

When Emma woke up again, she was lying instead in a hospital room. Jon hovered over her, his eyes red, his face dirty and tear-stained. The news played on a television in the corner.

And a team of orderlies had her pinned to the bed.

"*Nooooooo!*" Emma shrieked inconsolably. "Let me go!" She gasped and she choked and she cried. She fought desperately, with an unnatural, adrenaline-fueled strength, against hands and arms and even legs attempting to restrain her. She ripped the heart monitoring pads off her chest and the oxygen mask off her face and tried—unsuccessfully, thanks to the layers of bandage wrapped around it—to rip the IV out of her arm.

"Emma, you're okay!" Jon shouted at her, an arm against her chest. "Calm down! Everything is okay!"

But Emma knew better. Everything wasn't okay. It wasn't okay at all.

"Ahhhhh haaa haaa haaa!" she screeched, raspy and cracking. Hot tears poured down her face and pooled in dark, dirty streaks on the bedspread. "NO! NO! NO!" she cried, realizing by the hoarseness in her throat that she must have been screaming for several minutes before coming to.

She kicked and she wriggled and she cried and she pushed away hands that tried to hold the oxygen mask over her face, even though she was vaguely aware she was hyperventilating and probably needed it.

"Emma, please! *STOP!*" Jon said in a near panic, as if he was about to have a breakdown himself. "Just stop!"

Emma stopped fighting. She looked him over.

There wasn't a scratch on him.

"You're okay," he said quietly. "It's over."

And then Emma, whimpering and wheezing and exhausted, sank back into the pillows.

Someone handed Jon the oxygen mask, and she didn't fight him when he put it over her face. She just stared blankly up at the television in the corner, sucking in shallow breaths, her eyes heavy and her body spent.

"The death toll continues to rise," a reporter said, "as search-and-rescue efforts are extended to include the area surrounding the hotel, which, as you can see behind me, has been completely leveled. The current count—one hundred and thirteen—is expected to increase as rescue efforts continue through the night."

Jon grabbed the remote and muted the newscast. "How are you feeling?" he asked. "Better?"

Emma continued to stare at the television, at the scene of the explosion that she and Jon had somehow, miraculously, survived.

Finally she turned to him.

"You know," she answered slowly, between shallow breaths, "when I was sick, people would ask me that constantly. I never really knew what to tell them."

"So what did you tell them?"

"That I was still alive," she said quietly.

Emma sucked in deep breaths of the oxygen. She suddenly wanted nothing more in the entire world than to just go home. Recognizing she was in an intensive care unit, though, she feared that might not be possible.

"Was it bad?" she asked.

"Yeah, baby. It was bad," Jon said quietly.

"How long are we going to be stuck here?"

He shook his head and smiled. "They're turning you loose tomorrow."

"What?"

"I said it *was* pretty bad," he said, removing the mask and handing it across the bed. "But you had a pretty good doctor."

She followed his gaze. Standing next to the bed was Sarah.

Emma scowled and looked away.

"Oh, I see how it is," said Sarah, turning off the oxygen. "I fly four hundred miles to save your life, and that's the thanks I get?"

"*You* don't save my life. *Jon* saves my life. You swoop in to pick up the pieces," said Emma. "Like a vulture."

"Fine," said Sarah. "See if I ever help you again." She

headed for the door.

"Sarah, wait!" said Jon.

"And good luck getting them to release you into private care without my signature," she added as she disappeared around the curtain.

Jon turned back to Emma. "Why are you so mean to her?"

"Oh, please," said Emma, rubbing her now-pounding forehead. One of the many things she hated about anesthetics and painkillers was how quickly you could forget your body had just been beaten and mangled, and how suddenly you could be reminded of it. "You think that's mean? You should see how I treat people I *don't* like."

"You mean like me?" said Quinn.

Emma's head snapped painfully toward the doorway. Standing just inside the curtain was Quinn, still in his FBI jacket.

"My team is heading out," he said. "I just... I just wanted to make sure you were okay first."

Jon cleared his throat. Emma hadn't realized until then how completely exhausted he looked.

"Well," he said. "I think I'll go find Sarah and talk her into signing those discharge papers. Maybe I'll remind her I'm her ride home." He kissed Emma on the forehead. "I think it's about time you two cleared the air anyway."

Damn you, Jon. She knew his leaving her alone with Quinn was partially punishment for mouthing off to Sarah.

As Jon left, Quinn stepped to the end of the bed. He stared at his feet.

Emma decided this couldn't possibly be any more unpleasant than what she'd just been through. "So. FBI, huh?"

"Yeah, well, there isn't exactly a huge market for crisis psychologists since they shut down FEMA," he answered.

"You were always more of a bureau boy anyway. I don't even know why you went into the field in the first place."

"Because you asked me to," he said quietly.

Emma bit her lip and looked away.

On the TV, the news was replaying Sam's demands video. She had completely forgotten about Sam. Maybe it was a good thing Quinn had come to see her after all.

"Look, I need a favor," she said. "Sam Hackett, the guy up on the stage with us. He recognized you. Do you know who he was?"

He nodded. "It took me a while, but I remember him. I met him in Destiny."

Emma recognized the name. It was a town even smaller than the one she had grown up in. She wondered if Sam would ever get to go back there again. Or if he had even survived.

"He did everything he could to help us, Quinn. I need you to keep his name and his family out of the investigation. Can you do that for me?"

"That's an awfully big favor, Emmy."

"Yeah, well," she snapped, "I'm pretty sure you owe me one."

Quinn's jaw dropped. He stared at his shoes again.

Emma turned toward the window and squinted against the sunlight. Her heart raced in her chest—a reminder that she had probably just come through what must have been some pretty extensive surgery. Sarah might get on her nerves, but there was no questioning her ability.

Jon reappeared, stopping just inside the curtain. "So, are we good?" he asked, glancing back and forth between Quinn and Emma.

"Yeah," Quinn told the floor. "Same as always."

Emma watched Quinn's reflection in the window as he walked over and kissed her gently on the head before leaving. "I'll let you get some rest now," he said. "It was good to see you again, Emmy. I'm sorry it couldn't have been under better circumstances."

Emma squeezed her eyes shut, a tear rolling down her cheek. *Now I really, really just want to go home.*

"Larson, wait," said Jon.

Quinn stopped just inside the doorway.

"Richard told me what you did. Sneaking into the building like that took a lot of guts."

"I just didn't want her…" He stopped and took a deep breath. "I just didn't want anyone else to get hurt, you know?"

"Yeah, I know," said Jon, shaking his hand.

"Jon," said Quinn. He lowered his voice slightly, almost as if he still wanted Emma to hear him. "Do you think she'll ever forgive me?"

Jon crossed his arms. "Would you?"

Quinn rubbed a hand across his mouth and stepped out of the room.

"Well," said Jon as he rounded the end of the bed and

sat down beside Emma. "I think I've managed to talk Sarah into letting us out of here. Though I may or may not have had to promise her a Porsche to do it."

Emma would usually have had quite a bit to say about that, but right now she was too sore and exhausted. She turned away from him, letting her head sink into the pillow behind her.

That's when she noticed Sam's diary sitting on the nightstand.

Emma sat up slightly and stared at it, her lip trembling. There was only one reason it would be there.

Jon picked it up. "He asked me to give it to you," he said quietly. "And to tell you that, in the end, he knew everything was going to be okay."

Emma took the diary from him. The cover was singed, the edges of the paper frayed. It still held a faint scent of leather. She found the picture of Sam with his family tucked inside the cover. Emma held the photo in her hand, Sam's little boy smiling up at her.

How could he have possibly believed it would be okay?

Then she remembered the promise she'd made.

That's how Sam knew, she thought. Because he trusted her to keep her word, and when it came right down to it, saving his little boy was the only reason he had been there in the first place.

Emma put a hand over her mouth. Behind the photo was a folded piece of paper with Claire's name scribbled on it. "Oh, Sam," she whispered, the familiar sting of tears sneaking up on her. "I'm so sorry."

Jon pushed a lock of hair from her face.

As Emma looked up at him, she noticed something on the TV. She shot upright and grabbed the remote, anger suddenly pushing aside all the pain and fatigue. She clenched her jaw and stared at the sleazeball on the screen.

At Stephen Bennett.

She turned up the volume.

"In light of recent events," said the Speaker of the House, who stood behind the podium next to Bennett, "it has become painfully clear that we must band together in a more unified and centralized system. That is why, in a historical and unprecedented action, the surviving representatives of both the House and Senate have unanimously voted to take Minister Bennett up on his offer."

Emma grabbed Jon's arm. She was suddenly unable

to breathe again. "No," she mouthed wordlessly, tears streaming down her face. "No, no, no."

"Sam's Rebellion," Jon whispered.

"What?"

"Sam's Rebellion. It's something Jacob said to me when I called to let them know we were okay. He said Hackett had successfully managed to stage his own Shay's Rebellion."

Emma was numb. She was certain that wasn't at all what Sam had in mind.

"That is correct, Mr. Speaker." Bennett took the mic. "Barring any further hindrances, the United States of America will soon be known as the latest member"—he looked straight into the camera and smiled—"of the Global Order Government."

Emma sucked in shallow, rapid breaths, her eyes stinging.

Jon took her hand.

"A sad day indeed for the United States of America, folks," said the reporter from what Emma guessed must have been a local station.

Way to go, east Texas, she thought, though she was sure that reporter had just lost his job, at the very least.

"This latest development," the reporter continued, "comes on the heels of the passing of Vice President Allred, who, after having sustained a gunshot wound to the chest, died at three o'clock this morning."

Emma looked at Jon, who stared out the window, his eyes tinged red. She realized that some of the tears that stained his cheeks were for someone other than her.

They were for his Uncle Jack.

And somehow that was the very last straw. On top of everything else, knowing that Jon had lost his uncle—and that she'd had something to do with it—was more than Emma could handle. She buried her head in a trembling hand and began to cry.

"Emma?" said Jon. "Honey, look at me."

Emma was too physically and emotionally exhausted to even raise her head.

He put his hand beneath her chin and forced her to look him in the eyes. "Emma, listen to me. This—none of this—was your fault."

"Oh, Jon!" she cried, breaking into uncontrollable sobs. "*ALL of it is my fault!*"

Emma buried her face in Jon's shoulder and cried until she fell asleep, then spent the night tossing and turning through raging nightmares and fluctuating fevers. Jon stayed with her, crawling into the hospital bed beside her sometime during the night and slipping an arm under her shoulder. He sang to her softly until the sound of his voice and the warmth of his body calmed her enough for her to get in a few hours of uninterrupted sleep.

When she opened her eyes, the sun was somehow rising over another day in east Texas. For a long time she lay quietly, curled up under Jon's arm, listening to him breathing softly. Eventually she realized he was awake and watching her. She raised her eyes to meet his.

"Good morning, Mrs. Grant," he said with a grin, just like he had every morning for the last twenty-one years.

"Good morning."

"Has the nurse been in yet?"

Emma smiled. He'd been reprimanded more than once before for crawling into a hospital bed with her. "Not yet."

"Good." He pulled her closer. "Hey, we get to go home today. I don't know about you, but I think I'll take that raincheck on the trip to Eureka Springs now."

Emma nuzzled against his chest. She was more than ready to spend the next three days—the next three months—holed up in a cabin by the river with him, completely cut off from the rest of the world.

Until she remembered all the arrangements that would need to be made.

"Jon... I'm really sorry about Jack."

Jon took in a long, deep breath. "When I was a kid, I secretly wished my mom had married him instead of my dad. I loved him like a father, Emmy, and I don't think I ever even told him."

"There are so many things in life that we don't ever say. Then suddenly our chance is just gone. Makes you realize how little time we really have."

Jon was silent for a moment. He threw back the blankets and sat up on the side of the bed. "Emma," he said. "I know about the dreams."

Emma gasped and sat up straight.

"I'm so sorry, Em. I'm sorry for convincing you to take the sleeping pills when you didn't want to. I'm sorry for being so inconsiderate of everything you've been going through the last few months, for being so dismissive of whatever you've been seeing in your dreams. I just thought that if I could make them go away, if we could just ignore them, then maybe..." Jon shook his head.

"I know I haven't always been particularly supportive. So you don't have to go into any kind of detail about what you've seen, if you don't want to. I just want you to know that I'm here for you. That I love you, and I'll do whatever you need me to do. I just can't—" He took her hand. "I just can't lose you, okay?"

Emma stared down at her hand in his. "I thought you didn't believe in this stuff," she said quietly.

"Oh, I believe. I may not accept it. I may not understand it. But I believe. I've seen entirely too much not to."

Emma wrapped her arms around his neck and pulled him in to kiss him gently. He closed his eyes and rested his forehead on hers.

"Jon, do you remember how you said that when the time comes, I would know? Well, I think it's started."

Jon's shoulders sank. "I'm scared, Em."

"Me too."

CHAPTER 36

Matt sat alone by the lake, the cool moisture of the ground soaking through his jeans. It had rained every day that week, ever since his parents had gotten back from Dallas. But Matt didn't care that it was wet. He was tired of being cooped up in the house, where everyone sulked but didn't say much, and no one seemed to want to answer any of his questions. Eventually they had begun avoiding him altogether, and Matt decided that the chill of soggy shoes and muddy jeans wasn't any worse than a cold shoulder.

What was worse was feeling totally in the dark. Classes were canceled until further notice, and the paparazzi made it almost impossible to leave the house. The Grant kids had also been specifically forbidden to even so much as turn on the TV since the weekend of the bombing. It was one of the first things Matt's dad told them after walking through the front door with their obviously sedated mother in his arms.

"Look, your mom's still recovering, so let's just give her a chance to rest, okay?" he'd said. "She's already been through enough without being constantly reminded."

You were there too, Dad, Matt wanted to point out. His father, ever the tough guy, would never admit how much the entire ordeal had affected him. But Matt knew, and it didn't have to rain for a week straight for him to figure it out.

It wasn't just what happened in Dallas, though. It was what all of it meant, whatever that was. His parents were terrified. They were all terrified. He could *feel* it. Sarah. His grandfather. The sheriff who lived on the other side of the lake. Even Daniel seemed worried. Every so often Daniel would ask Sarah if she'd heard from Professor March, and she would simply bit her lip and shake her head. The strangest part was that Daniel would then hug her, as if he knew why she was so upset in the first place.

Matt, getting tired of everyone knowing but no one talking about it, finally cornered Daniel after a couple of days. Daniel bluntly told him to please not ever ask him about it again, and then began avoiding him too.

"Whatever," Matt mumbled to himself as he plucked a blade of grass and started tearing it into tiny pieces. "It doesn't matter."

But it did matter.

It mattered a lot.

Something was coming. No, worse than that, something had already begun. All the signs pointed to it: the military trucks that were rolling into the bigger cities like Houston and Atlanta; the Mexican and Canadian border systems that were slowly being dismantled; the sudden drop in the price of gas; the suitcases that Grandpa Scott carried into the guest room from his truck without so much as a word.

And the Global Order flag that now flew above the White House.

Matt knew that this—all of this—was the real reason his parents had spent most of the week in their bedroom and why his mother would wake up screaming.

Matt had tried more than once to get in to talk to her. He wanted to know what was going on. He *needed* to know what was going on. But each time, he was stopped at the door by his dad, arms crossed and eyebrows raised, as if to say, *What part of "she needs her rest" did you not understand?*

Matt would stare past him at his mother lying asleep in their bed, wonder just how much she'd been unwittingly drugged up, and then walk away. Matt was almost desperate enough to consider talking to his father for once, but knew his father wouldn't understand. No one else would ever understand the way his mom did, because no one else knew what his mom did.

No one else but him.

"Hey, Mattie," she'd said as she stepped into the hospital room where he lay the morning after his junior prom. She sat on the bed beside him and took his hand. "I heard you had a pretty rough night."

Matt stared silently out the window, not even looking in her direction.

"I guess that means you guys lost your deposit on the hotel room, huh?" she teased. "I know of at least a couple of girls who I'm sure are pretty disappointed over that."

Matt took a deep breath and turned to her. "Mom, I need to ask you something. And I need you to swear to me that you will be completely and totally honest with me."

His mom pressed her lips together. "All right then, Matthew. What do you want to know?"

"Mom," he said, his voice cracking as another sharp pain shot through his chest, "in all the things you've seen, all the dreams you've ever had about us—about our family—have you ever..." He paused, his eyes beginning to blur. He wasn't sure if it was from the pain or because of what he knew she was about to tell him. "Have you ever seen me as an old man? Have you ever seen me with kids? Or even married?"

Her eyes began to tear. Matt knew of her determination to never cry in front of any of them, but he'd noticed she'd found it harder and harder over the years to keep that rule with him.

"Am I even going to make it through college?" he added quietly.

"Oh, Matthew." She put her hand on his face and wiped a tear from his cheek. "Honey, do you know what this life is for? We're here to learn and grow. Through trials, and pain, and heartache. Through the hard times. And the good times. We're here to become the people we were meant to be. Now, for some of us, it doesn't take much. Some of us are strong enough, and special enough, and close enough, that all of that gets rolled into a short time. You are one of those special people, Matt. You have had to go through more hard times in your sixteen short years than some people do in their entire lives." She hesitated and lowered her voice, as if she were having trouble continuing. "And sweetheart... I don't even want to imagine you having to go through much more."

"But there's still so much I want to do," he whispered, hot tears running down his cheeks.

"Baby, I think you and I both know that this body wasn't meant to last for long," she said, putting a hand gently on his chest. "But I think that's because, in your case, it just didn't need to."

"Oh, Mom," he said, bursting into tears.

She pulled him to her, and he sobbed on her shoulder like a child.

"He has a great work for you to do, Mattie," she whispered to him then, on that day two years ago. "You and your brother. I just hope I'm still around to see it."

"*Matia mou?*" came a voice from the embankment behind him.

Matt didn't have to hear the nickname to know who it was. "Hello, Alex."

"Where is everyone?"

He wiped a tear from his face before answering. "Well, I think my brother and your brother have been perched up in a deer stand somewhere on the other side of the property all day. Leah somehow managed to sneak off with Daniel. And my parents were holed up at the cabin for the last two days before leaving for Allred's funeral this morning. I guess with everything that's gone on, they just felt like they needed some time alone."

"That didn't help you feel any better, though, I'm sure."

Matt bowed his head. She knew him so well. It was only going to make this harder.

"You haven't answered any of my calls," she said. "And you haven't shown up for any of your shifts, either."

"I've had a lot going on, Alex. I just needed some time to—"

"Luke told me you quit, Matt."

Matt rubbed a hand across his face. He knew if he was going to do this, he was going to have to look her in the eyes, no matter how much he didn't want to.

He stood, wiped his hands on his jeans, and turned around. "Alex, I don't think we should spend time together anymore."

Alex crossed her arms and looked away. "Damn it, Matthew Grant. You're going to do this to me again?"

"I'm serious."

"So am I!"

A lump started to form in Matt's throat as he watched her try to discreetly wipe a tear from the corner of her eye. "Look, I'm sorry, okay?"

"No, you're not. You don't care how I feel at all."

Matt stepped up to her then, staring down into those beautiful blue-gray eyes. "You're right. I don't," he said quietly.

Alex wrinkled her forehead. "What?"

"I'm an Empath, Alex. I don't feel about you the way you feel about me. Don't you see that? I don't feel anything, except for what other people feel. So, yes, I'm sure that when you're around me it seems like I do, but the truth is, when you're not around, I feel nothing for you. Absolutely nothing."

Her lip started to tremble. "I know what you're trying to do, Matt."

"Do you?"

"Yes," she answered, scanning his face.

Matt knew she was trying to get a read on how he was really feeling. But honestly, at that moment, all he felt was numb.

She lowered her voice. "Can you honestly look me in the eyes, *Matia*, and tell me you don't have feelings for me?"

Matt stared back at her with an expression of stone-cold seriousness. "I'm sorry, Alex. I don't."

She turned from him. "All right. You know what? Fine, if that's how you want it to be. But don't expect me to wait around for you to figure out whatever the hell it is that you want, Matthew Grant."

Matt stared at his feet as she walked away. A spider crawled through the grass in front of him. He lifted one soggy shoe.

And stomped it into the ground.

***

Thirteen hundred miles away, in Elizabeth City, North Carolina, Jonathan Grant stood in front of a mirror in a hotel room, fiddling with his tie for the second time in the last two weeks. Emma stepped out of the bathroom behind him, wearing a black dress almost identical to the one she'd lost in Dallas.

"You know, you really do look fantastic in that dress," he told her as she looped his tie around and pulled it through.

She gave him only the faintest hint of a smile. It was an expression they'd both unconsciously adopted over the last week. "I'm sorry it had to be for such a grim occasion."

For a split second Jon thought about suggesting they go out to dinner, so she could have the proper opportunity to show off her dress, but with the funeral and everything else that had happened, the idea seemed shallow.

He turned back to the mirror to finish adjusting his tie.

"Are you ready for this?" she asked.

"No more ready than I was the last time I had to do it."

She squeezed his hand. "Come on, sweetheart," she said. "Let's go."

They rode in silence as the driver took them to the old Waterfront Park on the banks of the Pasquotank River, where the service would be held. Jon hadn't set foot in Elizabeth City since Danny's funeral, but from the very moment they landed, the salty smell of the sea had washed up memories that had been all too easily forgotten in the landlocked life of southwest Missouri. Some of them good memories. Some of them bad. All of them, at that moment, very painful.

Neither he nor Emma noticed when their car fell into line behind the hearse. When the driver parked behind it,

Jon stepped out and offered a hand to Emma. She quietly kissed him on the cheek, then went to take her place in the front row, with Jack's wife Abigail and their closest friends and family.

Jon took his place at the back of the hearse with the other pallbearers, including his grandfather and President Saundra. Saundra, who had been Jack's closest friend, had taken it upon himself to make most of the arrangements—including, as his last presidential order before the United States was absorbed into the GOG, declaring Waterfront Park a national landmark so that Jack could be buried by the sea in the state he loved so much. He had even had the park renamed.

Allred Memorial Park. It had a nice ring to it.

Jon stared at the pavement beneath his feet as the driver came around to the back of the hearse to open the doors. The pallbearers, nodding to each other in silence, took their places on either side of the coffin as it was slid out, an American flag draped across the top.

Ironic, thought Jon as he put one hand on Saundra's shoulder and grabbed a handle, *considering that Jack died in the hopes of saving his country.*

It was a country that wouldn't exist for much longer.

They made their way slowly up the path toward the water, passing cameras and reporters, people standing with arms crossed reverently in the back, and row upon row of folding chairs set up on the grass to either side of them. Jon spotted Aaron and Rachael in the crowd. Aaron nodded. Rachael smiled.

They placed the coffin on a metal stand above the open grave. From what Jon understood, Saundra had commissioned a monument to be erected in Jack's honor after the funeral. Jon hoped it would be finished and in place before the GOG took control, otherwise it might not get done at all. Quite possibly out of spite.

Jon's grandfather and the other pallbearers went to sit with their families in the crowd. Jon followed Saundra up to the dome-covered Waterfront Pavilion and took a seat in one of the chairs behind the podium. He sat silently beneath "The Dome," the same dome that had once served as part of the entrance to the hospital where his grandfather was born and later to the college where his grandmother had graduated. He only halfway heard Saundra's opening remarks.

Then Saundra introduced him for the eulogy. Jon stepped up to the podium and looked out over the crowd.

"The last time I had to do something like this," he started quietly, "was when Uncle Jack asked me to speak at his son Danny's funeral. They were a lot alike, Jack and Danny. Though Danny would never admit it. They were both kind and sincere. They were dedicated and considerate. They were determined and unwavering, and unbelievably stubborn." He paused, the hint of a smile forming on his face.

It quickly faded.

"But most of all, they were loyal, loyal friends. Up until the very end. Today we celebrate and honor the memory of Jacob Allen Allred. A man without whom I wouldn't be standing here today. A man who…"

Jon turned his gaze to the people sitting in the front row. Emma, his grandfather, Aunt Abigail… A group of people he loved desperately. It was also a group, he sadly observed, that had gotten significantly smaller over the years.

Then Jon's eyes met Emma's, the woman he loved more than anyone or anything in the universe. He had told her that morning how beautiful she looked, but in that moment—in that grim and grievous moment—mostly, she looked tired. As if she had gotten less sleep in the last week than she had in all the restless, sleepless nights of the last few months. As if what happened in Dallas, and the war she continued to wage in her own head, weighed more heavily on her mind than all the horrible tragedies she had seen or endured over the course of her entire life.

And suddenly, Jon just couldn't handle it anymore.

He was so tired of losing people. All he'd ever wanted to do was protect her, protect everyone he loved. He'd thought that maybe if he parted ways with the world, everything would be okay. That he wouldn't have to lose anyone else. That he wouldn't have to do *this* anymore.

But the truth was, Jack was right. He couldn't just bury his head in the sand. Emma's desperate attempts to always save everyone were no different than his own desire to protect the people he cared about. Because in the end, the one thing she knew that he didn't—the one thing that played over and over in her mind—was that no matter how much they hid from the world, the world would eventually come to them.

The war would be on their doorstep.

And they wouldn't have anyone left to help them fight it.

Jon cleared his throat and continued. "A man who

taught me that you can't run from who you really are. Jack Allred lived every day of his life by a standard that few of us can ever even hope to achieve. He loved, and lived, and died for his family, his friends, his country, and his fellow man. May we all endeavor to live our own lives in such a way—" His eyes began to blur. "—in such a way that would make him proud. We love you, Uncle Jack. You saw the best in all of us, even when we didn't see it in ourselves. *Reveritas ad astra*. May you return to the stars."

"… to the stars," murmured the crowd as Jon stepped down and took a seat next to Emma.

Saundra returned to the podium. "Thank you, Jon," he began again.

"Although some of you may consider what I'm about to do to be in poor taste, those of you who knew the vice president well would also know he would find it to be ironically humorous and brilliantly strategic, which is one of the things that I personally admired and loved about Jack Allred. I would like to take this opportunity to say that this will be my last public address as president.

"Effective at midnight tonight, I am officially resigning from office—though at this point, I think the gesture is no more than a formality. Despite my best efforts to veto the questionable proceedings that occurred after the bombing in Dallas, the GOG will soon take control of what was once our beloved United States of America, and I have respectfully declined the position offered to me as chief of state under GOG rule."

Jon glanced sideways at Emma, who squeezed his hand. He looked past her to his grandfather, several seats down, and wondered if Pops had known that Saundra was about to jump ship.

"At this point I would like to open the floor to anyone who would care to share their own stories and thoughts about Vice President Jack Allred. As well as any"—he scanned the line of FBI agents that spanned the back of the park—"*concerns* they may share about the current state of affairs."

The remainder of the funeral went by in a blur of teary eyes and dry throats, with beautiful things said about Jack and disturbing things said about the GOG. Saundra was right—it was brilliant. This was quite possibly the largest gathering of influential people since the convention itself, and the GOG wouldn't dare have the audacity to try to censor a funeral being broadcasted live.

But eventually Saundra insisted that they wrap things

up, as it was starting to get dark, and with so many high-ranking officials out in the open, security was afraid it would be a safety concern. Jon was relieved. The hard metal chair, as well as the foreboding that had settled into the air, was making him uncomfortable.

"Jon, you did a fantastic job," Rachael told him as he, Emma, Aaron, and Pops stood talking while everyone else made their way to their cars. "Jack would have been proud, and I don't just mean about the speech."

"Thanks, Rachael," he said. "I really appreciate it."

Ostentatious clapping sounded just behind him. "I couldn't agree more, Captain. It really was quite *inspiring*."

Jon had hoped never to hear that voice again for the rest of his life.

"Well, Mr. and Mrs. Grant. Mr. and Mrs. Dallin," said Bennett as he joined their small group. "Jon Matthew," he added, glaring at Pops.

Pops didn't say a word.

"I was quite relieved to hear all of you somehow managed to survive that incredible ordeal in Dallas. Some of you," said Bennett, turning to Jon and Emma and raising an eyebrow, "quite *miraculously*, from what I'm told."

Emma stepped closer to Jon and took his arm.

"And us as well, of course, Minister," said Jon. "I'm sure we were all pleased to learn that you managed to find your way out of the building. We were especially worried," he added, "when you *completely* disappeared."

Bennett curled a lip.

"Oh, wait, I'm sorry. Do we even still call you Minister? Or will it be President Bennett soon?"

"How very intuitive of you to ask, Captain," answered Bennett with a smile. "That is, after all, the very reason I stepped over here. You're a hard man to get a hold of, Grant. I was hoping I might be able to have a word with you in private?" he said, nodding away from their group.

Jon crossed his arms and didn't move.

Bennett frowned. "Have it your way, then. Captain Jonathan Jacob Grant, on behalf of the Global Order Government, I would like to officially extend to you an offer for the position of chief of state over the geographical area soon to be known as the North American Faction."

Jon's jaw dropped. He glanced around to see if anyone outside their little circle had overheard Bennett's preposterous, and much louder than he would have liked, offer.

"You can't possibly be serious," said Pops.

Thanks for the vote of confidence, Pops, thought Jon. "Why in the world would the GOG want me as chief of state, Bennett? I'm no politician. I'm not even remotely qualified."

"Oh, I wouldn't sell yourself short, Captain. You're a decorated war hero, a brilliant strategist, a natural"—Bennett made a point to glance down at Jon's ring—"*born* leader. I personally think you'd make an excellent addition to the other nine heads of state, wouldn't you agree, Dr. Grant?"

Emma stared silently at the ground.

"Look, Captain, I'll be honest with you. You're not exactly my first choice for the job, but I've been directed to extend the offer nevertheless. Besides, you could always look at it this way: if nothing else, you'll have much more control over those 'current affairs' that you and Saundra and the rest of your ultra-conservative frat brothers are so worried about."

"You know what, Bennett?" said Jon. "I think I'm going to have to follow the lead of my good friend, *President* Saundra, and respectfully decline."

Bennett stepped uncomfortably closer and lowered his voice. "Make no mistake, Grant. This will be our only offer, and quite possibly your one chance to ensure you are," he said, glancing at Pops, "on the right side when the line is drawn in the sand, as it were."

Jon narrowed his eyes. "I think I know which side is the right one, Bennett."

Bennett took a step back. "I hope for your sake you're right, Captain." He looked at Emma. "Say hello to your children for me," he said, then turned and walked away.

"That was interesting," said Aaron.

Jon took a deep breath and stared at the stars. "Well, I think it's official. Things can't possibly get any more messed up than that. Makes you wonder what in the world we all did to deserve it."

"Oh, don't be so dramatic, Jon Jacob," said Pops. "Everything happens for a reason."

That was just a little bit more than Jon could handle. "Look around you, Pops! Jack is dead, the GOG is running the show, and the entire world is going to hell in a handbasket! So tell me, please, exactly what reason could there possibly be for all of this?"

Pops cocked his head. "Why, to bring us all to the point where we are right now, of course."

"What does that even *mean*?"

"It doesn't matter now, does it?" said Aaron. "Despite everything we went through, it looks like Bennett is going to end up getting his way after all."

Pops grinned. "Oh, I wouldn't go that far just yet."

CHAPTER 37

"Are you sure you even know where you're going?" said Sarah for the third time that afternoon.

Jon glanced at her in the rearview mirror. "Yes, Sarah. According to the coordinates Pops gave us, and the GPS on the dashboard, this is exactly the direction we're supposed to be headed."

She crossed her arms and turned to the window. "I don't know why we couldn't just fly. It would've been a heck of a lot better than being stuck in your truck for the last four and a half hours."

Jon looked sideways at Emma in the passenger seat. He kept expecting her to have fallen asleep, but she'd stayed awake the entire trip with her hands clasped tightly in her lap. "Because," said Jon, "Pops said we needed to be discreet, and the FAA has been under the GOG's thumb since before they even took over. So I'm afraid flying wasn't an option."

Not that it would have mattered. He scanned the endless stretch of highway and farmland that encompassed the whole of northern Missouri. *There isn't even anywhere out here to land.*

He checked the GPS one more time before making the turn onto the country road that didn't appear to lead to anything other than more farmland.

"Jon, are you sure we're really headed the right way?" Emma whispered. "I mean, there's absolutely nothing out here. How are we even supposed to know when we're in the right place?"

"Honestly?" Jon whispered back, glancing at the mirror to make sure Sarah wasn't listening. "I'm not even sure. All Pops said was, 'You'll know it when you see it.'"

They took one last turn onto an unmarked dirt road that led through a small grove of trees. At the end of that road, according to the GPS, were the coordinates that Jon's grandfather had written down for him—with the strict instructions to "guard them with his life."

Jon revved the engine up one last stretch of hillside, came to the end of the road, and stopped the truck.

A vast valley stretched out before them.

Jon and Emma exchanged a glance before getting out. An unmistakable tingling burned in Jon's chest as he stood beside the truck and stared out across the rolling hillside.

"Emma, I think I've—"

"—been here before?" she said without taking her eyes off the valley.

A UTV headed in their direction. As it came closer, Jon saw four men sitting inside.

One of them was former president Saundra.

"Jon," he said with a smile as the UTV came to a halt in front of them. The four men hopped out. "I'm so glad to see you both made it here safely. Dr. March, you as well, of course," he added as Sarah stepped out of the truck behind them.

Jon didn't know what to say. He wasn't even sure where "here" was.

Saundra took Jon's hand and pumped it vigorously. He smiled brighter than Jon had seen him smile in years.

"Jon, Emma," he said with a gleam in his sea-green eyes.

Jon would have thought his behavior out of place if not for the unexplained excitement in his own chest.

"Welcome to Ammon."

Jon looked at Emma.

She crossed her arms and turned her eyes to the ground.

At Saundra's request, Jon handed the keys to his truck to the other three men, who would move it to a more "secure" location—whatever that meant. He, Emma, and Sarah then climbed into the UTV with Saundra and rode across the valley. Jon wanted very much to ask Saundra where they were going, but got the impression that none of his questions would be answered until they reached their destination.

Jon couldn't, for the life of him, figure out what that destination might be.

They climbed the opposite side of the valley, then started another descent. Jon noticed a structure in the distance. An old barn rested on the side of the hill.

They headed straight for it.

As Saundra pulled into the barn, the smell of old hay filled Jon's nose. The UTV came to a halt, but Saundra didn't get out. He just sat there, as if waiting for something. Or someone.

Jon scanned the barn, noticing the darkness of the loft just above. He suddenly felt as if they were being watched.

Saundra turned off the headlights and flipped on the dome light on the UTV's roof, then said, "*Alons-y.*"

"Let's go?" Jon asked quietly, almost afraid to disturb

the stillness. "Go where?"

The ground beneath them started to move.

Jon took in a sharp breath as the UTV descended into the hillside, with all four of them still in it. He looked back at Emma, who hugged herself tightly, her hand sliding the pendant on her necklace back and forth with surprising vigor.

"Em," said Jon, reaching back and resting a hand on her leg. Her shallow, rapid breaths echoed off the metal walls of the shaft surrounding them. "Honey, are you okay?"

"She's fine," said Saundra. "Give her a moment to get her bearings, she'll be all right." He turned to smile at her. "Won't you, Emmy?"

Emma shifted in her seat and dropped her eyes.

"Okay, Saundra," said Jon. "I think we've all had just about enough of the secrecy. Where are we? What's going on?"

"All in good time, my old friend. Soon we'll be able to tell you everything. Or at least, everything we know."

Jon felt the air around them change suddenly. It was no longer thick with the musty smell of old hay and dirt, but was instead fresh and clean, most likely piped in through some sort of filtration system. The walls of the shaft transitioned from metal to solid rock.

"How far down does this thing go?" Jon asked.

"As far as it needs to, for our purposes," Saundra answered.

Saundra's ambiguity was now borderline annoying. *Okay, seriously*, Jon was just about to say, when he noticed the soft glow around them brighten. Three walls of the shaft vanished, and they now looked out across a massive underground bunker filled with people scurrying to and fro. The elevator lowered them onto a platform, then stopped.

"Mike!" Sarah shouted. She hopped out of the UTV and ran right past the two armed guards standing beside the platform. She disappeared into a crowd of people, where, sure enough, someone who looked just like her husband, Mike, was waiting for her.

What in the world would Michael March be doing here?

"Well, Jon," said Saundra, stepping out of the UTV. "You wanted answers. Are you ready to accept what you're about to see?"

No, Jon wanted to say, wanted to scream, into the

271

hillside around them. The warmth in his chest had long since given way to an uncomfortable foreboding. If any of those answers involved armed guards and underground bunkers, then he wanted nothing to do with any of it. He'd just as soon take his wife and his truck, turn around, and head straight home.

But if he was going to accept his fate, going to accept who he was supposed to be, then maybe this is where he'd have to start.

"Jon," Saundra said quietly. "It's now or never."

Jon turned to Emma. This was as much her choice as his. He reached for her hand.

It was sweaty and shaking.

"Em?"

She looked at Saundra and took a deep breath, then turned to Jon and nodded.

"This way, then," said Saundra.

Jon and Emma stepped out of the UTV and followed Saundra across what looked like some sort of service area. Men and women of all ages and ethnicities went this way and that, pushing dollies, directing forklifts, and staring down at clipboards. Some of them wore military fatigues, though Jon didn't recognize any of the insignia patches. The uniformed ones saluted Saundra and mumbled *Mr. President* as they walked by.

"What is all this?" Jon asked.

"We call ourselves the Consortium," said Saundra. "We're an international organization, most of us Marked, a handful of us not."

"You mean like the OGE?"

Saundra stopped in front of a set of double doors. "The Order of the Golden Eagle, the Shen Zi, the *Bojownicy o Wolność*, the Brotherhood of the Setting Moon, they're all no more than a face for the Marked. A way for us to blend in, to learn and grow, to fellowship, to contribute to the community. This—all of this—is where the real work happens. Here within the Consortium, we have one simple, solitary goal." He grinned at both Jon and Emma. "To do what we were born to do."

He pushed through the double doors, and the three of them stepped into a room much like the situation room at the emergency management department where Emma worked. Monitors covered the walls, and people sat stationed at desks all around the room, watching the monitors or their own computer screens. In the middle of the room the floor stepped down into a circular area that was sectioned off by a floor-to-ceiling glass wall with three open entrances. At the center of that area stood a pedestal, and surrounding that pedestal were six people, including the Marches, the Dallins, and Ephraim.

"Ephraim!" said Jon, stepping down into the small glass room and throwing his arms around him. "We've been worried sick about you ever since we left Dallas. Where have you been? By the time I came to see you before we left the hospital, you were already gone."

"I know. I'm sorry," said Ephraim. "As soon as Sarah got me all fixed up, I had to take off. Some work I needed to do."

Saundra and Emma joined them. Emma kept her eyes fixed on the floor. There was a paleness in her cheeks so profound it looked as though she was about to throw up.

Jon took her hand. "Emma, are you sure you're—"

"Deputy Grey, pleasure to see you again," Saundra interrupted.

"Mr. President." Ephraim saluted him. He turned to Jon and Emma and lowered his voice as Saundra walked off. "You guys have any idea what this is all about?"

Jon shrugged.

"Well, ladies and gentlemen, let's get started, shall we?" said Saundra. He nodded around the room as he made introductions. "Everyone, I would like you to meet Captain Jon Grant and his wife, Dr. Emma Grant. We also welcome Deputy Marshal Ephraim Grey, Professor Michael March and Dr. Sarah March, and Professors Peter and Dianna Godfrey." As he introduced Peter Godfrey, Saundra nodded toward a tall, curly-haired guy with glasses who hurried over from one of the computers by the wall. He put his arm around the redhead standing next to Saundra and shot everyone a toothy grin.

"And last, but not least, we have—"

"Aaron and Rachael Dallin," said Aaron, offering a hand to Peter and Dianna. "No Professor, or Doctor, or Captain, or Deputy, just Aaron and Rachael."

The Godfreys both shook his hand.

"Great, we're all introduced," said Jon. "So, are you ready to explain to us what we're all doing here?"

Saundra turned to Godfrey. "Peter, why don't you go ahead?"

"Sure," said Godfrey. "The reason we're all here…" He stepped up to the pedestal, removed a small brass sphere that was suspended in mid-air just above it, and carried it over to Jon. "… is this."

Jon stared down at the object in Godfrey's palm. It had strange markings on it, but otherwise it was just a round chunk of brass, not much bigger than an orange. "It's a ball."

"Yes, it is," said Godfrey. "And it's the only weapon we have against the GOG." He held it out to Jon.

Jon glanced around the room. The rest of the group stared at him, waiting. He offered Godfrey an open palm.

Godfrey dropped the ball into Jon's hand—then watched breathlessly, as if expecting it to do something. But nothing happened. Godfrey looked back at Saundra.

Saundra nodded.

"The problem," said Godfrey quietly, his shoulders sinking as he took the ball from Jon, "is that we still don't seem to know how to open it."

"I'm sorry, I'm confused," said Ephraim. "What is this thing supposed to do?"

"Well," said Godfrey, with a sort of growling nervous laugh that seemed completely out of place, "you see, we don't actually know."

"Then where did you get it?" Ephraim asked.

"It was left to us by our ancestors," said Saundra. "An ancient civilization of people who believed they existed before they were born. And that during that existence, there was a great war that nearly tore their world apart."

Jon noticed Emma shifting nervously from one foot to the other.

"*Their* world?" said Ephraim. "And exactly what world is that?"

Saundra put a hand on Ephraim's shoulder. "Ours," he answered, nodding around the group.

"Excuse me?"

Saundra pursed his lips together. He turned to Jon and nodded.

Jon took a deep breath. "From what we understand, the world in which we existed before we came here wasn't much different from this one. We lived, and learned, and loved," he said, turning to Emma and smiling, "long before the Earth itself was even formed. But then, something... happened."

Saundra continued from there. "There was a rebel force," he said. "They called themselves the Kieran, the Darkness. That's how the war began. Many of us were lost. Many of us weren't. When it was over, the Darkness was banished to the farthest end of the universe, to the most distant world. We knew, of course, that eventually it would make its way back here. So those of us who were left became guardians, sent to Earth for such a time as when the Darkness would return."

Ephraim was quiet for a long time before speaking. "So you're telling me you think that's what's going on now? That this Darkness has made its way here, and Bennett is a part of it?"

"No," everyone answered.

Except for Jon, who said, "Yes."

"What makes you think Bennett's one of them, Jon?" Rachael asked. "He's not even Marked."

Jon wrinkled his forehead. "Of course he is."

Saundra and Mike glanced at each other.

Everyone else just stared at him, open-mouthed.

"Wait. You're telling me you guys can't see it?" Jon asked. It was certainly possible. Pushers, who could make you see whatever they wanted you to see, could purposely hide their Mark from others. It made it much easier to Push someone if they didn't know you were capable of it. But for someone like Jon…

"Are you absolutely certain of this, Jon?" Saundra asked.

Jon narrowed his eyes. "Do you really have to ask?"

"Marked?" said Ephraim. "What does that mean, Marked?"

Jon hated talking about this stuff as it was, but trying to dump all this onto someone like Ephraim, someone he cared about, made him a thousand times more uncomfortable. "It's how we recognize each other. We're all born with a Mark that only we can see. One of your kind, they can be under the evil influence of the Darkness without even knowing it. But for one of us, with what we know and our"—he glanced sideways at Saundra—"our gifts… Well, let's just say it makes the choice to cross over much more intentional."

"And even more dangerous," Rachael said quietly. "For all of us."

"One of 'my kind,' huh? So what you're telling me is that the country is about to be taken over by an 'evil alien' who is something like the Antichrist, right?" he said with a grin, as if it were all a big joke. "Ooooo. What next? You going to tell me that the *Darkness* is led by the devil himself?"

Jon crossed his arms and sighed. This wasn't at all going the way he had hoped.

Ephraim's jaw dropped. "Now hold on just a

minute…"

"The truth is, young man, we honestly don't know who their leader was, or that much about him at all," said Saundra. "There are countless different beliefs and philosophies spanning the whole of human history, each of which has its own interpretations of good and evil, angels and ancestors, devils and deities. But what you must understand, Deputy, is that we remember very little of our lives and our world before we were born into this one. Most of what we do know has been passed down to us from parent to child, from generation to generation, over thousands of years."

Ephraim rubbed a hand across his mouth. "So let me get this straight. You're going to stand here and try to convince me that 'my' world is being taken over by some dark force that almost destroyed 'yours,' and you can't so much as tell me who's behind it all?"

Saundra bowed his head.

"Torren," Emma said quietly to the floor.

Jon's eyebrows shot up. "What?"

Emma raised her head slowly, her face pale, her lip trembling, and looked him straight in the eye. "His name was Torren," she said, then turned and headed for the door.

Jon stared after her.

"So it's true, then," Ephraim whispered, as if to himself. "Y'all a bunch of aliens."

"We prefer the term inter-dimensional beings," Godfrey answered with a grin.

"I'm glad you find all of this so amusing, Godfrey," snapped Jon. He took Ephraim's arm and pulled him aside. "Ephraim, look, you believe you have a soul, don't you? That there's some part of you that exists outside of human understanding? That we're not all just random balls of matter floating freely in space, born only to pay taxes and die? That somehow, some way, there has to be something besides just this body and just this life? Like you were meant for something more? And that when your body dies, maybe all the experiences and all the energy and all the consciousness that makes you *you* will move on? Will keep going?"

Ephraim shrugged. "Yes. I suppose I do."

"Well, so do we," said Jon. "Except when our body dies on this world, we don't just move on. We go home."

"I'm sorry, Jon, but I don't think I can take this," Ephraim said quietly. "I need to get some air."

"Ephraim, wait, please. Please, don't. I know this is a lot to handle. Trust me, it was a long, long time before I accepted any of it myself."

Ephraim narrowed his eyes. "Trust you? Don't you get it, Jon? I *do* trust you. I have always trusted you. And God forgive me, I think a part of me may actually believe you. For no other reason than because it's you! But that's what eats at me the most about this. I've known you and Emmy practically my entire life. Or at least, I thought I did. You're telling me in all the years that we've known each other, and all the conversations we've ever had about life and death and fate, you couldn't have once attempted to explain this to me? You had to wait until the entire world—my world—had gone to hell in a handcart?"

Jon looked at the floor. "I am so sorry, E. Usually the only time we're allowed to tell people who aren't like us is if they're family."

"You and Emmy *are* my family," he said, then walked off after Emma.

Jon took a deep breath and rubbed a hand across his face.

I should have stayed home.

"Jon," said Saundra. "I'm afraid there's more."

More?

Rachael reached into the bag that hung across her shoulder, pulled out a manila envelope, and handed it to Jon. Inside were several pictures she had taken while they were in Dallas.

"I told you I was there to snoop around," she said.

Bennett apparently hadn't wasted any time in pushing his agenda. Most of the pictures included him privately chatting with other attendees, one of which Jon recognized as the Speaker of the House, who was with Bennett on TV right after the bombing. How'd the Speaker even manage to make it out of the building? As if that wasn't disturbing enough, one picture included Bennett standing in a corner, talking to a man whose face still haunted Emma's nightmares.

Mac.

"Mac was working with Bennett?" said Jon. Sam's friend did tell Jon that Mac had mentioned a list just before gathering up a group of hostages. Jon knew Mac shot a few of them but wasn't sure what he did with the others. Based on the Speaker's unexplained survival, he now had a pretty good idea.

"I'm afraid so," said Saundra. "As was most of the

security detail, we believe."

That didn't surprise Jon at all, knowing what a joke security became once the convention began and how the one man who seemed to be asking questions—AD Tanner—had turned up dead.

"Up until this time, we had very little evidence that Bennett was Kieran. I mean, we certainly had our suspicions, but…"

Jon came to the very last picture. Another of Stephen Bennett, this time emerging from a pile of rubble at ground zero, where the hotel once stood, his tailored suit torn and covered in pulverized concrete.

He didn't have a scratch on him.

"Bennett was in the building?" Jon whispered.

Rachael nodded. "I watched him crawl out of that mess myself."

"Jon," said Saundra, putting a hand on his shoulder. "There are only three people we know of so far that survived the bombing, and I think we both know how close Emma came to not being one of them."

Jon's hand trembled, his vision beginning to blur. There was something about Bennett's face, covered in dust and smiling, a confidence in his eye that Jon knew he himself would never have.

It completely terrified him.

Rachael gently took the pictures from his hand. "Jon. If Bennett walked away from that explosion unharmed, the way you did, then what does that mean?"

"It means," said Jon, his voice shaky, "that Ephraim's description of Bennett was closer to the truth than even he knows."

Book Two:
When House Divides

When darkness builds
And house divides
When truth is lost
And kinship dies

Nine must depart
Ere break of day
A turning point
To show the way

To things above
And things below
Upon the Earth
And deep unknown

Your song is key
One Voice shall rise
On Seventh Day
Look to the skies

Look to the skies…

About the Author

Misty Sutton is a wife and mother of two, an instructor, a prepper, an agrarian, a hardcore home-economist, an Emergency Management and Political Science major, and (when she finds the time) an author of everything from apocalyptic fiction to preparedness curriculum for kids. She and her family enjoy spending their days in the beautiful and thriving area of Northwest Arkansas, where they hope to ride out the no-doubt ensuing zombie apocalypse with their equally quirky (and just as well trained) closest friends. You can follow her in all her adventures at www.fightingtherain.com.